BLACK WATER
SISTER

Zen Cho was born and raised in Malaysia and now lives in Birmingham. She was a finalist for the John W. Campbell Award for Best New Writer for her short fiction and won the Crawford Award. Her debut novel, *Sorcerer to the Crown*, won the 2016 British Fantasy Society Award for Best Newcomer. She is also the author of *The True Queen*.

By Zen Cho

Sorcerer to the Crown
The True Queen

Spirits Abroad

Black Water Sister

BLACK WATER SISTER

ZEN CHO

PAN BOOKS

First published 2021 by Ace,
an imprint of Penguin Random House LLC,
a Penguin Random House Company, New York

First published in the UK 2021 by Macmillan

This paperback edition first published 2022 by Pan Books
an imprint of Pan Macmillan
The Smithson, 6 Briset Street, London EC1M 5NR
EU representative: Macmillan Publishers Ireland Ltd, 1st Floor,
The Liffey Trust Centre, 117–126 Sheriff Street Upper,
Dublin 1, D01 YC43
Associated companies throughout the world
www.panmacmillan.com

ISBN 978-1-5098-0001-8

1 3 5 7 9 8 6 4 2

A CIP catalogue record for this book is available from the British Library.

Printed and bound by CPI Group (UK) Ltd, Croydon, CR0 4YY

Visit **www.panmacmillan.com** to read more about all our books
and to buy them. You will also find features, author interviews and
news of any author events, and you can sign up for e-newsletters
so that you're always first to hear about our new releases.

To Mom, Dad and Peter,
who make all things possible for me

ONE

The first thing the ghost said to Jess was:

Does your mother know you're a pengkid?

The ghost said it to shock. Unfortunately it had failed to consider the possibility that Jess might not understand it. Jess understood most of the Hokkien spoken to her, but because it was only ever her parents doing the speaking, there were certain gaps in her vocabulary.

Jess didn't take much notice of the ghost. She might have been more worried if she was less busy, but in a sense, she'd been hearing disapproving voices in her head all her life. Usually it was her mom's imagined voice lecturing her in Hokkien, but the ghost didn't sound that different.

Even so, the ghost's voice stuck with her. The line was still repeating itself in her head the next day, with the persistence of a half-heard advertising jingle.

She was waiting with her mom for the guy from the moving company. Mom was going through the bags of junk Jess had marked for throwing away, examining each object and setting some aside to keep. Jess had spent hours bagging up her stuff; this second go-over was totally unnecessary.

But it was a stressful time for Mom, she reminded herself. It was a huge deal to be moving countries at her age, even if she and Dad called it going home. *Back* to Malaysia, they said, as though the past nineteen years had been a temporary aberration, instead of Jess's entire life.

"We said we were going to cut down on our possessions," Jess said.

"I know," said Mom. "But this hair band is so nice!" She waved a sparkly pink hair band at Jess. "You don't want to wear, Min?"

"Dad gave me that when I was ten," said Jess. "My head's too big for it now."

Mom laid the hair band down, grimacing, but she couldn't quite bring herself to put it back in the garbage bag. Her innate hoarding tendencies had been aggravated by their financial instability. It seemed almost to give her a physical pain to throw things away.

"Maybe your cousin Ching Yee can wear," she murmured.

"Ching Yee is older than me," said Jess. She could feel her voice getting sharp. Patience didn't come naturally to her. She needed to redirect the conversation.

The line came back to her. *Does your mother know you're a—what?*

"Mom," Jess said in English, "what does 'pengkid' mean?"

Mom dropped the hair band, whipping around. "What? Where did you learn that word?"

Startled by the success of her feint, Jess said, "I heard it somewhere. Didn't you say it?"

Mom stiffened all along her back like an offended cat.

"Mom doesn't use words like that," she said. "Whatever friend told you that word, you better not hang out with them so much. It's not nice to say."

This struck Jess as hilarious. "None of my friends speak Hokkien, Mom."

"It's a Malay word," said Mom. "I only know is because my colleague told me last time. Hokkien, we don't say such things."

"Hokkien doesn't have any swear words?" said Jess skeptically.

"It's not a swear word—" Mom cut herself off, conscious she'd betrayed too much, but Jess pounced.

"So what does 'pengkid' mean?"

It took some badgering before Mom broke down and told her. Even then she spoke in such vague roundabout terms ("you know, these people . . . they have a certain lifestyle . . .") that it took a while before Jess got what she was driving at.

"You mean, like a lesbian?" said Jess.

Mom's expression told her all she needed to know.

After a moment Jess laughed. "I was starting to think it was something really terrible."

Mom was still in prim schoolmarm mode. "Not nice. Please don't say such things in front of the relatives."

"I don't know what you're worrying about," said Jess, bemused. "If they're anything like you, I'm not going to be saying anything in front of the relatives. They'll do all the saying."

"Good," said Mom. "Better not say anything if you're going to use such words."

The hair band lay forgotten on the floor. Jess swept it discreetly into the garbage bag.

"C'mon, focus," she said. "This is taking forever. Remember they're coming at four."

"Ah, Mom is not efficient!" said her mom, flustered. But this acknowledged, she went on at the same snail's pace as before, picking through each bag as though, with sufficient care, the detritus of Jess's childhood might be made to yield some extraordinary treasure.

Whatever the treasure was, it wasn't Jess herself. Everything had boded well when she was a kid. Exemplary grades, AP classes, full ride to an Ivy . . .

But look at her now. Seven months out from college, she was unemployed and going nowhere fast. Everyone she'd known at college was either at some fancy grad school or in a lucrative bigtech job. Meanwhile Jess's parents had lost all their money and here she was—their one insurance policy, their backup plan—still mooching off them.

"Ah!" cried Mom. She sounded as though she'd discovered the Rosetta stone. "Remember this? Even when you're small you're so clever to draw."

The drawing must have been bundled up with other, less interesting papers, or Jess wouldn't have thrown it away. Mom had kept every piece of art Jess had ever made, her childhood scrawls treated with as much reverence as the pieces from her first—and last—photography exhibition in her junior year.

The paper was thin, yellow and curly with age. Jess smelled crayon wax as she brought the drawing up to her face, and was hit with an intense shot of nostalgia.

A spindly person stood outside a house, her head roughly level with the roof. Next to her was a smaller figure, its face etched with parallel lines of black tears. They were colored orange, because as a child Jess had struggled to find any crayons that were a precise match for Chinese people's skin.

Both figures had their arms raised. In the sky, at the upper left-hand corner of the drawing, was the plane at which they were waving, flying away.

Jess didn't remember drawing the picture, but she knew what it was about. "How old was I?"

"Four years old," said Mom. Her eyes were misty with reminiscence. "That time Daddy still couldn't get a job in America. Luckily his friend asked Daddy to help out with his company in Kuala Lumpur, but Daddy had to fly back and forth between here and KL. Each time went back for two, three months. Your kindergarten teacher asked me, 'Is Jessamyn's father overseas?' Then she showed me this. I thought, 'Alamak, cannot like this, Min will get a complex.' I almost brought you back to Malaysia. Forget America, never mind our green cards. It's more important for the family to be together."

Jess touched the drawing, following the teardrops on the child's face. When was the last time she'd cried? Not when she'd said goodbye to Sharanya, neither of them knowing when they'd see each other again. She'd told a dumb joke and made Sharanya laugh and call her an asshole, tears in her eyes.

Jess must have cried during Dad's cancer scare. But she couldn't remember doing it. Only the tearless hours in waiting rooms, stale with exhaustion, Jess staring over Mom's head as she wept.

"Why didn't we go back?" said Jess.

"In the end Daddy got a job what," said Mom. "He was going back and forth for a short time only. It's not like you were an abandoned child. I was here. You turned out OK."

The words sounded like an appeal for reassurance. But the tone was strangely perfunctory, as though she was rehearsing a defense she'd repeated many times before.

"You turned out OK," Mom said again. She took the picture from Jess, smoothing it out and putting it on the pile of things to keep.

"Yeah," said Jess. She wasn't sure whom they were trying to convince.

AFTER THIS, THE ghost lay low for a while. It wasn't like Jess had time to worry about stray voices in her head. Masterminding an intercontinental move crowded everything else out. Her mom, a person to whom all matters were equally important, could probably have gotten it done given three years. Since they had three weeks, it fell on Jess to move things along.

Her dad had gone ahead to Malaysia to start the new job his brother-in-law had arranged for him. He looked tired on their video calls. He'd stopped dyeing his hair after the cancer scare; his head was now almost completely gray. Watching him, Jess noticed for the first time that the skin on his throat hung a little loose, creased with wrinkles. It made him look old.

The sudden disturbing thought came to her: *They've done it. They did it in the end.* After years of insults small and large—misunderstanding his accent, underrating his abilities, dangling opportunities in front of him only to snatch them away—America had finally beaten him.

Jess smothered the thought. Dad was only in his fifties. Asia was rising. This move to Malaysia wasn't a failure, for Jess or her parents. It was a new beginning.

Her subconscious wasn't convinced. In the manic run-up to the move, she started having vivid dreams about Malaysia.

At least, she assumed it was Malaysia. The dreams were permeated by overpowering sunshine, an intense glare she had never seen anywhere else. The perpetual sticky heat and vivid greenery were familiar from visits there. But nothing else was familiar.

She was almost always engaged in some mundane task—scrubbing plates, hanging up faded laundry on a clothesline, washing herself with a bucket of gaspingly cold water from a tank.

Sometimes there was a baby she was responsible for. It never seemed to stop crying. She found herself staring at its scrunched-up face with stony resentment, hating it but knowing there was nothing to be done.

In one dream she was outdoors, watching her own hands score lines in a tree trunk with a knife. Milky white fluid welled from the gash. Rows of trees stretched out around her.

She had started in the early morning, when it was dark, the air soft and cool on her skin. It grew warmer and brighter as she worked, the light turning silver, then gold. By the time she laid down her tools the heat was all-encompassing, the sun beating mercilessly down.

She carried her harvest to the river, where she paused to scoop water into the pails of white fluid—just enough so the agent wouldn't be able to tell when he weighed her yield. He still underpaid her. Everyone knew the agent was a cheat, as he knew they sought to cheat him, so that they were all bound by duplicity.

Getting her pay meant she could go to the shop to buy meat so they'd have something more to eat than plain rice. By the time she got home she was bone-tired, but she put the rice on to cook and started chopping the vegetables. She had to get the meal ready before sunset, before night came, before . . .

But Jess didn't find out what happened at night. She woke up in her sleeping bag, alone in a dark room.

For a moment she didn't know where she was. They'd shipped or sold off everything in the apartment. Empty, her bedroom looked different, the angles and shadows altered. She might still have been dreaming.

"Mom," she said later, "you know when you've got trees and you cut lines in it so the sap comes out—is that a thing? A Malaysian thing?"

She regretted the question at once. It had made sense in her head, but it sounded like gibberish once the words hit the air. But Mom only nodded, as though it was a perfectly normal thing to ask.

"Rubber tapping?" she said. "Malaysia still produce a lot, but not so much as before. Why?"

"I saw a video somewhere," said Jess.

She couldn't recall ever having seen or heard anything about rubber tapping, but her mom must have told her about it sometime. The rustling quiet between the trees, the red-faced baby, her own work-coarsened hands keeping strange rooms clean—they lost their reality in the light of day.

They were just dreams, Jess told herself, the result of her brain processing the move to Malaysia. The rubber tapping must represent her anxiety about her employment prospects—her nostalgia for a time when life was simpler, if harder. Probably the baby was her mom. A therapist would have a field day with her, Jess thought wryly, and forgot all about the dreams.

JESS AND HER mom were greeted at Bayan Lepas by what seemed like half of Penang's Chinese population. Jess hugged her dad while the flood of relatives swallowed up her mom.

Dad didn't say much, but he looked better than on their video calls, revived by the pleasure of the reunion. He smelled the same as ever—a comforting blend of Brut cologne and soap.

This is going to work, thought Jess, and then, *I have to make this work.*

"And this is Jessamyn?" said an auntie. "Grown up already ah! So pretty now! Last time I saw you, you were this tall only, you know."

They were staying at Dad's sister's house, in a well-off suburban neighborhood. Mom called it a bungalow—Malaysians seemed to use the word for any big house—but it was actually two stories. Past the wrought iron gates was a garden with bougainvilleas in extravagant bloom, magenta and peach and pale pink. The house, with its cream walls and brown tiled roof, had been built in the 1970s; the exterior had a slightly worn air that belied the family's prosperity.

Inside, the house was clean and comfortable and lived-in, as unpretentiously nice as its owners. The only luxuries were subtle ones—marble floors on the first story, Indonesian teak on the second. There was AC in the bedrooms and ceiling fans everywhere, and the house was designed to make the most of every breeze, with little holes for ventilation at the top of the external walls.

Kor Kor's kids had moved out—the eldest was working in Sydney, the younger two at college in Melbourne. Jess's parents had the daughter's bedroom, while Jess was given the room the sons had shared.

Mom and Dad had initially refused when Kor Kor invited them to stay at hers while they looked for their own place (as she put it, but they all knew it really meant "until they could afford their own place"). It had taken some persistence on Kor Kor's part to wear them down. In the course of a long-drawn-out video call, Mom had finally blurted, "My mother passed on few months ago. How can we stay at your house? By the time we come, it'll be almost Chinese New Year that time."

"Aiyah, don't worry. I'm Christian," said Kor Kor. "All this pantang all that, I'm not scared. More fun if you stay with me. My kids are overseas, not coming back for New Year. I have an empty nest. Lonely, you know!"

From this, Jess had imagined Kor Kor's house would be quiet. But even though they'd arrived in Penang with a few weeks to go before Lunar New Year, the house was perpetually full. Jess couldn't turn a corner without stumbling over a visiting auntie or uncle or their bored progeny.

Her aunt was retired and sociable, but they weren't all her friends. To Jess's surprise, it turned out the visitors were there on her parents' account.

She hadn't known her parents still knew that many people in Penang. She hadn't really thought they knew people anywhere. She'd always seen them as introverts, their investment in work and family leaving no space in their lives for so tenuous a connection as friendship.

She saw now that this was one of the unnatural changes being immigrants had wrought in her parents—one of the ways they had been warped under its pressures. Among their friends and relatives—people who shared their language, accent, values, preoccupations—Mom and Dad were different people: confident, gregarious and witty. It was Jess who was out of her element, navigating unfamiliar waters.

Her chats with the visitors were more like interrogations, with Jess's life choices as the topic du jour, but fortunately her active input was not often required. The aunties and uncles were perfectly capable of conducting conversations with Jess without any expectation that she actually speak.

"No job yet? Ah, Harvard grad like you, you'll have no problem finding."

"Must be she's waiting for the right opportunity," said another auntie. "Young people these days are picky. They won't simply take any job."

"You all are suffering from abundance," an uncle told Jess. Pleased with the phrase, he repeated, "Suffering from abundance," a beady eye shining judgment on Jess. "In my day having a job was more important. Never mind what job. No matter what it is, you can make it if you work hard."

Jess smiled vaguely. This was her habitual tactic with obnoxious men of any age. But Mom fired up.

"Why shouldn't she be picky? You have to work for most of your life. Might as well find something she likes."

"No point being an employee, working for other people," said Jess's aunt. "Better if Min does her own business."

Kor Kor scooped up a newspaper on the coffee table, showing it to Jess's mom. "Like this young fellow. He studied at Oxford, worked in US, then came back to do business. Now he has a chain, doing very well. Ching Yee took me to his café. One small coffee is twenty ringgit! Not like it's kopi luwak or what. Just normal coffee!"

"Where got people pay twenty ringgit for coffee?" said a skeptical auntie, but Kor Kor insisted:

"You go and see. All the young people go there. They all like that style. Hipster style." She pronounced the word "hipster" as though it was from an alien tongue.

"Twenty ringgit for one coffee," said Mom, impressed. "Nowadays the young people are so clever to make money."

She handed the newspaper to Jess, looking hopeful, as though if she only applied sufficient moral pressure, Jess might be persuaded to join the ranks of the young people who were clever at making money.

The paper showed a man in his twenties, dressed in the successful millennial uniform of crisp blue shirt, gray jeans and white Vans. He was light brown skinned and good-looking, suave but approachable. He looked like exactly the kind of person who would found a chain of hipster cafés.

The "suffering from abundance" uncle was peering over her shoulder, so when he burst out, "Ha!" he did it right in Jess's ear.

"Please explain the joke," Jess said acidly, driven beyond endurance.

The uncle ignored her.

"Ng Wei Sherng? That fellow is the last person your niece should copy!" he said to Kor Kor. "*His* cafés don't need to do well. You don't know ah, the father is who?" He tapped the young man's smiling face. "This is Dato' Ng Chee Hin's son."

"Really?" Mom peered over Jess's shoulder at the newspaper with fresh interest. "True hor, looks like him. I didn't realize because the boy is so dark."

"Mother is Indian," said the uncle knowledgeably.

Mom was talking over him, in her usual Mom way. "But he's so young! I thought Ng Chee Hin is in his seventies?"

A new voice said sharply, *Ng Chee Hin?*

It was the raspy voice of a habitual smoker, oddly familiar, though Jess didn't recognize it. She looked around for who had spoken, but she couldn't tell which of the aunties it had been. Everyone went on talking as though they hadn't heard the voice.

"Not bad what, still," Kor Kor was saying. "Even if the father is rich, doesn't mean the children will be successful. Most rich men's sons are playful, don't like to work."

"The problem is the father," said the uncle. "Ng Chee Hin is a rubber tapper's son. You ask yourself, how did he manage to become so rich, until the chief minister also goes to his house?" He shook his head. "Your niece better find some other model to follow."

"Aiyah, who are we to judge?" said Kor Kor. "Maybe when he's younger it's different, but nowadays Dato' Ng is very decent what. Kok Teng has a contract with his company. He says Dato' Ng is very religious, always donates to charity."

The uncle snorted.

"You know why the boy is so young?" he said to Mom. "Because he is the third wife's son. She was twentysomething only when she married Dato' Ng. He was fifty already by that time. Very pious man, Ng Chee Hin!"

Why are you talking about Ng Chee Hin? said the raspy stranger's voice.

The aunties and uncles were gossiping about rich people and their peccadilloes, Jess's career plans forgotten—except by Kor Kor, who withdrew from the general conversation, slightly put out.

"Only thing I'm worried is it's boring for you here, Min," she said to Jess. "If the children are around, they can entertain you. But there's only us old people. Nothing for a young person like you to do."

"Don't worry. I'm great at doing nothing," said Jess absently. She was trying to work out whom the raspy voice belonged to. She couldn't connect it with any of the women sitting around Kor Kor's living room, but then why was it so familiar . . . ?

A memory floated to the surface of her mind. The same voice saying, *Does your mother know you're a pengkid?*

Jess stiffened, cold with horror.

Outside in the world, Mom was saying, "Not good to do nothing! Why don't you help Kor Tiao?"

"I've got to go to the bathroom," said Jess, cutting her off.

In the bathroom she washed her face and patted it dry, listening to her own breath.

The stress was getting to her, making her think she was hearing things. It was nothing to freak out about. She'd had a lot to deal with in the past few weeks, and being lectured constantly by strangers wasn't helping. She needed to slow down, do some self-care. She'd book herself a manicure or something . . .

The voice sliced through all of this like a knife.

You never answered my question!

The speaker might have been standing next to Jess. She couldn't see them, but it was impossible to doubt their reality.

She gripped the sink, staring at her own terrified face in the mirror.

You're looking at what? said the voice impatiently. *What were they all saying about that useless bastard? Tell Ah Ma!*

TWO

"What the fuck?" said Jess out loud.

The sound of her own voice was reassuringly normal, grounding her in reality.

She had obviously imagined the voice in her head. She was the one who was in control of her brain. So as long as she kept telling herself that, the voice would go away—

Don't talk like that in front of your Ah Ma, said the voice.

"You're not my Ah Ma," said Jess, despite herself. "She's dead."

The death of her maternal grandmother the year before had been overshadowed by all the other crap going on in her life at the time. Dad had been in remission, but struggling with the fact that he'd lost everything he'd worked for. Jess had been trying to cobble together some kind of income from freelance photography work while applying for jobs that never got back to her and conducting a clandestine long-distance relationship with Sharanya, who was living with *her* family at the opposite end of the country.

As for Mom, she had been a straight-up mess. When she'd told

Jess one morning, "Ah Ma passed on last night," it took Jess a moment to remember who Ah Ma was.

They hadn't seen Ah Ma since they had moved to the States, though they met up with Dad's side of the family whenever they were back in Malaysia. Jess hadn't even thought to ask why they saw so little of Mom's relatives till their last visit to Malaysia a few years ago.

"Ah Ma doesn't like to serve people," Mom had said. "Better to visit people who like to have guests."

Sharanya could never believe that Jess had left it there. "You're not even a little bit curious? Your mom hasn't seen her own mom in two decades. That's not normal."

"Mom says she belongs to Dad's family now," Jess said. "It's a Chinese thing. Once a woman gets married, it's like she's left her family and joined her husband's."

"That's an Indian thing too," said Sharanya. "Before Skype was invented. This is the twenty-first century!"

"It's not like it's some big mystery. My grandmother's probably just an asshole," Jess told her. "Like my uncle. He only gets in touch to try to borrow money from Mom. It's like it's the 1800s and he thinks we went to Gold Mountain and we're millionaires now, while they're back in the old country eating millet. And Mom still talks to *him*, so my grandmother must be even worse."

The voice said now, *Of course Ah Ma is dead. If I'm not dead, how can I talk to you? Your mother never called.*

The bathroom seemed to contract around Jess. She'd been perpetually sweaty since arriving in Malaysia, but the sweat was cooling on her skin.

There was no such thing as ghosts, she told herself. Her subconscious was fucking with her. In an unprecedented, terrifying way, admittedly, but she didn't have time to freak out about that right now.

"Pull yourself together, Teoh," she said to her reflection. "Go out there and make nice with the uncles and aunties—"

You can't go yet, said the voice. *Outside is too noisy. Why does your aunt need to hold open house every day, she thinks she's a politician or what? Stay here and tell Ah Ma what they all were saying about Ng Chee Hin.*

"You're not my Ah Ma," said Jess. "You're not anybody! I'm imagining you!"

Don't shout, said the voice. *You want to talk, talk inside here. No need to open your mouth. After people will hear.*

By "inside here," the voice didn't mean the bathroom. It meant the inside of Jess's head.

What would the uncles and aunties in Kor Kor's living room say if they heard her talking to an imaginary voice? It wasn't like Jess cared what they thought, but they might be shitty to Mom about it.

She said, without opening her mouth, *If you're my grandmother, my dead grandmother, how can you be talking to me inside my head?*

I'm like the good brothers, said the voice, with the patience reserved by most people for children or idiots. *Not everybody can hear. But our family can do this kind of thing.*

What is that supposed to mean? said Jess. *I don't have any brothers!*

"Good brothers" also you don't know? said the voice. *Didn't your mother teach you* anything?

This is crazy, Jess said, or thought. It wasn't like she could really be addressing anyone but herself. She was the only person in the room. There was no one else she could be talking to. *What-*

ever this is, it has to stop. I have enough to deal with. I can't start hallucinating that I'm talking to a ghost who thinks it's my dead grandmother—

Hallucinating what? said the voice tartly. *If I'm not here, who do you think has been sending you all those dreams?*

The knock at the door made Jess jump. Mom said on the other side, "Min, you're inside? You're not feeling well, is it?"

Wait, said Jess. *Dreams?*

Mom banged on the door again. "Min?"

Jess recognized the trembly beginnings of panic in Mom's voice. She swore under her breath and opened the door. "I'm fine, Mom. What is it?"

"Auntie Poh Eng waiting to go so long already," Mom said. Then she got a proper look at Jess's face. "Your lips are so pale!" She took Jess's hands, pressing them between her warm palms. "So cold! Are you feeling dizzy? If you don't feel well, you must tell Mom. Mustn't suffer in silence."

Her expression pulled Jess out of her distraction. Mom had always been paranoid about health stuff, but Dad getting cancer had sent her anxiety into overdrive. She looked like she was already waiting for the doctor to pronounce Jess's prognosis.

"I'm OK," Jess said. "I'm jet-lagged, that's all. I'm going to go upstairs and take a nap."

"OK," said Mom, but she looked troubled. "After one week you still got hangover? You're so young, shouldn't be taking so long to recover. I think you don't have enough iron in your blood."

Surrender was usually the fastest way to cut short a bout of nagging.

"Yeah, I'll eat more spinach," said Jess. "Make my apologies to Kor Kor, OK?"

She was moving toward the stairs as she spoke, since even surrender didn't always work, but then a thought struck her. She paused on the first step, turning back.

"Mom, if I say 'good brothers'"—Jess said it in Hokkien, the same words the ghost had used—"what does that make you think of?"

"'Ho hia ti'?" echoed Mom. "Means 'good brothers.' Can also say to mean 'good friends.' 'Dad and Uncle Fahmi are ho hia ti,' like that. Why?"

"No reason," said Jess.

BY THE NEXT day, the impression the voice had left was fading. She had a call with Sharanya, which helped. It was surreal seeing her face on Jess's phone screen, but comforting too. It had been a couple of weeks since they'd been able to talk. Jess had been starting to feel like she'd made Sharanya up, like she'd never had a girlfriend at all.

She told Sharanya this.

Sharanya's eyes crinkled. "How is Penang?"

Jess shrugged, though her position made the movement awkward. She was propped up on her elbows on her bed, with the blanket over her head to muffle sound. "Same as ever. It's not like I get to see Penang. I just hang out at my aunt's house."

"Singapore's like that too," said Sharanya. "I'm looking forward to getting the chance to explore. It's going to be so great when we have our own place."

Jess was less confident than Sharanya that she'd be in Singapore by the fall, when Sharanya would be starting her PhD there. Jess had to get a job in Singapore for that to happen—and she'd have to leave her parents.

"Did you see that content manager job I sent you?" said Sharanya, before Jess could change the subject. "You'd be really good at that."

Jess could've pretended she was going to apply, but she'd always tried to be real with Sharanya. Lying to her family had become second nature; she didn't want that to be true of their relationship too.

"I saw it," said Jess. "But I'm not sure now's the right time. We've only just arrived, Mom's still getting settled . . . I need to be here for her and Dad."

Sharanya's face fell.

"I love that you're so supportive of your parents," she said earnestly. "But you have to live your own life, Jess. It can't always be about them. Your parents wouldn't want you to give up your dreams for them."

They wouldn't want her to move to Singapore to be with her girlfriend whom they didn't know about either. But Jess didn't point that out. She didn't want to keep talking about her parents; it was a topic that always went wrong with Sharanya. She cast around for a distraction.

"You know, I've been having these really weird dreams lately," she said.

She told Sharanya about the bizarre things her brain had been up to in the past few weeks. The dreams interested Sharanya less than the voice.

"You've been hearing *voices*?"

"It was only one voice," said Jess.

Sharanya wasn't listening. Because she was out to her family, she was making the call from her laptop, sitting at her desk with the door open behind her. Her brother passed by and waved at Jess.

Sharanya was typing and studying her screen, her brow furrowed in concentration. "This page says stress can cause auditory hallucinations."

Jess had undertaken the same hasty internet research into possible sources of the voice. "Hopefully it's that, and not brain tumors."

"I'm pretty sure it's stress, babe," said Sharanya. "I mean, look at your life. Maybe you should talk to somebody."

"I'm talking to you. I'm feeling better already."

"You know what I mean. Like, a qualified professional."

Jess looked at her unhappily. Sharanya was typing again. Probably looking up qualified professionals Jess could go and see.

"Do you think I'm going crazy?" said Jess. "I can't afford to be crazy. My parents have enough mental health issues for the whole family."

Sharanya finally looked back at her, though because she was looking at Jess's face on the screen instead of at the camera, their eyes didn't exactly meet. Being in an LDR was total bullshit. "You've been carrying a lot, Jess." Her expression was soft, the earlier tension between them forgotten in her concern. Jess wondered, not for the first time, how she'd managed to score someone like her. "This will help."

"What's wrong with repression and denial?" muttered Jess. "It's been working so far."

"The fact you're hearing voices suggests it isn't actually working," said Sharanya. "Hey, there's a psychiatric clinic in George Town. Is that near you?"

"It's Penang," said Jess. "Everything's nearby."

They managed to come up with a list of places to call, though it was hard to choose between them. There was limited information available online about any of the options.

"Can you ask around for recommendations?" said Sharanya. "Maybe your aunt . . . ?"

There was nobody Jess could ask without her parents finding out, and Mom and Dad had enough on their plate. They didn't need the discovery that Jess was going crazy, even if it was only a little bit crazy and she was dealing with it.

"I'll figure it out," said Jess.

THE CALL WITH Sharanya made Jess feel better about things, rooted in the real world. Of course she hadn't been talking to a ghost. Ghosts weren't a thing.

She had every intention of calling the clinics they'd found together, but she had limited opportunities to make a private call during business hours. She didn't have a car, so she was stuck in Kor Kor's house, unless her uncle or aunt or dad gave her a ride. She could get a cab, but not without attracting loud reproaches from Kor Kor, who seemed to take it as a personal insult that Jess didn't want to treat her as a chauffeur.

It was like being a teenager again, on a weird summer vacation. Without the framework of classes or a job, the days were simultaneously endless and not long enough for all she had to do. There was no need for Mom and Kor Kor to worry about her being idle. Admin ate up all her time. She had to arrange for their stuff to be put in storage, help her parents look for a place they could rent in Penang, and somehow find the time to job hunt amidst all the rest.

The last task was the worst. She felt guilty when she searched for vacancies in Singapore, and almost as guilty when she stuck to jobs in Malaysia. Every time she clicked on a job ad, it was like being asked to decide between her family and her girlfriend.

It didn't help that Kor Kor seemed to think Jess was there on holiday and needed entertaining. Kor Kor's idea of entertainment was sitting in her living room with a bunch of other retirees talking interminably about people they knew and what property they owned over cups of Lipton tea. Jess couldn't duck out, since it wasn't like she had anybody to see or anywhere to go.

The only silver lining to these auntie salons was that Kor Kor's friends lived in a completely different world from that constituted by reality. This occasionally proved entertaining.

"There was something dark right there," said Auntie Grace, gesturing at the ceiling. She was speaking English, which meant Jess could actually follow her. Her Hokkien was all right, but she couldn't keep up with the pace of the aunties and uncles' conversation. "I saw it few days ago."

Auntie Grace was the granddaughter of Jess's paternal great-grandfather's mistress. She wasn't actually related to Dad's side of the family, because she was the product of the mistress's first marriage to another man. Jess's great-grandmother had not been enthusiastic about the mistress or her children, which had resulted in an estrangement spanning generations. But it hadn't been able to survive Kor Kor's expansive hospitality. Auntie Grace was a regular visitor to the house.

"Could see out of the corner of my eye," she went on. "I didn't dare look directly. But it was like a black cloud like that, hanging there."

A frisson went through the assembled guests. The uncles and aunties were all unquestioningly superstitious. They talked about the supernatural with the same mixture of matter-of-fact acceptance and caution with which they discussed politics, and for much the same reason—you never knew who might be listening.

Kor Kor, owner of the maligned ceiling, shifted in her seat. She obviously wasn't thrilled by the suggestion that her living room was haunted.

"Maybe it was dirt," said Mom, trying to be helpful. "Malaysia so humid, easy to get mold."

Everyone raised their eyes to the ceiling. It was spotlessly white.

"We don't have mold," snapped Kor Kor. She turned to Jess, saying, with affected nonchalance, "Your interview with the American company is when ah? Will you have to fly to US?"

"No," said Jess. "We're doing it over Skype. It's for a job at their KL office."

"Not mold," said Auntie Grace, ignoring Kor Kor's attempt to change the subject. "I could feel there was something not right."

"Choy," said the aunties and uncles, looking at Kor Kor with pity.

"If you can feel there's something not right, why didn't you tell me?" said Kor Kor.

"You weren't there," said Auntie Grace, wide-eyed. "You went out of the room to talk to the contractor about your toilet. I was alone here and I was so scared! Didn't dare move. I held my cross"—she touched the silver crucifix on a chain around her neck—"and said the Lord's Prayer. After pray a few times, then only felt the room was lighter." She spread her hands, suggesting the dissipation of a presence. "I looked and the shadow went away already."

"This house was built when?" said an uncle. "Nineteen seventies? I tell my children, never buy an old house. You never know what's inside."

"Last week your husband had fever, right?" said Auntie Grace to Kor Kor. "For all you know, there is some issue. I can ask my pastor to come here. Pastor Cheah, when he prays, you can really feel God's presence!"

"I can ask my pastor to come also," said Kor Kor. "But there is no reason for us to be scared of this kind of thing. We are all Christians."

"Not everybody here is Christian," said Auntie Grace. She gave Jess's mom a pointed look.

The moment God had entered the conversation, Mom had exited it. She was discussing the stock market with an uncle and showed no sign of having heard Auntie Grace.

Undeterred, Auntie Grace raised her voice. "You're not Christian yet, right, Poey Hoon?"

"Poey Hoon Chee is a freethinker," said Kor Kor.

Auntie Grace nodded sagely. "When you are in between—not here not there—you're more likely to attract these things. You got feel or not, something following you?"

Mom said stiffly, "I am lucky. This kind of thing, I cannot sense one."

Jess had been enjoying the conversation, but her enjoyment dried up at Mom's expression.

"When you talk about attracting things, what kind of things do you mean, auntie?" she said.

She'd noticed that everyone had avoided naming what they were actually talking about. Sure enough, Auntie Grace looked uncomfortable.

"You know . . ." Auntie Grace glanced at Mom, who gave her no help. She switched from English to Hokkien. "Lasam eh mikia. Dirty things."

"But you said it wasn't dirt," said Jess in English.

"No, not dirt," said Auntie Grace. "I mean, those things, it's not so nice to talk about. You don't want it in your house."

Jess drew her eyebrows together. "Like flies?"

Auntie Grace was starting to look desperate. "No, not flies. Some people call aoboey kong."

"No lah," disagreed an uncle. "Aoboey kong is different. Aoboey kong is a god. People pray to aoboey kong to keep *them* out."

"What is aoboey kong?" said Jess. She rummaged in her rusty store of Hokkien. "The god at the back?"

"Yes, a god," said the uncle. "Sits by the back door there, protecting the house. Good things come in from the front one mah, right? From the back, it's all the not-so-good things, the floating things. You need a guardian to protect you from them. Aoboey kong is the guardian."

"Some people call the other things aoboey kong also," Auntie Grace insisted. "Nicer to say."

"Could be, could be," said an auntie peaceably. "People give different-different names. Some say 'ho hia ti.' Means the same thing."

Jess sat up, forgetting to look innocent. "People call ghosts 'good brothers'?"

The word "ghosts" sent a ripple of unease through the group. Kor Kor gave Jess a sharp look.

"Less scary to say 'good brothers' mah," said Kor Kor. "People don't like to talk about spirits directly. But this house doesn't have such things, so you all don't need to worry."

Her tone said the discussion was over.

Jess decided not to push her luck. She was feeling a little shaken herself.

This changed nothing, she told herself. She must have known that ghosts were referred to as "good brothers" in Hokkien, even if she hadn't consciously remembered it. The raspy voice hadn't told her anything she didn't know, because it was impossible for a voice in her head to belong to anyone but Jess herself.

Given what her family was like, it was no wonder her brain had decided to interpret her stress-induced auditory hallucinations as the rantings of a ghost. It was true Mom and Dad never talked about ghosts or spirits. They weren't especially pious and they tended to be wary of people who were. Their approach to religion was to leave the gods alone, in the hope the gods would return the favor.

But superstition was built into their worldview. A fundamental belief in the supernatural had permeated the home Jess had grown up in. Despite her Western acculturation, it was one of the things she'd absorbed passively from her upbringing, like a taste for spicy food and a familiarity with Cantopop standards. Officially she didn't believe in ghosts, but part of her wasn't a hundred percent sure.

Over the next couple of days, her unease faded. The voice didn't make a reappearance, and she was feeling OK. She'd managed to persuade herself that the voice had been a one-off—a weird side effect of jet lag—when the dreams started up again.

They weren't like the ones she'd been having before. In these new dreams, she was herself, with only her own burdens to bear— no screaming baby or household chores. There were no longer any rubber plantations or old-fashioned bathrooms with water tanks instead of showers. Instead, she was always in Kor Kor's house.

Yet she wasn't quite her waking self. Her vision was hazy, her center of balance altered. She stumbled around rooms that should have been familiar, bruising herself against furniture, stubbing her toes on doors. It was like she'd forgotten how to be in her body.

She didn't do much in these dreams. Only wandered around the quiet dark house, touching things, sometimes lifting them with great care. She didn't want to break anything, or give away her presence. She needed this time to work things out.

She always woke up exhausted.

She remembered the voice saying, *Who do you think has been sending you all those dreams?* But she pushed the memory away, squashing down the accompanying panic.

There was no need for an esoteric explanation of the dreams. In her waking life Jess felt like a tiny baby deer staggering around, perpetually on the verge of fucking things up irreparably. In the dreams, she was confused by things she knew, unable to master her own body. You didn't have to be Freud to work out the connection.

Still, after the third wandering-around-the-house dream, Jess finally rang the numbers Sharanya had found and booked an appointment. She didn't have health insurance, but she had some money saved up from photography jobs that her parents had refused to touch, and she'd benefit from the exchange rate. She'd be able to afford one session, at least. As for how she'd pay for more—and how she'd get to her appointment without her family finding out—she'd figure that out later.

THREE

Jess rose early for a job interview the next day. She was recuperating over a mug of Milo when her aunt came in from the garden.

"Min, you're up already?" said Kor Kor, glancing at the clock. She started working in her garden at six thirty every morning, when it wasn't even light out yet, so as to get in as much gardening as she could before it got hot.

"Skype interview." Jess rubbed her eyes. Last night's wandering-around-the-house dream had been especially long and tedious. She felt exhausted, even though she'd gone to bed at nine. "It was a guy in KL and his boss in California."

"Ah, your interview! Forgot it was today," said Kor Kor. "How was it? You made Milo, is it? Very good!" She said it as though pouring hot water on chocolate powder was an amazing feat of cooking. "You want to try chicken biscuit? Auntie Poh Eng brought from Seremban.

"You must eat. Gives you energy," she said when Jess tried to refuse. "Not good you're still suffering from jet lag. How long since you came back—two weeks?"

"Almost, yeah," said Jess.

It felt like longer. Her time in Malaysia felt like a dream. She couldn't quite make herself believe that she wasn't going to wake up to her real life in America.

Something niggled at her. What was it Kor Kor had said?

"I'm not suffering from jet lag," said Jess, but she was so out of it doubt crept up on her. "Am I?"

"So long already and you're still waking up at two a.m.," said Kor Kor. "You scared me. I thought must be a burglar. Otherwise why got people moving around the house in the middle of the night?"

Jess hadn't stirred till her alarm went off at five. "I didn't wake up at two a.m."

But Kor Kor had the typical auntie trait of being better at talking than listening.

"I didn't know your Hokkien is so good!" she said. "Can beat your cousins any day. Kor Tiao and I spoke English to them when they were small. Didn't want them to be confused. We thought English is better—they'll be able to read books, watch TV all that. Nowadays they say good for children to learn different languages when they're small . . . Aiyah, back then we didn't know!" She sighed. "Ching Yee they all can speak, but can order food and get around only. Not to your level."

Jess spoke Hokkien haltingly, liberally mixed with English, and only ever to her parents. Her first thought was that Kor Kor must have confused her with someone else.

"I can't speak that well," she said. She saw that Kor Kor took her self-deprecation as a social nicety, expected and meaningless. "Uh, when were we speaking Hokkien?"

"When you woke up in the night," said Kor Kor. "You don't remember?"

"I didn't wake up last night," Jess repeated, but her certainty faltered under Kor Kor's surprised gaze.

An indistinct image surfaced in her mind. Her own feet, going down the stairs, step by step . . . But that had been part of the dream, hadn't it?

Or had it? Other sensations returned to her. Making her way around a dark room, running her hand over a countertop, feeling cool tiles under the bare soles of her feet. A light had come on, the harsh glare startling her. Kor Kor's voice had said, "You're awake, Min? Why you didn't on the light?"

Jess passed a hand over her face, unnerved. "I forgot."

"We talked for so long some more!" said Kor Kor. "Must be you really went back to sleep afterwards. That's good. At your age you shouldn't take so long to adapt. My children, after a few days they're OK already—no more hangover."

Jess couldn't recall anything of the conversation they'd apparently had. It was strange feeling out the gap in her memories, like probing the space left by a missing tooth with her tongue. "What did we talk about?"

"Nothing much," said Kor Kor. "Talked about what is it like, working for Kor Tiao's company. How much is this house, all that."

Jess gaped. "I asked you how much your house cost?"

Kor Kor looked into Jess's face. "You really don't remember, hah? You must have been sleepwalking. All this stress sure will have some effect on your system."

She had come a little too close to the truth. Jess felt herself withdraw. She forced a smile.

"What stress?" she said. "I'm staying in my generous aunt's house with nothing to do but enjoy myself."

The charm assault always worked on Mom and Dad. Jess had forgotten she wasn't talking to them. Kor Kor patted her arm.

"You really know how to talk after you live in US," she said indulgently. "Don't need to worry so much. Your mother and father can handle themselves, you know. You're a good girl, but you don't have to think about them only. I always tell people, let the children live their own lives! But they don't listen to me."

Jess hadn't expected this, or the reaction it elicited from her. She looked down at her mug, blinking back sudden tears. She tamped down on the flare of unreasonable fury—the feeling both that she'd been found out and that Kor Kor had gotten everything completely wrong.

"I'm not worried about Mom and Dad. It's me I'm most worried about," she said lightly.

Kor Kor nodded, as though Jess had agreed with her.

"Correct. Better to think about yourself," she said. "We all older people give advice is because we want to help, but sometimes it's too much also. You have to stand up for yourself. You must say, 'Kor Kor! I don't want to open my own business. Keep your silly ideas to yourself.'"

Jess said, with a genuine smile this time, "I don't think my parents would be impressed if I talked to you like that."

"That's how Ching Yee talks," said Kor Kor, with a mix of disapproval and pride. "She didn't grow up in US also, but she's so clever to talk back. If it was her, she would have said to me in front of everybody, 'Haiyah, Mom, don't need to talk so much about this Ng Chee Hin's son. If you want your child to be like him, you should have married Ng Chee Hin!'"

Jess laughed. "I should've thought of that."

"When I told you about this Ng Wei Sherng the other day, it was just an idea only," said Kor Kor. "Uncle Hui says better not copy him. The Ng family are mixed up in all this funny business. How I know? Ng Chee Hin is one of Kor Tiao's big customers. Kor Tiao says he's very decent now, but last time, who knows?"

She shook her head. "Hai, Malaysia is like that. Cannot make money if you're completely straight. That's why. You must make your own decisions. You studied at Harvard what. I am just a kampung girl. Who am I to tell you what to do? Even helping Kor Tiao with his business, if you don't want, you must tell us."

They had evidently covered a lot of ground in this conversation that Jess had forgotten. She felt adrift.

"Don't worry, I wasn't planning on copying Ng Chee Hin's son," she said. "Uh, when you say 'helping Kor Tiao,' what exactly do you mean?"

"Good," said Kor Kor, talking over her. "You asked me so many questions about this boy, I thought, 'Cham liao, I make Min worried only.'"

"Wait, what?" said Jess. "I asked about Ng Chee Hin's son? When?"

"When we were talking at two a.m. that time. You forgot ah?" said Kor Kor. "You asked how many cafés does Ng Wei Sherng own, what property does the father hold. Must be you're really stressed, until even in your sleep you can ask this kind of thing. You must let go. It's OK one. Your father has recovered already what. I will pray for you all."

Jess put her mug carefully down on the table. Her hand shook slightly as she did it. She hoped Kor Kor didn't notice.

"Right," she said. "Thanks, Kor Kor."

"YOU WIN," SAID Jess. "You're real. You're haunting me. Now what?"

There was no answer. In normal conditions this wouldn't have been surprising, since no one else was there. Jess had locked herself in the bathroom because that was where the voice who claimed to be Ah Ma had last spoken to her.

She looked at herself, pale and sweating, in the mirror. She definitely looked like she was going crazy. But who wouldn't, with a ghost talking to them?

Part of her was still resisting the idea, holding out for a world where ghosts weren't real. So she'd had vivid dreams of places she had never seen, rich with intimate details of things she knew nothing about. They were probably things she'd absorbed when she was young, said the rational part of her brain. Impressions and experiences that had been stored in her subconscious without her realizing it.

As for the fact she'd had a whole conversation with Kor Kor and couldn't remember a word of it, there was nothing uncanny about that, said this part of her brain. She'd been sleepwalking. People could have conversations when they were sleepwalking that they had no memory of later.

There was no need for a supernatural explanation for the fact she had been asking Kor Kor about Ng Chee Hin's son. Jess had looked Ng Wei Sherng up online after hearing about him. He was only four years older than her, and he was everything she wasn't—straight, successful, certain of where he was going in life. He had degrees from Oxford *and* Stanford. Sure, his family was rich, but he was legitimately making money from his cafés—Malaysia's business press was clear on that. Plus he was dating a gorgeous heiress who was equally accomplished and glamorous, according to the several features Malaysian *Tatler* had done on them.

Admittedly it wasn't like Jess aspired to any of this—though she wouldn't have said no to the heiress. But Ng Wei Sherng had been held up to her as a model. It was natural that her sense of inadequacy should have fixated on him.

Yet even as her brain reeled off all the reasons why everything that had happened wasn't caused by her being haunted by a ghost, she tilted the mirror toward herself.

"Come on," she said aloud. "I said I believed in you. Stop hiding."

Something weird was going on. Jess wasn't imagining it. The

voice in her head wasn't caused by stress; it was *real*. The certainty of it lodged in her gut.

Wah, can order her grandmother around, hah? I told you, no need to talk so loud. Talk in your head enough already.

Jess started. It was like the voice had spoken in her ear. She was still the only person that she could see in the room, but she wasn't alone anymore.

The new presence was unmistakable. She could almost feel the warmth of its body. A smell that was a mix of cigarette smoke and talcum powder rose in her nostrils.

I said I believe you exist, said Jess, ignoring the terrified lurch in her chest. *Not that I believe you're my grandmother.*

You want Ah Ma to prove who I am? It was hard to tell whether the voice was amused or irritated. *Why you didn't ask your mother about your dreams?*

Disjointed images from the dreams came back to Jess. Worn clothes hanging on a line, the cool air of early morning among the rubber trees, the baby wailing as she chopped vegetables for dinner . . .

The baby was Mom? said Jess.

I only had one daughter, but she doesn't know how to give back to her mother, said the voice. *You saw what. Ah Ma's life was not easy.*

You gave me dreams of your life, said Jess slowly. It explained the vivid specificity of the dreams, how foreign they were and yet familiar. *Why?*

So you can understand Ah Ma, said the voice. *Your mother didn't know how to be filial. Even before you all went off to US, she didn't want to bring you to see me. I only had chance to go to your full moon because Ah Ku brought me. If it was left to your mother, hah! She won't even tell me she's having a celebration.*

Ah Ku was Jess's mom's brother, the one who was always trying to borrow money from her.

The story sounded legit, from the little Jess knew of her mom's family. It hadn't seemed necessary before to know any more than Mom wanted to share. For the first time, Jess found herself wishing she'd pushed Mom harder for answers.

Why didn't Mom want to see you? she asked. *Did you guys fight?*

Fight? The voice dripped with contempt. *Why should I fight with my daughter? Who is she to fight me? I am the mother. It's for her to listen, not to talk back.*

This definitely sounded like what an asshole would say. Jess felt a brief flush of vindication. *I told you, Sharanya!*

She pulled herself together. The voice hadn't proved itself yet. For all Jess knew, she was being haunted by some random spirit, assuming the guise of her late grandmother for nefarious ghost reasons.

What would her grandmother know that a spectral rando wouldn't?

Start with the basics.

If you're my grandmother, when did you die? said Jess.

The voice laughed. Except that it was hoarser and older, the laugh was eerily similar to her mom's.

After you die, it's different. Not like when you're living. No clocks, no calendars. What day, what time, I cannot tell you. Ah Ku brought me to hospital in the seventh month, Hungry Ghost Festival that time. After that, I don't know.

Ah Ma had died last September, so she could have been admitted in August. That had coincided with the seventh month in the Chinese lunar calendar. Jess knew that because they'd been going through an especially rough patch in August and she'd blown her fee from a corporate shoot on a spa day with her mom, as a much-needed treat.

It hadn't been a great success. Mom didn't like being hot, so she hadn't used the sauna or steam room, and she'd refused to go swimming in the fancy pool because it was the Hungry Ghost Month, when it was apparently bad luck to do anything that might—for example—carry a risk of drowning.

OK, then, said Jess, racking her brains for another question. *What did you die of?*

I don't remember, said the voice. *But what is surprising about an old woman dying? Actually my fate is not to have a long life. I should have died long ago. When I was your age, I got snake disease. You know what is snake disease? You get red spots all over. Very painful. The red spots spread around your waist and when they meet, you will die. I was like that.*

The voice had to belong to an old person, given how much it liked rambling about the past.

But you lived? said Jess.

The god saved me, said the voice.

So the ghost was religious, thought Jess. Could the ghost hear the thoughts that weren't deliberately addressed to it? It didn't seem like it, or presumably it would have jumped on Jess calling it an asshole in her head.

Of course, there was some counter-evidence. Jess remembered the first thing the voice had said to her. *Does your mother know . . . ?*

It was strange how hard it was to put the thought into words. The ghost already knew. And yet Jess felt hideously exposed. Her heart pounding, her palms damp, she said, *My grandmother wouldn't know that I was—that I'm gay.*

That one I didn't know before I died, said the voice. *I found out when I looked at the photos on your phone. Got a lot of you and that Indian girl.*

You looked through my phone? said Jess.

It was ridiculous to feel violated by this. The voice was in Jess's *head*. But she found she'd nevertheless been assuming a space sacred to herself, a locked room in her soul to which the ghost had no access. To have this belief ripped away made her feel as though the floor was buckling beneath her feet.

Get a grip, Jess told herself. The ghost didn't know everything she knew, or it wouldn't have had to ask what the uncles and aunties had been saying about Ng Chee Hin.

That was important to the ghost. It claimed to be Ah Ma, but it hadn't bothered trying to talk to Jess's mom, Ah Ma's own daughter whom she hadn't seen in years. Instead the ghost had used Jess to interrogate Kor Kor about the Ngs.

There was something there. But first, Jess needed to work out how much the ghost knew and what it was capable of. It had to be able to see and hear at least some of what she saw and heard, or it wouldn't have overheard the conversation about Ng Wei Sherng's hipster cafés. And it was able to assume control of Jess's body, even talk *as* Jess, without Jess's knowing it. There had been that lost two a.m. conversation with Kor Kor—but had the ghost talked to anyone else? What else had the ghost been doing with her body that Jess couldn't remember?

Panic surged inside her. She stamped it down. Whoever the voice belonged to, it was a person she had to have a clear head to deal with.

When did you see my photos? she said, as neutrally as possible.

When you were sleeping, said the voice.

Maybe the ghost was only able to take over when Jess was asleep. That would make sense. The past few weeks had been so busy that she would have noticed if she'd lost any blocks of time during the day.

If you don't want your mother to know about this girl, you must be more careful, the voice was saying. *Ah Ma is so old and even I knew how to find your photos. If I can do it, your mother sure can one. You better get rid of them.*

Jess was trying not to offend the ghost before she could find out what she needed to know, but she couldn't help an icy note creeping into her reply. *I've been a little busy. I was going to delete them anyway.*

Why? The voice sounded interested. *You and the Indian girl no more already, is it?*

It was actually because Jess had already decided she should start taking cybersecurity measures, now that she was living with her family without a job or an external social life or even a car to get her out of the house. Her parents were no great respecters of privacy. Jess could imagine them picking up her phone for some innocuous reason and stumbling onto her photos all too easily.

But she wasn't about to explain that. Sharanya was not something Jess was willing to discuss with any member of her family, living or dead—much less a ghost of dubious provenance.

The ghost drew its own conclusions from her silence.

Well, these affairs are like that, it said. *Woman going with woman, it won't last long. It's not like you're not pretty what. You should be able to find a boyfriend, no problem.*

Nothing you've said proves you're my grandmother, said Jess sharply.

The ghost lost patience with her. *You ah, if your head got chopped off, you'd ask Tai Su Yah to prove you're dead! If still need proof some more, why don't you ask your mother how old is she? Call her to show her IC. Then you'll have your proof. Such thing! If you don't want to layan me, just say. I am not the kind to go where I am not welcome.*

Jess could point out the flagrant untruth of this, but it would only piss off the ghost further. Instead she said, with the ingenuousness that always took authority figures off their guard, *What do you mean, her IC? What's an IC?*

IC also you don't know? It's a card. Got your photo, your name, address all that. If you're a citizen, you will have. America don't have meh?

Jess wasn't about to be drawn into a discussion of American identity documents. *I'll ask my mom about her IC*, she said. *I've got another question.*

You asked so many already, said the voice sullenly. *Ah Ma is tired of answering. You should talk less, listen more.*

Why do you want to know about Ng Chee Hin? said Jess.

After a brief pause, the voice said:

He is the enemy of the god.

Something in the voice made Jess shudder. It was as though a window had opened, letting in the chill air of the underworld.

What god? said Jess.

There was a silence, going on for long enough that Jess began to wonder if the ghost was sulking, or had gone off somewhere. *Could* it go off somewhere? Or was it in Jess's head all the time?

Jess tried again.

What happened to make you want to stay in this world? she said. *Why are you haunting me?*

So we can settle that useless bastard lah, said the ghost, sounding faintly surprised. *What else?*

FOUR

Jess didn't manage to extract an explanation from the ghost of what it meant by "enemy of the god." She was left to undertake her own investigations.

It helped that the ghost hadn't chosen just anybody as the object of her undead grudge. Dato' Ng Chee Hin was the fifth richest man in Malaysia, according to *Forbes*. Typing his name into a search engine brought up a ton of hits, even more than when Jess had stalked his son online.

You had to have a net worth of $250 million to even be on *Forbes*'s list. The first thing Jess had done after finding this out was check if there were any vacancies at Ng Chee Hin's company, but there was nothing she was qualified for, and everything required three to five years of experience anyway.

After this, she would not have been displeased to find evidence of the company's being shady. But as far as she could tell, Sejahtera Holdings had a clean slate. There was extensive coverage of the corporation and its owner in the press, but no trace of the funny business Kor Kor's gossipy uncle friend had mentioned. Ng Chee

Hin seemed to spend most of his time cutting ribbons at charity events. He made a lot of donations to Buddhist and Taoist organizations. It didn't really seem like "enemy of god" behavior.

The gossipy uncle had been right about one thing. Ng Chee Hin was close to the government. Jess could have made a decent-sized collage with all the photos of Dato' Ng shaking hands with various politicians. He didn't appear to have suffered from the regime change. When you were that rich, probably every political party wanted to be your friend.

It was only when it occurred to Jess to try searching Sejahtera Holdings together with the keyword "god" that she turned up something promising—a brief article dating from the previous year, with the headline "Appeal to Halt Temple Demolition."

> Devotees are urging the authorities to intervene to save the Heaven's Fortune Temple in Air Itam from demolition. Though small, the temple boasts a unique layout among Penang temples and is known for the bodhi tree in the temple courtyard, which shelters altars dedicated to different gods. The picturesque tree is said to be more than 100 years old.
>
> Developers served an eviction notice on the temple committee after the land was acquired by Sutera Sejahtera Sdn Bhd, a joint venture between Sejahtera Holdings and the Sutera Makmur Group.
>
> "We hope the developers will not take any hasty action," said the temple committee chairman, Barry Lim. "We are willing to discuss with them to find a good outcome for all parties, but we are not afraid to fight them in court. Their actions are insensitive to the religious sentiments of the devotees."
>
> The developers could not be reached for comment.

Jess couldn't find any further reports on what had happened. Searching the name of the temple didn't turn up any relevant hits.

There was plenty of news about the two companies mentioned in the article, Sejahtera Holdings and the Sutera Makmur Group, but nothing else on the joint venture. What any of this had to do with her supposed maternal grandmother was beyond her.

Maybe the ghost was one of the devotees who'd wanted to save the temple. It seemed a strange cause to remain on earth for, but then again, it wasn't like Jess was the best judge of Ah Ma's priorities. She literally couldn't remember the last time they'd met.

Of course, there was one person who might be able to tell her more.

She had to wait a few days before she had the chance to talk to Mom in private. It came when she was driving Mom around Penang in Kor Kor's car. They'd dropped Kor Kor herself off at a friend's house and would pick her up at the end of the day; Mom was using the intervening time and access to a car to run some errands.

"Mom," said Jess, "was Ah Ma religious?"

Mom was jumpy. "What? Who is religious? Watch out for the motorbike there! Must be more careful. Penang drivers cannot trust one. If you damage Kor Kor's car, then how?"

"Don't touch the steering wheel," said Jess irritably, leaning away from her. "You're going to get us killed. I know how to drive, Mom. Chill."

This was a misstep. Mom hated any reference to death or dying. Jess had to wait out a lecture on watching one's tongue, rejecting the American practice of saying everything that came into one's head, and indeed seeking to purge all inauspicious elements from one's thoughts before she could repeat her question.

"Ah Ma?" said Mom. "You mean my mother?"

"Yeah, your mother," said Jess. "My grandmother. Was she really into religion? Was there, like, a god she prayed to, or a temple she went to regularly?"

"Well," said Mom cautiously, "older people tend to be interested in religion. At that age, you start thinking about the next life."

Jess recognized this as Mom retreating behind the cloud of vagueness that was her customary defense against the awkwardness of not being able to tell the full truth.

Interesting, thought Jess.

"Why?" said Mom.

Jess shrugged. "Just wondering. Being here, it's made me realize I don't know as much about you guys as I should. I had no idea Dad used to be this bad-boy type, until Kor Kor got those photos out."

"Dad liked to ride motorbike and have long hair only," said Mom. "Actually he was a good boy. You ask Kor Kor. He was always careful what he said to his parents."

Clearly "you're going to get us killed" was still on her mind. Before she could get started down that road again, Jess said hastily:

"But it's weird, all the things I don't know. I don't know anything about your side of the family."

"There's nothing to know what," said Mom, contradicting herself immediately by adding, "Ah Ma had her own lifestyle. Where she prayed, what she did . . . I didn't know much. I was a small girl only. Some more she was a very private person, didn't tell people things. If you tell people about your life, they will sure comment one. She didn't like people to comment."

She sighed. "Ah Ma was different. Not like other people."

Jess snuck a look at her. She was gazing out of the window, a distant look on her face.

Jess wondered what it had been like to have a mother who had imparted so little of herself to her. Mom might not talk much about her family, but she overshared about pretty much everything else. Jess often wished Mom would exercise a little more restraint, but when it came down to it, she didn't really want a different kind of mom.

"Did you . . ." Jess hesitated. "Did you love her?"

She wasn't sure what answer she expected, but it was like she'd asked if Mom loved her. Mom replied, without hesitation or doubt, "Yes. She's my mother. No matter what, how can I not love?"

Glancing at her, Jess realized there were tears in her eyes. She reached out and patted Mom's hand. "Sorry, Mom."

Mom squeezed her hand. A brief silence fell. They were drawing up at a traffic light when Mom said:

"Min, I give you advice ah. You don't get angry at me."

This was standard Mom formula, prefacing unsolicited commentary on Jess's life and choices, from the trivial to the major. She could be about to recommend that Jess change her brand of deodorant, or tell her to go to law school.

"I'm making no promises," said Jess. "Hit me."

"When you start work on Monday, don't need to do too much," said Mom. "Just because Kor Tiao is your uncle doesn't mean you have to work so hard for him. They're not paying you also. Do the minimum, enough already."

It was a good thing they were still waiting for the light to turn green, or Jess probably would have swerved in a way that would give Mom legitimate grounds for freaking out. "Uh, what?"

"Not that I'm talking bad about Kor Tiao and Kor Kor," said Mom. "They are letting us stay in their house. Of course I appreciate. But at the end of the day, relative or not, people will always put their own interest first. You have to look after yourself."

"What are you talking about?" said Jess. "I'm not starting work on Monday. I don't have a job."

Mom blinked. "That's why. Because you're not working, you

can go help Kor Tiao at his company. They need somebody to design their leaflets, do the website all that. Their designer threw notice few weeks ago, they haven't been able to find a replacement yet. I told Kor Kor you're very clever at this kind of thing. They're very happy."

"Are they? Great. That's great," said Jess, her voice rising. "When were you guys going to tell me? Monday morning?"

"We told you what," Mom protested. "Kor Kor said she talked to you about it, few days ago. At first she wasn't sure whether you'll want to do it or not. She said, 'Min went to Harvard, she wants to work for our company meh? It's a SME only. Family-owned business.' She said she told you if you don't want to do, don't need. But you said you're OK with it."

"When did I say that?" Jess began, but the memory of her early-morning conversation with Kor Kor came back to her.

What was it Kor Kor had said? *Even helping Kor Tiao with his business, if you don't want, you must tell us.*

Jess had been too distracted by the discovery that she'd been talking to her aunt in her sleep to probe further at the time. Apparently among all the other things the ghost had done, she had committed Jess to taking a job at her uncle's kitchen appliance business.

Jess rubbed her temples.

"I wasn't really paying attention," she said. "So I'm starting on Monday. And I'm not getting paid?"

"Kor Tiao offered to give you the same salary as the last guy, but Dad said don't want," said Mom. "After all, you're helping Kor Tiao, but they're doing you a favor also. You can put it on your CV. When you get a real job, you don't need to work there anymore. Kor Kor and Kor Tiao understand."

Jess stared at the road.

Designing leaflets about fridges wasn't exactly what she thought she would be doing when she'd first left home for college. Even now, after the past couple of years had royally messed up all her ideas about herself and what her life was going to be like, she'd had other plans for how she was going to spend her time in Penang. Applying for jobs was like a full-time job in itself. Around that she'd been planning a project photographing old things in George Town. There was ample material—buildings, signs, walkways, picturesquely worn old walls with paint flaking off them . . .

Plus she was supposed to be talking to Sharanya on Monday morning. Not that she could use that as an excuse. The point of having the calls early in the morning was so no one in her family would know.

Her silence was making Mom anxious. "Min, you must understand. Dad is very paiseh. Kor Kor is his younger sister, but we're living in their house, eating their food. Dad is getting a good salary from Kor Tiao some more."

Jess could say no. They weren't entitled to her free labor. She had some savings, so if it was a question of paying rent, contributing to the household expenses, she could offer to do that instead.

But she knew she wasn't going to. The ghost agreeing on her behalf mattered less than the fact her parents had said she was going to do it. To contradict them would be to embarrass them in front of Kor Kor and Kor Tiao. She couldn't do that. Her parents had almost nothing left except their face.

"Actually I'm not so keen also," said Mom. "It was my idea. When Kor Kor said she's scared you'll get bored, it just came out. You know what Mom is like. But after that, I regretted. Why should you work for Kor Tiao's company for free? Are you a slave?"

This was classic Mom: zero to sixty in about a nanosecond. Torn between resentment and laughter, Jess said, "Mom . . ."

"Kor Tiao is a good brother-in-law, good uncle, doesn't mean he's a good boss," said Mom. "I'm worried about Dad, you know.

Kor Tiao knows he's not strong. He's not supposed to strain himself. But still they ask Dad to be the installer. If Kor Tiao wants to help him, he should give him a job where he's sitting in the office. Instead Dad is going out in the hot sun, carrying all these heavy items into people's houses. That's something wrong, isn't it?"

This gave Jess pause. Dad didn't talk much about what he did at work, so she'd only been distantly aware of the details. He didn't seem unhappy with his job. But it wasn't like he was going to be negative about it when he was living under his employer's roof, was he?

"Dad has been working long hours," said Jess slowly. Dad usually got home past eight, so tired he barely said anything at dinner. He even worked on Saturdays. Kor Tiao did, too, so Jess had assumed it was a Malaysian thing, but still . . .

"Too long!" said Mom. "Min, maybe you don't like this plan, working at Kor Tiao's company. But if you're there, you can watch out for Dad. Make sure they're not bullying him."

That made Jess grin despite herself. "I don't see anybody bullying Dad." He was quieter than Mom, but equally stubborn.

"You don't know," said Mom. "Dad is different now."

But she was wrong. Jess did know that. It was a good thing people didn't die of broken hearts anymore, or Dad would have been a goner.

As it was, he wasn't himself—hadn't been in a long while. Jess had hoped coming back to Malaysia and having a job would make a difference.

Guilt squirmed in her chest. It had been easy to hope, easier than actually doing something. It was time she got off her ass and tried to help.

"I'll do it," she said. As if there had ever been a chance she wasn't going to.

* * *

JESS DROVE MOM to the wet market and the post office. They picked up some clothes Mom had sent to a tailor for alterations, and then there was a place she wanted to try for lunch: "Kor Kor said the kway chap is famous. They serve with duck."

They passed a temple on the way. It reminded Jess of her original plan to pump Mom for information.

She was unlikely to get a better chance anytime soon, especially if she was going to be stuck in a nine-to-five office job starting Monday. It was worth a shot.

Jess said casually, "Did you ever go to that temple with Ah Ma when you were a kid?"

"What temple? Back there?" The temple was already receding into the distance. Mom twisted, craning to see it. "No lah. That's a Thai temple. We tend to go to Chinese temples."

"You guys switched it up?" said Jess. "There wasn't just one you used to go to?"

"Temple is not like church," Mom explained. "Most Christians don't go to different church every week. But Taoist, you can pray to a lot of gods. The gods don't mind."

But Mom was holding something back. The fog of vagueness had risen around her again.

Jess said suspiciously, "So was there not a main temple Ah Ma liked, or . . . ?"

"Do you have any appointment tomorrow?" said Mom, as though she hadn't heard her. "Tomorrow you can drive me to JPN. Have to go in the morning, otherwise have to wait for a long time. I need to change my IC. The new one is biometric, it has a chip inside. When you go KL you can use to take the MRT."

Jess had no idea what she was talking about, but if she asked she would just be enabling Mom in her transparent attempt to change the subject. Jess was opening her mouth to call her out on it when a recollection pricked at her. The ghost had said she should ask to look at Mom's IC.

"IC's identity card, right?" she said. "Can I see yours? I've never seen one."

"While you're driving?"

"I meant later lah," said Jess, because Manglish in her accent always made Mom laugh. It worked this time too.

The place they went to for lunch was a classic Penang establishment, in a shophouse with tables spilling out onto the road. The food was served from a stall at the front, with meat and offal stacked on a metal table and two sweaty chefs ladling soup out of huge pots. They only served one dish: a bowl of wide rice noodles in a savory dark broth redolent of cinnamon and star anise, piled high with braised duck meat, pig intestines and other viscera Jess couldn't identify.

It was the kind of thing that would have been hard to explain if she'd brought it as a packed lunch to school—but all of that belonged to a different life, in a different world. Here, there was no shortage of appreciation for the restaurant's offering. Jess and her mom joined a line of hungry Penangites and tourists, drawn there by food bloggers and recommendations passed through the auntie network.

After they'd gotten a table and ordered, Jess studied Mom's identity card. Mom looked like a youthful stranger in the photo, as yet untouched by the rigors of her years in America.

To hide how much the image moved her, Jess said, "That was a really unfortunate perm."

"Back then very trendy," said Mom absently. She was busy glaring at the people lining up at the stall, as though she suspected them of having designs on her kway chap.

"Wait," said Jess. "This says you were born in 1963."

"I think we're supposed to go there and wait for our food," said Mom, half rising.

"Sit down. I'll go," said Jess. "That's wrong, isn't it? You were born in 1962."

"Oh, that," said Mom. "My father was slow to register me, so birth cert and IC say 1963. Actually I'm born 1962, tiger year. But my parents told people I'm born one year later, rabbit year. Tiger girls supposed to be fierce, hard to find husband."

"Oh," said Jess. "So nobody else knows?"

"You and Dad only," said Mom. "No harm people think I'm younger, right? Min, don't you think you better go now? After someone take our food. These Singaporeans don't give chance one."

"OK, Mom," said Jess. She got up, handing the card back to her mom. "Don't worry."

WHAT'S YOUR BEEF with Ng Chee Hin? said Jess.

The voice said, *Why you always want to talk to Ah Ma in the bathroom?*

Mom doesn't knock before coming into the bedroom, said Jess. *Is it because of the temple?*

The ghost said, *How come you know about the temple?*

I Googled Ng Chee Hin's company, said Jess. She remembered the ghost—Ah Ma—was an old person. *I mean, I looked it up online. There's this thing called the internet, you can type in any word and find out about it—*

I know what is Google, said Ah Ma. *I only died last year! They wrote about what that bastard is trying to do to the temple on the internet, is it? What did they say?*

There was a piece from last June about Sejahtera Holdings taking over a piece of land with a temple on it, said Jess. *Is that what you were talking about when you said Ng Chee Hin was the enemy of the god?*

They wrote about it in June? said Ah Ma. *What happened since then?*

I don't know, said Jess.

She could feel the presence bristle. *You don't think you can bluff me! Ah Ma is very clever to find things out. You saw what, even things your mother doesn't know I know.*

I'm not trying to bluff you, Jess protested. *I don't know what happened. I couldn't find anything else about it online.*

There was a brief silence.

Only one article, hah? Then after that no more, said Ah Ma. *Could be. All the newspaper reporters are scared of him.*

Why? said Jess.

There was no answer.

Jess said, *If you want me to help you, I need to understand what's going on.*

You're willing to help me? said Ah Ma.

Are you going to get out of my head if I don't help you? said Jess.

I cannot die yet, said the ghost. *I have things to do in this life.*

Then let's get them done, said Jess. *You are my grandmother. I guess I kind of have an obligation to help you move on.*

Oh, now you believe? said Ah Ma acidly. *Last time you were like the police only. Kept asking for proof.*

My mom has the wrong date of birth on her IC, said Jess. *You were right.*

You asked her? Ah Ma sounded a little surprised.

Jess raised her eyebrows, though she wasn't sure if Ah Ma could even see her do it. *You told me to.*

Hmm, said Ah Ma—but she was pleased. *Who knew you're so guai?*

Every one of Jess's relatives knew she was guai—that was to say, good, obedient, compliant, filial, never giving her parents a moment's worry. She found things were easier that way.

Now you know, she said lightly. *I'm so guai I'm going to do what you tell me to. But I need you to do some things in return.*

Ah, here it comes, said Ah Ma. *You want 4D numbers, is it?*

Uh, no, that's not what I meant, said Jess. She paused. *Wait, can you help me win the lottery?*

No, said Ah Ma. *If anybody tells you they can give you winning numbers, whether it's a god or a ghost, you don't believe them. You think bookies don't know how to pray ah? They all pray to the rice sieve. The spirit stops people from guessing the number.*

The spirit of the rice sieve? Jess wondered if her Hokkien had failed her. *You mean, the thing you wash rice in?*

Yes. Very powerful spirit.

Right, said Jess. She couldn't afford to get distracted, she reminded herself. *I didn't mean favors. We need some ground rules if you're going to be riding around in my head. That's fair, isn't it?*

What rules? said Ah Ma cautiously.

Rule number one is, you can't take over my body unless you ask me first.

Even at night? said Ah Ma.

So the night *was* different, thought Jess.

Especially at night, she said firmly. *You've been taking over when I'm asleep, haven't you?*

The silence was as good as an admission.

No more talking to people when I'm asleep, said Jess. *If you want to talk to someone, you can ask me. But you can't just talk through me whenever you feel like it. What was up with you telling my aunt I was fine with working for my uncle?*

What else are you going to do? Not like you have a job, said Ah Ma. *You're living in people's house. Helping their business is a small thing only.*

That's not the point, said Jess. *If you keep doing stuff like that, people are going to notice. I don't speak fluent Hokkien!*

I talked to your aunt once only, said Ah Ma. *I asked so many times also, you didn't want to tell me about Ng Chee Hin. If you told me, I won't need to go ask other people. Not like I want to talk to your aunt. I cannot stand these Chinese people who run off and worship the white people's god.*

Yeah, OK, fine, said Jess. *Do you agree with the rule, though? No talking to anybody through me. And no more of this getting up and doing stuff when I'm asleep.*

Even if I just want to walk around only, I have to ask you first?

Yes, said Jess. *It's my body. I can't be doing ten thousand steps a night, it's tiring! And if people find me walking around at three a.m., they're going to ask questions. It'll start with seeing a doctor, but who's to say it won't end with an exorcist?*

The point went home.

Fine, said Ah Ma grudgingly. *What else?*

No looking at my phone, or my computer, or going through my wardrobe, or any of that stuff.

I can't do anything what. You said already.

Yeah, but you can't peek when I'm looking at my phone or whatever. And no eavesdropping on my conversations.

That one I cannot, said Ah Ma, delighted to have an excuse to be uncooperative. *If you see or hear anything, I see and hear also. Your eyes are my eyes. Your ears are my ears.*

Really? You experience everything I experience? said Jess. *Don't you, I don't know, sleep sometimes?*

I'm dead already. Why I have to sleep for what?

Jess thought of the first time she had realized Ah Ma was talking to her, in Kor Kor's living room, with the uncles and aunties talking about Ng Chee Hin and his son.

If you overhear everything I hear, said Jess, *why would you need me to tell you what Kor Kor's friends were saying about Ng Chee Hin?*

Sometimes I don't pay attention lah. You think your life is so interesting meh?

Then you can zone out when I'm doing personal stuff, can't you?

Jess was rapidly losing credit with the ghost.

You're very choosy, hah, said Ah Ma, peeved. *What other rules you want to impose?*

Just one more, said Jess. *If I ask you a question, you have to answer. And you have to tell me the truth. OK?*

This time there was a pause.

Ah Ma said, *Some things, you have to be ready before they can be told.*

Try me, said Jess.

You have what questions to ask?

There were so many it was hard to know where to start.

What's so special about the temple? said Jess finally. *Why does it matter?*

Ah Ma sighed. *If I want to explain, it's very difficult. Especially for you. Everything also you don't know.*

Jess frowned.

That's not my fault, she began, but Ah Ma cut her off.

You want to know about the temple? she said. *Better I show you.*

FIVE

Driving Ah Ma to the temple the next day laid to rest any remaining doubts Jess might have had about the voice in her head being her grandmother. The ghost was precisely as annoying in a car as Mom was.

Go left after McDonald's, Ah Ma said. Then, *Why you didn't go left? You're supposed to go left back there, that road there. You're wrong already!*

The road before McDonald's? You said after *McDonald's,* said Jess. *Where should I go now?*

How am I supposed to know? said Ah Ma. *If you went left back there, then I can tell you. Here, I don't know. Why you don't want to use Waze? Ah Ku always uses Waze.*

I put the name of the temple into Waze, said Jess, gritting her teeth. *It didn't come up. It's not* in *Waze.*

So many people go there to pray. Cannot be it's not in Waze, said Ah Ma. *You wrote the name in English, is it? You should write in Chinese.*

I don't know Chinese!

Why your mother didn't teach you how to write Chinese? Aren't you Chinese?

They drew up at a traffic light. Jess began to say, "She didn't teach me Chinese because she couldn't read it herself and anyway we went to live in America and she didn't think I'd need it because she had no idea I'd come back to be haunted by my dead grandmother!"

But the man in the next car over was giving her a funny look. Jess realized she was talking out loud. She swallowed her irritation with an effort.

I'll go back to McDonald's, OK? she said—inside her head this time. She smiled reassuringly at the man and sped off when the light turned green.

There were no further misadventures. At Ah Ma's direction she parked in an open space next to a hawker center. There was a ticket booth at the entrance manned by a drowsy Nepali guy, but otherwise not much effort had been made to distinguish the space as a parking lot. It was unpaved, the ground uneven, and there was no lighting. On the far side was a threatening dark mass of trees—undeveloped jungle, Jess supposed. Once it got dark, the only light would be from the hawker center.

Mom would kill her if she got murdered here, she thought.

She got out of the car, locking it. *Are you sure this is it? It looks like somewhere the Mafia would bring people to finish them off.*

I went to this temple every day, said Ah Ma. *You think I don't know where it is? What is Mafia?*

Oh, gangsters, said Jess. *You know, like in* The Godfather.

What nonsense are you talking? said Ah Ma. *A temple is a holy place. People come here to pray, not to fight or do bad things. You should learn to respect. Don't simply talk.*

OK, OK, sorry, said Jess. *Where is the temple?*

There, said Ah Ma.

Where?

There, repeated Ah Ma, in the tone she adopted when she thought Jess was being stupid. Come to think of it, it was the tone she used pretty much all the time. *Where you're looking right now.*

She meant the jungle.

THERE WAS IN fact a sign. As Jess got closer to the trees, she saw a red gate, like a humbler version of a Chinatown gate. It had a roof on it with curved ends, like the roofs on Chinese temples, and a black board inscribed with what Jess assumed was the temple's name, in gold Chinese characters. But any grandeur it might once have had was faded—the gilt had come off a couple of the characters, and the red paint on the gate was flaking off in patches. Beyond the gate was a path leading to a flight of worn steps, also painted red.

The signs of human habitation should have been reassuring. Yet Jess couldn't shake a feeling that she was walking into danger, going somewhere she wasn't supposed to. The trees lining the path gave off a good green smell, but also a sense of oppression; darkness seemed to gather around them. She went through the gate, the skin prickling on the back of her neck. She kept glancing over her shoulder to check she wasn't being followed.

What's there to be afraid of? she asked herself. *You're already haunted.* Ah Ma was such a prosaic ghost it was hard to find her spooky, but objectively she had to be scarier than anything Jess was likely to encounter going along the path.

It was still light, but evening was on its way. The glare of late afternoon had subsided and the color of the sky had softened. Soon the light would turn blue. Jess looked back longingly at the hawker center, coming to life with early dinner customers. It seemed to represent everything ordinary and human, falling away with every step she took.

At the top of the steps the path petered out, swallowed up by long grass. There wasn't even a building. A huge tree towered over a mess of scrub, weeds and wild banana trees growing in tropical profusion.

This is just jungle, Jess said to Ah Ma.

Then the music started up.

It was more noise than music, a cacophonous jangling layered over the deep thudding of a drum. It sounded like there was a lion dance going on or something. The smell of incense came to Jess on a gust of soft air.

It's a garden, said Ah Ma. *You think that big tree will simply grow anywhere? That kind of tree, Buddha meditated under it. It's a special tree.*

Jess looked at the tree again. This must be the bodhi tree the article had mentioned, the one that was over a hundred years old. It looked like several smaller trees had been stuck together to make it. Tangled vines hung down from its spreading branches. Jess stepped gingerly over knobbly roots humping out of the ground.

Now that she was studying the place more closely, she could see it was a garden, a space laid out by humans. Some of the plants, overgrown and jungly as they looked, were in pots. Through the wild grass she could make out paths with cracked paving.

They're behind the tree, said Ah Ma. Her voice in Jess's head vibrated with impatience.

Jess went toward the noise.

There was a crowd of people in the clearing on the other side of the bodhi tree. Jess hung back, not wanting to be seen, but the crowd seemed engrossed in the performance.

It had clearly been going on for some time. The musicians consisted of two men playing a drum and a gong respectively. They were sweating, like they had been at it for a while. But it wasn't a lion dance.

In the center of the clearing a scrawny Chinese man in yellow satin pants was doing what looked like kung fu. He had a sword in his mouth, his teeth gritted on the blade, and a flag in one hand. He was topless except for a satin bib tied around his neck.

The watchers were mostly middle-aged men and women, nearly all Chinese. Their expressions, grave and slightly bored, gave the scene a surreal air of mundanity.

There were a few altars right under the bodhi tree—small, red-roofed structures like miniature houses, sheltering the statues of gods. An incense urn crammed with joss sticks stood before the altars, filling the air with smoke. A cough rose inexorably in Jess's throat, escaping despite her efforts to stifle it.

One of the watchers turned around and saw her. He seemed mildly surprised by the sight of a girl lurking in the shrubbery.

"Are you looking for the god?" he said in English. "You can wait here. He hasn't started consultations yet."

Jess emerged cautiously, joining the circle of watchers. The performer looked familiar, now that she had a better view of him. She'd seen him before, but where?

The man who'd invited her into the circle smiled at her. He was wearing mirrored sunglasses and a red baseball cap with AIR-ASIA on it, but close up, Jess could tell he was younger than most of the other people there, around her own age. It was hard to peg his background—with his skin tone, he could have belonged to almost any of the major or minor ethnic groups resident in Penang.

"Pretty weird, huh?" he said. His accent sounded American. That wasn't what she would've expected in a place like this.

"Yeah," said Jess. "Not really my scene."

"Me neither," said the man. He was listing slightly toward her, speaking in the half shout used to order drinks and conduct flirtations in noisy clubs all the world over. The association made him seem even more incongruous. "My father asked me to come. I'm not very religious."

"What's he, um—" An auntie was peering at them. Jess lowered her voice. "What's that guy doing?"

"You mean the medium?"

The man they were all watching gave an indistinct yell. He seized the hilt of his sword and started slashing industriously at the air.

Nobody seemed alarmed by this behavior. The peeping auntie started recording him on her phone.

"He's gone into a trance and Kuan Kong has entered him," the man in the AirAsia cap explained. "The God of War, you know?"

Jess's expression must have made it obvious that she didn't know.

"They have an altar with him in all the Chinese restaurants," said AirAsia. "He's the one with the red face and the beard. He's a powerful general. That's why the medium's got that sword."

"So he's acting as the god?"

AirAsia's forehead wrinkled. "No, he *is* the god. He'll start taking questions after this." He looked at Jess's face, which was no doubt doing all kinds of things. "You're not from around here, are you?"

I didn't ask you to come here so you can pak tor with boys, said Ah Ma. *Tell the god I'm here.*

What, talk to that *guy?* said Jess, looking at the performer. *I can't interrupt now. Everyone's watching him.*

The medium turned. His eyes locked with Jess's. His face twisted.

He charged directly at Jess, screaming.

Jess recoiled. "What the hell!"

Call him to stop! Tell him it's me, said Ah Ma, sounding panicked. *Faster!*

"Don't worry," whispered AirAsia. "He's just getting rid of the bad spirits. He's not actually attacking you—"

The medium grabbed Jess by the front of her T-shirt, swinging his sword over his head. The auntie who'd been recording him scuttled out of the way, squeaking. "Oi!" said AirAsia. A couple of men in matching polo shirts detached themselves from the circle of watchers and rushed toward the medium.

Jess was raising her hands to shove the medium away when her eyes met his. She froze.

Whatever it was looking out of the medium's eyes, it wasn't a man. It wasn't human.

What are you doing? said Ah Ma. *Tell the god who I am! Once he knows, he'll be OK.*

Jess couldn't talk. Her terror of the thing inside the medium was immediate and visceral, drawing every muscle taut, locking her mouth.

AirAsia grabbed the medium's arm before the sword could descend. "Hey, uncle, cool down!"

The medium—man—*thing* wrenched his arm back from AirAsia. But before the medium could do anything else, the guys in the polo shirts pulled him away.

Jess struggled, hurling herself against the wall of her paralysis, until a crack appeared. Her voice escaped through it, thin and wavering with fright.

"Don't," she said. "I brought somebody with me. She wants to see you. It's . . ."

This was when she realized she did not know Ah Ma's name. Mom had always referred to her as Ah Ma. Her actual name had never come up.

As she stuttered, the thing in the medium looked right through Jess and said:

"Eh, you came back?" The voice was surprisingly deep; it didn't seem like it should be coming out of the medium's thin chest. It spoke Hokkien with a strange accent.

The medium shook off the polo-shirted men absently. It didn't look like he was exerting any effort to do it, even though the men were trying their best to hold on to him. "You didn't say it's you! I thought it was some naughty ghost. You want me to call Little Sister?"

No, no, said Ah Ma hastily. *Tell the god I came to talk to my family only. Ask if I can talk to Ah Soon.*

Jess opened her mouth. Ah Ma added, *Say nicely! Gods, you must ask nicely.*

"She says she wants to talk to Ah Soon, please," said Jess. "Can she?"

"Right now?" said the thing grumpily. "We just started only. Come back tomorrow cannot ah?"

"No," said Jess, before Ah Ma could tell her what answer to give. Ah Ma could say what she liked. Jess was *never* coming back here.

The medium's face frowned, but the thing inside him said, "OK. But don't talk too long. All these people are waiting." It gestured at AirAsia and the other devotees, who were gaping at Jess. Jess gave them a weak smile.

The medium slumped suddenly.

Help him! said Ah Ma.

Jess managed to catch the man before he fell. His chin hit his chest, his arms going slack. The polo shirts took over from her, taking the flag and sword from the medium's limp hands.

"Is he OK?" said Jess tentatively.

She had the impression the polo shirts weren't too pleased with the interruption to the proceedings, but they didn't say anything, only glanced at her briefly before looking away. It took Jess a moment to register that they were afraid of her.

She was still processing this when the medium opened his eyes, raising his head. He blinked and looked around as though he was surprised to find himself where he was.

"What happened? Where did the god go?" he said to the polo shirts.

Then he saw Jess. His eyes widened.

"Ah Min?" he said.

There was a reason the man had looked so familiar, Jess realized. She had seen the way he turned his head innumerable times before. It was the same way Mom did it. Which made sense, because he was Mom's brother.

"Ah Ku," she said.

SIX

Ah Ku led Jess deeper into the garden, away from the crowd.

As they went, Jess glimpsed the statuette of a goddess, lurking in one of the shrines under the bodhi tree. The statuette was of coarse make, the details nearly effaced by time and weather, but it was draped in yellow satin, like an empress. Some of the face could still be made out—thin eyebrows curving over staring, expressionless eyes, a narrow unsmiling mouth. It seemed to be looking directly at Jess.

A shiver ran over her skin. She turned away, unnerved.

"Ask everybody to wait first," Ah Ku had told the guys in the polo shirts, who appeared to be his assistants. "This is my niece from America. I must talk to her."

"It's almost seven p.m. already," one of the polo shirts objected. "The devotees will complain."

"If they want to complain, ask them to complain to the god," said Ah Ku. "He's the one who wants me to talk to my niece. If not, he wouldn't have gone off."

"The god told the girl not to talk too long," said the polo shirt. "Relatives can come to your house what."

But he muttered this last part under his breath. Ah Ku ignored him.

"Come, girl," he told Jess.

She followed her uncle past altars veiled with greenery, then across a bridge arching over a brown pond full of terrapins.

There was a ramshackle structure at the back of the garden—a zinc roof on metal poles, with fluorescent light bulbs strapped to the ceiling. It housed a jumble of old altar tables, candles and other prayer goods, chairs and—for some reason—a mini fridge and a shelving unit piled with snacks. Ah Ku pulled out a red plastic chair for Jess and gave her a carton of chrysanthemum tea.

As Jess struggled to get the straw out of its plastic wrapping, he sat down, lighting a cigarette.

Jess could see why his assistants had been worried. Her uncle had the air of someone settling in for a while.

"Long time haven't seen you," he said. "Last time your mother brought you to visit Ah Ku was when? Eleven, twelve years ago? That time you were a small girl only."

Jess vaguely remembered the visit. Wriggling on a pleather sofa, sticky from the heat, while next to her Mom unsmilingly declined all the food, drink and friendliness Ah Ku offered. On their way out to the car, Ah Ku had asked Mom for money.

"How did you know it was me?" said Jess.

"Oh, Ah Yen showed me your photo on Facebook," said Ah Ku.

Jess had forgotten she was Facebook friends with her cousin. Yew Yen mostly posted Chinese memes Jess didn't understand.

"Who knew you'll be so pretty when you grow up?" Ah Ku marveled. "Last time you're so fat and speccy. Got boyfriend ah?"

Ask him what's happening with the developers, hissed Ah Ma. *What has that bastard been doing?*

Jess was still jumpy from the encounter with whatever it was that had been inside her uncle. Maybe she'd only thought she had seen it, just as she'd half imagined a flash of intelligence in the eyes of the statuette under the tree.

On the other hand, she was in a garden temple overrun by wilderness, watching night advance across the sky, because the voice of her deceased grandmother had sent her there. The sooner she did what she had to do and got out, the better.

"No boyfriend yet," said Jess. "Listen, Ah Ku—"

"You've been in Penang for how long?" said Ah Ku. He showed no surprise when Jess told him it had been a couple of weeks, though the fact this was the first time they were seeing each other was somewhat awkward. "Staying with your father's relatives, is it?"

It struck Jess that Mom might not want Ah Ku to know where they were staying. She didn't even know if Mom had been in touch since they'd arrived in Malaysia.

The pause had gone on for too long.

"Your mother is sensitive, is it?" said Ah Ku. "Don't worry, I won't go and bother her. Hai, if she hasn't invited me to her house, you think I don't know what that means?

"I am not angry," he added reassuringly. "You don't know Ah Ku. I am very cincai. Ah Ma was different. She wasn't happy your mother didn't give her face. I told Ah Ma, aiyah, Ah Chee married already, she belongs to the husband's family now. She doesn't have time to come and layan you. She must look after her husband's family, isn't it?"

Where got she looked after your father's family? Your mother, she looks after herself only, said Ah Ma. *Ask Ah Ku about the temple.*

"Do you work here, Ah Ku?" said Jess. She'd had an idea that Ah Ku ran his own garage, but he could have moved on without telling her mom. Clearly the communication between the siblings wasn't great.

"Work here?" Ah Ku seemed surprised by the question. "No, I do business. Fixing people's cars. You came to my shop what, when you were small. You don't remember?"

"I remember the shop," said Jess. "But I thought, from what you were doing back there . . ."

"I'm the chairman of the temple committee," said Ah Ku.

The article about the temple had quoted a Barry Lim, Jess remembered. Lim was Mom's surname, but it was so common in Malaysia that the name hadn't pinged her when she'd read the article. She'd never heard Mom refer to Ah Ku as anything but Ah Soon, short for Beng Soon, but people often adopted English names in addition to their Chinese names.

"But this is not work," continued her uncle. "All this"—his gesture took in the garden, its altars and the devotees waiting for the stalled ceremony to continue—"is to help people. People come here to ask advice from the gods."

He was a hundred percent serious, as serious as AirAsia had been when he told Jess her uncle was the God of War.

Jess wasn't sure how to react. Fortunately, Ah Ku didn't wait for a response.

"Medium's job is to save the world," he went on. "I don't do it for reward. You think the devotees give big angpow? It's hardly enough to cover the costs of maintenance. Some more you are my niece. Don't need to worry. Tell Ah Ku what you want. I will sure ask the god to help you."

Jess realized he thought she'd come to pray for a blessing, like the men and women waiting to consult the god.

"No, uh," she said, embarrassed. "Thanks, Ah Ku, but I didn't come to ask for anything. I want to know what's happening to this place."

Ah Ku's forehead furrowed. "What's happening?"

Ask about Ng Chee Hin, said Ah Ma. *Ah Ku got all Ds and Es in his exams. He doesn't understand hidden meanings.*

"I heard some developers wanted to demolish the temple?" prompted Jess. "Ng Chee Hin's company was involved?"

The name had a galvanizing effect. Ah Ku had been relaxed and friendly, about to tip another cigarette out of the packet. He jerked upright as though Jess had pricked him with a pin, slamming the cigarette packet on the table.

"That useless bastard!" he shouted. "How did you hear about him?"

"There was an article in *The Star*," said Jess. "It said his company was trying to take over this land, get rid of the temple. But it was from a while ago. I couldn't find anything else on the story."

"You found the article on the internet, is it? That was a long time ago already." Ah Ku calmed down. "They reported one time only, in *The Star* and *Sin Chew*. After that, the newspapers didn't want to print anymore. We made a lot of noise, you know! But after that bastard talked to all his big friends, they didn't want to listen already."

"But what happened?" said Jess. "Are they getting the land, or . . . ?"

"So long as I'm here, that bastard doesn't need to think about touching the temple," said Ah Ku. "The newspapers may be scared of him, but we don't care. The gods are on our side!"

This boy is talking bullshit, said Ah Ma. *Ask him what's really happening. They said they were going to sue the temple, ask the judge to kick us out. Did they win?*

"What happened to the lawsuit?" said Jess.

"We're fighting them," said Ah Ku. "The lawyer says now must wait for the judgment. Until then, the developers cannot do anything. If they want to build, they have to build around the temple."

He narrowed his eyes. "How did you know about the court case? When they sued us, we told everybody also no use. They didn't want to write about it."

Jess hesitated.

Ah Ma said, *You're being shy for what? Say Ah Ma told you.*

But you're dead, said Jess.

Ah Ku is a medium, said Ah Ma. *When you came, he was dancing Kuan Kong. This gods and spirits business, nobody is more used to it than him. You tell him and see.*

"Um," said Jess. "Ah Ma told me about the case. She's, uh—" Jess caught herself before she said "haunting." "She's been talking to me."

Ah Ku's eyes widened. "Ah Ma is here?" He looked at Jess with new respect.

Ah Ma was right, though. There was no trace of skepticism in Ah Ku's expression. He was studying Jess as though he was trying to find some sign of his mother in her face.

"She asked me to come here," said Jess.

Ah Ku said something, but Ah Ma was talking over him in Jess's head, telling her what to say. Jess waved her hand as if to bat away a mosquito, wishing it was as easy to get rid of her grandmother's unquiet spirit.

"Hold on a second," she said out loud. "Take it easy! I'll tell him." To Ah Ku, she said, "Ah Ma's worried about the temple."

Ah Ku glanced around, checking for listeners. It was getting dark, the deep soft shadows cast by the trees and bushes spreading across the garden. He got up and turned on the light before he sat back down again, leaning forward.

"What did Big Sister say?" He said "Ah Chee," the same term he used to refer to Jess's mom, but Jess had a feeling he wasn't talking about Mom this time.

Ah Ma told her the answer, adding, *Don't talk so loud. When you speak about gods, it's better to whisper.*

"Ah Ma didn't ask," Jess told Ah Ku, lowering her voice to the requisite whisper. "But Big Sister should be happy, right? This is her place. Ah Ma wants to look after it."

Ah Ku puffed up like an irate chicken. "You tell Ah Ma, no need to worry. I'm handling it. The case is finished already, now waiting for the judge to decide only. The lawyer says our chances are good. Ah Ma should think of herself. For humans, life and death are our fate. After dying, we must move on to the next life. It's not good to hang around."

"Yes," said Jess, editorializing somewhat. Ah Ma had rich words for sons who presumed to lecture their mothers when they (the mothers) knew more than they (the sons) ever could about the operations of fate. "But Ah Ma can't go until the business is settled. She says you can't trust Ng Chee Hin."

"True also," Ah Ku allowed.

"She says she'll need a medium."

Ah Ku looked alarmed. "I cannot do. The god won't like it. Ah Ma knows also. The gods they all don't like . . ." He cleared his throat instead of saying the word.

"Good brothers?" suggested Jess.

Ah Ku nodded. "If Ah Ma enters me, the god will be angry."

Ah Ku cannot do, agreed Ah Ma. *He must keep his body pure. If not, he'll offend Kuan Kong. But what about Yew Ping?*

Jess relayed this to her uncle, who looked troubled.

"My son?" he said.

"Ah Ping is playful," said Jess. "But he should know how to be a medium. He's been coming to the temple since he was a small boy. He knows all the rites and ceremonies. With Ah Ma's guidance, she thinks he can do it."

Ah Ku shook his head. "Ah Ma doesn't know. Ah Ping is in UK now. He was selling DVDs, but the police caught him."

"Caught him?" said Jess. "What was he doing?"

"Selling DVDs," repeated Ah Ku.

Ah Ma said impatiently, *He means pirated DVDs. You're not supposed to sell.*

"He went and punched the policeman," continued Ah Ku. "I had to give them money, or else Ah Ping would have gone into the lockup." He sighed. "That time, Ah Ma was in hospital. She didn't understand things already, so no use to tell her also. After the funeral, we sent Ah Ping to UK to keep him out of trouble. He's working there now, in a restaurant."

He reflected, puffing on his cigarette. "There's the girls. How about Yew Ling? Or Yew Yen?"

"Ah Ma doesn't want a girl as her medium," said Jess. "She says they're useless. Every month you have to take a break and can't do anything for a few days."

"Ma, you must be more modern." Ah Ku was talking directly to his mother, as though Jess wasn't even there. "Nowadays, men and women, there's not much difference. A boy who is not reliable is useless every day of the month. Isn't it better to have a reliable girl?

"Both the girls are very responsible. You don't," said Ah Ku, with a touch of vinegar in his voice, "see them fighting with policemen. Ah Ling is working in KL now, but Ah Yen is quite big already—eighteen years old."

Ah Yen is going to university, no? said Ah Ma sharply. *I don't want her. She should be studying, not talking to spirits. What about your wife's nephew, Ah Tat?*

Jess relayed this, but Ah Ku wasn't listening. He'd had an idea.

"Why don't you use Ah Min?" he said. "You entered her already. She can hear your voice, means she can do it."

"*No*," said Jess, horrified. "And that's me talking!"

Ah Ma was equally appalled by the suggestion. *Ah Min doesn't know anything. She grew up in US. She doesn't know how to talk properly also.*

Jess had actually been patting herself on the back over how well she had been doing speaking Hokkien. Whether it was Ah Ma's influence, or the effects of immersion, her Hokkien was better than it had ever been. It was true she still mixed it with English when she couldn't remember the term for something, but everybody in Penang spoke a heterogeneous Hokkien, jumbling Malay, Chinese dialect and English together.

But this wasn't the moment to be defensive about her linguistic abilities.

"Ah Ma thinks it's a bad idea," said Jess firmly. "She says I don't know anything. And she's right!"

Ah Ku frowned. But before he could start arguing, they heard raised voices from the other end of the garden. Ah Ku got up, looking annoyed.

"Must be the devotees are scolding my assistants," he said. "They don't know how to respect the gods ah?"

There was the sound of running feet. One of the polo-shirted men burst out of the bushes. The fluorescent light threw his face into stark relief, highlighting the sweat and fear.

"Master, some men came and they're trying to halau us," he said. "We asked them to leave, but they don't want. They're carrying parang all that. How?"

Ah Ku and Ah Ma said at the same time, "That *bastard*!"

"WHAT'S THE MATTER, friends?" said Ah Ku, in the expansive manner of a host at a party.

His arrival interrupted a disagreement between the devotees and a group of strange men. The devotees looked frightened and indignant, but the new arrivals looked like men on a job. They had the air of someone who had come to fix the plumbing, which sat oddly with the cleavers they carried—the parang used to clear intractable jungle.

"You're the boss?" said one of the men in Malay. He was no taller or larger than any of the others, but:

That's the chief, said Ah Ma.

How do you know? said Jess. The man wasn't even holding a parang, unlike the others. His hands were empty.

Like that also you must ask? said Ah Ma contemptuously. *You see him already you can know. His angin is different. The others cannot compare.*

Oh, sorry I can't distinguish between thugs, said Jess. *It's not like I have any experience!*

Ah Ku didn't seem bothered by the knives.

"I am the medium," he said. "The ceremony just started only. If you want to consult the god, you must wait. These other people came first."

Ah Ku had been about to put on a shirt before coming out to confront the men, but Ah Ma had intervened.

Wear the god's clothes, she'd said. *Like that only they'll be scared.*

But the chief thug didn't seem intimidated by Ah Ku's satin pants and bib. Not that Jess blamed him. He probably wasn't even a worshipper of the Chinese gods. She found it difficult to place him—not helped by the fact that night had fallen and the garden was poorly lit—but the fact he'd addressed Ah Ku in Malay suggested he wasn't Chinese.

The remainder of the group appeared to be a mix of ethnicities, and some of them did seem wary. It wasn't only the Chinese among them who glanced nervously at the altar and the incense urn with its smoking joss sticks.

"You all must get out," said Chief Thug to Ah Ku. "Tell everybody."

What right does he have to come to this temple and tell people to get out? said Ah Ma, furious. *Who sent him? You ask!*

I'm not asking that guy anything, said Jess. *I don't know if you've noticed, but his friends all have knives! Anyway, I thought you knew who sent him.*

I want to hear him say that bastard's name!

"Boss, we are praying right now," said Ah Ku. "It's not good if we suddenly stop. The spirits will be angry."

A devotee chimed in, "Abang, you should respect people's religion." It was AirAsia. He looked apprehensive and his Malay was awkward, like he wasn't used to speaking it, but he forged on. "This is a sensitive issue. If you try to interfere, you'll cause offense."

This increased the other thugs' nervousness, though it was probably the prospect of angering the spirits that worried them more than offending religious sensitivities. One of them said to Chief Thug, "Maybe we should let the ceremony finish first."

Chief Thug ignored him. He stepped forward, looming over Ah Ku.

To Ah Ku's credit, he didn't flinch or back down, though Jess saw his throat move in a swallow.

"This is not your land. You all are squatters," said Chief Thug. "You want to go or not?"

"We don't want to fight," said Ah Ku, spreading his hands. "But we have a right to be here. This temple has been here a long time. You ask anybody, all the neighbors know. Under the law, we can stay here until the judge gives the order—"

Chief Thug punched him in the face. As Ah Ku's head snapped back, the thug smashed a fist into his gut.

The devotees shrieked and scattered. Ah Ku fell to the ground, and the thug started kicking him in the stomach. His expression hadn't changed at all.

Ah Soon! screamed Ah Ma.

Jess's throat was tight with terror. She looked around for someone to help, but most of the devotees had cleared out. AirAsia was nowhere to be seen. The men who'd been playing the drum and the gong were still there, as were the polo-shirted assistants, but they hung back, uncertain.

Help him! said Ah Ma. *Stop them!*

There was only Jess.

"Don't," she said. Her voice was pathetically wobbly. She cleared her throat. "Leave him alone!"

Chief Thug ignored her. Every fiber of her being was urging her to turn and run.

Ah Min, do *something!* said Ah Ma.

Jess shot forward before her body could rebel against the dumb orders her brain was giving. Chief Thug had stopped whaling on Ah Ku for a second while he wiped sweat off his brow. Jess bent, slipping her hands under Ah Ku's arms and dragging him out of reach.

"Stop it," she said. "He's a medium! If you kill him, what do you think his god will do to you?"

Left to himself, Chief Thug probably would have smacked her out of the way and kept on kicking Ah Ku. But her words went home with his companions. A couple of them stepped in, pulling Chief Thug back.

The polo shirts took Ah Ku from Jess's hands. Ah Ku stirred, groaning, so at least he wasn't dead.

Ah Ma was going wild. *That bastard! He doesn't want to wait already. His men won't go until the temple is no more. You saw, that dog was willing to kill Ah Ku!*

Her rage and fear washed over Jess, but they didn't touch her. Everything had gone very clear. Jess knew she was scared, but it was like her emotions had been packed away behind several protective layers. She felt preternaturally calm.

She looked up at the polo shirts. "We've got to get my uncle to the hospital."

The men looked at each other, hesitating.

"If we go, they all will spoil the temple," said one of the polo shirts.

"Would you rather they wreck the temple or wreck us?" hissed Jess. "You can move! Rebuild the temple somewhere else!"

It was like she had run headfirst into a wall. The devotees didn't say anything, but they didn't need to. They radiated negation.

They're scared the gods will be angry, said Ah Ma. *Gods are like humans. Some will forgive, they won't hold a grudge. Others don't give face. If they're not happy, you will feel it.*

Chief Thug said to the other men, "We're supposed to clear the site. What are you doing? Wasting time only!"

"If we kill people, it'll make trouble," protested a fellow thug.

"Who said we're going to kill people?" said Chief Thug. "Beating is not killing. You think they dare to report? Who are they going to report to? Police won't help them."

Ah Min, said Ah Ma.

Not now, said Jess. She said aloud to the devotees, "Please. We have to go."

Ah Min, repeated Ah Ma. *Let me do.*

Do what?

I can settle these men, said Ah Ma. *After you die, you become strong, stronger than the living. I'm not scared of them. But I need a body.*

Pressure descended in Jess's head. It was like the harbinger of a migraine, or the oppression exuding from a lowering sky when a storm is brewing. She resisted it instinctively, pushing back.

I don't understand, she said.

But she did. She understood fine. She was just frightened of what it would mean to say yes.

You don't need to understand, said Ah Ma. *I will do everything. But you must let me in.*

"Abang," said Jess aloud, calling Chief Thug "big brother," as AirAsia had done. "Why don't we all go home and wait for the court to decide? If the judge says the temple's got to go, I'm sure the temple committee will comply. Right?"

She turned to the polo shirts. But before they could answer, Chief Thug grabbed her and slapped her. He seized her hair, wrenching her head back.

"You'll go now!" he said. He started shaking her back and forth. "You think you can tell me what to do? Bitch!"

The other devotees were shouting, but that was as much as they dared to do. Chief Thug was roaring at her, shaking her, his face purple with rage, spit flying from his lips. She couldn't tell what he was saying; the world was going past her in a blur. She cut the inside of her mouth on her own teeth, tasting blood.

Ah Min, let me in. Ah Ma's voice was calm inside Jess's head, a steady point to cling to. *I can get rid of them. Let me do.*

Beneath the ghost's calm, Jess heard something that echoed her own feelings—a rage that had been festering for longer than she had been alive.

OK. OK, said Jess. She was still in control, just. What was it she wanted to say to Ah Ma?

Oh, yes.

But you have to promise me one thing, said Jess.

What? This time there was a trace of impatience in Ah Ma's voice.

Fuck him up, said Jess.

She let go, allowing herself to be subsumed by the pressure in her head.

A blinding light washed over her. White noise filled her mind—voices she'd never heard, faces she'd never seen, memories that weren't hers. Someone turned her head easily, as though Chief Thug wasn't holding a fistful of her hair. Someone spoke through her mouth:

"Ah Hock"—she was addressing one of the polo-shirted assistants—"you go now. Take Master Lim to Dr. Rozlan. Not the hospital, remember! I will handle this."

Confusion crossed Chief Thug's face. Awe and dread dawned in the assistant's.

Jess thought, *This must be what it's like to be God.*

And then the light blotted everything out.

SEVEN

Someone was prodding at her eye and it hurt. Jess struck out, snarling, "No!"

She was in her own room in Kor Kor's house, sitting at the desk with a small vanity mirror in front of her. It was dark outside, but the light was on, and the air from the open window smelled like morning.

She wasn't alone. There was someone else reflected in the mirror, standing behind her.

Jess spun around, but that was a bad idea. Pain scythed through her head. She jammed her hand against her temple, whimpering.

"Who asked you to move like that?" said Ah Ma.

"Wait," said Jess. "How come I can see you?"

Asked to envision Ah Ma, she would have imagined a cantankerous old woman, but in fact the ghost's appearance was constantly shifting. One moment Ah Ma was a middle-aged woman, like the aunties who crowded Kor Kor's living room, only less well-dressed—Kor Kor's friends wore nice dresses and skirts and capri pants, good quality and new-looking. Middle-aged Ah Ma wore a faded pink T-shirt and black shorts, the kind of cheap clothes sold at pasar malam.

But the next moment her face shimmered and she turned young, around Jess's age. Now she was in laborer's clothes—a wide-brimmed hat, long-sleeved top and trousers. Her skin was tanned a deep brown from the sun, but apart from that, she looked familiar. She looked like a shorter, less well-fed version of Jess.

That was creepy, but fortunately it didn't last long. Jess blinked, and Ah Ma was old again. Her skin went from dewy to wrinkled, her hair from black to gray and back again.

The only thing that stayed the same was her expression, which was exactly what Jess would've expected. She looked like something had crawled up her butt and died in 1953 and she'd never gotten over it.

"You want to wake up ah?" said Ah Ma. "I haven't finished yet." Her voice sounded strange coming from outside Jess's head.

Which was throbbing. In fact, Jess ached all over, and there was something weird going on with her vision. She closed her eyes again, opened them—then, as an experiment, squeezed first one eye shut and then the other.

She was seeing two different images at once. Her left eye saw her room, with her cousins' old posters of race cars and soccer players on the wall, and Ah Ma frowning at her. Her right eye saw the same room, posters and all—but no Ah Ma.

Ah Ma peered at her suspiciously. "You look you want to vomit like that. Let me go inside. Then I can get the dustbin."

She came closer, looking determined. Ah Ma intended, Jess realized, to enter her and take over her body. Jess squirmed away until her back hit the desk.

"No!" she said. "I'm not going to puke. I'm fine." She did in fact feel nauseated, but she would have thrown herself out of the window before she let Ah Ma possess her again.

She closed her right eye, which helped. She still felt incredibly rough, but seeing only one version of the world steadied her stomach.

"What's going on?" she said. "What happened last night?"

"What happened? That bastard sent his samseng to beat Ah Ku. You saw what."

"I mean, after that," said Jess. "After I"—she swallowed—"let you in."

"Oh, I got rid of those men," said Ah Ma. "I told you I'll settle them." She made a fist.

It should have been funny. Ah Ma was tiny, no higher than Jess's shoulder. But it wasn't.

"You beat them up?" said Jess. Except Ah Ma had been doing it with her body, so . . . "*I* beat them up?"

"This type of man, you cannot negotiate," said Ah Ma. "They're not scared of anything. You must beat them, then only they'll respect you."

"You're kidding me," said Jess. "How could I even—that big guy was twice my size!"

"You don't believe? You look at your hands and see."

Jess looked down. She raised her right hand to her face, gingerly straightening the fingers. The bruising on her knuckles was already going from red to purple.

"No matter how big that samseng is, he is a human," said Ah Ma. "I am a ghost. It's not the same."

"No," said Jess. "I can see that."

"You're OK already? Let me in," said Ah Ma. "I haven't done the other eye yet."

Jess leaned away from her. Ah Ma couldn't actually possess her without her consent while she was awake, she reminded herself. "What are you talking about? What have you been doing with my eyes?"

"Don't touch!" snapped Ah Ma. "You can see me is because I'm opening your eyes. But I only did one, then you woke up and I couldn't do already."

Jess was inspecting herself in the mirror. When she shut her left eye, opening her right, Ah Ma vanished, but she could see the large red dot on her left eyelid. A red marker pen lay on the desk—and there was red ink on Jess's fingers too.

"Did you draw this on me?"

"I did it so you can see," said Ah Ma. "When you get the new idol of the god, it's empty. You have to open the eyes first, then only the spirit can go in. Right now you're like the new idol, blind, cannot do anything. How are you supposed to be my medium if you cannot even see the spirits?"

Jess stared, forgetting to close her right eye, so that she saw two worlds at once. The world without Ah Ma, peaceful and blessed—and the fucked-up actual world, in which she was being haunted by the worst ghost ever. "What do you mean, how am I supposed to be your medium?"

"You're supposed to use the god's blood to open the eyes," said Ah Ma. "But don't have god's blood, so I used the red pen. This Ah Ku, he always thinks you have to buy special things to do the rituals. He doesn't listen to me. If you want to do, if you have the strength, you can do it. You don't need all those expensive things."

Jess ignored this. "I'm not going to be your medium."

Ah Ma assumed a patient expression. It did not look natural on her. "Ah Ma told you, without a body, I cannot do anything. You saw what. That bastard doesn't care! Even at the temple, he's willing to beat people. Ah Ku is a good boy, but he cannot face up to that bastard. If I don't help, there'll be no more temple."

"If Ah Ku can't face him, what makes you think I can?"

"*You* don't need to do anything." Ah Ma didn't even seem annoyed by Jess's resistance. It was as if Jess was a toddler protesting bedtime. "Ah Ma will handle it. You just relax only, like last night. Come, let me go inside and finish your eyes. Then we can call Ah Ku and tell him he don't need to worry, Ah Ma will handle everything."

It seemed to Jess there must be simpler solutions to the problem of the temple than picking a fight with the fifth richest man in Malaysia. "Can't you just move the altars? It's not like the temple has to be there, right?"

Ah Ma said, in a voice like a shutter closing, "Better not talk about things you don't understand. Do what Ah Ma tells you, enough already."

"No," said Jess. "I don't want to be your medium."

She braced herself for scoldings, guilt trips, emotional blackmail—all the tools with which Asian elders were wont to apply pressure to their wayward descendants.

But Ah Ma laughed. "You think it's so simple? Say you don't want, enough already? Nobody wants to be a medium. Medium has to suffer. If you can choose, who wants to do? But it's not you who chooses."

"This is ridiculous," said Jess.

Her Asian friends had always considered her lucky for having parents who weren't that exercised about her choice of career. Mom and Dad were anxious that she stay out of trouble and get decent grades at school, but compared to some of her friends' parents, they hadn't really pushed her. They'd been pleased but slightly taken aback when she got into Harvard: "Who knew you're so smart!" Dad had told her, with more candor than tact.

So much for being lucky, thought Jess wildly. It figured that she'd avoided getting nagged to go to law school, only to get nagged to become a vessel for the dead.

"Ah Ma was like you," said the source of the nagging. "Didn't want to do."

Jess blinked. "You were a medium too?"

But it made sense. Jess should have guessed it. That was why Ah Ma was so obsessed with the garden temple. It was the family business.

"I told you what. I caught snake disease," said Ah Ma. "Almost wanted to die already, but the god saved me. In return I had to serve her. What to do? These matters, fate decides. That's why you can be a medium also, because you are my granddaughter."

Jess was busy processing this new information. "You were a medium, Ah Ku's a medium. Was Mom . . . ?" It was a profoundly weird thought. Of course Jess knew in theory that Mom had had a whole life before she'd had her, but it was hard to really *believe* it.

Ah Ma sniffed. "Your mother! No lah. She's useless. Cannot see, cannot hear. Not good for women to be mediums. When you're dirty, at that time of the month, the gods don't like it. If a spirit enters you and they realize you're not clean, they'll suddenly leave. Then don't know whether your soul will come back into your body or not. Very dangerous."

"You're not really selling it to me here," said Jess.

"If I can choose another medium, I will also," said Ah Ma. "But there's no choice. Now I understand. After I died, I woke up and you were there. I didn't know what was happening also. But must be the god sent me to you."

Jess was screwed if this became a matter of divine diktat. "How do you know? Did the god tell you that?"

No answer. Jess saw a glimmer of hope.

"It must be a mistake," she said. "Why would the god appoint me as your medium? I'm totally unsuitable. You said so yourself. I can't even speak Hokkien properly."

Ah Ma waved a dismissive hand. "That's a small thing lah. I've been talking to you for a short time only, already you can speak better. You saw what, when you were talking to Ah Ku, you understood everything. Malay also you can manage now, right? You could follow what those samseng were saying yesterday."

Jess was about to disagree, and also to tell her grandmother to fuck off. But then she remembered Chief Thug, his expression of boredom verging on annoyance, telling Ah Ku, "You all must get out."

In Malay. The entire interaction with the intruders at the temple had been in Malay. And Jess had understood it all.

But she couldn't speak Malay. It wasn't like Hokkien, which had been the aural backdrop of her life even after they'd moved to America. She understood slightly less of Malay than a bright dog might understand of human speech.

Jess clasped her hands, feeling her own bones against her fingertips. She wasn't going to scream or throw up. "What have you done to me?"

"I didn't purposely do anything," said Ah Ma. "But if you share the same body, your heart will change. My English also is very good now," she added, with pride. "I can understand all your American slang."

"Oh yeah?" said Jess. "How about this? *Fuck. Off.*"

She expected Ah Ma to be pissed off. But the ever-shifting face—eerily familiar at some times, wholly strange at others—smiled.

"Even your mother didn't dare talk to me like that," said Ah Ma. "That's why I know the god chose you."

There was a strange note of satisfaction in her voice.

"You're like Ah Ma," she said. "You're clever at being angry."

Jess had nothing to say to this.

It struck her, as she stared at herself in the mirror, that Ah Ma was the only member of her family who knew this about her. It was a lonely thought.

* * *

JESS PHONED AH Ku up, partly to get Ah Ma off her back and partly because she wanted to know he was OK. The memory of the thug kicking him while he lay on the ground kept recurring.

Nobody picked up. It was seven a.m., probably Ah Ku was still asleep, Jess told Ah Ma.

Fortunately, Ah Ma had the number of the doctor he'd been taken to. They were both jumpy until the doctor picked up.

Her uncle had a couple of broken ribs but no more serious injuries, said Dr. Rozlan. He had been sent home to rest. The doctor recommended painkillers and avoiding certain unsavory persons.

"To be fair, the unsavory persons came to him," said Jess.

"Then I would say Mr. Lim should avoid certain places, for their tendency to attract unsavory persons." For some reason, Dr. Rozlan had a British accent, overlaid on a base of Malay uncle. "I hope you will advise your uncle accordingly. He may be more likely to consider it now your grandmother is no longer with us. I know the old lady's wishes are important to him, but after all, bones are more important than bricks and mortar, aren't they?"

"Uh, yeah," said Jess.

When she relayed the doctor's message, Ah Ma snorted. "He's a Muslim. What does he know about temples?"

"Who is he, anyway?" said Jess. "The family doctor?"

Ah Ma ignored this. "I want to go to Ah Ku's house. I can tell you how to drive there."

"We made a deal. I asked a question, so you have to answer," said Jess. "We had rules, remember?"

"Something like this also you must know meh?" said Ah Ma irritably. "Ah Ku helped this Malay boy's brother last time. So now he gives discount if Ah Ku needs medicine. Enough or not? Come, let's go."

"No," said Jess. "I made the call. Ah Ku's fine. I've got to go to work."

Ah Ma started to protest, but Jess said, "You're the one who accepted the job, remember?" and shut the bathroom door on her.

Doors presumably weren't an actual problem for Ah Ma. Jess wasn't sure what she'd do if Ah Ma followed her into the bathroom—probably start throwing things—but to Jess's relief, she refrained. Jess had a blissfully undisturbed half hour getting ready, taking her time over her makeup.

By the time she was done, nobody would've guessed she'd spent the night getting into altercations with gangsters and performing mysterious eye-opening rites on herself. She opened the door, closing her right eye, and scanned the room with the left.

Ah Ma was nowhere to be seen. Maybe she'd gone off to check on Ah Ku herself. Could she do that?

Whatever. Jess wasn't about to question her good fortune.

Dad was already having breakfast. He did a double take when he saw her.

"You look nice ah!" he said, with unflattering surprise. He narrowed his eyes. "Did you cut your hair?"

Jess had had to go with a bold eye to hide the red dot on her left eyelid. It was an eccentric choice for daytime, but she'd figured Dad and Kor Tiao weren't likely to notice.

"It's makeup, Dad," she said. Maybe it was just as well she was having to go to the office and make some minimal efforts at personal grooming. It was a good thing Sharanya loved her for her personality, given how little attention she'd been giving her looks of late.

She needed to reply to Sharanya's last message so they could reschedule their call. She couldn't do it now, with her dad around, but hopefully there'd be a chance after they got to the office to WhatsApp her privately.

Dad grunted, but he sounded a little impressed. "Don't forget to bring your camera. Kor Tiao wants you to take photo of the units."

It wasn't yet as unbearably muggy as it would get later, but when she got in the van, Jess reflexively adjusted the AC up to the highest setting.

"Hot, is it?" said Dad. There were already beads of sweat on his nose and upper lip, but he turned both the AC vents between them toward Jess. Cool air washed over her.

She meant to ask Dad about what was going on with his job. But "hey, what's up with Kor Tiao forcing you to do manual labor?" didn't seem like the best approach, and Dad was humming along to the Chinese ballad on the radio, breaking out in song at the chorus.

She hadn't heard Dad sing in a while. He had an unexpectedly beautiful voice, deep and resonant. Jess herself wasn't especially musical, though her parents had forced her through piano lessons till she went to college, because they thought it would make her good at math.

It was comfortable in the van. Dad didn't expect her to talk unless she felt like it, wouldn't nag her or require her to manage his feelings.

Her thoughts bumped around in her head like balloons. If Dad had had the resources spent on her, she thought sleepily—all those years of piano lessons; of music teachers visibly reminding themselves to be patient while she fucked up her scales—what could he have done? What would he be like if he'd been able to afford the space in his life for art?

She dozed off with the AC blowing full in her face, feeling safe.

EIGHT

When Jess woke up, Dad was parking the van. Through the window she could see temporary fencing along the road, a row of green panels reflecting dazzling sunshine. Part-built structures loomed beyond the fencing. In the near distance, a tower crane rose into a vast blue sky.

Jess rubbed her eyes. "Are we at Kor Tiao's office?" She'd been imagining something a little more developed.

"No, this is the construction site," said Dad. He rummaged around his feet, pulling out a steering wheel lock. "Went to the office just now, while you were sleeping."

"You should have woken me up." Jess yawned. "Why are we at a construction site?"

"Supposed to install appliances in the show unit," said Dad. "Kor Tiao wants you to take photo after I install. This should be a high-spec unit. The condos are very expensive. The developer said we can use the photos in advertisements all that." He had a worried wrinkle in his forehead when he looked at Jess. "You slept late last night, is it?"

Jess twisted around to look in the back of the van. None of the boxes looked especially portable. Dad hated it when you even tried to take his bag for him. "We're carrying those in together, right?"

"No need," said Dad. "The other handyman, Ah Chong, is coming also. He's meeting us here."

Jess downgraded Kor Tiao from "definitely exploiting my dad" back to "only potentially a secret asshole."

"If you want to sleep more," said Dad, "you can stay in the car. On the aircon but open the window, should be OK."

"No, no," said Jess, stifling another yawn. "I'll come in with you."

It was already unbelievably hot, though it was only nine a.m. They got out of the van, passing a sign advertising the development. Rexmondton Heights, it was called, which was exactly the kind of dumb-sounding fancy name Jess would have expected.

The sign featured an artist's depiction of what the squat structures beyond the barrier were supposed to turn into—a condominium complex, with a fountain in the middle for some reason. There were little people chilling out in a lush green courtyard, as though any Malaysian would ever hang around outdoors under the sun if they could avoid it.

Jess followed her dad to a low, temporary-looking office building next to the construction site. She noticed a small altar toward the back of the building, like the ones at the garden temple.

You saw altars like that all over the island—at roadsides, down back alleys, in parking lots, behind restaurants. But there was something striking about this one, with the green of the site walls behind it and the tower crane rising above. It would make a great shot.

Jess filed the thought away for later, stepping into the building. A welcome gust of cold air blew down the back of her top. It was polyester and already sticking to her; she'd dressed for spending the day in an air-conditioned office, not for traipsing around a building site in the heat.

Dad was wearing a cotton polo shirt and khakis. He looked cool and competent, in control, like he was in his native habitat.

Jess guessed he was. It was weird to be reminded that she'd seen him at a disadvantage all her life.

"Mr. Ho?" he said to the lone person there, a Chinese man in office wear. "I'm from Eurasia Appliances."

The man rose. "You're here to install the cooker hood all that, is it? The unit is at the back there."

There were fake condos at the back of the building, set up to give buyers an idea of the bliss in store for them as residents of Rexmondton Heights. While the man showed Dad around the kitchen, Jess checked her phone. Sharanya had sent her a link and a voice note.

"Dad," said Jess, when Mr. Ho left them alone in the show unit. "I'm going to go out and make a call, OK? It's to do with this job application."

Dad paused whatever it was he was doing with the kitchen cabinets to peer at her. "You want to go outside ah? Construction site, better not go here go there. Not safe. The ground got nails all that, you know."

"I'm not going to the construction site. Don't worry," said Jess. "I'll be right back."

Outside, the sun's glare struck her full in the face. The overhang afforded some shade, though Jess had to press herself against the wall to keep out of the sun. She went round to the back of the building where she could be alone, out of sight of everyone except the small god in the altar.

She had to turn up the volume so she could hear Sharanya's voice note over the distant clank and grind of machinery. Before her lay the construction site—an unfinished place, bare orange earth and the beginnings of buildings. At one end was a strip of jungle, dark green in the sun. Either that was where the development stopped, or they hadn't gotten around to razing the greenery yet.

It was nice having Sharanya's voice in her ear. The link she'd sent was to an ad for a job at the university she was going to in the fall.

"You could totally teach freshmen how to write essays," said Sharanya. "I know teaching's not really what you want to do, but you could look for other stuff once you were there.

"Good luck with your first day, babe. Hope there haven't been any more, you know, voices. I can't believe your family's making you work for your uncle's company when you're already dealing with so much crap. Let's talk again soon, OK? I love you."

Jess recorded her response, gazing distractedly at the tower crane. The strap of her camera case dug into her shoulder. She should have left it in the building, but she'd been in a rush to get out before Dad could stop her.

She'd canceled her appointment with the psych Sharanya had found, but Jess told her they were booked up and wouldn't be able to see her for a month. "It's OK, though. I haven't heard anything else since. It must have been the stress of moving."

She didn't mention Ah Ma or the garden temple. Sharanya lived in a wholly rational world, rolled her eyes at astrology and tarot cards and poorly sourced parental WhatsApp forwards alike. There was no way she'd believe in what Jess was going through. And the last thing Jess needed right now was her girlfriend freaking out about her going crazy.

She was sticky with sweat, even in the shade. She was about to go back inside when she looked up and saw the altar.

It wasn't like Dad was going to be done yet, and she had her camera with her.

The altar held a smiling pink-skinned statue of an old man with bushy white eyebrows and a white mustache. He looked like a Chinese Colonel Sanders. He was even dressed in white, with gold buttons running down the front. His bottom half was clad in a gold sarong.

Someone had draped a garland around his neck. By his feet, along with the usual offering of joss sticks, sat a small pyramid wrapped in brown paper and banana leaf.

"Nasi lemak?" said Jess aloud. Nasi lemak was the closest thing Malaysia had to a national dish and one of the few Malay dishes her relatives ate regularly, so she'd seen such pyramids before. There'd be rice wrapped up in the banana leaf, along with sambal, half a boiled egg and a bunch of other stuff Jess couldn't immediately recall.

It seemed an odd offering. Maybe someone had been praying and had forgotten their breakfast there.

She raised her camera and took a few shots.

It really was unbearably hot. Jess wanted to get back indoors, but she hesitated. It felt somehow disrespectful to leave without giving the statue anything in return. She rummaged in her pocket and dug up a couple of tissues—yeah, no—and half a tube of mints.

She set the mints on the base of the altar, next to the nasi lemak. She was stepping away when a voice said right in her ear:

"What are you doing?"

Jess jumped, just about managing not to drop her camera. Out of her left eye she could see Ah Ma glaring at her.

"Warn me if you're going to do that!" said Jess.

"Ah Ku's house you don't want to go, but you're willing to come to this place?"

"It's for work," said Jess. "Where've you been?"

Ah Ma didn't answer. She was looking around, jittery, as though she expected to be ambushed at any minute. "What are you doing here? Why are you taking photo of this for what? It's a Datuk Kong only."

"Really?" Jess had been planning to ask Dad about the idol, but since Ah Ma had brought it up . . . "What's a Datuk Kong?"

"He's the spirit who jaga the area. They all pray to him so the construction won't have problems," said Ah Ma. "But I tell you, no use to pray to him if the god is bad mood. When the god is bad mood, I also don't want to be here. Why you came here for what?"

"I told you, it's for work," said Jess. "What's wrong with coming here?"

Ah Ma looked like the only thing stopping her from slapping Jess was her incorporeality. "You don't know ah?" She turned, pointing at the patch of forest Jess had noticed earlier. "You see over there? That's where the temple is. You cannot see only, because of the trees." Ah Ma gestured at the construction site. "The buildings all that, that bastard's company owns one."

"Wait," said Jess, "this is Ng Chee Hin's development?"

The man's voice, when it came, made them both start.

"Siapa kacau aku?" it snarled.

The voice belonged to a Malay uncle, his face scrunched up with irritation underneath his cap. He was standing by the altar, formally dressed in baju Melayu, crisp white and gold, as though he was going to a wedding. It was a strange look given where they were, but that wasn't the only weird thing about him.

"You called me for what?" he said. "What do you want? I'm busy, you know!"

"Nobody called you," said Ah Ma. "If you're busy, you go off lah! I'm talking to my medium."

"I'm not your medium," said Jess automatically.

She blinked, but that didn't change anything. Her right eye saw the altar with the Chinese Colonel Sanders statue, his eyes narrowed in a beatific smile, and nothing else. According to her right eye, she was all alone.

Her left eye told a different story. It saw the Malay uncle, getting mad at her terrible grandmother.

"If your medium didn't want to call me, then she gave me an offering for what?" The uncle pointed at the mints Jess had put down on the altar. "This kind of offering, even if there's no trouble, I don't want. All the more there's a hantu attacking people, you think I want to eat this kind of thing? You should teach your medium to think of other people. And give better offerings! The packet is half-gone already!"

"What's attacking people?" said Jess.

Both spirits ignored her.

"Is the god here?" said Ah Ma. She hesitated. The next words came out in a near whisper. "The Black Water Sister?"

She said the name in Hokkien instead of Malay, but the uncle—or rather, the Datuk Kong—seemed to understand her. He shuddered. "Don't say so loud! You want to call her to come ah?" He looked around furtively. "That damn woman is waiting for me to relax. If I'm not careful, she'll come in. She wants to chase out the humans. If I wasn't fighting her, she would have killed them already."

"You'd better go and hide somewhere, rather than fighting," said Ah Ma. "You think you can beat the god, small spirit like you? She doesn't care one. If she can eat one hundred souls, she'll do it."

"You think I want to fight?" said the Datuk Kong unexpectedly. "I only became a Datuk recently, when the old Datuk here moved to another place. If I can run, I'll run. But what can I do? The humans there"—he pointed at the construction site—"they give me nasi lemak every day. They all are not rich also. They're construction workers, from Bangladesh. Half of them don't have permits. You think that Chinaman will pay them a lot? How can I not protect them?"

Ah Ma was taken aback. "They're Bangladeshi also they pray to you?"

"When you're scared, you'll pray to anybody," said the Datuk Kong. "Before they started giving me the offerings, there were a lot of accidents. The tower crane didn't want to work. The metal rod fell, almost kena the humans. All these things happening. They complained, but that Chinaman doesn't care. He wants them to be quiet and finish the job."

"Who's 'that Chinaman'?" said Jess. "Do you mean Ng Chee Hin? Is he employing undocumented migrants?"

"He means the contractor," said Ah Ma irritably. "That bastard is the developer, but it's not his company that will do the construction. They call a contractor to do it. Ah Ku used to do construction work, so I know."

"But this is happening on his site," said Jess. She'd been feeling like an outsider stumbling into half-understood conversations, a puppet jerked around on Ah Ma's strings. But now the same triumphant rush went through her as when she took a perfect photograph. "There are safety issues and he's ignoring them."

Ah Ma didn't get it.

"All these contractors are like that lah," she said impatiently. "They don't want to hear this excuse that excuse. They want to do the job and get paid." She turned to the Datuk Kong. "So far how many people died?"

"Nobody has died," said the Datuk Kong in glacial tones, "because I have been there to jaga. So long as I'm here, that woman doesn't need to try bothering the humans—"

He cut himself off, listening intently.

Over the distant whirring from the construction site came the sound of human voices, upraised.

"She's here," said Ah Ma.

It took Jess a moment to recognize the expression on her shifting features. It was something she had never seen on Ah Ma before—fear.

The Datuk Kong was engaging in swearing so fruity even Jess's newfound Malay proficiency couldn't keep up with it. "You see! You called me away and now she's don't know doing what! I have to go back."

"We should go now," Ah Ma said to Jess. "Quick, call your father to go home—"

But Jess said to the Datuk Kong, "I'm coming with you."

"Crazy ah, you?" Ah Ma sputtered. "You don't know only. Even the Datuk Kong is scared of the god."

"Very scared," the Datuk Kong agreed.

"You want to die, is it?" said Ah Ma.

Dying was extremely low on the list of things Jess wanted to do, and going with the Datuk to confront a god capable of making Ah Ma blanch wasn't a lot higher up. But being an immigrant and dealing with all the ways that had sucked had shaped a good 70 percent of her personality. She shared little else with the men who'd left offerings for a foreign god, hoping he'd protect them when no one else would. But this was one thing she could do to honor that commonality.

"Who are you to go and face up to the god?" said Ah Ma. "You won't be able to do anything also."

Jess adjusted the strap of her camera case, resettling it on her shoulder. She had a feeling she might be needing it.

"If I can't do anything else," she said, "I can be a witness."

She looked at the Datuk Kong, squeezing her right eye shut to bring him into focus. "Shouldn't we be going?"

* * *

AH MA CAME along, complaining all the way.

"You don't know this god," she kept saying as they followed the Datuk Kong around the construction fencing. "If you know, you'll be scared."

"OK, then tell me!" said Jess. "Who is this god?" She cast her mind back to the discussion between Ah Ma and the Datuk Kong. "She's called the Black Water Sister?"

Ah Ma hissed at her to shut up. "Cannot simply say her name. Say 'god' enough already. Or you can call 'Big Sister.' This god, I know very well. I was her medium."

"You're the medium?" yelped the Datuk Kong.

"I'm talking to you meh?" snapped Ah Ma. "Mind your own business!"

"Why are you so scared of her?" said Jess. "If you're her medium, can't you, like, talk to her?"

"God, you cannot answer back like that," said Ah Ma. "When your father and mother are angry at you, do you try to answer back?"

Jess was about to point out that she did, in fact, regularly answer back. But they had come to a gap in the fencing, obscured by some straggly bushes. The Datuk gestured at Jess to enter. She squeezed through, metal snagging on her top.

While she was disentangling herself, she looked up and saw the spirits step through the fencing as though it wasn't there. *That* was a weird moment.

"When the god talks to you, you listen," Ah Ma continued. "She said, 'Don't come here and build in my area. Don't go and disturb my temple.' If people don't want to listen, then they kena, it's their fault. She warned them already."

"The workers didn't choose to disturb her, though," said Jess. "It's the company who decided to develop the site. It's not like the workers have any power to change that. Isn't it unfair to punish them?"

"Where got gods care about fair or unfair one?" said Ah Ma.

Jess didn't see what gods were for, if not to care about fairness. Before she could say this, there was an outburst of shouting up ahead.

It came from a group of men, almost all dark-skinned South Asians, in hardhats and high-vis vests. They were arguing with a Chinese man.

"Where is that damn woman?" said the Datuk Kong to Ah Ma. "I can feel she's here. You're the medium. Can you see?"

"I'm dead already, how can I be anybody's medium anymore?" said Ah Ma. "If I can see also, I don't want to see. I didn't want to come here in the first place."

"Nobody asked you to come," Jess pointed out. "You're free to go whenever."

"If I go and something happens to you, how?" said Ah Ma. "Who's going to be my medium then?"

The Datuk Kong was searching for the god. He kept darting off and circling back, muttering, "Don't have, don't have. Where has she gone?"

Jess was more interested in the humans. There was something about the ongoing argument that worried her—an ugly energy in the men's voices and gestures. She went over to the group, impelled by an obscure sense of urgency.

The dust rose up from the ground before her. The men looked around, suspicious. Jess had never felt so out of place in her life— and she would've said, before that moment, that hers was an existence featuring some pretty striking instances of feeling out of place.

It was so hot it was hard to think. She was sweating already, but fresh perspiration sprang up on her palms, from plain old fear.

But her feet were braver than her head. They kept going, and she heard herself speaking, her voice bright and confident.

"What's going on here?"

She'd gone instinctively for English. The men stared at her like she'd gotten out of a UFO and started beeping at them.

"Who are you?" said the Chinese man.

"I'm from Sejahtera Holdings," said Jess, imbuing her tone with surprise that he even had to ask. "I presume you're the contractor?"

The name of the company did most of the work, but her accent helped, as did her office-ready outfit. She saw the change ripple through the man's expression, smoothing out the beginnings of a frown, effecting subtle changes in his posture.

"Yes," said the man sullenly. "I'm Mr. Yong."

Jess gave her camera case what she hoped was a discreet nudge, pushing it further out of sight. "What's the problem here, Mr. Yong?"

"No problem," said Mr. Yong, glaring at the other men. "I'm discussing with the workers."

The workers were conferring with one another, talking in low voices. Jess didn't recognize the language, but she assumed it was Bengali.

"They all are saying they don't want to operate the tower crane," said the Datuk Kong. "Maybe she's there." He vanished.

Jess hadn't gotten used to how spirits came and went without warning. She hoped Mr. Yong hadn't noticed her smile wavering.

"I heard there's an issue with the tower crane," she said. "It's malfunctioning?"

"There's nothing wrong!" said Mr. Yong. "They all cari pasal only. Want more money to do their work, so they say tower crane got problem."

The other men seemed to have come to a decision. One of them spoke up, a man in his forties.

"We all are not trying to cause problems, madam," he said. His English was notably better than Mr. Yong's. "There is a hantu spoiling the machines. Recently many accidents. We are worried about safety, that's all. If it's safe, we will work."

"I see," said Jess. "I'll report back to my boss." She turned to Mr. Yong. "I suggest you get someone to look at that tower crane. Mr. Ng would not be happy if there were any safety incidents on this site."

When the man opened his mouth to protest, she added, "He doesn't want any bad publicity around this development. Do you think people will buy condos if they think the site is haunted?"

Mr. Yong went ahead and protested anyway. "The machine is OK one. You don't listen to these foreigners, they simply talk only . . ."

A bloodcurdling yell drowned him out.

"Auntie! Help, auntie!"

It was the Datuk Kong. He pelted toward them, holding on to his cap.

"She's coming," he shouted to Ah Ma. "You have to talk to her, auntie. She don't want to listen to me!"

"You want to run now?" Ah Ma said. "I thought you came here is because you wanted to fight her?"

Mr. Yong was starting to look at Jess funny. *Can you shut up!* she thought at Ah Ma—but then she saw the god.

The Black Water Sister was too far away for Jess to make out her features. She could only tell that the god was a woman, probably Chinese, with short dark hair.

Yet Jess recognized her. She was the goddess she had noticed at the temple garden—the weathered little statuette in yellow satin, under the bodhi tree.

Jess couldn't have said how she knew the statuette was meant to represent this god and no other, but she did. There was nothing mystical about it. It was like smelling something burning and knowing there was a fire, or seeing lightning and thinking of rain.

The statuette's eyes had seemed to be watching her, Jess remembered. She knew now that the Black Water Sister *had* seen her—remembered her—and was looking at her now, with intent. It was a terrible thing to know.

"You see?" hissed Ah Ma. "I told you to run away, you don't want. Now only you know!"

It didn't seem like the men could see the god. Jess heard Mr. Yong say, "Miss?" but fear had dried up all the spit in her mouth.

She'd thought she believed in spirits before. It was hard not to when one as loud as Ah Ma was riding around in your head. But she saw now that she hadn't known what it was to believe. There was a reason why Christians called it "God-fearing."

The god held up a pale hand. Jess couldn't move. Every muscle in her body was rigid with horror.

The god rushed forward, but not at Jess. The men scattered, shouting. The hideous attention that had been holding Jess immobile relaxed, leaving her weak with relief.

But the relief was fleeting.

"Eh, what are you doing?" shouted Mr. Yong. "Stop!"

The Bangladeshi guy who'd spoken to Jess was staggering drunkenly, shaking his head like he was trying to get water out of his ears. The others were arguing with him, trying to hold him back, but he shook them off and broke free.

He headed toward the partly constructed buildings, running

as though he was fleeing a nightmare. The god was nowhere to be seen.

"The god went inside him already," said Ah Ma.

"You mean she's possessed him?" said Jess. "Why? What's she trying to do?"

"This god is very fierce," said Ah Ma. She sounded resigned, like she already knew what was going to happen. "If you make her angry, she will eat you up. They should know by now."

"We have to help him," said Jess. She wasn't sure she was strong enough to restrain the man. But she had a ghost right next to her who had a proven track record of granting supernatural powers. "Can't you possess me, like you did last night?"

"You want me to fight the god?" scoffed Ah Ma. "Forget about it! This is none of my business. If you want to fight, you go and do yourself."

"OK, well, fuck you too," said Jess, and started off after the man.

He'd had a head start, but he wasn't running all that fast. His gait was strange, stumbling, as though the god wasn't used to his body. Maybe the man was fighting for mastery over the spirit.

If so, he didn't win. Jess was only about six feet away from him when he put on a burst of speed and dashed into the scaffolding covering the foundation of a building. Steel and concrete beams rose starkly out of the scaffolding, bare of the plaster and paint and glass and wood that would turn the building into somewhere people could live.

The scaffolding trembled, a shudder going through the interlocking metal poles. Jess's stomach dropped.

"Shit!" She sped up, as though she could actually do anything, help the man in any way. But then Ah Ma was in her face, screaming:

"Go back, go back, stupid girl!"

She shoved Jess in the chest. It was like being hit by a very small, concentrated gale. As Jess went down, the Datuk Kong raced past her, his face grim with intention.

There was a grinding shriek of metal giving way. The noise was apocalyptic, drowning out all other sound. Jess was on her ass on the ground, and she could feel the vibrations from the crash travel up through her body, jarring her bones. Dust stung her eyes.

When she could see again, the scaffolding was a heap of broken cement and jagged metal. And the man was in there.

The looks on the workers' faces were almost the worst thing. They didn't look sad or angry or horrified. They looked like they had seen it coming.

"We have to—" said Jess, but her voice came out as a nearly soundless croak. She cleared her throat and tried again. "We have to call somebody. The fire department. What's nine one one?"

Mr. Yong stared at her blankly.

"Nine one one," Jess repeated. "How do you call the police here?" She turned to Ah Ma. It didn't matter if they noticed she was talking to a ghost. Nothing seemed to matter right now, except doing something about the man under the rubble.

She half expected Ah Ma to go off on her, tell her, "I told you so." But it appeared Ah Ma was in fact capable of mustering a sense of the occasion.

She said, "Nine nine nine. But that fellow won't want to call."

"Police?" said Mr. Yong, coming back to life. "No need to call police." He barked some urgent Chinese into a walkie-talkie, adding, "We can handle it."

Jess didn't know what expression her face was making, but she was gratified, in a detached way, to see him wilt under its effect.

"There is a human being in there," she said. It felt like the top of her head would come off if she got any angrier. "He might be seriously injured, or dead. This is an emergency and we need the emergency services."

She took out her phone to dial 999.

A shell-shocked quiet hung over the men. The background sound of machinery had paused, as though out of respect for what had just passed. So they all heard it when the voice spoke from inside the rubble, shaky but clear:

"Hello? Hello? Help, please!"

NINE

The guy's name was Rijaul and he didn't have a scratch on him. It only required a brief exchange with Rijaul to confirm that. It took longer to get him out from under the rubble.

Mr. Yong and his colleagues seemed hopeful they could arrange this themselves, without any external interference. Jess was pretty sure they would be forced eventually to accept they couldn't cover up the incident—a massive pile of collapsed scaffolding was hard to hide.

But she wasn't about to wait around for them to change their minds. While Mr. Yong was shouting into his walkie-talkie, she slipped away and made a call.

It was a challenge relaying the necessary information to the operator on the line. The reception wasn't great, they were both having problems with each other's English, and Ah Ma was bawling in Jess's other ear.

"Police won't help one!" said Ah Ma. "They want to take your money only."

"Uh, we're in Air Itam," said Jess. "Hold on, let me get the address . . ." She lowered the phone, snapping, "Can you give me a moment!"

"You think the workers want you to call the police?" said Ah Ma. "If they don't have visa all that, the police will catch them. Then how? Malaysia is not like US, you don't know only—"

"Look, I get it. There are problems with the police in the States too," said Jess. "But that guy is under a shit-ton of metal and concrete, somebody needs to get him out, and I don't trust Mr. Yong and his buddies to do it! What else do you want me to do?"

"This is not your business also," Ah Ma said. "Who asked you to be a busybody? If you simply do, you'll make things worse only."

Jess rolled her eyes and stuck a finger in her free ear. Ah Ma kept talking inside her head, but at least it blocked out the background noise from the construction site.

Jess had finished her call and wandered back to the collapsed scaffolding to take some discreet shots when someone said behind her, "Awak ambil gambar?"

It was one of the construction workers. Jess looked around, but Mr. Yong was nowhere to be seen.

"Uh, yeah," she said. There didn't seem any point in trying to deny it, given she was holding a huge camera. "I'm taking photos."

It was weird hearing the Malay words drop from her lips, a gift from the unwanted presence in her head. She closed her left eye so she wouldn't have to see Ah Ma, pretending she was squinting because of the sun.

"How many Facebook friends you have?" said the worker.

"I—what?"

"If you put on Facebook, how many people will see?" said the worker. "Four hundred, five hundred?"

"Um. Maybe fifty?" said Jess. "I don't really use Facebook—"

"Fifty?" said the worker, outraged. "Like that, what's the point you put on Facebook? Might as well you give me the photos." He lowered his voice. "I have a friend, he had to go to hospital so cannot work, but the NGO is helping him. I can contact them."

"I was planning to send the photos to the press, not put them on Facebook," said Jess. "But I can send them to you too. What's your number?"

The worker's name was Kassim. He typed his number into Jess's phone, glancing over his shoulder to check no one was watching. "Very good, you send to the newspaper. Might as well you put on Facebook also. Even fifty people is better than nothing. The bosses all want it to be quiet, don't want people to know. You go and show everybody."

"OK," said Jess. The only people who followed her on Facebook were her relatives. But it was impossible to disagree with the man; his urgency compelled assent.

"This is not the first time," said Kassim. "This hantu, she'll sure come back. Then how? It shouldn't be like that. We have rights also. You tell people. Show them your photos. Yeah?"

"Yeah," said Jess. "I will."

She didn't know what else to say, but that was all he wanted from her. He nodded and turned away.

Jess watched his retreating back till she heard the distant wail of sirens. She shook herself and went out to the entrance to greet the arriving firefighters and paramedics.

"The accident was over there," she said, pointing. "They're trying to get the guy out now. He's conscious and talking. He says he's OK, no injuries."

Then she kept walking, out and along the road, back to the sales office where Dad was—hopefully—not freaking out too much about her absence.

"You don't want to stay ah?" said Ah Ma, looking back toward the construction site. She seemed nonplussed.

"He's going to be OK, right?" said Jess. "That spirit's with him. The Datuk Kong?"

Out of her left eye she saw Ah Ma nod.

"Not bad this Datuk," she said grudgingly. "Can help people. Datuk are the same as humans, some you cannot trust. At least this one can stand up to the god, protect that Bangladeshi."

This was a little surprising. "I thought you were on the god's side."

Ah Ma snorted. "When your mother was small, I used to go and plant vegetables on the vacant ground there so we can eat. You think the cangkul was on my side? When the god chooses you to be their medium, it's not you're on the god's side or against the god's side. You are the tool only."

"Ah Ma," said Jess, "who is Ng Chee Hin, actually? Why are you so mad at him?"

Ah Ma sniffed. "You ask your uncle, your father's brother-in-law. He should know about that bastard what. He's the one doing business with the bastard's company."

"You're the one who wants me to be your medium," Jess pointed out.

"I thought you don't want?"

Jess stopped on the sidewalk, even though the sun was blazing so hard it was giving her a headache. The air wavered in the heat.

"Look, I've seen your god now." A shiver ran over Jess's skin, despite the intolerable heat. "I know what she's capable of. If saving the temple from this development is the only thing that will stop her, then I'll help you do it. I didn't understand before. I thought it was just, like, a place. I didn't realize she was going after *people*.

"But you've got to tell me the truth," said Jess. "It's not going to work otherwise."

Ah Ma looked at her, her expression opaque.

It was a rare moment when Jess couldn't tell what she was thinking. It was a strange realization to have, that she understood Ah Ma that well.

"Ng Chee Hin is a samseng," said Ah Ma. "He's the biggest gang boss in Penang. That's why that bastard is not scared of anything. The police also don't want to fight with him."

Jess let out a breath. So that was what Kor Kor had meant by the "funny business" the Ng family were mixed up in. "Why didn't you tell me before?"

"Like that also must tell you?" said Ah Ma. "I thought you're so clever, went to university. I have to tell you Malaysia is hot and chili is spicy also, is it?"

Jess started walking again. "I think telling me yesterday that we might encounter dangerous criminals at the temple would have been relevant information, yes!"

"Dangerous what dangerous? Ah Ma protected you what."

"The god's not like the cops," said Jess. The scream of the scaffolding coming down was still resounding in her ears. "Why isn't he scared of her?"

"He hasn't learned to be scared," said Ah Ma. "This kind of man, they think they're above everything. Heaven also they don't respect. If that bastard builds condos here and sells, he can make a lot of money. He doesn't care about anything else."

It made sense. You probably didn't get on the Forbes rich list by being easily intimidated.

They turned off the main road. Dad and Ah Chong's vans were still parked outside the sales office.

"Why is the temple even here?" said Jess. "If the temple committee doesn't own the land, who built it?"

"This place, last time got rubber plantation," said Ah Ma. "The workers built the temple so they can pray. This god, she's been here for a long time already. Now the humans have gone off, but the gods are not so easy to chase out."

She gave Jess a sidelong look. "If you're willing to help Ah Ma, means we're going to Ah Ku's house after this, is it?"

"No," said Jess. "We're going to go to Ng Wei Sherng's café."

DAD DIDN'T SEEM like he'd been too worried about Jess being gone. She'd been spending so much time with her mom that she'd forgotten Mom's level of parental paranoia wasn't normal.

Dad only glanced at his watch and said, "So long ah, your phone call? So how, you got the job or not?"

"It was a phone screening. They said they'd let me know in a couple of days if I'm getting into the next round," said Jess. "Are you guys done?"

While Dad and Ah Chong packed up, she took photos of the appliances they'd installed—a range cooker, a cooker hood and a fridge. It wasn't the most exciting shoot she'd ever done, but it gave her time to think.

Ah Ma had disappeared the moment Jess stepped into the show unit. She suspected the ghost was avoiding Dad.

She was half waiting for someone to burst in demanding to talk to her about the accident at the construction site, but nothing like that happened. When they went through the office on their way out, the guy who'd greeted them earlier was on the phone, talking in a low urgent voice. He gave them a tense smile and a wave, but didn't say anything.

The fire engine was parked in the road outside the construction site, but the ambulance was gone. Jess hoped that meant they'd gotten Rijaul out.

"Something going on," said Dad. He glanced over at the construction site, but you couldn't see the collapsed scaffolding from where they were. "Must be some accident or what."

It would have been a good moment to tell him what had happened. But Jess hesitated and then he was getting in the van, the moment lost.

There was no more humming on the drive back. Dad was quiet, engrossed in navigating the rush-hour traffic.

Jess said, "You OK, Dad?"

"Hmm?" Dad glanced at her like he'd forgotten she was there. "Yeah, OK. How is it, working for Kor Tiao?"

Jess tried to study him without making it obvious she was doing it, something she'd gotten very good at when he was sick.

He sounded fine. Was he pretending? Managing her mom's feelings took up so much of Jess's emotional energy that she rarely had much left to spare for her dad. He'd always been easier to handle. Even after he'd gotten sick, he'd held as much as he could inside himself, asking as little of Mom and Jess as he could get away with.

He'd spent the afternoon engaged in manual labor. He was probably tired. This wasn't the time to interrogate him, but the question came out almost against Jess's volition.

"Dad, why is Kor Tiao making you do this?"

"Hah? Do what?"

"I thought when you said you were going to help with his business, you were going to be advising on strategy, or doing his accounts or something," said Jess. "A desk job. Instead he's sending you out to construction sites and people's houses. It's not like he doesn't know you're—you were sick."

An unexpected lump in her throat stopped her from going on. She turned to look out of the window, blinking furiously.

There was a startled silence on Dad's side of the car. Then he said, "Mom talked to you, is it?"

Jess ventured a look at him. He was half smiling, but he looked a little annoyed as well. Not at Jess.

"This Mom ah, she stress you out only," he said. "Told her already, but she don't want to listen. I asked Kor Tiao if I can do this job. Actually he give me face. You think normal handyman can earn six thousand ringgit a month? If I'm not the brother-in-law, he won't bother with me."

"Oh," said Jess, a little taken aback. "You wanted to install fridges?"

Dad shrugged. "I can do this kind of thing what." It was true he had always been handy around the house. Their old house—the one they'd had to sell when Dad got sick—had been full of things he'd built or fixed. "At my age, learning a new skill is good, right?"

"Mom's got a point, though. Shouldn't you be taking it easy?" said Jess. "It seems like a lot to be doing at your age."

"I'm not even sixty yet," said Dad. "That's not considered old. There's a lot of things I still want to do."

They'd come to a stop at a traffic light, but it flipped to green. He paused while changing gears.

"The doctors said I'm OK," he said. "I told Mom, if I act like I'm sick, then really cannot already. Might as well I go and live in the old folks' home. We all must move on, Mom also. Cannot be so kiasi, everything also don't want to do.

"If I want to go and sit in the aircon office, write emails, of course Kor Tiao will let me do. He is helping me only. You think he needs a fifty-year-old staff? But with this job, I can learn something new, talk to people, drive around. End of the day, I go home, don't stress. You tell Mom, don't need to worry so much. Aiyah, if I cannot handle myself by this age, there's really no hope lah."

This was Dad as he had been before he'd lost his job and fallen sick—brisk, competent, unflappable. Jess had been conditioned to find his manner reassuring. She relaxed almost despite herself.

With that came an old impulse, so layered over by more recent impressions that it felt fresh—a longing to lean on her dad's strength the way she used to, back when she'd thought it would never give out.

She hadn't even considered telling her parents what was going on before. Her instinct for hiding the unwelcome parts of her life from them had kicked in automatically. For the first time, she thought about it.

She was no longer used to seeking help from her parents. It was simultaneously true that they had given her everything she had and were the reason she could do all she did, and that they were unequipped to deal with 90 percent of the problems she had as an adult. They'd set her up to have a life different from theirs, free of the hardships they'd had to endure. The result was that almost all her troubles were exciting new troubles, beyond their skill set to address.

But Ah Ma and her god didn't belong to that category. It wasn't as though, in telling Mom and Dad about ghosts and spirit possession and vengeful gods, Jess would be presenting them with an unfamiliar concept, like—to take a random example—the idea that your daughter could be gay and it might not be the end of the world. In their version of reality, people had unlucky encounters with spirits all the time.

For most of her life, Mom and Dad had been living in her world, a world Jess had been trained to deal with by education and socialization in a way they hadn't. Now she was living in theirs.

Maybe she could let them in. Maybe they could help her.

"Dad," she said, "that development we were at, it's owned by Ng Chee Hin, right?"

"Hmm? Yeah," said Dad. "Sejahtera Holdings is Dato' Ng Chee Hin's company. This project, he joint venture with the other company." He seemed surprised. "How you know who is Ng Chee Hin?"

"Kor Kor and her friends were talking about him the other day." Jess hesitated. "Is he—I mean, isn't he a gangster?"

It sounded stupid once she said it out loud. She remembered the clean-cut old guy she'd seen in the newspaper articles, cutting ribbons. It was hard to imagine anything less like a gangster.

"No lah," scoffed Dad.

"It's just that I've heard things—"

"That one was back then, when he was starting out," said Dad. "Nowadays no more already."

This wasn't quite the denial Jess had been expecting from his initial response.

"Is Kor Tiao OK with that?" she said. "I would've thought, with him and Kor Kor being Christians, they wouldn't want to be doing business with criminals."

"This project is legal what," said Dad. "Aiyah, this Dato' Ng has so much capital, why he want to do illegal projects for what? If you look at all the gangsters, it's the same. Once they build up, they don't want to be involved in crime anymore. That kind of business is not sustainable. The real money is in the legal industries."

"Oh," said Jess.

"Malaysia is like that," said Dad. "Cannot be so choosy. Dato' Ng behaves decently, donates to charity . . . A lot of people, if they have his money, they won't bother to stay in Penang. They'll go off to KL or Hong Kong. But this is his hometown, he wants to invest in it.

"Have to be fair to him also. His father was a rubber tapper, the family didn't have money. When he was young he had to go out and work, no chance to go to school. For someone like him, how can he progress? Nowadays it's the Indian boys. You see them, by the time they're in secondary school they'll be in a gang."

Jess sighed. It wasn't the first time she'd thought that, even if everything had been different, she wouldn't have wanted to introduce Sharanya to her parents anyway. There was too much of a risk that they'd embarrass her by being hideously racist. "Dad . . ."

"They have no choice," said Dad. "The teacher don't want to waste time on them. They cannot find a job. The gangster comes to them, helps them, tells them now you have all these brothers. End up they go down that road." He shook his head.

"Dato' Ng is lucky," he said. "To achieve until his level, normal people cannot do it. But Dato' Ng is different. From young already the police can see he's going to be the boss. They can beat him, but he won't say anything."

Jess was about to ask how he knew so much about Ng Chee Hin when Dad added:

"Ah Ma was like that also. Very tough lady. Things other people don't dare to do, she can do."

Jess hadn't expected this. Dad never spoke about Mom's side of the family.

"Really?" she said. "Like what?"

"She's the one who cari makan for the family," said Dad. "She went out to tap rubber so they all can eat. Hard life. Some more the man she married, your Ah Kong, he's not easy to live with."

Jess knew pretty much nothing about her maternal grandfather. He had died when Mom was a kid, young enough that she didn't remember much about him. That's what Mom had always said, anyway. "What was wrong with Ah Kong?"

"Shouldn't speak ill of the dead," said Dad.

There was a long enough pause that it became evident that he meant to leave it there.

"Come on, Dad!" said Jess. "He's my grandfather. It's not like I'm going to tell anyone."

"Ah Kong was not responsible," said Dad reluctantly. "That's why I tell Mom, Ah Ma managed to bring up two children. It's not bad already. In this life, who is perfect? You have to forgive. Cannot simpan dendam. It's your own mother what."

"I don't get it," said Jess. "What did Mom have to forgive Ah Ma for?"

But they were rounding the corner into the street where Kor Kor's house was, and the conversation was over from Dad's point of view.

"That one you better ask Mom," was all he would say.

"Fine," said Jess, exasperated. "I will!"

MOM HAD GONE to bed by the time they got home, so interrogating her would have to wait. It wouldn't happen in the morning, though. Jess had other plans.

At five a.m. the next day she was huddled under her blanket with her phone, smiling down at Sharanya's grainy image.

"How was your first day on the job?" said Sharanya.

Jess remembered the way the construction worker had run toward the scaffolding, the god's blank face when Jess had looked up to see her across the construction site. She shivered.

"It was weird," she said. "It's not exactly what I was planning on doing after graduation, you know?"

She paused, studying Sharanya's face.

It was strange, not feeling able to tell Sharanya what was going on. Before all of this, Jess would have said she was the one person she could trust with anything.

If they were able to talk in person, it would have been different. Jess would have been able to whisper what was happening into the tender place where Sharanya's shoulder joined her neck. She wouldn't have been afraid of the judgment in that direct gaze.

But it was impossible to explain everything on a video call. She didn't know what she'd do if Sharanya didn't believe her—have a screaming meltdown, probably. That would definitely reassure Sharanya that Jess was fine and not having a break from reality.

"Yeah," Sharanya was saying, with ready understanding. "I was going to say, I know I sent you that job, but it's OK if you're not interested. I just thought it'd be fun if you ended up teaching at my university."

Jess had forgotten about the link Sharanya had sent.

"Actually, that looked cool," she said, with a pang of guilt. "I probably will apply."

Sharanya brightened. "Really? You know, I think you'd be a great teacher. You're so charismatic."

"You are literally the only person in the world who thinks that," said Jess, but Sharanya's affectionate delusion was heartening.

Maybe Jess *could* tell her about Ah Ma and the god and the garden temple. The problem had definitely expanded beyond the bounds of what Jess was able to handle alone. It wasn't like Sharanya could do anything from where she was, thousands of miles and several time zones away, but being able to confide in her would be a relief in itself.

She didn't feel quite ready to announce that she believed the voice in her head belonged to her dead grandmother, especially since she'd told Sharanya the voice had gone away. She would build up to it.

"You know, one of the aunties was talking about seeing a shadow on the living room ceiling the other day," said Jess. "It took me a while to work out what she was talking about, but I think she was saying she thought it was a ghost."

"Wow," said Sharanya. "What did everyone else say?"

"I don't think anyone else saw it," said Jess cautiously. "But they all seemed like they believed her. Except my aunt. She didn't really like the idea of a ghost being in her house."

Sharanya laughed. "My aunties would be exactly the same. They totally believe in all that stuff. It's wild. Most of them went to college. I guess it's a cultural thing?"

Jess had been planning to say she thought she knew what had cast the shadow Auntie Grace had seen—that she had seen the same ghost. It was Ah Ma, whose voice had been troubling Jess even before she arrived in Penang, whose life had threaded itself into Jess's dreams.

She looked at Sharanya's amused, skeptical face and couldn't do it.

"Yeah," she said. "Must be."

It was nearly seven by the time she went downstairs to get some breakfast. The house was quiet—weirdly so, until Jess remembered it was a Tuesday. That meant Kor Tiao and Kor Kor were out with their exercise buddies—they were part of a posse of middle-aged fitness freaks who met up regularly to walk backward and do tai chi in the Botanic Gardens. Mom and Dad were probably still asleep.

She was wandering into the living room with a mug of Milo in one hand and a plate of Hup Seng crackers in the other, when she looked out of the sliding doors facing onto the garden and saw Mom sitting on the swing outside.

Jess didn't know why Kor Kor had a swing in the garden. It was a romantic spot, veiled by flowering bougainvilleas and almost comfortable in the evenings when the heat of the sun had died down, but nobody ever used it. The one time Jess had tried, Kor Kor had hared out of the house to tell her to come indoors: "You'll get bitten, so many mosquitoes here. After get dengue then how?"

Jess's mom clearly had bigger things than dengue on her mind. She started fumbling with a tissue when she saw Jess, but it would have taken more than a Kleenex or six to hide the fact she'd been crying. Jess knew all the signs.

"Hey, what's up?" said Jess. A chill passed over her. "Is Dad OK?"

"What? Dad?" said Mom. "He didn't wake up yet. Still sleeping. Why?"

"Why are you crying?"

"I'm not crying." Mom blew her nose.

Jess gave her a look. Mom crumbled.

"What's wrong if I'm crying?" she said. "I'm not allowed to cry meh? I have so much to cry about!"

"Do you?" said Jess. "You have an amazing daughter and a nice husband. You get to live in a literal tropical paradise. Instead of lying on a beach drinking piña coladas, you're hiding in some bushes at the crack of dawn, crying. What happened?" She put her arm around Mom and gave her a little shake, but gently.

Mom wasn't smiling yet, which meant it was serious.

"Nothing happened," she said.

Jess waited. After a pause Mom said, "I applied for a job, but they didn't want. Last night heard back from them. Small thing only lah." Her voice broke on the reassurance. She sniffed and looked, woebegone, at the crumpled ball of tissues in her hand.

"I'll get you some more tissues," said Jess.

She came back with a box of Kleenex and waited till Mom had had the chance to destroy a couple before saying, "I didn't know you were looking for a job."

Mom shrugged. "You and Dad are working. I should work also, right?"

Jess could hardly deny they needed the money. "What job was it?"

"Businessman's secretary," said Mom. "I thought I can do it. The salary is not much, but not many places want to interview me also. So long I haven't worked."

She'd looked after Jess full-time when Jess was little, and then when Jess was older, Dad had been doing well enough that Mom hadn't needed to go out and find a job. For a while she'd sold sambal to other homesick Malaysians, but Mom took so long making the sambal and was so uncompromising about the results that it had been hard to make the venture profitable. When the neighbors had complained about the smell, Mom had scaled back.

It hadn't mattered anyway. They had been comfortable enough. Even Dad's redundancy hadn't worried them too much initially. At the time they'd assumed he'd get another job soon. They hadn't expected him to get sick.

"I went for interview, thought it went well," said Mom. "Then got phone call. They said they want a young person. They're scared I cannot keep up."

"Are they allowed to say that? That's, like, age discrimination, isn't it?"

"In Malaysia they don't care one," said Mom. "Last night I had to pretend to go to sleep early, otherwise I'll sure tell Dad. You mustn't tell him, OK? Don't want him to be disappointed." Her voice wobbled on the edge of a sob.

"Dad doesn't expect you to get a job," said Jess. "Don't worry, Mom. We're doing OK, right? Dad's getting a regular paycheck, we've got somewhere to live . . ."

"Better if we have our own place. Not good for different families to stay in one house. Sooner or later they will fight."

"Yeah, OK, but—"

"Chinese New Year coming soon some more."

"You said we won't be celebrating. Because of . . ." Jess hesitated over the name, but it would be incredibly tactless even of Ah Ma to show up now. "Because of Ah Ma." The fact Mom's mother had died recently apparently meant she, Dad and Jess were tainted with bad luck. They wouldn't be visiting any relatives for Chinese New Year.

"But Kor Kor and Kor Tiao will visit people, and they all know we're here," said Mom. "So must give angpow. Even if we give small angpow, have to give so many . . . People will say, wah, they all went US, earned USD, still give so little!"

"Fu—never mind those people, Mom. Who cares about them?"

"And there's our debts," said Mom.

It was not a good idea to start thinking about their debt. Jess found it easier than Mom did, because the numbers were so astronomical. "Forget about the debt. The debt collectors can't get you here."

Mom wiped her eyes. "At least it doesn't affect you. You can still go back to US."

"What, and leave you guys here?" said Jess. "How would you manage without me?"

Mom drew herself up. "We can one. You think we're so helpless?"

This was so exactly what Jess thought that it was hard for her to control her face. "I don't need to go back. Maybe I'll just stay here."

Saying it gave her a surprisingly acute pang. She hadn't thought she'd miss America. She'd always felt out of place there, with the immigrant's tenuous claim to belonging.

That was nothing to how foreign she felt in Malaysia, though. She didn't even blend in visually, although Penang was majority Chinese. Something about the way she dressed or held herself tipped everyone off, before she even opened her mouth. Hawkers and Grab drivers and people in shops all looked taken aback when she addressed them in Hokkien.

They were only going to keep being surprised, if her Hokkien kept improving thanks to her being haunted by a native speaker.

Mom's eyes had filled with tears again.

"You know how many people want US passport?" she said. "We sacrifice so much so you can be American citizen. If you don't go back, what's the point we work so hard?"

"Mom," said Jess, as the tears spilled over. "C'mon, Mom. You're wallowing now." She gave Mom a reassuring squeeze. "I'm just saying, you don't need to worry. Dad's working—and he's fine, by the way. We talked about it. He says he likes the job and Kor Tiao is definitely not exploiting him. Soon we'll be able to get a place of our own. Everything will work out, you'll see."

But Mom had tipped over the edge. She was sobbing in a way that Jess knew from experience had to be left alone to run itself out. Trying to comfort Mom in this mood was pointless, because she was no longer crying about any one disappointment or mischance, but all of them—all of the accumulated blows and pricks and grazes life had dealt her.

"We cannot start over already," she told Dad when he'd first proposed moving back to Malaysia to take up the job Kor Tiao was offering. "We're too old. Cannot take it anymore."

Her optimism had been restored by the next day, or at least she'd acted like it had. But Jess hadn't forgotten that glimpse of a chink in what she'd come to realize was her mom's armor.

Had she really thought of confiding in Mom and Dad about what was going on? Jess wondered at her own forgetfulness.

The past couple of years had stripped her of many illusions about her parents that none of them would have wished away. It made it all the more vital to preserve their illusions about her.

Finally, Mom wiped her eyes, smiling unsteadily at Jess.

"Mom is too emotional," she said.

Jess patted her on the shoulder. "It's OK." All Jess wanted to do was go back to her room and sleep for a week.

"How was it yesterday?" said Mom, attempting to sound normal. Her breath hitched, but they both pretended not to notice it. "Is it OK, working for Kor Tiao?"

"Yeah," said Jess. "It was fine."

TEN

The approach of Chinese New Year meant Kor Kor's social calendar was even more packed than usual. Jess's parents might not be doing any New Year visiting themselves, but the unceasing stream of relatives and friends to the house meant they were seeing everyone they would have visited anyway.

There was one advantage to the fact Jess was working for Kor Tiao. Sure, she was spending her days freezing in an over-air-conditioned office, designing flyers she wasn't sure anyone actually needed. But at least she was no longer expected to sit and smile while aunties and uncles she barely knew discussed her professional, marital and general life prospects all day.

There were still dinners where this happened, but at least she'd get to skip one of them when she made her planned trip to Ng Chee Hin's son's café. She told her family she was going for a networking event for young professionals in Penang.

The red dot on her left eyelid had faded by now, taking with it her ability to see Ah Ma. It hadn't done anything to her ability to *hear* Ah Ma, but Ah Ma had piped down a little after Jess had managed to get through to Ah Ku on the phone. He'd sounded OK—not *great*, but not like he was dying either. He'd dismissed Ah Ma's anxious questions about his health, and refused Jess's offer to visit.

"Hai, don't need lah. After your mother find out, she'll be angry. I'm OK. I'm sitting at home, not doing anything. Don't want that bastard to find me. You better be careful also, Ah Min. That bastard won't give chance one, even to a young girl like you."

Tell Ah Ku he don't need to worry, said Ah Ma. *I'm here to jaga you. You don't need to be scared of that bastard.*

Jess relayed the message, but Ah Ku was not convinced. "Ah Ma's a ghost already. What can she do? Better you stay away from Ng Chee Hin. Don't go and make noise. We fought them in court. There's nothing more for us to do."

He hadn't seen the Black Water Sister at the construction site, or the workers' faces as they looked at the scaffolding the god had brought down. But there was no point worrying him.

"It's OK, Ah Ku," said Jess. "I'm not planning on making noise."

The morning before she was due to visit Ng Wei Sherng's café, she made sure her photos of the accident at the construction site were backed up in multiple places—on her computer, an external hard drive and a couple of different cloud storage sites.

She hadn't sent the photos to the press yet. She had thought the incident would have come out in the news anyway—the Rexmondton Heights development was a major one, and the place had been swarming with emergency services personnel. But there was no coverage that she could see, though Kor Tiao got all three major English-language newspapers and she'd been diligently going through each of them since the day of the accident.

Ah Ma snorted when Jess mentioned this to her. *I told you. They all are scared of him. If they write about it, that bastard won't pay them for advertisements anymore.*

If that was true, there didn't seem much point in sending the photos to journalists. But Jess wasn't sure how much she could believe what Ah Ma said about Ng Chee Hin. The ghost was hardly objective.

One thing she could and did do was send the photos to the construction worker who'd given her his number. Whatever happened, at least Kassim would have the evidence of what had gone down at the site.

Jess laid down one ground rule for the visit to the café.

You can't come, she told Ah Ma. *If I see you or hear you, I'm turning around and going straight home.*

Ah Ma was predictably put out by this. *Where got medium talk to the spirit like that? Cannot do this, cannot do that. Some more I'm your grandmother!*

Now that she'd seen Ah Ma, it was a little weird going back to talking to a voice in her head. Jess would have been tempted to ask Ah Ma to redo the eye opening, and mark both her eyes while she was at it, but for the thought of what else she might see. The Datuk Kong had been all right, but if it meant she started seeing spirits like the Black Water Sister everywhere . . . Jess shuddered.

You forgot ah, Ah Ma saved you? Ah Ma went on. *If I didn't come to the development the other day, you think what will happen? You'll die and be a ghost like me already.*

I know you saved me, said Jess. *I owe you one. That's why I'm doing this. You think I want to go to Ng Wei Sherng's café? I beat up his dad's men!*

Though as a matter of fact Ng Wei Sherng's café was the kind of place she totally would have gone to if not for the minor fact that his dad was a gang boss who was beefing with her relatives. She'd checked out the Facebook page for the flagship branch. It was a converted shophouse in George Town which served fusion takes on local cuisine and hosted slam poetry nights.

There was something annoying about the café's combination of international hipster aesthetic and local charm, from the lovingly restored Peranakan tiles juxtaposed against exposed brickwork, to the selection of novelty ice creams. Durian ice cream was standard, but Jess had never seen anything like their nasi lemak sundae—scoops of coconut gelato on a base of pandan chiffon cake, scattered with caramelized peanuts and dusted with fried anchovies crushed to a powder. She found it all so appealing she felt faintly manipulated.

Not like you wanted to fight those men also, said Ah Ma. *They're the ones who bullied you.*

I don't think Ng Chee Hin is going to take that into account, said Jess drily. *If he figures out who I am, I won't be the only one who's screwed. He's a major client of my uncle's. I can't afford to get in trouble with him. If I'm going on his turf, I need to bring my A game. I can't afford to lose focus.*

If I don't say anything, should be OK what, said Ah Ma. *What's there to distract you if I'm quiet?*

Nothing. Jess had been prepared for an argument. This acknowledgment on Ah Ma's part that there might be circumstances in which her silence would be more valuable than her opinions was surprising. *If you're sure you can stay quiet.*

Ah Ma is so old, said the ghost with hauteur. *You think I don't know when to talk and when to don't talk?*

After a moment she added, *Your uncle really give you all face. Letting you live in his house, eat his food . . . Your father is the older brother some more. When people help you, you shouldn't cause issues for them.*

That's what I'm saying. Jess hesitated. *So you promise you won't come?*

If you go alone and that bastard sends his samseng to beat you, then how? I won't say anything. You won't even know I'm there.

By way of a commitment to noninterference, that was probably the most she was going to get from Ah Ma. It was true there might be benefits to having her there—Jess had no wish to face Ng Chee Hin's gangsters alone, supposing any did show up. Most importantly, it wasn't like Jess could stop her. Ah Ma was in her head, and she'd stay there till Jess found a way to resolve this mess.

"Great," said Jess. "It's a deal."

JESS WASN'T PLANNING to spend a long time at the café. She figured she'd look around, talk to the staff, see what she could find out about the Ng family.

The café was one of a row of traditional shophouses, with shuttered first-floor windows and attractive ornamental plaster molding on the facade. There were some hip, uncomfortable-looking metal chairs and tables set out on the covered five-foot way that ran along the front of the shophouses.

Jess went through rust-colored double doors, decorated with intricate carvings, into a surprisingly large interior space. The floor was of polished cement, the walls painted in pastel hues and distressed in a highly intentional way. She walked through a bustling bakery, an adjoining restaurant and a kids' playroom before emerging into a tree-lined courtyard. There was a pool with white and orange koi swimming lazily in the water. People sat at small tables under the trees, smoking and chatting.

At the other end of the courtyard was another building. Through open doors she could see what looked like a bar, crowded with people.

"What the hell," said Jess aloud. "There's more of this?"

"It used to be two shophouses, back to back," said a voice behind her.

Jess turned. The voice belonged to a guy around her age of indeterminate race, in a gray shirt and dark jeans. He gave off an air of being suave and trustworthy and cool, like someone who would know how to fix your MacBook if you'd spilled coffee on it.

There was something vaguely familiar about him. Jess was trying to work out what it was when he saw her face and did a double take.

"Oh my God, it's you," he said. "I thought I'd never see you again!"

The mirrored shades and cap had obscured his face and hair before, but the accent—a thick frosting of American on a base of Penangite—was unmistakable.

"AirAsia," said Jess. It was the young guy from the ceremony at the garden temple, the one who'd intervened when Ah Ku rushed her while he was possessed by Kuan Kong.

"What?" said AirAsia.

Jess gestured at her head. "Your cap."

"Oh right," he said. "I was going hard on the Tony Fernandes look. This is wild. I was wondering what happened to you! What brings you here?" He paused. "Wait, are you here for the event?"

"Yeah, sure," said Jess. "Um, which event are you talking about?"

"The singles' night." For some reason, AirAsia was blushing. He pointed at the bar across the courtyard. "It's through there. It's getting pretty crowded, though. We're buying the place next door, so next year we'll have more space."

"'We'?" said Jess.

AirAsia smiled. It was a peculiarly attractive smile—conscious of its own charm, but not offensively so.

"I own this place," he said. "Call me Sherng."

It was then that Jess realized where she had seen his face before. It hadn't been at the temple.

"Ng Wei Sherng?" she said, adding, "I saw the piece about you in *The Star*."

But she saw there was no need to explain herself. Ng Wei Sherng was used to being recognized.

"That's me," he said. "What's your name?"

"CRAZY, MAN, WHAT happened that night," said Sherng. "Do you know what happened to the medium? Is he OK?"

They were sitting at a round metal table in the courtyard, with an abandoned cigarette stub still smoking in the ashtray. It wasn't precisely cool yet, but enough of the day's heat had faded that being outside was pleasant.

Jess looked down at her iced tea. "On the house," Sherng had said when she tried to pay. He was leaning forward slightly in his chair, looking like he meant to be there for a while. Either he was hitting on her—which, if you believed Sharanya, was always happening to Jess—or else he had some nefarious motive for talking to her.

Perhaps he knew who she was—the niece of the temple caretaker who was blocking his father's development, the woman who'd chased away Ng Chee Hin's men. But how could he have found that out? It wasn't like they'd exchanged names before.

Sherng hadn't acted like he was on the gangsters' side when they'd showed up at the temple. She hadn't really been paying attention to him that night; there had been too much going on. But he'd stood up to Chief Thug, hadn't he? He'd spoken up in support of Ah Ku.

It wasn't like that had prevented Chief Thug from beating the shit out of Ah Ku. And hadn't Sherng said his father had asked him to go to the temple? "I'm not very religious," he'd said.

Maybe it was all some elaborate setup. Maybe Ng Wei Sherng had known about Jess even before she'd turned up at the temple and that was why he had been there. It was all a trap, designed to catch Ah Ma . . .

But there was no way Sherng could know about Ah Ma. Nobody had known Jess was going to the temple that day, not even Jess. It had been a spontaneous trip, instigated by Ah Ma. Ah Ku had clearly had no idea she was coming. She'd even surprised Kuan Kong, and if anything or anybody was capable of knowing things they shouldn't, it would have been the intelligence possessing Ah Ku.

The thought calmed Jess down.

She studied Sherng. He looked genuinely curious. Everything about him seemed genuine. He projected an authenticity that fit better with their surroundings—the intelligence and sympathy with which the shophouse had been converted—than it did with the idea of his being the son of the fifth richest man in Malaysia.

If it was a facade, he was a good actor. But wouldn't you be a good actor if your dad was a gang boss? Having family ties to organized crime seemed like it would give you a lot of practice in deception.

She glanced around the courtyard, but there was no sign of Ah Ma. She should have come up with some kind of signal for if she wanted Ah Ma's advice. At that moment being told what to do seemed attractive.

But then again, she knew what Ah Ma would say. She'd say Ng Wei Sherng was the son of a no-good bastard and Jess couldn't trust him.

"I think the medium's OK," said Jess. "Someone took him to the doctor. You left, right?"

Sherng looked away. "Yeah, when that guy punched the medium. I went to call for help."

"Oh yeah?" Jess stared at Sherng's averted face. He was embarrassed, but there was more to it than that. He was hiding something.

"That's strange," said Jess. Her voice was overly bright. "Nobody came."

Sherng looked uncomfortable. "You got out OK, right? I wanted to stay, but my parents would have freaked out. I was supposed to go to a function with them that night. Didn't want them getting suspicious."

"Yeah?" said Jess, her eyes still fixed on him. "I thought you said your dad asked you to go to the temple."

Sherng went red. "Oh God, I did say that. I didn't want you to think I believed in all that crap. I didn't realize you knew the medium."

Jess stiffened and took a slug of iced tea to hide it.

There were at least two alternatives. Either Sherng was in on everything his dad was up to—he knew about Jess's connection to the temple, he'd witnessed or heard about what Ah Ma–in–Jess had done to his dad's thugs, and this was all part of some intricate plot to lure her to her doom.

Or he wasn't acting. He was a normal guy who hadn't known that his dad was sending in gangsters to clear the squatters off his land.

Jess looked around. She was in a public place, surrounded by people who—she realized—were discreetly watching them. Of course, Sherng was a minor celebrity. Pictures of them were probably being shared on social media at that very moment. She was as safe as she was ever likely to be in the presence of the son of Penang's biggest gang boss.

"And I didn't realize you were the son of Dato' Ng Chee Hin." The name was like a magic word; it drew Sherng's eyes irresistibly back to hers. Jess said deliberately, "The company that's developing the temple land. He owns it, doesn't he?"

She watched Sherng's face change. His expression, so open and sincere a moment ago, shut like a door.

"I see," he said. He drew back into his chair, crossing his arms. "You're accusing my father of sending those guys to the temple, is it? That's why you came here?"

Before Jess could answer, Sherng added, "Which publication are you with? *The Edge*? Tell your boss he needs to get over his grudge. He's been trying to get dirt on my father for years. It's never going to happen."

"You think I'm a journalist?" Jess laughed, though it was slightly painful contemplating the alternate reality in which she was an investigative reporter hunting down a lead, rather than a mooch plagued by the ghost of her dead grandmother.

"Not a great one, if you can't come up with a better cover story," said Sherng. "We have plenty of events on. You couldn't have chosen another? Who's going to believe *you'd* need to go to a singles' night to find a guy?"

"You'd be surprised," said Jess, thinking of the various relatives who were constantly trying to set her up with young men they knew. "Can we get back to what your dad's gangsters were doing at the temple?"

She spoke louder than she'd intended to. People's heads turned toward them, some staring openly now. Sherng smiled at them nervously.

"That's great," he said to Jess. "Really great delivery. You're going to kill it at the audition."

Whatever Sherng was, or knew, he wasn't a good liar. Nobody would have believed Jess was rehearsing lines for an audition. But the people at the other tables took the real point, which was that Sherng didn't want their attention.

Sherng lowered his voice while his customers pretended to look away. "Look, if you want to talk about this, we can talk. But not here."

Even if he wasn't acting, that didn't mean Jess could trust him.

"I'm comfortable here. Where people can see us," she said pointedly.

Sherng stared. "You—what, you think I'm dangerous or something?" He sounded hurt. "I'm not going to do anything. You know, you're the one who came to my café. I don't have to talk to you."

Jess said, "You're right. I'm sorry."

She could almost hear Ah Ma imploding from sheer rage. Bulldozing everyone she met might work for Ah Ma, but she was dead; she had nothing to lose. If Jess was going to stay alive, she had to do things her way. Which included, sometimes, saying things she didn't mean.

"I want to talk," she said. She lowered her voice. "But given who your dad is, I think it's fair for me to want to do it in public."

"I just want to go outside," said Sherng, adding over his shoulder, "Miss, if you take one more photo of me, I'm going to have to ask you to leave the café."

He pushed back his chair, standing up. "Come on. I need a cigarette."

ELEVEN

On the five-foot way outside the café, Sherng tapped a cigarette out of a packet and offered it to Jess.

She shook her head. "I don't smoke."

She wondered why Sherng hadn't kicked her out. He'd had a point when he said he didn't have to talk to her. Surely it wasn't merely that he wanted to rehabilitate himself in the eyes of a pretty girl? Jess wasn't *that* hot.

"I shouldn't smoke either," said Sherng, but he did, puffing morosely on his cigarette. "My ex hated it."

Jess had been wondering if he was going to mention the heiress. She had been judging him over his silence on the subject, but her estimation of him underwent a rapid readjustment. The next moment she felt annoyed with herself for caring.

"So tell me," she said. "What happened that night at the temple? You didn't call the police."

"No." Sherng hesitated. "I'm only talking to you if you agree to treat this conversation as off the record."

"I'm not actually a journalist," said Jess.

Sherng glanced sidelong at her. "Why are you so interested, then? Who are you?" A thought struck him. "Is your name even Jess?"

"Yeah," said Jess, though on some views that was a lie. Jessamyn wasn't technically her real name. Mom had chosen it when they moved to America, to make things easier at school. Jess's passport and birth certificate proclaimed her to be Teoh Sze Min.

She'd always had a conflicted relationship with her name, all the more so when she'd come reluctantly to the conclusion that she wasn't straight. It felt way too pat that the name she called herself in her head should be invisible in her official records.

"I went to talk to a medium at a temple and he ended up getting beaten up by thugs," said Jess. She folded her arms. "Call me an interested bystander."

Nothing in Sherng's face suggested he knew she'd glossed over the precise nature of her relationship with the medium in question. He said:

"If you must know, I called my dad. Not because I thought he sent those guys," he added quickly. "But if anyone could find out who sent them, it'd be him. I knew he'd be able to help, better than the police."

"Because he's got his own guys?" said Jess.

Sherng glared at her. "I don't know what you've heard about my dad, but you can't trust what people say, OK? People love talking shit about my dad. Being successful means you make enemies. But I can tell you he wouldn't do something like that."

His Malaysian accent got stronger when he was upset. *De-escalate*, thought Jess. She didn't want him so mad he stopped talking.

"I know he's your dad," she said carefully. "But we don't always know what our parents are capable of."

"I'm not saying he wouldn't do it because he's *nice*," said Sherng. "He's a businessman. He's tough—but he's fair. Most importantly, he's not stupid. Why would he need some strongmen to clear the site for him? His company owns the land."

"There's a court case, isn't there?"

Sherng dismissed this with an impatient puff of smoke. "The case isn't going to go against him. The law's on his side. There's no reason for my dad to do something so risky when all he needs to do is wait it out."

This sounded plausible. But it was just what Ng Chee Hin *would* say, wasn't it? It wasn't like he'd want to own up to employing thugs. "Is that what he told you?"

"It's common sense." Sherng sighed. "I've been telling him all along he's mishandling this issue. It doesn't look good to be the Goliath in a David and Goliath situation. Now there are gangsters getting involved? Threatening little old aunties and uncles praying at the temple? I told Pa, whoever did this, he's going to screw it up for everybody."

Now they were getting somewhere.

"You think it's somebody he knows?" said Jess.

"It has to be somebody involved with the development, right?" Sherng seemed to have forgotten she wasn't on his side. He sounded like he was thinking out loud. "It's a big deal. Sejahtera's only one of the partners. There's a lot of money riding on it, enough to make people reckless."

"What makes you so sure it's not your dad?" said Jess, genuinely curious.

"Trust me, my dad already has a lot of money," said Sherng. "He's in the next phase now. He wants to give back to society. If you open a newspaper, you'll see he's always helping people out, donating to charity. That's why I told him, he needs to crack down on the troublemaker."

"What did he say?"

Sherng rolled his shoulders irritably. "I mean, he's an Asian dad. Do you try giving advice to your parents? What do they say?"

Jess thought about this. "They mostly ignore me. I take your point."

"Yeah." Sherng took a gloomy draw of his cigarette. "It wasn't a successful conversation. Pa was mad at me anyway, for going to the temple. He's been trying to keep me away from it."

"Really? Why?"

"Look at this place!" Sherng gestured at the café. "Does it look like it belongs to somebody who likes destroying heritage sites? I want them to leave the temple alone. I told my dad they could build around it. But he thinks it wouldn't work with the plans. They want a modern development. Some people don't want to live next door to the gods."

"So what were you doing there?" said Jess. "Taking the chance to look around before it's gone?"

"I was scoping it out. I have this idea for the site," said Sherng. "I thought I should see the place before I pitched it to my dad, in case it wasn't right for what I had in mind. But it's perfect. You saw! That temple is cool, right?"

Jess had been too apprehensive when she'd visited the garden temple to admire it. She remembered it now—the bodhi tree and the way the garden had seemed to cohere around it; the wandering paths, smothered with weeds; the small gods in their crumbling shrines.

"It was pretty cool," she admitted.

"Penang is full of places like that. Hidden gems," said Sherng. "It's hard to get people to see it, though. Especially people like my dad. He's had to fight for everything, so he's practical. His generation, the people he works with, they look at land and they think condos, they think shopping malls, they think offices. They think that's the only way they can make use of land. But that temple is special. It'd be a waste to destroy it. It'd be criminal."

It was impossible to doubt his passion.

"What would you do with it?" said Jess.

"What couldn't you do with it?" said Sherng. "I'd start with F and B. Imagine having a drink with all those trees and altars around you. It's so atmospheric. People would go nuts. But you wouldn't have to stop there. It's such an amazing space, the potential is endless. You could do all kinds of events—wedding shoots—hell, why not weddings? There's a growing market for quirky venues."

"You want to turn the temple into a hipster café?" said Jess.

She was surprised by her own revulsion, as at a sacrilege. It was strange, given she'd only been there once and planned to avoid it in the future, but she found she had strong feelings about the garden temple. She saw again in her mind's eye the wind-ruffled curtain of vines hanging from the bodhi tree, the faded red altars amidst the roots. Sherng couldn't have been paying attention, if he could think of the garden and its shrines as no more than set dressing.

"What's wrong with leaving it as it is?" she said.

Sherng gave her a look that said she was being disappointing. "That temple is sitting on land worth millions. If you don't find a way to make it profitable, sooner or later it's going to be destroyed. Isn't it better if it's preserved? If you want to keep that kind of place around, it needs to work for people now. For the young people, not just some uncles who want 4D numbers and a cure for gout."

Jess must still have looked skeptical. Sherng laughed suddenly.

"Basket! There's no reward for trying to find the middle ground," he said. "You think I'm this big corporate villain and my dad thinks I'm a bleeding heart. He thinks I have no sense. When I first opened this café, he was like, 'Who's going to come? Building so old. Furniture so lauyah.' The vintage furniture, he hated that the most. He was like, 'If you can't afford to buy new chairs, why you didn't ask me?' He couldn't believe it when we started making money. He thinks I'm weird about old things. He doesn't see that it's practical."

"If by 'practical' you mean 'profit driven,'" said Jess.

"Yeah, it's money. But it's also soul," said Sherng. "My idea wouldn't make as much as a high-rise—mixed use, shopping, F and B, residential. I can't match the yield from a bunch of premium condos. All my idea does is keep a part of old Penang alive for new Penang."

Jess thought of Ah Ma. "Maybe it's OK to let old things pass on."

Sherng looked betrayed. "Don't you want to save the temple?"

"I think it should be what it is," said Jess. "It doesn't have to be anything else. It's OK if it fades away. But it shouldn't be torn out and it shouldn't be made over."

Sherng smiled. "And Pa thinks I'm a romantic. He should meet you."

Jess looked down to avoid giving away how much she never wanted to meet Ng Chee Hin.

A brief silence fell. Sherng lit another cigarette.

"What happened after I left, that time?" he said. "I came back to the temple after the function, but you guys were gone by then. You said the medium's OK?"

"Yeah," said Jess, after a pause. "I think those guys got scared after they beat him up. They started arguing among themselves and then they went off."

Let Sherng call her out for lying if he found out who had really gotten rid of the thugs that night. Jess would deny everything. Who would believe she was capable of roughing up a gang of thugs anyway?

"Shit," said Sherng. "I'm going to have to talk to my dad." He didn't seem delighted by the prospect.

He did appear to be on the level. Maybe he was telling the truth. At the very least, Jess could believe he thought his dad hadn't sent the gangsters.

That didn't mean he was right. But it might mean she'd found a way in. A potential ally.

She remembered the construction worker, Kassim, interrogating her about her social media reach. Here was an opportunity to talk to someone who could make a real difference to Kassim and the other workers' situation, if he cared to do it.

"There's another thing you might want to talk to your dad about," she said. She took out her phone. "You know about the accident at the development?"

Sherng looked blank. "What accident?"

Jess handed him her phone. She heard his sharp intake of breath as he took in the image of the collapsed scaffolding.

"It happened on Monday," said Jess. "There was a guy under there. He could have died. The workers have been complaining about safety issues for a while—equipment failing, that kind of thing—but they say they've been ignored." She met Sherng's eyes. "Your dad has a big problem on his hands."

AH MA WAITED with surprising patience till Jess was a couple of blocks away from the café to speak.

You don't want to take taxi? she said.

Night had fallen, but George Town was still full of life, people spilling out onto the streets now that the heat of the day had been quenched. Jess passed crowded restaurants and backpacker bars full of tourists.

It was nice, being out of the house. She hadn't realized how much spending all her time around her family was getting to her. The living members were almost as stressful as the dead.

"I wanted to think," she said.

She felt dissatisfied, the kind of restless that needed walking off, even though her encounter with Sherng had been reasonably successful. She was uninjured, unthreatened, and she had a promise of action from Ng Chee Hin's own son.

Sherng had been convincingly shocked by her account of the incident at the construction site—a heavily edited account. She'd mentioned that the workers believed the accident had been caused by a disgruntled spirit, but that was as much as she'd said about the supernatural aspect of the matter. Sherng had said he didn't believe in all that crap, after all.

When he'd said, "Do you know why that guy ran toward the scaffolding?" Jess had shrugged.

"There was a lot going on," she said. "Apparently these equipment failures and accidents have been happening for a while. He was probably stressed out."

Strictly, nothing she was saying was incorrect. Jess had plenty of experience in lying by telling the truth.

Sherng ran a hand through his hair. "I had no idea. Crap. This is really, really bad." He hesitated. "Have you shown anybody else these photos?"

Jess raised her eyebrows. "Why do you ask?"

"Can I ask you not to tell anybody? I know what that sounds like," he added hastily. "But I'm telling you this in good faith. If you publish these, you lose your leverage. If I talk to my father and I can tell him we can handle it confidentially, he'll be more likely to listen."

"I've sent the photos to some people," said Jess, watching him. "I haven't heard that they plan to publish them yet. I haven't shared them anywhere public."

"OK," said Sherng. "So we still have time. My dad probably doesn't even know this is going on."

"Really?" said Jess despite herself. What did she think Sherng was going to do, put his hand up and admit his dad was a conscienceless gangster?

"He's the last person the contractor would want to tell, if things are going wrong," said Sherng. "They've been having issues with the contractor already. The development's behind schedule and it's not just because of the court case." He looked at her. "Give me a chance."

He'd promised she would hear from him in a week's time. ("Pa's in Bangkok. This kind of thing, it's best to discuss in person.")

That was a win. No one was in a better position to persuade Ng Chee Hin to do something than his son and heir.

Sure, Jess could've told Sherng to fuck off and gone ahead with plastering the images all over social media, despite her pitiful number of Facebook followers. She could have emailed them to every media outlet she could find.

But if the press was scared of Ng Chee Hin—if even the police wouldn't go against him—how much traction was she going to get that way?

"Go and show everybody," the worker had told her. But what he wanted was his rights, not a social media campaign that might not go anywhere. He'd asked her to tell people and she'd told somebody. It wasn't like she'd agreed not to publish. She was just holding off to see what Ng Wei Sherng was able to do.

"What did you think of him?" she asked Ah Ma. She only realized she was speaking aloud when a guy passing by gave her a funny look. She fumbled in her bag, popping an earbud in her ear so it would look like she was on the phone. She could always think at Ah Ma instead, but talking gave her a reassuring—if illusory—sense of distance between them.

Good boy, said Ah Ma judiciously. *That bastard is lucky. Most rich men's sons don't know how to behave.*

That this broadly matched Jess's assessment surprised her. She hadn't expected Ah Ma to be anything but suspicious of him. "You think I can trust him?"

No lah. If he's guai, listens to his father, that means all the more cannot trust. What's wrong?

"Nothing," said Jess, but the denial was pure reflex and both of them knew it. She said, "He said he'd talk to his dad about what happened at the site. But I don't know how much that's going to help."

Ah Ma snorted. "No use. That boy says whatever also, that bastard isn't going to stop the development."

Jess had come to the end of the five-foot way she was walking along. A road ran between the rows of shophouses, busy with cars and motorbikes. She paused, waiting for a gap in the traffic so she could cross.

"Ah Ma, you know the god. You were her medium. What would actually get her to back off?"

Ah Ma didn't answer immediately. Jess had crossed the road and was making her way along the next block when the ghost spoke.

God is very simple, said Ah Ma. *If you pray to them, give offerings at the right time, they'll be happy. If you go and kacau their temple, don't respect them, they won't be happy. These people want to destroy her place, how can she not be angry?*

"What if we could get Ng Chee Hin to pray to her?" said Jess. "Would that work?"

If somebody gives you a present, but they still want to spoil your house, will you accept?

"Obviously, Sherng will have to get him to agree to leave the temple alone," said Jess. "But say that happens, and we get him to make her an offering—"

The god won't layan that bastard. Ah Ma's tone was freezing. *You think she's stupid? If you want to pray to her, your heart must be sincere. A useless man like that bastard, the mouth says one thing when the heart is different, what god wants his offering? He can buy however many suckling pigs he wants and pay for all the joss sticks. When he dies and goes to hell, he's still going to suffer!*

"OK," said Jess, with an effort at patience. "What if we get Sherng to do it? He seems pretty sincere."

You want to ask the son to go to the temple and pray to the god?

"He likes the temple," said Jess. "If I tell him that my grandmother was a medium there and he needs to pray to show respect—"

That one cannot say. You cannot tell him about Ah Ma.

So much for that idea. "Then . . ."

Tell him it's Ah Ku who asked him to do it, said Ah Ma. *But cannot say he's your Ah Ku. Just say the medium told you.*

Jess blinked. "You think it's worth doing?"

Could be. If the son makes an offering to the god, asks her to stop disturbing the construction workers, maybe she'll be willing to forgive, said Ah Ma. *Then Ah Ma can move on also.*

Jess hadn't even thought of that side benefit of propitiating the god. "Oh, would you go?"

You think I like ah, being a hantu? I'm like a hungry ghost like that. Neither here neither there. If I can, of course I'll go on to my next life. I must stay here is because of this problem with the god.

"OK." Jess took a deep breath, letting it out in a rush. "I'll ask him to meet me at the temple."

She'd been trying to block out her memory of the Black Water Sister, but inevitably the god's image recurred now—the small figure dwarfed by incomplete buildings, squinting against the sun.

Goosebumps rose on Jess's skin despite the warmth of the evening. She was grateful for the bustle of people around her.

"The god won't . . ." Jess paused, swallowing. "She won't *do* anything, will she?"

Why? You're scared ah?

"I watched her try to murder a man, so yeah, I'm a little nervous!"

You're not the one building condos in her place, said Ah Ma. *You don't need to worry. Just listen to Ah Ma. You must WhatsApp Ah Ku, ask him to come also.*

"Uh, it's OK," said Jess. She couldn't see Ah Ku being that useful if the god decided to turn nasty. "I don't think we need to bother him. Shouldn't he be resting?"

He's the caretaker. If we're going to the temple, we must call him, said Ah Ma. *You tell that boy, don't need to tell the father. After he makes trouble only.*

TWELVE

Sherng seemed enthusiastic when Jess suggested a meetup with the caretaker at the garden temple so Sherng could explain what he had in mind for the site.

Yeah, definitely happy to talk, said his text. After CNY?

Chinese New Year would go on for two weeks. Kassim had messaged Jess on WhatsApp, asking if she'd published her photos anywhere yet. He and his coworkers were talking to an NGO about demanding better protections from the contractor, but it sounded like they'd appreciate any publicity she was able to drum up.

If she was going to put the photos up online, the holiday period would be a good time, when everyone was home and checking their phones. But she wanted to see what Sherng could offer first.

Can you do tomorrow? she replied.

She was pushing it—Saturday was only two days before the eve of the New Year, when people had reunion dinner with their families—but he said yes.

Jess held off on mentioning the whole "there's a vengeful god preying on your dad's development and you need to propitiate her" thing. That was an explanation best made in person, ideally via Ah Ku.

"You might need to make an appearance," she said to Ah Ma. "In case he doesn't believe it."

You don't need to worry, said Ah Ma. *He'll believe.*

IT WAS LATE morning when Jess pulled up in the parking lot in front of the temple. Sunshine flooded the parking lot. The hawker center was experiencing a lull in business—it was too late for breakfast, too early for lunch—but a comforting blend of human noises still came from it: pots and pans clanging, oil hissing, people shouting orders over a stream of Cantonese from the TV. Against all this, the jungle looked like nothing more than some trees, denuded of mystery or threat.

Sherng was already at the temple. He was absorbed in his phone, but he looked up when Jess got to the top of the stairs, his scowl of concentration turning into a smile.

Jess didn't smile back. She was too startled.

The garden was teeming. People perched on the roofs of the shrines, smoking, drinking and eating snacks. Others were gliding along the paths or clustered around the plants. A small wild banana tree had three women somehow sitting *in* it, gossiping.

Except they weren't women, but spirits. They were all spirits.

Jess had asked Ah Ma to mark her eyes, opening them again to the spirit world. If she was venturing into the Black Water Sister's domain, she'd figured she'd better be able to see what was going on. She hadn't bargained on there being so much to see.

Fortunately the spirits didn't seem interested in Jess. They glanced up briefly at her approach before going back to what they were doing, though a couple nodded to Ah Ma as if they recognized her.

"Eh, how are you?" they said pleasantly. "Died already, is it?"

This was all lost on Sherng.

"Weird, I don't have reception," he said. "Is your phone working?"

A notification popped up as Jess checked her phone—a message from Mom, reminding her not to eat the nangka in the Tupperware in the fridge, but only the nangka in the plastic bag, because the Tupperware nangka was Kor Kor's, and if Jess touched it she would inevitably spark a civil war. Jess didn't even like nangka.

"Yeah."

"You're with Digi, is it?" said Sherng. "Maybe I should switch."

He scanned the garden. Jess could imagine how peaceful it must look to him under the sun, the long grass swaying in the breeze. She kept her gaze resolutely averted from the shrines underneath the bodhi tree.

"It's beautiful, isn't it?" said Sherng. He sighed. "I've got to get my dad out here. Maybe if he saw it . . ."

But Jess could see how the temple would strike Sherng's dad, the same way it would strike her parents, even if they couldn't perceive the spirits crowding it. Viewed through uncle-vision, the place was messy, overgrown, full of hazards both physical and spiritual. The picturesque vines and creepers whispered of bugs; the undergrowth was undoubtedly crowded with snakes; the pond with its placid terrapins basking in the sun might as well have had a sign up saying COME CATCH YOUR DENGUE HERE. As for the quaint altars and the gods and goddesses they held . . .

"It might not make a difference," said Jess, swallowing a squeak. She'd just registered that the women in the banana tree had feet that were fixed on their ankles the wrong way around, pointing backward. She wrenched her eyes away from them. "We, uh, we don't all see the same thing when we look at something."

"True," said Sherng. He probably thought Jess was reciting a platitude, instead of making a statement that was very literally true for her at that moment. "You said the medium's willing to talk? How do you know him, anyway?"

Before Jess could answer, Ah Ku emerged from behind the bodhi tree. He was dressed a little more formally than when Jess had last seen him, in a polo shirt and Bermuda shorts, and he was bearing a tray with drinks on it.

"Hello, hello," he said. "This is the boy, is it?"

"I'm Ng Wei Sherng," said Sherng. "How are you, uncle? Terrible, what happened that time. I want you to know we're very concerned. We want to resolve this." He hesitated. "Were you badly injured?"

"Aiyah, I'm OK lah," said Ah Ku, dismissing the whaling he'd gotten from Chief Thug with a wave of the hand. He winced, which rendered the gesture somewhat hollow. "You want chrysanthemum tea? I made for you all. Today so hot, better drink more."

Sherng declined courteously. "Thanks, uncle, but I'm doing keto."

"You like chrysanthemum tea, right?" said Ah Ku to Jess. "Come, drink. This is very cooling, good for your body."

There was a weird vibe coming off him. Despite his expansive greeting, he wouldn't meet Jess's eyes. He almost seemed embarrassed.

She accepted the cup at his insistence, glancing discreetly at Ah Ma. The ghost's ever-shifting face gave nothing away.

"I don't know who sent those men," said Sherng. "But we're going to find out and deal with them. What happened was unacceptable."

He'd said, "*I* don't know," thought Jess. Not *we*. She wondered if his dad even knew what he was up to, if Sherng had told him he was going to the temple again.

"Medium's life is like that," said Ah Ku. "Cannot predict what will happen. You want to see the temple? I can give you a tour."

"A tour would be great," said Sherng politely, but he gave Jess a puzzled look. He'd clearly been expecting somewhat more hostility from the caretaker of the temple his dad was trying to bulldoze.

Jess couldn't help him. *Ah Ma, what's going on?*

"What are you talking about?" said Ah Ma. "Nothing's going on also." Her voice vibrated with barely suppressed excitement.

Jess couldn't have said why apprehension was flooding her body. Maybe it was the spirits she was carefully not looking at, or the proximity of the Black Water Sister's altar, brooding under the bodhi tree. Despite the sunlight and the heat, a chill ran down her spine.

Something was wrong.

We had an agreement, she told Ah Ma. *If I ask a question, you answer. And you tell me the truth.*

"You always want to quarrel with Ah Ma only," said Ah Ma. "Faster drink your tea."

"Why don't we tell Sherng why we asked him to come here?" Jess said aloud to Ah Ku.

"You drink finish the tea first," said Ah Ku. "Then I can put the tray back." He was twitchy, far more nervous than the circumstances seemed to warrant.

"You know what, I'm not thirsty right now," said Jess. "I'll have it later." She reached out to put her cup of tea back on his tray.

"Ah Ku told you to drink, you drink!" snarled Ah Ma.

Jess hadn't thought Ah Ma was capable of interacting with the physical world without a body. Surely that was the whole reason she needed Jess's help. So she wasn't prepared when Ah Ma grabbed her arm.

The touch of Ah Ma's hand was delicate despite the force she was evidently exerting—Jess could barely feel the pressure of ghostly fingers on her flesh. It was only because Ah Ma had taken Jess off guard that she managed to bring the cup to Jess's lips.

Startled, Jess swallowed some liquid despite herself. The rest of the tea sloshed down her front.

One more cup! said Ah Ma.

The ghost had vanished. Jess saw her own hand reach toward the tray Ah Ku held, her fingers curling around a second cup of tea. She had gulped down half of it before Jess managed to get ahold of herself and fling the cup away. It dropped to the ground, rolling.

She took a deep breath, trying to clear the clouds from her mind, but this only made her feel queasier. The world spun around her, the ground unsteady beneath her feet. Through her dizziness she saw distress written across Ah Ku's face, as though this wasn't his fucking fault in the first place.

"Jess?" said Sherng. "What's going on?"

"What did you put in my drink?" Jess tried to say to Ah Ku.

But her mouth was no longer her own. Her voice said, in a familiar hectoring Hokkien, "Why you put so little? She's still awake!"

Because that was where Ah Ma had gone, of course. Back inside Jess, where she definitely did not belong.

You fucking dumbass, thought Jess blurrily to herself. *You walked straight into this.*

She should have guessed the tea was spiked. They had been too insistent that she drink up. Plus it made no sense that Ah Ku had gone to the effort of brewing actual tea when he'd regaled her with Yeo's cartons before.

She should never have come here in the first place, never agreed to get involved in something she only half understood. She'd been lulled into thinking she could trust Ah Ma, believing they were on the same side.

Stupid of her. It wasn't like Ah Ma hadn't shown her who she was. Jess thought of the construction site, the god driving that man to his destruction. Ah Ma would have left him to die, crushed by the scaffolding.

"Cannot give too much, Ma," said Ah Ku. "After she has brain damage or what, then how? Ma can use the body, means enough already what. Shouldn't waste time. You want to settle the boy, better do it quickly."

Thinking was like swimming through caramel. *Settle the boy*, thought Jess. *What does that mean?* Then, *Oh FUCK*.

"Jess, are you OK?" said the boy in question. Sherng laid a hand on her shoulder, glancing distrustfully at Ah Ku. "Looks like she's not feeling well, uncle. I think we'd better go. We can meet another day. Come on, Jess."

The shot of pure horror had burned through Jess's haziness.

"She's not going anywhere," Ah Ma–in–Jess was saying, when Jess seized control of her mouth. With a huge effort of will, she choked out:

"Run!"

"What?" said Sherng.

Jess shoved him to make the point, but she only succeeded in making him stumble. He was righting himself and turning to give her a betrayed look when Ah Ma took over again, pushing Jess to the back of her own mind and assuming control of her limbs. Ah Ma picked up a length of pipe lying in the grass and hit Sherng on the back.

Sherng fell to the ground.

Jess looked around wildly for help, but there was no one. A couple of the spirits were watching with cool interest, as though the scene was some random documentary about Peruvian skateboarders they'd only clicked on because they were bored. Most didn't even seem to have noticed that anything out of the ordinary was happening.

What the fuck *are you doing?* said Jess to Ah Ma.

But she didn't really need to ask. She knew.

Ah Ku hovered behind her, all but wringing his hands, even though he'd probably planted the pipe in the grass for Ah Ma to use. The whole thing was a setup. Mom had been right to avoid these assholes for all those years.

"Ma, you don't want to wait ah?" said Ah Ku. "They all should be coming already. They can do for you."

"Wait for what? I can do," said Ah Ma.

Sherng groaned.

"Jess," he said thickly, "what the hell, man?"

He tried to get up. Ah Ma dealt him another blow with the pipe, kicking him for good measure.

"Better finish him off now," she said. "You've got what?"

Ah Ku produced a parang, offering the hilt to Ah Ma. Jess felt Ah Ma's dissatisfaction course through her body. It was as though her body belonged to Ah Ma now, and so it felt her emotions, carried out her intentions, while Jess was left to rage ineffectually, locked inside her own head.

"This only?" said Ah Ma.

"It's sharp," said Ah Ku. "You try first."

But Ah Ma shook her head. "Dirty lah. After the blood spill, then how? Ah Min must go home after this. I'll strangle him."

Sherng rolled painfully onto his back. His eyes were wide and glassy with fear.

"Jess," he said. "Are you in there?"

Ah Ma flung down the pipe and stretched her hands out toward Sherng.

Not her hands. *Jess's* hands. They were Jess's own two hands and she couldn't let this happen.

She forced her right hand up, throwing all her willpower into it.

It was like straining to push a boulder uphill. For what felt like forever, nothing happened.

Her fingers twitched. All at once Ah Ma's will gave way under Jess's resolve. Her hand shot forward and grabbed Sherng by the arm.

Jess helped him to his feet while in her head Ah Ma snarled, *Naughty girl! You don't interfere!*

Each movement was slow and effortful. It was like she'd clamped weights onto her limbs, like when she did a hard workout and her muscles no longer wanted to function. Jess had to concentrate ferociously to push past Ah Ma's resistance. If her attention so much as flickered, the ghost would take over again.

"You've got to get out of here," she tried to say, but English felt foreign in her mouth, her tongue tripping over its ponderous syllables. The sound that came out of her was garbled and meaningless.

Sherng pulled his arm out of her grasp, looking wary. She didn't blame him.

"Must. Go," said Jess, forcing the words out. "Go. Now!"

"Is that you, Jess?" said Sherng. "What's wrong? Why are you doing this?"

He was staring intently at her, as though he could somehow see through her skull and discern the ghost inside.

Useless girl! snarled Ah Ma. *Your own family you're willing to betray. You're not ashamed ah?*

She tried to smack Sherng, but Jess was watching out for any attempts at violence. She grabbed her own hand, drawing it back.

"I'm not helping you murder anybody, whoever they are," she said out loud, in Hokkien. "What the hell is your problem?"

"Who are you talking to?" said Sherng.

Everyone ignored him.

"Ah Min ah, let her do," said Ah Ku. "You don't know only. Actually it must be done. If you let him go, you think what? He'll go home and won't disturb us anymore? This kind of business, once you start, you must finish."

"Are you kidding me?" said Jess. "Who came up with this stupid idea in the first place? 'Let's kill Ng Chee Hin's son, he'll definitely leave us alone after that.' The guy is a *gang boss*. Piss him off and he'll send his gangsters after us!"

She could feel Ah Ma's answer coming up her throat. She tried to seal her mouth shut, choke the words down, but despite herself her mouth opened and she heard her own voice saying:

"You think Ng Chee Hin is the only one who can call people? We also have supporters. How come your phone can work, but the boy's cannot? You think about it."

Jess managed to wrest her voice back. "What are you talking about?"

"Ah Ma means, you don't have to worry," said Ah Ku soothingly. "We have the god on our side."

"Oh, she's talking about divine support? Is that it?" said Jess. "Great! That's great. We have a god who can mess up people's reception. His father has men who can beat us to death and throw us in the drain afterward. We're definitely going to win."

You think we don't have that also? said Ah Ma.

A motorcycle horn blared in the distance. Ah Ku brightened. "They're here already."

"Who?" said Jess.

But the men were already coming up the stairs, spilling into the garden. There were around ten of them, all Chinese.

That wasn't the only difference between them and the thugs Jess had seen the last time she was here. Chief Thug and his buddies had been sleeker, better maintained. These guys were scrawny, dressed in shabby pasar malam clothes—worn singlets and T-shirts with incongruous logos on them, flip-flops on their feet, shorts that had seen better days. Some of the men had knives, but others were holding wrenches or rusty metal bars, as though they'd snatched up the first weapon to hand before rushing over.

That didn't make them any less menacing. They looked just as happy to cut your throat as the other thugs had been, only these guys would probably give you tetanus while they were at it.

"Shit!" said Sherng.

Till then he'd been weirdly relaxed for someone who was the subject of an attempted murder, even if the murderers were proving somewhat inept. But at the sight of the men, he made a break for it, dashing toward the jungle at the back of the temple.

He took everyone by surprise. Ah Ku and Ah Ma started yelling, but Sherng might well have made it, if not for the terrain. A piece of cracked paving tripped him up, arresting his flight for just long enough for the men to catch him.

Two men brought him over to Ah Ku, clocking him on the head casually when he wouldn't stop struggling.

"You're late already!" said Ah Ku. "My mother had to try to do by herself. Is it right you let an old lady do your dirty business?"

"Had to close shop first what," said one of the men sullenly. He looked barely out of his teens, younger than Jess. He was fair-skinned, with a sulky red mouth and a mole on his cheek like an Old Hollywood actress.

The other guy was uncle-aged. Ah Ku's reproof didn't seem to bother him.

"Don't need to answer back, Ah Tat," he said to the boy. To Ah Ku he said, with the ease of long acquaintance, "It's OK what, we came in time. The business is not done yet also."

The truth of the situation burst upon Jess with all the force of a revelation. But it felt as though a part of her had known all along— a part of her that had grown closer to Ah Ma in the shadowy corners of Jess's own mind, where the ghost's secrets lurked.

"You're not fighting Ng Chee Hin because you're different from him," Jess sputtered. "You're fighting him because you're *competitors*."

"Who's this girl?" said the older man to Ah Ku.

"That's why you didn't go to the hospital," Jess went on. "They'd ask questions at the hospital. You went to Dr. Rozlan instead. You have your own guy. Because that's what gangsters do!"

Sherng raised his head, looking at Jess. His eyes were suddenly fierce. "Who are you? What's your full name?"

"Shh," said Jess, worried they'd hit him again.

Fortunately the men were still busy talking to each other.

"My niece," said Ah Ku. "You remember Ah Min? Used to come to the shop when she was small. Poey Hoon Chee's kid."

"Oh, Ah Min, is it?" said the older man holding Sherng. His face transformed, friendly wrinkles emerging around his eyes. "Grown up already! You remember me or not? I'm your mother's cousin."

Of course he was. No wonder Mom never hung out with her relatives, never talked about them if she could help it. They were all in it together—Ah Ku and the rest of them. Only a gangster would use his niece to lure the son of a magnate to his temple so he could murder him.

And only a gangster would come back from the dead to take vengeance on her rival.

Why didn't you tell me? said Jess to Ah Ma.

Unexpectedly, Ah Ma answered.

Like that also need to tell you? she said. *You think normal people dare to fight Ng Chee Hin? It's not my fault if like that also you don't know!*

Jess had dropped her guard in her shock. She only realized when Ah Ma seized control of her voice and spat:

"Bring the boy here! I'll settle him."

"Ma, there's no need for you to do," said Ah Ku. "We can handle it."

"You all don't do!" said Ah Ma. Her voice came out in a strangled shriek as Jess tried to clamp her mouth shut.

Ah Ma kept going, in a breathless squeak, "You mustn't do anything strenuous, Ah Soon. After you hurt yourself."

"The boys can do it, then," said Ah Ku.

Ah Ma wasn't having it. "No, no. I'll do. I'm dead already. What for you all get in trouble?" She stopped, panting as though she'd been sprinting.

"But if you do it, it's Ah Min whose hands will have the blood on them," said Ah Ku. "That's not fair to Ah Min also."

"That's right it's not fair," said Jess. "This is total bullshit!"

She spoke in English, as a matter of principle and to make it clear it was her talking, not the unwanted tenant in her head. The words were slurred, but that was fine. Nobody was paying attention to what she was saying anyway. What mattered was who was speaking.

"Nah, you see! You can't even control the body," said Ah Ku. He wasn't speaking to Jess. "How can you deal with the boy like that?"

"You think I'm so useless, I cannot even control my own granddaughter?" said Ah Ma.

Ah Ma's raspy smoker's voice resonated inside Jess's head, even as Jess heard her own voice speak the words aloud. Ah Ku might have asked the question, but Ah Ma's answer was intended for Jess.

"You said what, Ah Soon," said Ah Ma. "I have the god on my side."

And with that, the god was there. She stood by Ah Ku as though she'd been there all along.

No one warned Jess, so she looked incautiously right in the Black Water Sister's face. It was only for a moment, before the terror hit, the bone-deep knowledge that she'd fucked up. It was the same terror she'd felt meeting Ah Ku's eyes at that first encounter, when she'd seen the god in him—a precipitous feeling, like vertigo, as the world jerked into true perspective.

Instinct dragged her gaze downwards. She hunched her shoulders, as if she could make herself small enough to escape divine observation.

The Black Water Sister didn't have one of those startling blue-black faces some idols had, wasn't attired in period robes or anything you'd expect to see on a deity. She looked like an ordinary Chinese woman, in her twenties or thirties, wearing a light top and trousers. Physically, she was like anyone you might pass on the street.

But she wasn't like Ah Ku or Sherng or the gangsters. She wasn't even like Ah Ma or the Datuk Kong or the other, ordinary spirits in the garden temple. She was a hole punched out of a sane world, a channel for the sublime—or the horrific. Through her, the unthinkable was made real.

She came toward Jess.

I'll die if she touches me, thought Jess, but the god touched her and Jess did not die.

It was the softest brush of a fingertip on Jess's top lip. All at once inanimation settled on her, a heavy blanket, muffling thought and feeling. Blessedly removed from herself, she heard her own voice say gently to Sherng:

"You didn't pray to me. You don't know how to respect me. This is my place. You dare to come here?"

The words were in a dialect Jess didn't know—not Hokkien or Mandarin or Cantonese, the latter two of which she didn't speak but usually recognized. Yet she understood it all, the god's speech translated, as she spoke, into the wordless language of the heart.

"Jess?" said Sherng stupidly.

His voice quivered. He had learned to fear now, but it was too late, for him and for Jess.

She saw without surprise that Ah Ma was standing next to her again. The ghost had to have stepped out of Jess's body, because—

oh fuck, oh God—the goddess was using it, speaking to Sherng through Jess.

Ah Ma put her hands together, bowing her head.

"Ah Chee," she said, calling the goddess "elder sister." "You want to do, or I do?"

The impassive face, with its deceptive youthfulness, turned to Ah Ma. "You do."

The goddess raised her hand.

Jess saw that what would happen must happen. Her terror hadn't gone away, but it was muted now. She felt almost comfortable, relaxed in her powerlessness. If she let go, she could fall asleep, and no one could blame her for what came next . . .

The goddess put her hand on the nape of Jess's neck. It was like having a hot iron pressed against her skin. Jess screamed, convulsing, trying to jerk away.

Her whole self sprang back to life. She was afraid, yes, scared shitless—but she was also rich, thick, concentrated with rage.

Ah Ma melted into Jess as the goddess held the way open. Jess's body was limp, submission forced from her by the hand on her neck. Only her pain was her own.

Ah Ma jerked Jess's head from side to side, cracking her neck, rolling her shoulders. She reached out and settled her hands around Sherng's throat, squeezing.

Sherng struggled, his arms and legs flailing. He kicked Jess in the stomach, taking her breath away, but Ah Ma only pressed harder.

The men stood around them, watching with respectful faces, like people who didn't know anything about classical music listening to an orchestra. Mole Boy—Ah Tat, they'd called him—looked entranced, his mouth half-open with excitement.

I'm going to kill a human being, thought Jess. Agony shrilled through her entire body, pulsing out from the goddess's hand on her neck. *It will be my hands that do it.*

The thought galvanized her. If it could hurt this fucking much even when Ah Ma and the god had taken her over—if Jess's pain belonged to her—then her body was still hers, despite anything gods or grandmothers could do. They could take everything, they could swallow her whole, but her hands she would keep to her own damn self.

She tore her hands from Sherng's neck. Gasping, he fell back. She wrenched herself out of the goddess's grip and bent over, shaking until the teeth rattled in her head, shaking Ah Ma off her.

The scalding pain of the god's touch had burned away the last traces of dizziness from the spiked chrysanthemum tea. Without the god's help, Ah Ma couldn't get a purchase on her. Jess heard the ghost shriek, "Useless girl!"

For a crystalline moment, she knew she had all of her mind and body back.

The men scattered, leaving the way clear. Jess noticed suddenly that the spirits were gone. Their absence was weirdly spooky, in this garden that was their place, their home as much as the Black Water Sister's.

She snatched up the length of pipe Ah Ma had used to hit Sherng, and sprinted toward the bodhi tree.

She didn't look back to see if the god or Ah Ma was following her. She slipped in the final stretch, but managed to avoid face-planting on the ground. Instead she landed heavily on her knees in front of the Black Water Sister's worn effigy, in the perfect position to wield her pipe.

Jess heaved the incense urn out of the way. There was a handful of joss sticks in it, smoldering gently. The smell of incense was in her nostrils as she brought the pipe down on the statuette.

The idol's face cracked. The men were shouting behind her, but she couldn't hear the god or Ah Ma.

Jess bashed at the idol again. Adrenaline—and possibly the

drugs—was affecting her coordination, but at such close range it didn't matter, and maybe she had some supernatural strength left over from having been possessed. The pipe crashed into the goddess's side, and the statuette shattered.

The men had stopped shouting. Jess didn't bother looking back at them. She got to her feet and went to work on the altar.

It was easier than she would have thought to break it down. Time and exposure had done most of the work for her. Soon she'd reduced the altar to a jumble of splintered wood, the shards of the idol mixed up with the jagged panels of its shelter.

Jess straightened up, panting.

The incense urn stood at the side where she'd put it. Jess overturned it with her foot and smashed it with the pipe.

There. She was done.

She turned around.

The god was gone. So was Ah Ma. Only humans remained.

Sherng had picked himself up, but the men hadn't tried to recapture him. They were all staring at Jess in dead silence.

Finally a man broke the silence.

"You're crazy," he said in Hokkien. He walked away, toward the path back to the parking lot. He picked up the pace as he went, and then he started running.

It was like a dam breaking. The other men followed, scrambling away as though the goddess herself was after them.

Jess dropped her length of pipe and looked at Sherng.

"Are you OK?" she said.

If she were Sherng she would be halfway across Penang by now, but apparently Sherng didn't have any self-preservation instinct. His eyes were huge.

"What the—" His voice was hoarse. He paused, swallowing painfully. "What the hell was all that?"

Before Jess could answer, Ah Ku moved. Jess hadn't realized he was still there.

Neither had Sherng, apparently. Alarm crossed his face and he bolted, heading off in the opposite direction from the other men.

Ah Ku didn't even spare him a glance. He trudged over to Jess and looked down at the ruins of the altar. He sighed.

"Like that, we might as well clear out," he said. "Stay here for what?"

Jess should probably run for it. Ah Ku had been in on Ah Ma's conspiracy against her. He'd literally tried to poison her.

But weirdly, she didn't feel afraid of him. Next to the god and Ah Ma, he felt like, if not an ally, a fellow victim, as vulnerable to the whims of gods and ghosts as Jess.

Then Ah Ku turned and slapped her.

"Stupid girl!" he said. "What will I tell your mother now?"

THIRTEEN

Jess held her stinging cheek, almost too shocked to be mad.

"My mother doesn't even know I'm here!" she blurted.

It was the first thing that came into her head. But before she could find the words fully to express her indignation, Ah Ku walked off.

"Your mother is smart," he said over his shoulder. "She don't want to see, don't want to know. I told Ah Ma, what do you expect? She's educated. You think she wants to be involved in this not-three not-four business? Cannot say she's wrong also.

"If you followed your mother, there won't be all this trouble. Your surname is not Lim also. This"—Ah Ku's gesture took in the garden temple, broken altar and all—"is not your affair. You shouldn't have come here in the first place."

Jess opened and closed her mouth like a fish, so outraged she felt winded by it.

"You're standing there for what?" said Ah Ku. "Come, come."

Jess hurried after him.

"I came because of Ah Ma," she said. "She's the one who dragged me into all of this. How was I supposed to know you guys were going to use me to attempt a murder?"

Ah Ku had the grace to look embarrassed.

"I didn't want to be involved also," he said. "But what can I do? Ah Ma is like that. Everything must do her way. If you don't follow, even her own son she'll curse. Old people are like that."

"I disagree, I happen to know most old people are not murderers!" said Jess. "What were you guys thinking? It's not like killing Ng Chee Hin's son would have made him back off. All you would've done is piss him off and turn it into a big gang war." She paused, disturbed, as the implications of what she'd said sank in. "Is that what Ah Ma wants?"

"No lah," said Ah Ku. "Ah Ma is not like that. She's clever to fight, but she doesn't fight for no reason. She wanted to scare off that bastard, make sure he won't come and kacau us anymore."

"But—"

"If a human kills the son, Ng Chee Hin will be angry," said Ah Ku. "Humans, he's not scared."

It took a moment for Jess to process this.

"So that's why Ah Ma wanted me to do it?" she said. "She wanted Ng Chee Hin to know the—" Even the thought of saying the Black Water Sister's name made the hairs stand up on the back of Jess's neck. "To know the god killed his son."

What was it Ah Ma had said when Jess asked why Ng Chee Hin wasn't scared of the god? *He hasn't learned to be scared.*

"Ah Ma wanted to teach him to be scared," said Jess slowly. "But how would he have known? I would've been the sucker who got arrested."

Ah Ku scoffed, "If you offend Ng Chee Hin, you don't need to worry about getting arrested. His men will come to your house at night and catch you."

"Great. Thanks, Ah Ku. I'm definitely not worried anymore."

"You don't need to worry. That bastard isn't stupid," said Ah Ku. "You think he'll believe a small girl like you is willing to kill people? He knows one lah! When he finds out you're Ah Ma's granddaughter, he'll understand. He'll know, better not meddle in the gods' business. If you offend the gods, they will punish you.

"But instead you went and broke the shrine." Ah Ku shook his head. "I told Ah Ma she shouldn't force you. If you don't want to do, it won't turn out well. But she said got no time to find another candidate. Ah Ma wants someone strong to be her medium."

Jess stared at Ah Ku, incredulous. She couldn't even take the lids off jars of pasta sauce without assistance—Sharanya was the lid remover of their relationship. "Then why me? Yew Ping can't be the only young man in the family."

"I'm not talking about whether you can beat people," said Ah Ku. "What Ah Ma cares about is whether the spirit is strong. You're so troublesome, it shows your spirit is strong. If not, how can you fight Ah Ma?"

"I'm the troublesome one? I'm not making her murder anyone!"

Ah Ku didn't bother answering this. He went round the back of the roofed structure where he'd entertained Jess the first time she came to the temple, emerging laden with various cleaning implements—a broom, a bucket, a dustpan and brush.

"Nah." He held the broom out to Jess. It was the old-fashioned kind they sold in sundry shops, nothing more than a bundle of long twigs tied together.

"What's this for?"

"To clean up." Ah Ku nodded at the broken shrine.

Jess looked down at the broom in his hand, then up at his brown, creased face, the eyes squinting a little in the sunlight. "You *drugged* me!"

"Aiyah, I made sure it's a small amount only," said Ah Ku. "I was trying to help you."

"You also slapped me," Jess reminded him.

"You think I'll slap you if I don't care?" said Ah Ku. "If you're not my sister's child, I would have run away already. Where's everybody else? They cabut. You know why?"

He paused, looking expectantly at Jess.

"Because I destroyed the shrine?" she said.

"They're scared the god will be angry," said Ah Ku. "I'm your uncle, that's why I'm here cleaning up. If not, I'll be at another temple asking for charms already."

He let out a deep hacking cough, grimacing. Jess had almost forgotten he had broken ribs.

She snatched the broom from him. "Why did you even come? You should've told Ah Ma you need to stay home and recover. You can't let her bully you."

"Hah!" Ah Ku seemed genuinely amused. "You should know what. That's easy to say, hard to do."

JESS WAS HOPING to avoid her parents when she got home. The events of the day had left her with limited resources to deal with familial demands.

But luck was not with her. Mom was in the living room when Jess let herself in at the front door. Mom was riffling through Kor Kor's shelves, her back turned to the door. Jess thought of dashing for the stairs, but Mom turned before she could do it.

Jess froze. She'd tried to make herself presentable using the tissues in the car, but there had only been so much she could do. She still looked sweaty and disheveled, not like someone who'd spent the past five hours in an air-conditioned café working on job applications.

"Min, have you seen my book about herbs?" said Mom. She sounded frazzled. "Kor Kor wants to show Auntie Cheryl. Cannot find."

She was evidently consumed by the problem of the missing book. Jess would be safe so long as she didn't draw attention to herself. "Bedside table? I'll go check. You guys going out?"

Mom avoided her eyes. "Kor Kor asked us to come to her small group."

Jess was already making for the stairs, but she stopped with a foot on the first step. "Isn't that a church thing?"

Mom had been steadily refusing Kor Kor's invites to church-related events since they had arrived in Penang. She was always polite when she did it, but Kor Kor's attempts to proselytize were one of her many grievances against her.

"The host is a doctor, he lives in Jesselton Heights," said Mom. "Kor Kor says he always serves good makan. I told Dad, why not? It's a chance to make friends."

Feeling like she'd extended a foot over solid ground only to step into quicksand, Jess said:

"You *have* friends. You were just saying you know too many people in Penang. You can't go anywhere without running into them."

"Is there anything wrong if we go?" said Mom. "Go and see only, cannot meh?"

Jess swallowed her indignation with difficulty. Knowing it was unjustified didn't make it any easier.

"Of course. I don't care," she lied. "You guys can go to all the church things you want. I'm not the boss of you."

Despite her defiance, Mom was starting to look anxious. "You don't like, is it? Why?"

Before Jess could answer, Dad came barreling down the stairs, waving a thin paperback.

"Nah, here's your book," he said. "Let's go. Late already. Eh, Min, you're back? Finished already, your applications?"

Jess felt a pang of guilt. She hadn't applied to a single job in the past week. "I got some in."

Now that she had the book, Mom transferred her attention to Jess. "Maybe we should go to the temple and get a charm for you, Min."

"What?" said Jess. "What for?"

Mom couldn't know what had happened, could she? She couldn't have found out from Ah Ku, surely. It hadn't even been half an hour since Jess had dropped him off at his house.

"So long you've been applying for jobs, still not getting much interviews," said Mom. "Sometimes the temple can help. They can give you a charm to change your luck. I got for you when you did your exams, remember? It worked, right?"

The memory caught up with Jess. The morning of her SATs, Mom burning the slip of yellow paper, covered with Chinese characters, over a bowl of water. The black specks floating in the water as Jess brought it to her lips . . .

"I aced my SATs because I worked like a dog and had no social life," said Jess. "It wasn't because of the magic ash you made me drink!"

"Don't be arrogant, Min," said Mom. "If you don't understand, better don't say anything. Don't cause offense."

Jess thought of herself an hour ago, crouching under the sun, sweeping the debris of the goddess's altar into a dustpan. It was a little too late to take "don't cause offense" as her rule in religious matters.

"Shouldn't you guys be going?" she said. "Ask Kor Kor's church friends what *they* think of charms."

She felt strangely deflated as she shut herself into her bedroom. Of course there was nothing wrong with her parents attending Kor Kor's small group for the food and a discreet snoop around

Penang's fanciest neighborhood. They could even be attending for the Christianity. That would be fine. Wouldn't it?

Jess found that it wouldn't. Yesterday—half an hour ago, even—she would have said with complete confidence that her parents would never consider converting to Christianity. Now that certainty was taken away.

She was surprised by how much it shook her. Religion wasn't something Jess would've said was important to her and her parents, in either its presence or its absence. But the idea that Mom and Dad might change that dramatically made her feel as though she didn't really know them. As though they were leaving her behind. She felt like a child standing at a station, watching a train pull away from the platform with her parents in it.

What else did she not know about her family? Her assumptions about their relationship to religion had been wrong. Religion must have been important to Mom once upon a time, with a mother and a brother who were both spirit mediums.

And gangsters, thought Jess. *Don't forget the part where they're gangsters.*

Maybe Ah Ku was right.

"Better you go back to US," he had said as they tidied up the mess Jess had made. "Safer."

"Couldn't Ng Chee Hin find me in America?" said Jess. "It's not that far away. Especially for a millionaire. He probably has a private jet."

"Who's talking about Ng Chee Hin?" said Ah Ku. "You let us handle him. He is a human being only. You should be worrying about this." He nodded at what was left of the altar.

"You think I've offended the god?" said Jess. Ah Ku's expression rendered an answer unnecessary. "OK, stupid question. But I can't escape a god by moving, can I? They don't even need private jets."

"In these matters, location is very important," said Ah Ku. "This big sister, she likes this place only. Other places, she doesn't want to go. That's why we had to fight that bastard no matter what, even if he tried to bully us. She is not willing to move."

He sighed, his shoulders slumping. "But now, might as well we move the temple. The other deities are more flexible."

"You think the goddess might agree to move now that her altar's gone?" said Jess.

The look Ah Ku gave her was familiar. Jess had seen it, at different points, on Ah Ma, Mom, Dad, Kor Kor, Kor Tiao and their friends. It was a look of realization that here was an alien to whom even the most basic things, things everyone understood, would have to be explained.

"No," said Ah Ku. "We didn't want to move is because we were scared the big sister will be angry. But now you spoiled her shrine. So makes no difference if we move also. Either way, she will want to punish us.

"But mustn't be hasty," he added. "See how first. We can rebuild the shrine, pray to the god, ask her to forgive." He sounded singularly unconvinced.

Jess had to give Ah Ku a lift back to his house. His motorcycle had been stolen.

"Probably they all took when they were running away," said Ah Ku. "It's so old, nobody else would want." He was remarkably philosophical about having been robbed by his fellow gang brothers. "If this is my punishment, considered very lenient already."

His house was a terrace house with a concrete yard and a stainless steel gate, blinding in the sun. Jess pulled the brake and said:

"What about Ah Ma?"

There was a red altar in Ah Ku's front yard. Jess tried not to look at it.

"Maybe she'll have some idea about how to deal with the god," agreed Ah Ku. "She was the medium."

"No, I mean," said Jess, "she's going to be mad at me, isn't she? For messing up her plans."

"Oh, that one you don't need to worry," said Ah Ku. "At the end of the day, you're Ah Ma's granddaughter. You're in this bad position, how can she not give chance?"

He paused, looking like he wanted to say more, but nothing came at first. The silence hung heavy between them. Jess thought he was going to ask her for money, but instead Ah Ku rummaged in his pocket and held out a couple of crumpled blue-green bills.

"Nah," he said. "I don't have angpow on me, but you take."

Over Jess's protests he folded the money into her hands. Jess's initial position was that she didn't need money and he shouldn't give her any. When this failed, she fell back to:

"You don't have to give me a hundred ringgit. That's too much."

Ah Ku waved this away too. "Small thing only lah. Aiyah, nowadays hundred ringgit cannot buy much. It's for good luck. Give your mother my regards."

"My mother doesn't know I've been meeting up with you," said Jess.

"Oh yeah. Forgot," said Ah Ku. "Maybe I'll see her another time. You look after yourself, yeah? Don't stress. All problems can solve one."

If the money hadn't given it away, his voice would have, with its put-on optimism, gentle and unpersuaded. It was the tone in which one soothes a man on his deathbed, when lies no longer matter.

Lying in bed that night, Jess remembered Ah Ku's seamed face, stamped with the conviction of her doom. Her skin prickled beneath her blanket, foreboding washing over her.

If she could go back to America, she thought drowsily, if she could go home, she would. But there was nothing to go back to. Her family was here; new tenants lived in what had been their apartment. Her friends were scattered. And Sharanya . . .

Sharanya was coming to her, kind of, eventually. All Jess had to do was find a way to move to Singapore, once all of this was over. Home wasn't a place, Sharanya always said. It was people.

Jess reached for her phone, flicking open WhatsApp. Sharanya had forwarded an old group photo including the two of them. It wasn't a great shot—Sharanya had red-eye and Jess had blinked at exactly the wrong moment.

The messages from Sharanya read:

Looking through old photos and found these dorks

I miss you

Jess remembered when the picture had been taken. It was at the café where they had first met, both of them nervous freshmen tagging along with new friends to a meetup neither felt in the mood for. The café had been nothing special, the meetup as awkward as Jess had dreaded it might be. But still the encounter was a warm golden moment in her memory, flooded with autumn sunshine. Sharanya's hair had glowed in it, rich shades of brown and red shining out of the black . . .

Jess fell asleep smiling.

IN HER DREAM she was running.

It was nighttime. Soft earth squelched under her feet, long grass scratching her calves. Her legs ached. Her chest felt like it was being squeezed in an inexorable grip.

But she couldn't stop. There was someone behind her.

She was in an open space, a field or something, hurtling toward a dark mass. It wasn't till she was nearly up against it that she saw it was a stand of trees. The jungle swallowed her whole.

The canopy overhead blotted out the moonlight. The undergrowth slowed her down. She heard her pursuer bellowing like a bull, enraged by the same stray logs on which she stubbed her toes, the slippery leaf matter beneath their feet.

Fear quickened her pace. She stumbled over a root, twisting her ankle, and fell heavily against a tree. The bark scraped her face as she pushed off.

She struggled to her feet. Her face was wet, blood seeping from the raw skin. Agony flared from her ankle as she started to hobble, picking up speed.

But it was no good. The delay had cost her. Her pursuer caught up with her.

He did not reproach her and she did not plead with him. Their relationship was a long-standing enmity; they knew each other too well for words to be useful at this point. Anything that was left to be said between them would be said through action—the arm upraised, the face averted, the hand warding off the blow.

She was scrambling away, still thinking she might live to repeat this scene, as she had survived so many scenes before, when she saw the knife in his hand.

It was then that she saw what was coming. Terror froze her flailing limbs in place, but she had her voice. She was screaming when he slit her throat.

Jess woke with her mouth open in a soundless shriek. It was dark. The Black Water Sister stood at the foot of her bed.

The god leaned over. There were beads of perspiration on her upper lip, even though the AC was on. Jess could smell her.

It was the smell that turned Jess's stomach. It was the same smell that came off everyone at the end of a Malaysian day—the sweaty funk that filled buses and wafted off kids in uniform as they headed home from school. It made everything too real.

The god touched Jess's forehead. The back of Jess's neck burned where the god had held her before. It was like having hot wax dripped on her, individual points on her skin blossoming into pain. Jess yelped, trying to jerk away, but the god's fingertips on her forehead wouldn't let her move.

"You saw what happened," said the god. "Now you know. You think you can run from me?"

She lifted her fingers and let Jess go, and Jess woke up for real.

She was alone in her bedroom, drenched in sweat despite the AC. She rolled over, the sheets sticking to her, and lunged for the trash can.

She didn't throw up, but it was a close thing. She lay on her front, panting and swallowing, as weak as if she had been felled by a fever.

The god's words echoed in her head. *Now you know.*

Jess wanted to get up, get a drink, creep into her parents' room and climb into their bed, as she used to do when she had nightmares as a kid. But fear kept her pinned to the bed, listening to the sound of her own breath. At that moment she would have been glad to hear Ah Ma's voice, just to know she wasn't alone.

It never came. Jess stayed where she was, tucked up in her blanket as though it would keep her safe, until the lightening sky through the window heralded the end of the night.

FOURTEEN

What Jess really wanted was a Milo and unchallenging human conversation, unrelated to gods or ghosts. But she emerged from her room at around seven a.m. into a quiet house. Kor Kor was apparently sleeping in for once.

Jess could have tried calling Sharanya, but she wasn't sure she'd be able to make it through the call without breaking down and telling her everything. And she didn't want to tell Sharanya anything. She didn't want to think about what had happened. Talking about last night would make it feel too real.

The Milo at least was available. Jess made herself a large mug, inhaling the comforting milky malt chocolate scent.

She would answer Sharanya's WhatsApp messages. She'd fallen asleep before she had been able to reply. She opened the app on her phone.

What happened yesterday? Are you OK?

The message was from Sherng. Jess stared.

She hadn't decided what she was going to do about Sherng.

Keep her head down and hope he didn't report her to the police, probably.

She'd assumed he wouldn't want to have anything more to do with her. Apparently she was wrong.

She shouldn't respond. Ah Ku would say it was a setup—would remind her that, at the end of the day, Sherng was the son of a gang boss.

But he had stayed at the garden temple when he could have run away. He had asked her what was going on, as though he trusted her to tell the truth.

Her fingers hovered over the screen.

She had to engage with Sherng, she told herself. If she didn't explain what had happened last night—if she left him thinking she wanted him dead—she might find herself running into Chief Thug and his friends the next time she went out. Maybe she wouldn't even have to go out. How had Ah Ku put it? *His men will come to your house at night and catch you.*

There were way too many things lying in wait to catch Jess at night as it was.

Shouldn't I be asking if you're OK? Jess replied.

What did Ah Ku know? He was the one who'd tried to poison her. All Sherng had done was try to interest her in his gentrification project.

If she was being honest with herself, despite everything, on some level she'd enjoyed talking to Sherng at his café. It wasn't that she was attracted to him—thankfully. Being able to be attracted to men would have made Jess's life easier overall, but not on this specific occasion.

It had just been nice hanging out with someone her age, someone who was more like her than her parents. Jess could guess what kind of restaurants Sherng went to, what he did for fun, what he was watching on Netflix. Even the fact that he almost certainly had a Netflix subscription marked him out as a member of the same species as Jess, a species with which she'd had minimal in-person contact since she'd graduated.

Sure, Sherng was rich, successful and socially adept, and she was a depressed shut-in who was only getting out of the house because of her dead grandmother's posthumous mission of revenge. Jess still had more in common with him than with anyone else she knew in Penang.

Sherng was up early, or maybe he hadn't slept. His response came promptly:

This is going to sound stupid. But was it you trying to choke me? You didn't seem like yourself.

Jess typed, It's hard to explain. Can we meet? NOT at the temple. You decide. You can bring a bodyguard.

It struck her that that could be misread.

I'm not going to do anything, she added. It's just in case. I don't think she's coming back for a while, though.

Sherng's reply said, She?

Can I tell you in person?

This time Sherng took a while to get back to her, long enough that Jess put down her phone and went upstairs to brush her teeth and change out of her pajamas.

Her reflection in the mirror startled her. Her eyes were hollow, her skin grayish. She looked more like a dead person than Ah Ma did.

She wasn't used to being displeased with the way she looked. It offended her sense of self—and it might make Mom ask questions. She spent some time restoring her face to something that might belong to a youthful, reasonably happy person, covering up the marks left by sleep deprivation.

When she got back to her phone half an hour later, Sherng had answered.

OK. Meet at Tau?

Tau was a restaurant specializing in soy-based food and drinks ("We serve everything starting with 'tau'!" said their Instagram profile). Jess was eating kaya toast, scrolling through photos of tofu-flavored gelato and braised pork in soy sauce, when Mom came in.

"Yesterday how ah, when you went to the café?" said Mom. "Forgot to ask last night."

"Did you?" said Jess absently. "I thought I told you. I worked on some applications. Made some progress."

"You can focus in the café? It's not too noisy?"

There was something wrong. Mom hovered by the table, picking stuff up and putting it down again. She was radiating nervous energy.

Jess could ask what was up. But she felt exhausted, bled dry by everything that had happened. Maybe it would be OK to leave Mom to deal with her own feelings for once. Couldn't she talk to Dad about them? Wasn't that what people got married for?

"It was fine," said Jess. "How was last night?"

"Last night?" Mom seemed to have forgotten she'd gone out. "Oh, Kor Kor's small group? It was OK. Nothing much."

She sat down. To Jess's horror, she saw Mom was welling up.

"Kor Kor is lucky," said Mom. "Her children are far away, but they tell her everything. Ching Yee calls her every day, you know! What she's eating for lunch also she tells her mom. What to do? I always want you to feel you can tell me anything. I must have done something wrong if you don't trust me. How to blame you?"

Mom was full-on weeping by now.

"What didn't I tell you?" said Jess. She found the rapidity with which Mom had gone from zero to meltdown as irritating as it was alarming. But at the thought of all the secrets she was keeping from Mom—how justified she was in reproaching Jess for her lack of candor, even if she didn't know it—Jess softened. She got up and went round the table, putting her arm around Mom.

"Hey, come on," she said. "What is it?"

Her mind was riffling through the things she didn't want Mom to know. What was the worst secret her parents could learn?

The truth about Sharanya, of course, and what that meant about Jess. That was still the worst. Jess would rather Mom and Dad knew she'd spent the afternoon yesterday trying to strangle a man than that they find out about Sharanya. They would probably be more understanding about the former than the latter.

Mom spoke, but her voice was so clogged with tears she had to repeat herself before Jess understood.

"Ah Kim told me she saw you," she said.

"OK," said Jess. Ah Kim must be someone Mom had seen at the small group meeting, one of the aunties who regularly crowded Kor Kor's living room. "Which one is Ah Kim again . . . ?"

"My sister-in-law," said Mom. "Ah Ku's wife. She phoned just now. Said why you didn't come inside and greet her when you came to her house? So long never saw you and you didn't pay your respects. She wasn't happy you didn't give her face. Told me off."

Jess's heart sped up.

But she was good at hiding. She let her face relax into an expression of apology, free of defensiveness or suspicion.

"Oh jeez," she said. "Sorry I let you in for it. I didn't even realize she was there. How is Ah Kim?"

"Why you didn't tell me you went to Ah Ku's house?" said Mom. "You used to be such a good girl, so open. Now you meet my brother also I must find out from Ah Kim. What more you haven't told me?"

Jess had resolved to be patient, but this annoyed her enough to make her incautious. She withdrew her arm from around Mom's shoulders.

"I mean, it's not like you've been super open with me," she said. "Like, when were you going to mention the fact your mother was a spirit medium and a gangster?"

Jess wasn't sure whether Ah Ma had actually been a gangster or if it was just Ah Ku and his associates. Ah Ma had certainly had enough murderous intent to suggest she'd been accustomed to criminal activity in life, but maybe ghosts had fewer inhibitions about killing people.

But Mom's answer confirmed it.

"What for Ah Ku's going around telling people things like that?" she said sharply. "He should learn to keep his mouth shut. Ah Ma's passed on already."

So Ah Kim hadn't told her about the ghost. You could call Ah Ma a lot of things, but "passed on" wasn't one of them.

Mom was clearly wondering herself what Jess knew. "What else did Ah Ku tell you? He's not doing any funny business, right? He told me all that no more already."

It sounded like she hadn't heard about the run-ins with Ng Chee Hin's men at the temple. Maybe she didn't even know Ah Ma and Ah Ku were quarreling with Ng Chee Hin. It wasn't like the dispute about the temple had been in the news recently.

"Why didn't you tell me about this stuff?" said Jess. "It's kind of a big thing for me not to know about my own relatives."

"Why you want to know for what? This kind of thing, better not to know," said Mom. "I also don't want to know. You think it's easy ah, moving to US? But I have to think about you. You are my daughter. If I don't look after you, who else will do it?"

It sounded like a non sequitur, but Jess knew how Mom's

mind worked. It made strange-seeming leaps, devised unexpected connections—but the connections were always present. This time, it wasn't hard to work out what she meant.

"Hold on, are you saying we emigrated because of Ah Ma?" said Jess.

"I don't want you to get involved," said Mom. "Ah Ma's life is like that, she has to be tough. But why should you suffer? You know or not, the police went and caught Ah Ku's son Ah Ping? Lucky thing he didn't go to jail." She looked at Jess. "You went to Ah Ku's house for what?"

Jess had had enough time to construct a story by now. It came out smoothly.

"Ah Ku said since I didn't go to Ah Ma's funeral, I should pay my respects," she said. "He took me to pray to her. He's having some trouble with his business or something. I think he thinks Ah Ma's, like, cursed him from beyond the veil."

"Choy," said Mom. "Don't simply talk like that. This Ah Ku is too superstitious. Ah Ma is his own mother, where got she'll curse him?"

She was frowning, but the story must have seemed plausible. She didn't question it further. "Next time Ah Ku tries to contact you, you let me know. I'll deal with it. Why you didn't tell me about him?"

Jess shrugged. "I didn't want to worry you. I know you've got issues with Ah Ku. It didn't seem like a big deal, praying to Ah Ma."

"Issues? I don't have issues with Ah Ku. He's my brother."

"I don't know, I think it'd be fair to have an issue with the fact he's a ga—an ex-gangster." Jess glanced at Mom. "So were *you* a gangster before you left Malaysia?"

Mom had calmed down a little. The question didn't seem to offend her. "No lah. Do I look like I can be a gangster?"

"No," agreed Jess. It was hard to imagine Mom with a rusting length of pipe, or looking tough in any way. "But maybe you did their bookkeeping or something. How am I supposed to know?"

"I was lucky," said Mom. "After Ah Ku came along, Ah Ma couldn't cope. She had to go out to work, so she put me with my grandmother, Ah Chor. I didn't live with Ah Ma after that, stayed with my grandparents until I went to uni. Ah Chor didn't like Ah Ma's lifestyle—the spirits business, and the other things. She kept me away from all that. Taught me to study hard, behave myself."

Mom had never said so much about her family before. Feeling like a *National Geographic* camerawoman approaching a famously jumpy animal, Jess said, "What about Ah Ku, did he stay with Ah Ma?"

Mom nodded. "He's the son mah."

So that was what Dad had been talking about when he'd said Mom needed to forgive Ah Ma. It had to have been hard, being the child who had been given away. "Is that why you weren't close to Ah Ma?"

Mom sighed. "You know, Mom was a good girl. From young also I was scared of all these spirits things. I cannot see and I don't want to see.

"Ah Ma was different. From the beginning she was wild. Ah Chor was so strict, but even she couldn't handle her. If you knew Ah Ma, you'll understand."

Boy, do I, thought Jess.

"You cannot blame her also," said Mom. "For you and me, why should we go and do this kind of thing? We can find a decent job. Don't need to carry heavy things, burn under the sun. Ah Ma was not educated. Eight years old already she had to leave home and work."

Jess blinked. "What, really? What kind of work can an eight-year-old do?"

"A lot. Jaga the stall at the market, clean the house," said Mom.

"You don't know only! Your life is so comfortable, but not everybody is as lucky as you. Ah Ma wanted to change her fate. Of course if she can become a clerk or a teacher, she'll do it. But what can she do? She cannot read or write, how to find an office job? Some more she lived in a small village, didn't have the chance to meet anybody. She only met people like the man who sold scrap rubber.

"When she's young she's very pretty, you know," Mom added. "Dark only, because she had to work outside in the sun. But pretty. All the men liked her. I'm not saying it's right, but she was so young when she got married. Not like she married because she loved the man. The parents chose for her. Last time it was like that, arranged marriage."

This was opaque even to Jess, but after a moment comprehension dawned.

"Wait, wait, wait," Jess said. "You're saying Ah Ma cheated on Ah Kong with the scrap rubber guy?"

"She was only eighteen when she got married," said Mom. "Younger than you. Ah Kong was so much older than her, he was in his thirties already when they met. When they fight he can beat her one, you know! Ah Ma beat him back, but he's stronger than her. Aiyoh, sometimes after they quarrel, her face become like pizza like that."

Jess thought of the dreams Ah Ma had given her—the squalling baby, the smell of rubber trees in the morning, the unending round of tasks to be done. In the dreams she had rushed to prepare dinner once she got home, because something was going to happen at night.

Ah Ma had never shown her what it was that happened at night. It appeared there were some species of suffering she wasn't willing to share.

"But what's the scrap rubber boyfriend got to do with anything?" said Jess.

"He's the one who dragged her into that world," said Mom. "The gang world. This guy, his business made enough money that he had surplus, so he can make loans to people. Charged high interest. If they cannot pay back, his men will chase them. He's a powerful man in their village, even though he's so young. Younger than Ah Ma some more. But she's pretty and her character is something different. Not many people you can meet like her."

"Grandma was a gangster moll," said Jess. "It sounds like the title of a movie."

"What? What is 'moll'?"

"So did Ah Ma divorce Ah Kong?"

"Back then there's no such thing as divorce," said Mom. "But after Ah Kong passed on, Ah Ma went to live with the man. That's when she sent me to Ah Chor. Ah Chor was so angry. I remember when Ah Ma took me to her house, she won't even speak to Ah Ma." She shook her head.

"What, because Ah Ma left Ah Kong?" said Jess. "Even though he was abusive?"

"That one not so much," said Mom. "If Ah Ma went back to Ah Chor's house, it won't be so bad. But to go and stay with the boyfriend . . ." Her voice dropped. "Ah Kong died when Ah Ma was pregnant with Ah Ku. She didn't even wait to give birth first. Pregnant and she went to the other man's house!

"Ah Chor was right," she added. "This kind of relationship cannot last one. Short time only she stayed with the boyfriend, then he kicked Ah Ma out. After that she lived by herself with Ah Ku."

"She didn't take you back then?"

"No," said Mom. "She didn't take me back."

Maybe it was the effect of the dreams Ah Ma had given Jess. Somehow it was easy to imagine the little girl Mom had been—straight black hair, skinny legs and wary eyes.

Jess touched her arm. "Did it bother you, being sent to live with Ah Chor?"

"Yes." Mom rubbed her eyes. "But it's OK. I have you and Dad now. I don't need any other family."

This was touching, but also like having an executioner tighten a noose around Jess's neck. She looked down to avoid betraying her reaction.

"Min?" Mom's voice changed, no longer wobbly.

She looked ghastly, the bones standing out on her face. It was as though Jess had been vouchsafed a glimpse into the future. This was how Mom might look on her deathbed.

It was a horrific thought, unthinkable. Jess pushed it away, burying it beneath all the other things she wasn't allowed to think or feel.

"Mom, are you OK?" she said.

But Mom was reaching out, touching the back of Jess's neck, pushing the hair out of the way. Her fingers were trembling.

"What's this?" she said. Her voice was resonant with dread.

"What?" said Jess, but some part of her already knew. When Mom brought a mirror and showed her what was on her neck, she felt no surprise.

There were five welts in a semicircle, the skin red and raised. They looked like fingerprints, marks someone might leave if they had been holding Jess by the neck.

Bile rose in Jess's throat.

"What did Ah Ku make you do?" said Mom.

FOR A SHORT time Jess had been freed from the horror of the night before, distracted by her conversation with Mom. But now the dream rushed in on her again—the hunt through the forest, the knife opening her flesh. She put a hand to her throat.

"Min?" said Mom. Her voice sounded like it was coming from a great distance away. "You OK?"

"I'm fine," Jess heard herself saying. She wanted to crawl away and hide herself, like an injured animal.

"What did Ah Ku do?" said Mom. "See lah, you keep secrets from Mom. If you told me, I would have warned you. I should have told you, stay away from Ah Ku. But how I know he'll contact you without asking me? I've been patient, you know. Not like he does so much for me. When Dad was sick also he didn't call me. Didn't offer to help out, even though I gave him so much money over the years. I don't mind. I don't expect him to give me money. But he cannot even leave my daughter alone! My poor girl! What did he do?"

"It's not him," said Jess. She was getting a grip on herself. Mom's ready flow of words was helping. Irritation cut through the haze of terror, bringing Jess back to the mundane world. "It's not Ah Ku. I saw him at the garden temple, but—"

"He took you to *that* temple?" said Mom, her voice rising.

Jess looked up. "He didn't take me there. I—"

It might all have come out then, Ah Ma and the whole improbable nightmare. But that was when Jess saw the god.

The Black Water Sister stood outside the glass sliding doors, framed by Kor Kor's bougainvilleas, sickeningly real against the vivid-hued blooms.

Jess froze, her voice drying up in her throat. She tore her gaze away, but she had looked now. There was no taking that back.

"You what?" said Mom.

"I, uh—" The instinct to hide descended on Jess. She needed to keep talking or Mom would realize something was wrong. "I went to the temple myself. I saw an article about it online."

She barely knew what she was saying. Her thoughts were scurrying around in her head, frantic. What should she do? She needed to get Mom out of this room, away from the god. But would the god follow them?

"You shouldn't have gone there!" said Mom. "Why you didn't tell me? I would have warned you . . . Let me see your neck. Don't know why Kor Kor likes this old light, even when it's on, you cannot see anything. Come, come to the window."

Mom tugged her toward the glass sliding doors where the god stood. Jess resisted.

"I don't—Mom, no!"

Mom reached out to the curtains, apparently intending to let the early-morning sunlight in.

For the first time, the god took her eyes off Jess. She looked at Mom.

Jess's body moved without the intervention of thought. She threw herself at Mom, dragging her away from the sliding doors.

"What are you doing?" said Mom. "What's wrong?"

"Don't freak out, OK?" said Jess, giving up on discretion. She could keep lying or she could cope with the fact that the god was standing *outside their house* staring at them, but she couldn't do both at the same time.

She moved to put herself between Mom and the god so she could form a barrier, however inadequate, and lowered her voice. "The god is over there."

Mom's forehead wrinkled. "What?"

"Ah Ma's god is at the window," said Jess.

She watched the emotions chase themselves across Mom's face: bewilderment, followed by understanding—and horror.

"You can see?" whispered Mom.

You think you can run from me? the god had said.

"She's following me," said Jess, heartsick.

"Following you? Why?"

Jess remembered the dark night of her dream and how it had ended, with her blood soaking the forest floor.

The dream had been a lesson. The dangers of this shadow-world of spirits Ah Ma had drawn her into were not merely spiritual, but horribly tangible. If you offended a god, they wouldn't stop at cursing you with some vague form of bad luck. They would fuck you up.

And Jess had offended a god.

"I destroyed her shrine," she said.

"*What?*"

"I had to," said Jess defensively. "She was . . ." But a lifetime's habit of caution clamped down on her, pushing the words back down her throat. Did she really want Mom to know the full extent of what had been going on? Best to portion it out. Jess needed time to think, and they had better things to worry about just then anyway. "I'll tell you later. What do I do, Mom? She's still there."

"She's doing what?"

Jess wasn't going to attempt a second inspection, but she didn't need to look at the god to know the answer. "Waiting for me."

Mom stood looking at her for a moment. Jess braced herself for a meltdown, or a reaming out, or a combination of the two.

Instead Mom turned and shouted, like a waiter in a kopitiam yelling out orders to the kitchen, "Ah Yit ah Ah Yit!"

She had to shout again before Kor Kor came bustling down the stairs. She was wearing black leggings and a baggy pink T-shirt with the words *California Dreamin'* on the front. "What's the matter? I was Skyping Ching Yee, didn't hear you."

"Min collided with a spirit," said Mom.

Kor Kor's eyes widened. "When?"

"My brother took her to his temple the other day."

Mom and Kor Kor exchanged a look that was the equivalent of several involved conversations.

"Kor Kor *knows* about Ah Ku and Ah Ma and everything?" said Jess, with dawning indignation. "And you didn't tell me?"

Mom ignored this. "Is the god still at the window there?"

"The spirit is here?" said Kor Kor. "In my house?" They were both speaking in whispers.

They needn't have worried about attracting the god's attention. As far as Jess could tell without looking directly at her, the god had gone back to gazing fixedly at Jess.

"She's outside, by the sliding doors," said Jess, but Kor Kor was already striding to the dresser in the hallway, her face set with determination. She snatched up an olive wood cross, a souvenir from a Holy Land tour she and Kor Tiao had gone on a couple of years ago.

"Which window?" she said. She was pale.

Mom pointed.

Jess said, "Kor Kor, I don't think you should . . ."

But Kor Kor went over to the sliding doors, holding the wooden cross aloft in one hand. The other hand was pressed against her chest, clasping the silver crucifix she always wore around her neck.

"Kor Kor, come back!"

Jess might as well have kept her mouth shut for all the effect this had. Kor Kor went right up to the glass.

"In Jesus's name, I command you to leave this place!" she proclaimed, waving her cross.

Jess hung back at first, uncertain. But then she saw the god's head turn, her eyes falling on Kor Kor and her little cross.

Jess darted after her aunt. "Kor Kor, let's not . . . let's go back there, OK? We can talk about what to do."

"Our Father in heaven, hallowed be your name," chanted Kor Kor. She slid open the glass, sticking the cross out through the grille. "Your kingdom come, your will be done, on earth as it is in heaven."

The god raised her hand.

It came to Jess that she could not bear for the god to touch Kor Kor, or Mom, or anything Jess loved. She wouldn't let the god have a single petal off a single blossom on the bougainvilleas. Jess might have betrayed herself into the Black Water Sister's keeping, like Persephone recklessly swallowing pomegranate seeds, but her family hadn't done anything to deserve the god's vengeance. None of them belonged to the god. They belonged to Jess, and the god had *no right*.

The god was reaching out to Kor Kor when Jess pushed her aunt back, making her stumble. Jess put herself between Kor Kor and the window, shoving her face up against the grille.

"Fuck off!" Jess shouted. "Don't you know when you're not fucking welcome?"

The god turned her chill gaze on Jess. Jess felt the phantom bite of the knife at her throat. She swallowed.

"You owe me," said the god, in that dialect Jess shouldn't understand.

"You started it," said Jess absurdly, saturated with terror. It didn't matter what she said so long as she kept talking, kept the god's attention on her. Mom was holding Kor Kor back, thank God, though she was also yelling something irrelevant at Jess about coming away from the window. "You're the one who took over my body. I didn't do anything to you."

"You came to my temple," said the god. "You spoiled my shrine. How are you going to pay me back?"

"What if I don't?"

The god didn't answer. She only reached through the grille and laid her fingers on Jess's forehead, as she had done in the dream. The touch was as tender as a lover's.

Agony flared across the back of Jess's neck. It hurt so much she only had the breath to gasp, which was lucky because it meant she didn't alarm the women behind her. They were freaking out enough as it was. Kor Kor was praying loudly, and Mom was saying, "Min, you come here right now!"

"How are you going to pay me back?" said the god again.

Jess could hear Mom and Kor Kor approaching. She had to get rid of the god.

"I'll find a way," she said, breathless. The pain was subsiding, which made it easier to think. "Leave my family alone. It's nothing to do with them. I'll handle everything. I'll go to the temple. I'll pray to you—"

"You must bring me a sacrifice."

"I'll bring it to the temple," said Jess. "But you have to go away. This is my aunt's house, a Christian house. You don't have a right to anything here."

The god looked at her.

"OK, fine. You get me," said Jess. "Just me. Nobody else."

The god turned her eyes toward Mom and Kor Kor before looking back at Jess.

"Bring me the sacrifice," she said.

Her message couldn't have been clearer. *This is the price of your loved ones' safety.*

And then she was gone. The bougainvillea blossoms shook, stirred by a passing breeze.

Kor Kor tugged at Jess, drawing her away from the grille.

"You don't interfere," she was saying to Mom in Hokkien. "You all are not Christian. I am! These spirits cannot hurt me." Switching to English, she said loudly, all in one breath, "But deliver us from evil, for yours is the kingdom and the power and the glory forever! Amen."

"She's gone," said Jess.

"The god's not there anymore?" said Mom.

Kor Kor was flushed and exultant. "Thanks be to God! See, Poey Hoon Chee, this is the power of Jesus!"

Mom ignored her. "You said you'll pray to her? That's all? She's happy already?"

She had the same look in her eyes as when Dad had been sick, as though she had lost something precious and couldn't find it.

Jess reached for the comforting lie. "Yeah, it's fine. I'll go burn some joss sticks for her at the temple tomorrow."

"That same temple you want to go back?" said Mom, her voice rising. "Cannot! If I knew Ah Ku was taking you there, I wouldn't have let you go."

"You want to pray to the spirit?" said Kor Kor, talking over her. "That's all wrong already!"

Mom turned on her, glad of a target, even though Kor Kor was agreeing with her. "If Min has to pray to be left alone by the spirit, better she pray. Nobody asked you to comment also!"

Kor Kor took a deep breath.

Jess said hastily, "You asked her, Mom. You're the one who called Kor Kor in."

But it was too late. Mom had finally exhausted Kor Kor's capacious reserves of patience. Kor Kor let out her breath in one big rush.

"Poey Hoon Chee," she said, "you are *too much*!"

FIFTEEN

T au and its soy-based delights would have to wait for another day. Jess messaged Sherng to postpone their meetup from the back of Kor Kor's car, feeling like a teenager in disgrace.

Mom and Kor Kor were being scrupulously polite to each other in the front, saying nothing that was not strictly necessary. The temperature was arctic.

Jess had never seen them really fight before. The quarrel had rapidly taken on a life of its own. Kor Kor and Mom had started hashing out all the bad life decisions Mom had ever made, starting with emigrating to America and ending with returning to Malaysia, as well as the reasons none of Kor Kor's kids were living near her as adults.

Jess had had to intervene to drag the focus back to her spiritual difficulties. She didn't *actually* want Mom and Kor Kor involved in the dumpster fire that was her life, but it was that or let Mom fatally offend Kor Kor and get them all kicked out.

At first Jess's strategy had seemed to work.

"We must pray," said Kor Kor.

"Correct," Mom agreed. "This issue man cannot solve."

"Jesus will protect you," Kor Kor continued. "You just have to ask him for help only. Put your hands together and say, 'Jesus, I accept you into my heart.'"

"I'll take you to Master Yap's temple," said Mom. "They pray to Tai Seng Ia, the Monkey God. You know the Monkey God? He was born from the rock, that one."

"You mean the Monkey King?" said Jess, bemused. "From *Journey to the West*?"

Mom nodded, as though it was totally normal to have a temple dedicated to a fictional character. "We call him the Great Sage. More respectful. When it comes to this kind of issue, he's very good, very powerful."

"You want to go to Chinese temple some more ah?" said Ah Kor. "They're the ones who caused the problem in the first place." She turned to Jess. "Why don't you come to church with me? My pastor has experience with exorcisms. She's a lady-pastor, but very tough. Indian lady, so she's not scared of all these Chinese gods."

Jess could tell Mom was starting to fume. She said quickly, "Aren't Christians not supposed to believe in other gods? I thought there's only meant to be one God."

"Only one with capital *G*," agreed Kor Kor. "These other gods, the small *g* one, are spirits only. Spirits, the Bible also got. Jesus cast out a lot.

"Our congregation has such cases, you know," she added. "Some people, they want to convert, but they're scared the spirits will keep disturbing them. My pastor helps them. Their altars, the idols all that, she's willing to pick up from people's homes to dispose of them. People don't dare throw away themselves. You have to be very strong in faith to do this kind of work."

"This spirit is Chinese what," said Mom. "Who is your pastor to her? Jesus also she hasn't heard of. That's why when you prayed earlier it didn't work, Ah Yit. This spirit only respects the Chinese gods."

Kor Kor bristled. "Where got it didn't work? Jesus sent the spirit away. The spirits are scared of his name. They don't dare come near to the cross. True or not, Min?"

"The god went off because you promised you'll go back to the temple in Air Itam and pray to her, right?" said Mom. "I heard you say."

Jess found two pairs of eyes fixed on her, demanding validation. She cleared her throat. "Well . . ."

The god hadn't seemed to notice Kor Kor's cross, but who was Jess to say that it wouldn't have worked if she hadn't stepped in?

In her mind's eye she saw the god's face again—the dark hair in which the sunlight was swallowed up, the inhuman blankness of her expression. Jess couldn't find it in herself to regret pushing Kor Kor away from the grille.

"I don't know," she said truthfully. "The important thing is, she went away. But she'll be back. Unless I offer her a sacrifice."

"What sacrifice?" said Mom.

"I don't know for sure," said Jess.

But she had a suspicion. The back of her neck twinged, the marks the god had left on her skin reminding her of their presence. The god had shown what she considered a meet tribute the day before, when she had held Jess still so death could be dealt through her.

"I'd prefer not to find out," said Jess. "But if I don't go back to the temple . . ."

"Cannot go back," said Mom at once.

"Yes, better not go," said Ah Kor.

"We'll ask Tai Seng Ia what should we do," said Mom. "I know the medium at the temple. He'll help us."

"No use you talk to all these mediums," said Kor Kor. "Let me call my pastor, see if she's free."

They glared at each other. Jess could see storm clouds amassing.

"Why don't we do both?" she said.

"Good idea," said Mom instantly. "Come, we go to the temple now."

"Now?" Jess glanced at the clock. She was supposed to be meeting Sherng in an hour's time. "Can't we go tomorrow?"

"Better go now, before Dad wakes up," said Mom. "Cannot tell Dad about this. He's so stressed already, working so hard."

Jess glanced at Kor Kor, worried this would spark another argument, but Kor Kor nodded. Apparently she and Mom had found the one thing they could agree on in this situation.

"I told your father, he must rest more," said Kor Kor. "But he don't want to listen. Keeps pushing himself. Men are like that, they have their pride. If he hears about this some more, scared he cannot handle it."

"He might have a breakdown," said Mom darkly.

"Mustn't disturb your father," said Kor Kor. "You know how to drive to this temple, Hoon Chee?"

Despite this rapprochement, neither she nor Mom relaxed for the duration of the drive. The journey was weirdly long, even allowing for the Friday jam as people left work for prayers. Jess peered out of the window and found she didn't recognize anything.

"Where are we even going?" she said.

"The temple is in Balik Pulau," said Mom. "Very far."

They passed dinky villages and durian farms and paddy fields, green and gold in the sun. Jess dozed off.

She only woke up when the car came to a stop. Mom was getting out.

"Awake already?" said Kor Kor. "Your mom was going to go find the medium first. Wanted to let you nap some more. If you're getting out now, I'll come also."

Jess yawned. "You don't have to come in, Kor Kor. You could wait in the car."

"No," said Kor Kor. "Better I come in case something happens. I brought my Bible." She held up a small thick volume covered in blue leather. She'd brought the olive wood cross as well.

"Oh," said Jess. "Good."

It wasn't like she shared Kor Kor's faith, or believed in the efficacy of these artifacts against the god's implacable persistence. Yet she felt obscurely comforted. It was something not to be dealing with this alone.

The temple was a modest structure with a corrugated zinc roof, nothing like the elaborate clan houses in George Town to which tourists flocked. But behind it was a dramatic blue-green hill, its peak rising to a dazzling blue sky.

It was only once they got closer to the temple that the mundane intruded. There was a brave attempt at landscaping out front, featuring a human-sized statue of the Monkey King, looking like he'd leaped out of a nineties Hong Kong TV series. He could have done with a paint job.

The red paint was peeling on the grille doors of the temple too. There was a design of a tree on each grille door, with twining green leaves, but the patches of rust somewhat detracted from the effect. Beyond the doors was an altar with a much smaller statue of the Monkey King, draped in an embroidered satin robe.

The only person there was a bored teenage boy. When Mom asked if Donald Sim was around, he nodded and ambled off, leaving them to wait.

Mom and Kor Kor were still enclosed in a bubble of tension. Jess looked around, trying to ignore it.

The Monkey King wasn't the only god worshipped at the temple. There were other idols on either side of him. Jess didn't study them too closely. It felt somehow impolite—and the last thing she wanted was to draw more divine attention to herself.

Averting her eyes, she noticed a framed painting on the wall. It was a portrait of a bald Chinese man with a kindly wrinkled face. He looked like a nice grandpa.

A caption in Chinese and dodgy English explained that Master Yap had been born in Canton and had come to Malaya in the 1900s. Desiring solitude so that he could devote himself to meditation, he had retreated to a remote part of the island. He was a virtuous man who did many good deeds. As his reputation grew, people came from far and wide to seek his wisdom. After his death, he had come to a follower in a dream and told him to build a temple by the hill where he had resided.

Jess wondered if the dream had been a one-off appearance, or if Master Yap had pestered his follower until his wishes had been fulfilled. If Master Yap was like his picture, Jess thought she wouldn't mind so much being haunted by him. At least he was virtuous and had done good deeds. You wouldn't see anyone putting up that epitaph for Ah Ma.

Donald Sim turned out to be a stout man around Mom's age, wearing—of course—a polo shirt.

He seemed pleased to see Mom. It turned out they had known each other at school; Mom addressed him by a nickname that had no apparent connection to "Donald" or "Sim."

While they chatted, Kor Kor waited with her arms crossed. Her hands were tucked into her elbows, as though to avoid the risk of touching anything and catching a spiritual infection.

But it was not in Kor Kor's nature to stay frosty when met with warmth. All Mr. Sim had to say was, "Your sister-in-law? Very good. Welcome!" for the arms to uncross.

"So pretty here, with the mountain behind there," said Kor

Kor. "You must get a lot of tourists. All the Singaporeans, KL people like this kind of thing."

Mr. Sim laughed, but in a nice way. "No lah. We have hardly any visitors. It's so far. Some more we don't give 4D numbers all that." He spoke surprisingly good English. Jess would have pegged him as a retired civil servant or something, not a spirit medium. "Hard to survive. The statue outside we only got because a devotee donated money after Tai Seng Ia helped him."

"We also need help, Ah Paut," said Mom. She put her hand on Jess's shoulder. "My daughter is in trouble."

Mr. Sim composed his face into somberness. "What happened?"

"You don't mind I show him?" said Mom. Her hand was hovering over the back of Jess's neck.

Jess kind of minded. But if there was a chance Mr. Sim and his god could fix this, make the Black Water Sister leave her alone . . .

She nodded. Mom pushed the collar of her T-shirt down, holding her hair up so Mr. Sim could see the god's marks on her skin.

Mr. Sim's polite expression slipped, revealing real emotion. Shock, followed by a spark of professional interest.

"I see," he said. "Come with me."

"TAI SENG IA is a big god, you know," said Mr. Sim. "Just because you call, doesn't mean he'll come."

They were in a back room of the temple. Mr. Sim had called in an assistant, a young man maybe a few years older than Jess. He wasn't wearing a polo shirt, but Jess presumed he hadn't expected to be on duty that day. He looked grave and a little bored as he lit joss sticks and dressed Mr. Sim in black satin.

Jess was jittery, and Mom and Kor Kor weren't helping. Kor Kor was clutching at her Bible and her olive wood cross as though she was scared they would fly out of her hands. Mom looked like she was in a hospital waiting room.

It would be fine, Jess told herself. The Monkey King was a fun god. Dad used to bring back DVDs of Hong Kong TV series from their trips to Malaysia. She'd enjoyed the adaptation of *Journey to the West*, with its ebullient Monkey, unafraid of gods and demons alike.

Sure, Monkey got into fights. Sometimes Tripitaka or the Goddess of Mercy had had to remind him to behave. But he had a good heart. He had ascended to become a Buddha at the end, hadn't he?

Jess didn't know what had happened after that. She hadn't watched the second series.

"Because he's an animal, he can be fierce," Mr. Sim continued. "He tends to express himself through action, using the physical. But you don't need to worry. Ah Huat will help to restrain him."

The idea that the god might require restraint by Mr. Sim's assistant wasn't especially reassuring. Mr. Sim seemed to realize this, because he added:

"In the end, he is a god. When he comes, it's to do good to humans. Because he's strong, he's not scared of demons."

"This is not a demon," said Mom. "I told you, this god, my mother used to pray to last time."

"Well," said Mr. Sim, "these smaller gods, there's not so much difference with the lower kinds of spirits. They can be very troublesome. But Tai Seng Ia can settle it—if he comes. I will try for you."

His quiet civil servant's voice sat strangely with his outfit. He'd swapped the polo shirt for a heavily embroidered black satin suit, with a collar of the same material around his neck. It looked like armor, or what the costume designer for a budget-strapped Chinese opera troupe might imagine armor to look like.

Mr. Sim got up and prayed to the Monkey King, a bundle of joss sticks in his hands.

Kor Kor prayed along, her eyes shut and her hand pressing her Bible open. "Even though I walk through the darkest valley, I will fear no evil, for you are with me."

For you are with me. The image of the Black Water Sister's face rose before Jess, the sweat gleaming on her upper lip. She shuddered.

Mr. Sim's assistant brought him a thronelike red chair, highly decorated with gilt. He placed squares of paper beneath Mr. Sim's feet. They looked like the yellow paper people folded into ingots to burn when praying to Ti Kong on the ninth day of Chinese New Year. But when Jess whispered, "What are they doing? What are those?" Mom shook her head.

"Better not ask so much," she said.

Mr. Sim sat with his eyes shut for what felt like a long time. He looked like he was meditating. Jess was wondering if it would be rude to take out her phone when he started convulsing.

Mom clutched Jess's hand. Kor Kor chanted louder, her voice high and frightened.

The medium slumped over, eyes closed, and retched. A thin white liquid dripped onto the concrete floor. His head started turning round and round, his arms swinging. His body was vibrating as though shaken by some overpowering force.

The contrast between the gentle, serious Mr. Sim and the shuddering, senseless creature he had transformed into was profoundly unsettling. It was like something out of *The Exorcist*. Only here Mr. Sim was both exorcist and possessed, victim and avenger.

Mr. Sim's body seized. He sprang to his feet, standing on the chair with one leg uplifted and crossed over the other, his arms curved as though he was preparing to attack. It looked like a kung fu stance, something you might find Bruce Lee doing in a movie still. Leashed power thrummed in his limbs.

Then he scratched himself.

Jess grinned involuntarily. The Monkey God turned and looked right at her. Out of Mr. Sim's narrow sunflower-seed eyes shone an inhuman consciousness.

The grin dropped off Jess's face.

The Monkey God bounded over to her, Mr. Sim's middle-aged body moving with an implausible fluidity. The assistant cried out, running after him.

But the god in the medium was already bending over Jess, inspecting her, hot breath gusting on her skin. He picked up a lock of Jess's hair, sniffing it.

There was no ill will in the Monkey God's bright animal gaze, but there was no mercy either. If Jess made the wrong move—startled or annoyed him—it would not be much to the god to break her neck. She almost wouldn't blame him. You might put down a grizzly bear that had killed a hiker, but you wouldn't fault it.

She stayed very still, barely breathing, tense with dread.

Ah Huat spoke to the Monkey God, drawing him away. Jess's hair slipped through his fingers. She sat shivering, feeling like a prison escapee over whom the searchlight had passed.

Ah Huat tied a headdress to the Monkey God's head and bound his waist with a belt. He pried open the god's mouth and put a piece of yellow paper on his tongue. It looked a lot like the charms Mom had used to burn and make Jess drink.

The Monkey God said something to Ah Huat. His voice was deep and rusty, as though it didn't get used often. He sounded nothing like Mr. Sim.

Kor Kor was holding her Bible before her like a shield, but she looked interested despite herself.

"What's he saying?" she said to Ah Huat. "What language is that? Never heard before one."

"Tai Seng Ia speaks deep Mandarin," said Ah Huat. "They spoke in China back then. Not like today's version."

Kor Kor looked skeptical. "If it's so deep, you can understand meh?"

"It's part of our training," said Ah Huat with dignity. "So we can translate for the devotees."

"He's saying what?"

Ah Huat didn't go quite so far as to say, *If you must know*, but the sentiment infused his voice as he said, "Tai Seng Ia asked why does your niece smell like that."

"Like what?" Kor Kor sniffed Jess. "She smells OK what. You showered this morning, right, Min?"

"It's fine, Kor Kor," Jess muttered, but she should have kept her mouth shut. The searchlight of the Monkey God's attention veered back to her. He said something to Ah Huat, sounding agitated. Ah Huat answered, his voice placating, holding up his hands.

Primed by fear, Jess's body knew that the Monkey God was coming toward her before her mind caught on. She bolted out of her chair, but she only made it halfway across the room before the Monkey God caught her.

The room went sideways.

I'm going to die, thought Jess. The hand that had grasped her was Mr. Sim's hand, wide and calloused, but the power in it was beyond nature, more than muscle and sinew and bone alone could muster.

Jess struggled, resisting the god, making herself as heavy as possible. She was distantly conscious that Mom and Kor Kor were screaming bloody murder.

The Monkey God swung her around like she was a rag doll. His strength was unbelievable. Mr. Sim was Mom's age, there was no way this was all coming from him—

Out of the corner of Jess's eye, she saw that Mom and Kor Kor had rushed Ah Huat. Kor Kor seemed to be bashing at Ah Huat with her cross. Jess opened her mouth, about to do something reckless, like swear at the Monkey God or bite him or—

"Ah Ma!" she gasped. "*Help!*"

No one answered. The Monkey God dropped her on the floor. She hit the concrete, rolled over and sat up, her head ringing like a bell. She was in front of the altar. A blow on her back forced her down again.

She heard Ah Huat shouting unintelligibly. His feet in flip-flops appeared beside her. He knelt, helping Jess up and pressing something into her hand.

It was a bundle of joss sticks.

"You light," he said, gesturing at the incense urn.

The Monkey God grabbed her arm, growling, but Ah Huat made him release Jess. The assistant turned back to Jess.

"Don't worry. You light and pray to Tai Seng Ia. If you show him respect, he'll see you are OK one."

"Where got my daughter disrespect him?" said Mom. Her voice was quivering, but she looked more angry than scared. "We came to ask for help and my daughter is being treated like this. What kind of temple is this?"

"It's a misunderstanding, auntie," said Ah Huat. "Tai Seng Ia is confused. He thought your daughter was a spirit, a bad spirit."

Kor Kor was equally outraged. "Let's go," she said to Mom. "I told you we should see my pastor. When you are a Christian, you don't have to be bullied."

Ah Huat said to Jess, "I told Tai Seng Ia you are human. The bad spirit is bothering you only. But you must pray. Then he'll believe."

The Monkey God glared at her, twitching and scratching, looking like he was half a second away from pouncing on her again. He didn't look like he'd be propitiated by prayer, but Jess wasn't in the mood to argue.

She edged toward the incense urn and touched the ends of her joss sticks to the burning joss sticks in the urn till they blackened and started to smoke. She turned back, ready to wave the joss sticks at the statue of the Monkey God on the altar, when the Monkey God–in–Mr. Sim snarled and broke past Ah Huat.

Kor Kor darted before him, waving her cross, but the god knocked her over. Mom was next, armed with her handbag—but Jess had had enough.

"What the fuck is your problem?" she roared. The sound of her own voice broke through her terror. Beyond it, she found rage— and in its blazing heart, power.

The power coursed through her veins, making her feel reckless, invulnerable. The back of her neck throbbed with a dull ache, but she barely noticed it. She pushed between her mom and the Monkey God. "Leave her alone!"

The Monkey God grabbed Jess's hair, pulling it so hard it felt like he might peel her scalp off her skull. Jess jabbed her fistful of joss sticks up at him and felt the tips smash against his face before she remembered that face belonged to Mr. Sim.

The Monkey God let her go, eyelids fluttering, but he didn't seem to feel any pain. He knocked the joss sticks from Jess's hand, scattering them. Jess ducked before he could hit her, landing on the floor.

The scent of incense was joined by the smell of something burning. Her clothes were getting singed where they caught on the red-hot ends of the joss sticks on the floor. As she pushed herself off the ground, her palm came down on a burning joss stick. She felt the sensation of heat against her skin and knew it should hurt, but it didn't. It was like the power surging inside her had thickened her skin, numbing her to sensation.

The Monkey God loomed over her. His face was distorted with berserker fury, no longer recognizable as Mr. Sim's.

Jess's fear was like a physical reflex, a leg bouncing at the tap of a kneecap. The power drowned it out, spilling out of her like a white light shining out of a lamp. It rushed out in the unfamiliar accents of a language she didn't speak:

"Don't fucking touch me!"

She smashed her head against the Monkey God's chest. He staggered back, letting out a winded breath.

But in a moment he had recovered. He raised his hand, snarling. She could hear Ah Huat expostulating with the Monkey God from a safe distance.

Jess thought, *If I die, you die first.* The thought wasn't in English or Hokkien; the language was one she had never learned. She seized the Monkey God's arm, twisting—

But then the Monkey God froze. His arm went limp in Jess's grasp. His mouth fell open.

The animal intelligence animating Mr. Sim's face fell away, leaving his eyes vacant, his body a shell. The medium's eyes rolled back in his head, showing the whites. His body trembled all over.

Mom came up behind him and thumped him on the back of the head with her handbag.

"Stop, stop!" cried Ah Huat.

Jess released Mr. Sim's arm. It took her a moment to find the words in English.

"Don't, Mom," she said. "Something's happening."

"What's that? What's happening?" said Kor Kor. Her hair was disheveled, but otherwise she didn't look any the worse for having been bowled over by the Monkey God. She turned to Ah Huat. "He's having a fit or what?"

But it was evident from Ah Huat's expression that he didn't have any answers. He looked like he was having the worst day at work ever.

"Better you all stay back," he said. He beckoned to Jess. "Miss, come here!"

The medium's eyes snapped open. He looked around.

"Master?" said Ah Huat.

"Ah Paut?" said Mom.

"No," said Jess. She hadn't taken her eyes off the medium. "It's someone else."

"Sorry, Big Sister," said the god in the medium. He spoke in a light baritone with a creak in it, an old man's voice. His gaze as he squinted at Jess was an old man's, too, shortsighted and mild. "I came as fast as I could. What brings you here?"

THE MEDIUM SPOKE the tongue of the Black Water Sister—the same language in which Jess had sworn at the Monkey God.

"He's speaking what? Hakka?" said Kor Kor, agog. "Tai Seng Ia got speak Hakka meh?"

"It's not Tai Seng Ia," said Jess. "It's a different spirit."

"What do you mean, it's a different spirit?" said Mom. "How do you know?"

Jess couldn't believe she couldn't see the difference. The medium even looked shorter than he had been a few moments ago.

"You can't tell?" she said. "For one thing, he's not trying to murder me!"

Ah Huat said tentatively, "Master Yap?"

"Why you didn't call me in the first place?" said the new god. "I am the one who knows Big Sister. This is not Tai Seng Ia's business. He knows how to fight and chase demons only. He doesn't know how to layan people."

"What's happening? What spirit is this?" said Kor Kor to Ah Huat. "What did you call him, 'Master Yap'?"

"He's the founder of the temple," said Jess.

"How do you know that?" said Mom, wide-eyed.

She was clearly in a mood to read signs and portents in everything. Jess could hardly blame her.

"I mean, it's called Master Yap's temple. Plus I read the sign out front," said Jess. "But I thought he was—" *just some guy*, she was going to say, before it struck her that this might come off as disrespectful.

"A human being," she said instead. "Why is he possessing Mr. Sim?"

"Ti Kong, the Jade Emperor, promoted Master Yap to become a god after he died," explained Ah Huat. "Master Sim is the medium for Master Yap also. A lot of people come to ask him for advice."

Master Yap was staring intently at Jess.

"Eh? But she's just a girl," he said to Ah Huat. "I'm wrong already. I thought she was someone else." He squinted at Jess, as though trying to make out her features. "She has the same aura as Big Sister, that's why. She is the medium?"

"No, no," said Ah Huat. "She collided with a spirit, a god. That's why Master Sim invoked Tai Seng Ia. But something went wrong. Tai Seng Ia thought she was a demon. He got very angry, until he wanted to attack her."

Master Yap nodded. "A big god like him, whether it's a small god or a demon, it's hard for him to distinguish. The medium should have prayed when she entered the temple. If she greeted Tai Seng Ia properly, he won't be angry. You should know what, when different gods meet each other, they can end up fighting."

"But the girl is not a medium," said Ah Huat patiently.

"At least this god is not violent," said Mom to Kor Kor. "Maybe should have asked to see him in the first place. The other one"— she meant the Monkey God, but she didn't want to say the name—"is too unpredictable." She turned to the assistant. "Can Master Yap help my daughter?"

Ah Huat translated the question for the god's benefit.

"What is the trouble?" said Master Yap, Ah Huat interpreting.

Jess told the story she had workshopped with Mom and Kor Kor before they'd left the house. "My uncle brought me to a temple to pray, but there was an accident and I damaged a shrine."

"She tripped," said Kor Kor. "The path wasn't even. Dangerous, you know! They should maintain the place properly."

"The altar was very old already," said Mom. "My daughter fell and it went just like that. Maybe got termites in the wood?"

Jess intervened before her relatives could make Master Yap suspicious with all this helpful over-elaboration of detail.

"I offended the god," she said, "so now she's stalking me. She appeared in my dream and threatened me, but now she's showing up even in the day. Is there a way to make her stop?"

Master Yap looked thoughtful.

"Usually if this kind of thing happen, you must propitiate the god," he said. "Pray to them. But in this case, I'm not sure . . . You said the god came to you in a dream. What happened in the dream?"

Jess hesitated, but Ah Huat nodded at her encouragingly, and Mom said, "Tell him, Min. If you don't tell, how can Master Yap help?"

It was like being a kid at the doctor's. Reluctantly, Jess said, "I was in a wild place. A jungle."

It was hard to talk about it. The words fell lifeless from her mouth, stripped of the dark mystery of the dream.

"It was nighttime and I was running. A man was chasing me. He caught me and he—" Embarrassingly, Jess's voice broke. She cleared her throat. "He killed me."

Master Yap's gaze was intent, judgment suspended behind it. "How did he kill you?"

Mom made a movement as though she wanted to stuff the question back in his mouth. Jess twined her hand around Mom's.

The way Master Yap was listening steadied her. He seemed to have no doubt of the dream's significance.

"He cut my throat," said Jess.

Master Yap let out a triumphant exhalation. "And then?"

"I saw the god and she spoke to me." Jess swallowed. "She said, 'Now you know. You think you can run from me?'"

"You didn't tell me that!" said Mom reproachfully.

Jess bit back the honest response that she never told Mom anything worrying if she could help it. "Uh, yeah. I guess I forgot to mention it."

"I thought so," said Master Yap, before Mom could start haranguing her. "I will tell you the meaning of your dream. The god didn't threaten you. She was blessing you."

"What?" said Jess.

"This god, her temple is at Air Itam there, right?" said Master Yap. "The temple in the garden."

Kor Kor murmured, "How did he know that? We didn't tell him also."

Mom shushed her. "Isn't he a god? Of course he knows. Don't talk so much, I want to hear."

"This deity, you know who is she?" said Master Yap.

Jess's throat was dry. It was hard to get the words out.

"Black Water Sister," she said.

Mom flinched.

"That's what people call her, because they don't know her name," said Master Yap. "When she was alive, she had a name. But by the time I came to Penang, nobody remembered already, even though she died not many years ago.

"She used to be a woman who lived in that area. Her husband chased her into the jungle and killed her. She was young—twenty, twenty-one years old only."

The man standing over her, murder in his face. Jess made a faint affirmative noise, conscious of Mom and Kor Kor's eyes on her. She wasn't going to throw up. All she had to do was keep her mouth shut, her teeth together.

"Where she died, where her blood spilled, a tree grew," said Master Yap. "Her ghost haunted the tree. The ghost was fierce, but if you gave her face, she would help you. People prayed to her, left offerings at the tree. She helped a poor man become rich and he built a temple for her there, cleared the jungle and planted a garden. The tree is still there. A big tree, very old. True or not?"

"That's true," murmured Mom to Kor Kor.

"This story everybody knows," said Kor Kor skeptically.

"*I* didn't know it," said Jess. It was a different story from the one Ah Ma had told her about the origins of the temple—wasn't it? Maybe the rich man who had turned the temple into a garden had worked on the plantation there before he had gained his wealth.

"Of course this kind of thing we won't talk about if we can avoid it," said Mom. "Ask Master Yap what to do about the god."

"You don't need to be scared," said Master Yap. "The god was showing you her death. Not everybody gets to see. This is her way of honoring you. Other people, she won't send such dreams."

"Oh," said Jess. "Great. Cool. How do I get out of being honored?"

"All the girl needs to do is accept," continued Master Yap, as though she hadn't spoken. "Big Sister has chosen her as her medium. She put her mark on the girl. True or not?"

Jess's hand crept to her neck. Ah Huat, who had seen the god's fingerprints on her skin, said, "It's true! The mark is on her neck there. Master Sim saw."

"But this makes no sense," said Jess. She felt like she was being swept down a river by a swift current.

Kor Kor was clutching her cross to her chest. Mom's face was bloodless, the corners of her lips pulled down as if by an invisible weight.

"I destroyed her altar," said Jess. "Why would she choose me as her medium?"

"Her old one passed on." Mom's voice came out in a whisper, flattened by horror. Clearing her throat, she said, louder, "My mother was her medium. She passed on last year."

"That's why," said Master Yap, nodding with the satisfaction of a detective happening on the final missing clue. "This girl has the grandmother's blood, means she can do it. Because she spoiled the shrine, she owes the god a debt. So the god chose her.

"Go back to the temple there and rebuild the shrine," he said to Jess. "For training, ask the medium." He patted Mr. Sim's chest. "He can teach you. Then it will be OK. This god, Black Water Sister, she must have a priest to serve her. She had no children to do the rites for her, so the medium must do. If not, she can become dangerous. She can hurt people."

Both he and Ah Huat seemed to feel this resolved the issue. Ah Huat said to Master Yap, "There's nobody else already. Today only this girl. Please go back to heaven, tomorrow come again."

"Wait!" said Jess.

"She can't be a medium," said Mom. "She graduated from Harvard!"

But Master Yap had lost interest, no doubt thinking of the plumes of incense smoke awaiting him on his heavenly cloud. "Want or don't want, there's nothing to be done. It's not the human who decides."

The light went out of Mr. Sim's eyes. He slumped as the spirit left him, Ah Huat catching his limp body with practiced ease. He helped Mr. Sim to a seat.

Mr. Sim opened his eyes. He looked bleary, as though he was waking up after a bender.

"So how?" he said. "Settled already?"

It turned out Kor Kor had brought a sheaf of tracts in her handbag. She handed them out as they said their goodbyes.

"You can come to my church anytime," she said. "I'll introduce you to my pastor. Our congregation has people like you, used to be involved in this kind of thing. There's no need to stay inside. You can step out."

Mr. Sim accepted the tract politely, but Jess could tell he wasn't convinced.

"If I can choose, who will want to do this work?" he said. He pointed at his face. Livid marks stood out on his skin where Jess had shoved her bushel of burning joss sticks at him. "The god is the one who fought with you, but I'm the one who has the injury."

"Sorry," said Jess guiltily. "He was coming for me and I didn't think."

Mr. Sim waved her apology away. "It's the god who attacked you. Of course you will defend yourself. When I come back, I'm the one who must deal with the consequences. To be a medium is like that. What the gods want to do, you cannot stop. You have to accept it."

"No such thing," said Kor Kor. "Try and see! Ask Jesus to save you."

Mr. Sim shook his head.

"It's not for the medium to choose," he said. He met Jess's eyes, but she looked away, unwilling to find recognition there.

SIXTEEN

Mom turned to Kor Kor as they came out of Master Yap's temple.

"Did your pastor reply to you yet? She's free when?"

Kor Kor looked surprised. "You want to consult her?"

"You said she can help Min, means I want to see her," said Mom. "If she wants to baptize Min today itself, she can do it."

"Uh, she can?" said Jess. "Do I get a say?"

"Being a Christian is no big deal what," said Mom as they got into the car. "Just do the ceremony. Don't need to go to church if you don't want."

"Hoon Chee, cannot like that," Kor Kor objected. "If Min wants to convert, she must take it seriously."

"I am not converting to Christianity!" said Jess.

"Whatever the pastor wants, we can do," said Mom, ignoring her. "If she wants, Loke Khoon and I can convert also. After all, our parents have passed on already. Better we all become Christian than Min has to be the medium." Her gaze when she met Jess's eyes in the rearview mirror was steely.

She was a woman on a mission, but it was an unpropitious season for getting things done. Jess and her parents might not be celebrating Chinese New Year due to Mom's recent bereavement, but that wasn't stopping the rest of the island. While the non-Chinese took advantage of the public holiday to crowd the shopping malls, the Chinese closed up shop and went home to their families.

"All the mediums will be busy," said Mom. "Maybe Kor Kor is right also. These mediums are not the answer. They are part of that world, so they have a certain mindset. If the god says you must do like that, they follow only. This lady-pastor will be different."

But the lady-pastor was vacationing in Langkawi. Kor Kor wasn't sure when she'd be back.

"Cannot be she's the only pastor in Penang," said Mom. "Who else is there?"

Kor Kor was very willing to help despite her busy social life. Every affluent boomer in Penang with dead parents and children overseas had been congregating in her house for the past week or so, eating truckloads of peanuts, drinking tea and comparing WhatsApp forwards of dubious provenance.

But the day after their visit to Master Yap's temple, Kor Kor's eldest daughter made a surprise appearance. She turned up at the door with her bags and a huge grin, just in time for reunion dinner.

Mom took one look at Ching Yee, fresh from her twelve-hour flight from Sydney, and sighed.

"We'll go and see Kor Kor's pastor next week," she said to Jess in an undertone.

There wasn't much opportunity for private conversation after that, what with all the visitors and the various entertainments Kor Kor immediately began planning for Ching Yee.

Jess didn't mind. It was a relief to be restored to the mundane for a while. Caught up in family commitments, she was forced not to think about the god.

Ching Yee was sharing her bedroom, which ruled out calls with Sharanya. This obviously sucked, but it was also kind of a relief. It would be too weird having to pretend to Sharanya that everything was normal when it was so profoundly not.

It was nice how happy Kor Kor was. Her only grievance with the world was that Ching Yee was spending no more than a week in Penang.

"Why you didn't take more leave?" said Kor Kor. "One week is not enough. Should be ten days, two weeks at least."

"Cannot lah, Ma. I'm on this big project at work, I can't afford to be out for too long," said Ching Yee. "And I have to get back to Oz. My friend's wedding is next week. I'm the maid of honor."

"What friend is this? Australian?"

"He's Malaysian, actually," said Ching Yee. "Haffiz. My good friend from secondary school." She looked out of the window. "The garden's looking good. How's the passion fruit you got from Auntie Grace? Got fruit or not?"

"The Malay boy? I remember, you used to go to tuition with him," said Kor Kor. "Eh, I saw his parents the other day, at Queensbay Mall. They didn't say they're going to Australia also."

"Haffiz's parents aren't going to the wedding," said Ching Yee.

Something in the tone of her voice put Jess on guard. She was braced even before Ching Yee said, "He's marrying a guy."

"Oh," said Kor Kor.

Her face looked like she'd bitten into an orange, only to find out it was a lime. Jess didn't dare look at Mom.

"Like that also you want to go?" said Kor Kor. "You know, the Bible says—"

"The Bible says we should love our neighbors as we love ourselves," said Ching Yee. "Haffiz is one of my oldest friends. Whether I'm going is not up for debate. If you don't like it, you don't need to comment."

"Girl . . ."

"I'm going to get a top-up," said Ching Yee, raising her glass. "Jess, you want more soya bean?"

The look she gave Jess as she went off to the kitchen was definitely a meaningful one, but what it meant was hard to parse. It was apologetic, a little guilty, a little amused. Was it an "I'm sorry for having a scene with my mom and making things awkward" look? Or was it specifically an "I'm sorry for provoking our family into displaying their latent homophobia to you" look?

Jess couldn't help suspecting it was the latter. But Ching Yee didn't *know*, did she? There was nothing on Jess's social media that could have given her away. She was never in any of Sharanya's pictures either. She was so careful.

It wasn't that she'd mind Ching Yee herself knowing she was gay. But if Ching Yee knew, that was only one degree away from Kor Kor knowing, and Kor Kor knowing was as good as Jess's parents knowing.

And Jess's parents had enough crap to deal with as it was. Chinese New Year was stressing them out. At the end of the first day, when Jess was stretched out on her bed, trying to persuade herself to get up and have a shower, she heard them arguing in their room.

"Why you gave Loke Keong's kids fifty ringgit angpow for what? Not like you're so close," Mom was saying. "You're his older brother and he only visit us after we're in Penang for two weeks already."

"Aiyah, shouldn't hold a grudge over this small matter," said Dad. "To these young people, fifty ringgit is not to say a lot also."

"All the more you shouldn't give so much, if they don't know how to appreciate. In our position, who are we to splash our money? Everybody knows we're struggling."

"Gave already, don't need to talk so much. Loke Keong gave Min fifty ringgit also what."

"But Loke Keong has three children," said Mom. "We have one only. He knows he won't lose money. Just because he's your brother, doesn't mean you should let him take advantage of you—"

"Enough lah!" snapped Dad. "You're always so scared my family take advantage of us. Who let us stay in this house? Who gave me a job? Your family hasn't contributed one sen also."

The silence that followed was so awkward that Jess got off her bed and went to the bathroom just to put some distance between it and herself.

Then there was the incident with the uncle with the Rolex. It wasn't like Jess was able to distinguish a Rolex from any other watch; she only knew the uncle had a Rolex because he talked to Kor Tiao about it for the entire duration of his visit. Jess hadn't known it was possible to have so many feelings about watches.

She would have forgotten all about Rolex uncle if she hadn't come upon Mom a few hours later, hiding in her room and wiping her eyes.

"Have you guys been fighting again?" said Jess.

"What? Who's fighting?" said Mom. "Oh, with Dad? No lah, we're OK. Dad's too generous, that's all. He's such a good man, you know. But still people treat him like this."

"Like what?" Jess sat down next to Mom on the bed. "What happened?"

"You saw how that Uncle Gordon treated him?" said Mom. She meant the Rolex uncle.

Jess hadn't really been paying attention, for the obvious reason that the conversation had been somewhat less interesting than watching paint dry. "Did he say something to Dad?"

"He didn't talk to Dad at all," said Mom. "Talked to Kor Tiao only, like he doesn't know Dad. Dad was his senior at uni, you know! He helped Uncle Gordon get his first job, recommended him to the boss. Now he's rich and Dad's not doing so well, he doesn't even want to look at Dad. Did you know there's such people in the world?"

She was welling up as she spoke. Jess's heart twisted in her chest. She leaned over Mom to grab a tissue off the bedside table.

"He sounds like an asshole," said Jess, handing Mom the tissue. "He'll probably die alone and get eaten by his Rolexes. Who cares about somebody like that?"

"I told Dad also, but he's the old friend from uni. How not to care?" Mom blew her nose. "Don't tell Dad I told you. He doesn't want you to be upset."

Jess thought about all the secrets they were keeping to spare one another's feelings. Mom was the weak link. Anything you told her you knew Dad would hear, and she regularly told Jess all the things Dad tried to protect her from. Mom could never keep anything to herself.

But that wasn't true, was it? It turned out Mom had the biggest secrets of them all.

"Mom," said Jess, "what if there's nothing we can do about the . . ." She swallowed. "About the god? What if I'm stuck with her?"

Mom stiffened.

"That won't happen," she said. "We'll solve it. You haven't seen anything since we went to Master Yap's temple, right?"

Jess shook her head. She hadn't seen the Black Water Sister again, sleeping or waking. There had been no trace of Ah Ma either—not that Mom even knew about Ah Ma.

"Maybe the cleansing ritual worked," said Mom.

Donald Sim had given her a bag of rice grains and told her to sprinkle some in the corners of each room to bless the house. Not to be left out, Kor Kor had gone around the house hanging up crucifixes and torn-out pages of an old calendar bearing Bible verses. If the Black Water Sister were a movie vampire, Jess would be feeling pretty secure right now.

"For all you know, she won't come back," said Mom.

"Yeah," said Jess, but she wasn't convinced.

She'd promised the god a sacrifice. The god was waiting for her.

It was easier to believe that Ah Ma might have been kept away by the blessed rice and crucifixes. It was either that, or Jess had managed to make Ah Ma mad enough that the ghost was finally leaving her alone.

She hoped it was one of those, and not that something had happened to Ah Ma. What if the Black Water Sister had done something terrible to her—devoured her soul or something—because of what Jess had done? Ah Ma had lied, attempted murder, done her best to screw Jess over. But Jess still didn't want to be the cause of her grandmother's ghost having been devoured by a vengeful goddess.

She slanted a glance at her mom. At least Mom didn't seem to have any suspicion about Ah Ma's involvement in all of this. Jess wasn't planning on telling her, so long as she could avoid it. It was bad enough losing a mother about whom you had complicated feelings. Hearing she'd returned as a ghost but hadn't bothered trying to speak to you *and* her ghost had gone missing would be even worse.

"We'll see if Kor Kor's pastor can help," said Mom. "Even if she cannot, there'll be some other way. In the end, god is not so different from human. They want you to respect them, give them presents. You look at even the richest, most powerful man, like that guy . . . who is he?" Mom paused, her brow furrowed in the effort of recollection.

"Ng Chee Hin?" Jess suggested.

Mom blinked. She'd probably been thinking of Jeff Bezos or somebody. "Yeah, like him. How did you hear of Ng Chee Hin?" She must have forgotten that Jess had been there when the aunties and uncles were discussing him in Kor Kor's living room.

"He's one of Kor Tiao's biggest customers," Jess reminded her. "I Googled him. He's the fifth richest man in Malaysia, did you know that?"

"Wah," said Mom, impressed. "Fifth richest! When he started out, he didn't have any money. Now he's so well-off."

The thought seemed to make her pensive. She said, "When my mother passed on, she still didn't have any money. Holiday also, the farthest she went was to Genting."

"Genting Highlands?" Jess vaguely remembered a trip to the amusement park at Genting when she was a kid. She'd been entertained by the locals bundled up against the seventy-degree chill. "Was Ah Ma a big fan of roller coasters?"

"She liked the casino," said Mom absently. "What I was saying is, even Ng Chee Hin, even if he's the number one richest man in the world, you can negotiate with him. If he doesn't know how to compromise, he won't be able to do business, right?"

"I guess," said Jess. "I'm not sure gods are really into compromise, though."

"Can one," said Mom. "You can bargain with anybody, spirit or human. All you need to know is what do they want and what are they scared of. That's all."

Jess made an affirmative noise. It wasn't like she even disagreed. She thought the Black Water Sister probably would be open to striking a deal. The problem was, Jess suspected, none of them was going to like her price.

IT WAS THE fourth day of New Year by the time Jess was able to speak with Sharanya, and she was so tired she overslept. Sharanya had been waiting for forty-five minutes by the time Jess woke and remembered they were supposed to be having a video call.

It hadn't even been two full weeks since their last call, and it already felt weird seeing Sharanya. She was a relic of Jess's previous life, when Jess had been a normal person with a girlfriend and plans for her future that went beyond "extricate self from terrifying goddess's grasp."

Except Sharanya wasn't a relic. She was a real live person—and she was annoyed.

"I was wondering if you were actually going to show up," she said.

Jess was hunkered down in bed, the sheet pulled over her head as usual to reduce the risk of being overheard. The harsh light from her phone screen picked out every unflattering detail—her egregious bedhead, the dark circles under her eyes, her millions of pores. She wished she'd taken a moment to wash her face and brush her hair before getting on the call. "Yeah, sorry, babe. This week has been an utter shitshow. I can't even tell you."

Sharanya softened. "Holidays, huh? Has your mom been totally unbearable?"

Most of the time Jess and Sharanya had an understanding about Jess's mom and it was OK for Sharanya to dunk on her. But right now, it wasn't.

"She's having a rough time," said Jess. "Your mom wouldn't love it if she was having to live off her sister-in-law's charity. My aunt's younger too. It's a whole thing."

"Yeah, I can see that's hard," said Sharanya, sounding unconvinced. "But isn't it your mom who's been shooting down all the options you've found for places to rent?"

"It's not like there've been that many options," said Jess. "We haven't had time to look."

"You guys have been in Malaysia for a month now."

Jess couldn't really say, "Yes, but I've been busy being haunted first by my grandmother and now by something even worse. You thought being manipulated into working for my uncle was bad? Try being forced to become the vessel of a murderous god!"

She said instead, "We've been busy. Dad's taken up with his job, and I guess we're still finding our feet . . ."

"But your mom's not working, right?" said Sharanya. "Can't she take the lead on finding you guys a place? It sounds like she's the one being picky."

The thought that Mom might search for a property for them, given she had the fewest commitments, had occurred to Jess before. But now that it was Sharanya saying it, she felt the need to defend Mom. "She doesn't do that stuff. I think she lacks confidence. Dad always handled that kind of thing for her, and now me."

"How's she going to get confident if she keeps relying on you guys to do everything for her?"

Jess should have reminded herself that she'd kept Sharanya waiting; that she'd barely responded to her messages over the past couple of weeks; that she wouldn't hold hands with her in public when they were at college, for fear of getting caught by her Asian friends, who might tell their parents. But she was feeling too raw and exhausted to filter herself. She kept thinking of Mom's face, twisted in grief because she couldn't protect her husband from the small poisonous cuts attending failure.

"I know my mom has her issues," said Jess. "But if it doesn't bother me, why do you care?"

"It does bother you. We talk constantly about how much it bothers you," said Sharanya. "Why are you suddenly pretending it doesn't?"

"You know," said Jess, "if you're in a bad mood or whatever, we don't have to talk."

"*I* don't want to talk?" said Sharanya. "You're the one who kept me waiting for forty-five minutes!"

"Oh, sorry for oversleeping when it's five a.m. here—"

"You're the one who wants to speak at five a.m.," said Sharanya. "I could do another time. I'm right here. I answer all your messages. I don't keep you hanging. All you have to do is tell me what time works for you."

Jess ignored the gibe about answering messages. She said in a low voice, "You know why we have to talk at this time. There's always people around in this house. It's like my aunt has a pathological fear of solitude. I can only speak now because my cousin's staying over with a friend."

"You know, it's not like you have to only talk to me when other people aren't around," said Sharanya. "There are other options."

Jess could not believe this. Sharanya was always the first to say nobody should feel pressured to come out if they weren't ready, to remind their white friends that even in the twenty-first century there were people for whom being out came with a risk to their job, their family and social connections, even their lives.

"Oh yeah?" said Jess. "Like what? Tell me."

She glared at Sharanya, daring her to say it.

For the first time in the course of their relationship, Sharanya didn't back down. She glared back.

"You want to do this? Let's do this," she said. "You tell me, Jess. How long are you planning to hide for? Are we going to be roommates in Singapore ten years from now?"

"You know what it's like with my parents," said Jess. "They couldn't even begin to deal. I can't do that to them, after all the shit they've been through."

"I'm not asking you to tell them now. I'm asking you, when are you going to be ready? You can't hide behind your parents forever."

"I'm not hiding behind my parents," said Jess. It was weirdly hard to get the words out.

Sharanya exhaled. Jess could almost hear her reminding herself to be patient.

This made Jess feel worse than ever. She and Sharanya had never had to be *forbearing* with each other before. It had always been—maybe not easy, but simple. The most straightforward thing in her life.

"I know it's not easy," said Sharanya. Jess could tell it was taking effort on her part to be gentle. "When I came out to my parents, my dad didn't talk to me for months. But he got over it. You've got to give your parents a chance. Maybe they'll surprise you. They can't accept what they don't know."

"I know how they'd react," said Jess. "I just—you've got to trust that I know my parents. Your family's different. You've got siblings, there are three of you. My parents couldn't take it. And I'm all they've got."

"I know you want to be a good daughter. I get it, it's important to you to be filial, but—"

"Filial?" Jess stifled a wild laugh. "I'm not fucking *filial*. It's like I'm under an evil spell. They made me, so now I'm in debt and I can never pay it off, no matter what I do. But I don't get to stop trying. I get to carry this debt for the rest of my life, because I love them, and if I make them unhappy, I'll know I really am completely useless!"

Sharanya had frozen on the screen, but Jess heard her take a deep breath and expel it in a sigh. She waited for Sharanya to say something soothing and unhelpful, like she always did. Like "Who told you you had to be useful?" or "You know you're not required to make your parents happy, right?"

Instead she said, "You know this is a prison of your own making."

There was a hardness Jess had never heard in her voice before.

"It really isn't," said Jess.

"It *is*," said Sharanya. "And if you can't even recognize that, how are things ever going to change? It's not like your family's going to magically become not homophobic if you just leave the issue for long enough. I'm willing to wait to be a part of your life. But not forever."

"What are you talking about?" said Jess, baffled. "You are a part of my life."

"I *was* a part of your life," Sharanya corrected her. "Living thousands of miles apart, talking not even once a week . . . I spend more time with my Pilates instructor than with you. This isn't a relationship."

It looked like her eyes might be filling with tears, but it was hard to tell for sure on the phone screen. Guilt squirmed in Jess's stomach.

"I'm sorry I've been unresponsive," she said. "I've just been busy."

"With what?" said Sharanya. "Your uncle doesn't even pay you. You can't take five minutes to answer my messages? I mean, are you even applying for jobs in Singapore? What about that job we were talking about, the one I sent you?"

Jess hadn't done a single job application since Ah Ma had first taken her to the garden temple. The guilt died, drowned out by a rising sense of injustice.

"Look, I have a ton of shit on my plate, and it's not a priority right now," she said. "If you had any idea what I'm going through—"

"I would, if you told me," said Sharanya. "Like I said, I'm right here. But I can't keep coming bottom of the list, Jess."

"You're not. That's not what I meant!"

"That's how I feel," said Sharanya. "That's how you're treating me. And I don't know if I can keep doing this."

Jess stared at her, dazed at the speed with which the conversation had spun out of control.

"Are you—" Her voice wobbled, breaking embarrassingly, like a teenage boy's. "Are you breaking up with me?"

"No." But then Sharanya's face crumpled and she said, "I don't know. Maybe."

"Sharanya—"

There was a knock on the door. Jess's head whipped around despite herself.

The next moment she'd turned back to the screen, but it was too late. Sharanya was looking at her like Jess had only done what she had expected. She didn't even look annoyed, or disappointed. She looked resigned.

"You've got to go," she said. "Bye, Jess."

"Wait, Sharanya—!"

But she'd ended the call. Jess gaped at her phone, stunned.

"Min?" said Kor Kor's voice on the other side of the bedroom door. "What are you doing? You're talking to somebody, is it?"

"No," said Jess.

She got out of bed on autopilot, glancing mechanically at herself in the mirror. She was surprised by how OK she looked. She was pale and mussy-haired, but her face bore no signs of recent disaster.

"Sorry, did I wake you up?" said Jess. "I was watching a show."

She smiled at Kor Kor, though it made her face feel like Play-Doh, pummeled into the required shape. *Nothing to see here. Everything's fine.*

SEVENTEEN

Jess didn't feel like going to see Sherng the next day, especially when she woke up and saw that Sharanya hadn't replied to the messages she'd sent after their call. Earnest, groveling messages, running to several paragraphs each, baring her heart as she rarely did even to Sharanya.

The only thing Jess hadn't told her was everything that was going on. Jess had gone too far down this path of not talking about her dead grandmother and her run-ins with gangsters and her entanglement with a creepy god to turn back. She couldn't dump it all on Sharanya now. Sharanya had taken enough shit from her as it was.

Though it was starting to look like she'd officially had enough.

Jess was tempted to roll over and pull the covers over her head, try to sleep the day away the way she had sometimes when Dad was sick and the world felt like too much to deal with.

She only managed to drag herself out of bed by reminding herself there would be worse consequences for a no-show than merely offending Sherng. His dad had hit men in his employ. She needed to make sure Sherng understood she wasn't a murderer, contrary to appearances.

She should also find out whether he'd talked to his father about the accident at the construction site. The photos she'd taken that day were still sitting on her computer; as far as she knew, the construction workers hadn't deployed them yet either. She hadn't heard anything of what they were planning since Kassim had messaged her to ask if she'd sent the photos anywhere.

No wonder Sharanya had accused her of not showing up for their relationship. Jess hadn't been showing up for anyone recently. The least she could do was go and talk to Sherng.

She knew Mom would raise a ruckus about her going out, so she'd scheduled the meetup for noon, when everyone was going to be out of the house. Ching Yee was seeing old school friends, and the aunties and uncles were having lunch with Kor Kor's small group. The average age of the group was around sixty—Mom and Dad would be the youngest people there—so Jess wasn't expected to come along.

The house was quiet when she emerged from her room at eleven a.m., both cars gone from the driveway. Jess was ordering a Grab and congratulating herself on how well she'd managed things when Mom said behind her:

"Min, I've been thinking."

"Argh!" said Jess. "I thought you went out for lunch!"

"No mood to go," said Mom. She didn't look like she'd gotten any more sleep than Jess had. Her lips were pale and there were shadows under her eyes. "I told Dad to go without me. I was thinking, we should ask Ah Ku to help you."

"Uh, yeah?" Jess glanced out of the window. No sign of her taxi.

"He's a medium, like my mother," said Mom. "But for a different god, Kuan Kong. Last time Kuan Kong was a general, so he knows how to behave, not like Tai Seng Ia. Maybe he'll know how to handle Ah Ma's god."

It seemed unlikely Kuan Kong would be inclined to assist an altar destroyer. If Ah Ku had believed otherwise, he wouldn't have given Jess that RM100. "But you said you didn't think mediums would be helpful."

"Unless you try, you won't know what," argued Mom. "We should explore all the options."

A car drew up outside the gate.

"That's my ride," said Jess. "I've got to go, Mom."

Mom said, predictably, "You ordered taxi? Now also you want to go out? This is not the time to hangkai, you know!"

"Why not?" said Jess. "It's not like it makes a difference where I am. I'm being haunted by a god, not stalked by the Mafia."

Of course, if a gang did have a hit out on her, she was going out to meet the likeliest reason why. But Jess shook the thought off. Sherng wasn't going to arrange for her to be assassinated at a novelty tofu restaurant, surrounded by hipsters with smartphones. The footage would be on Facebook before she hit the ground.

"She could come find me here as easily as anywhere else," she said.

"Choy," said Mom automatically. "No need to talk like that. At least if you're in the house, Kor Kor and I can help you."

The car started blaring its horn.

"Look, I'll be back as soon as I can, but I have to go," said Jess.

It wasn't like Mom would believe her if she said she was going for an interview. But there was one thing that might convince her to let Jess go. Jess only hesitated for a moment before saying, "The guy I'm meeting is waiting. I've already canceled once."

"What guy is this? You tell him you have emergency, cannot make it . . ."

"It's a guy I'm seeing," said Jess. "If you must know, I'm going on a date." Even though the date was invented, Jess felt, weirdly, like she was cheating on Sharanya, adding to the long list of ways in which she'd failed to be the girlfriend she deserved. She turned her face to hide her expression from Mom.

Luckily, Mom wasn't really paying attention.

"You don't have time to yumcha all that," she was saying.

Then she registered what Jess had said. She looked comically astonished—as though part of her knew how unlikely it was that Jess would ever go on a date with a guy.

"Date?" said Mom. "But who is this guy?"

"He's a friend of a friend," said Jess. "He's from here, but he studied in America. My friend set us up."

Mom was torn between alarm and delight. "What college did he go to? Why you didn't tell me?"

Jess's phone started ringing. She glanced at the screen. "It's the driver—hey, I'll be right out, sorry!" She hung up. "I didn't tell you because I knew you'd freak out."

"Who's freaking out?" said Mom. "Sure or not he's OK? You shouldn't meet strange men by yourself. Better to go on group date. Oh, but you don't have girlfriends here. Want or not, I come? I'll sit at another table. You can pretend I'm not there."

Being told she didn't have girlfriends was a little too close to the truth right now. It was with a poker face developed through years of practice that Jess said lightly:

"I'm not going to have to pretend, because you are not coming on my date." She kissed Mom on the cheek and grabbed her bag off the coffee table. "I'll tell you about it when I'm back. Don't worry, Mom."

She managed to get to the end of the driveway before Mom called out after her, "He's Chinese, right?"

Little did she know. It was both funny and sad to think how

much Mom would love Sherng. If only his dad weren't Ng Chee Hin, but a different, less felonious millionaire, he'd be pretty much perfect—well-off, personable, accomplished. Good-looking, but nerdy enough to ping aunties and uncles as a "good boy." Admittedly there was the fact his mom was Indian, but at least his dad was Chinese. With everything else Sherng had going for him, Jess couldn't imagine his being mixed race would be an issue for long, even though Mom's worst fear for her love life was that she'd get together with a man who was neither Chinese nor white.

Well. That was her second worst fear. Her *worst* fear was that Jess would end up forever alone. What Jess was was an eventuality beyond conception; a fear lurking beneath the level of acceptable thought, as nameless and dreadful as any spirit. Even to articulate the possibility to herself would, for Mom, be a betrayal of Jess.

Jess needed to stop thinking about this now.

She looked at her phone to distract herself. Still nothing from Sharanya. The way things were going, she probably *would* end up forever alone, and her parents would never need to know there were worse things than having a spinster daughter.

She was in a foul mood by the time the Grab driver dropped her off at the end of a row of shophouses. She stepped over the drain up onto the five-foot way. The café was at the other end.

Sherng had messaged. I'm on my way.

Jess might have passed most of her life in America, but she was Malaysian enough to know what this meant. She was in for a wait, then. She didn't mind. It would be nice to hang out with a drink by herself and not have to pretend to be fine for a little while.

She had a premonition of danger before she saw the guy. A shiver ran up the back of her neck. She spun around, half expecting to see Ah Ma, or—*please, no*—the Black Water Sister.

When she saw the man parking his motorcycle, her first sensation was of relief. Then he leaped off his bike and came toward her.

She recognized him, though it took her a moment to place the face, with its prominent black mole on the cheek. It was Mole Boy—Ah Tat, they'd called him. The young man who'd turned up with Ah Ku's raggedy posse at the garden temple. His intention was written across his face.

Jess started running, even as her brain chattered, *But he's not going to do anything, not out here in front of God and everybody—*

It was a mistake to assume any gods were on her side. Mole Boy caught her arm, smothering her scream with a hand over her mouth.

Jess bit down, tasting salt, and heard Mole Boy swear. His grip loosened. She tried to bolt, but he hung on to her, twisting her arm painfully.

"Let me go!" she snarled, trying unsuccessfully to tug her arm away. "What the hell is your problem?"

Mole Boy didn't answer. He looked mad and scared, but determined.

There were only the two of them on the five-foot way. Jess's Grab had driven off. But there had to be people in the shops, people who would come out if she managed to make enough of a commotion . . .

"Fuck off!" she yelled.

The door to the restaurant where she was supposed to meet Sherng opened. A young man stepped out. He was wearing a blue and yellow apron, with a cartoon of a smiling soybean on the front.

"Hello?" he called, his voice wavering. He wasn't a local. Burmese, probably. "Are you OK, miss?"

Jess saw a row of curious faces behind the glass frontage of the restaurant, watching the confrontation in air-conditioned comfort. She felt a jolt of mixed anger and pity. Of all the people who could have tried to help, it was the migrant worker who'd come out to check on a stranger.

Mole Boy ignored the waiter, digging his fingers into her flesh. She drove her heel into his foot, trying to get free of him.

"Excuse me, sir," said the waiter.

Jess leaned away from Mole Boy, putting all her weight into resisting him, so when he released her arm, she collapsed to the floor. Triumph flared in her chest, but then she saw his knife.

The waiter had seen it too. He froze. There was a disturbance inside the restaurant as people realized what was going on, but nobody else came out.

The waiter was yelling something. Jess couldn't hear the words over the panicked hammering of her own heart.

I'm going to die, she thought. *I'm going to—*

But suddenly she was no longer alone. Someone else was on the floor with her, and it was someone who understood, who had gone through the same thing, who knew what it was like.

The Black Water Sister told her what would happen next. The man would cut her throat and her blood would pool on the ground. It would soak into the moist earth, turning the fallen leaves black. She would be unmoored from her past and future lives, kept hungry by what had been done to her. For more than a hundred years, watching the living as if through smeared glass, except for the brief brilliant moments when she was able to smash the glass and reach through . . .

Horror shivered through Jess, her own fear tangled with the god's remembered dread. Then a red wave of fury crashed over her, sweeping away fear and dread. In it, the distinction between herself and the god, that had seemed so vital, was submerged and lost. Cringing on the ground, they were one person.

Over them—over *her*—stood her fate, ready to strike. But she had already died once.

She had been given a second chance. She was not about to waste it.

She reached for power and it came to her hand, flowing into her smoothly—the destructive power of the unforgetful dead.

She wrenched the knife from the man's hand. She cut herself on the blade as she did it, but the pain was no more than a whisper, drowned out by the roaring in her head. She scratched absently at the back of her neck to ease the itch there.

The knife was slippery with her blood when she slashed at her attacker. That was the only reason she missed.

The man dodged when she tried again, flinging himself backward. She rolled onto her knees and got up. Her attacker was struggling to his feet. She seized the back of his shirt before he could get away.

A man stabbed in the back made a choking noise as he died. That was something she had learned after her death. She was looking forward to hearing the sound again.

But there was something she didn't know, something she wanted to ask him. She shook her head to clear it. The question bubbled to the surface.

"Why did you come after me?" she said in the god's tongue. "What did I do?"

"Jess?" said Sherng. "What are you doing?"

The sound of her name cut through the noise in Jess's head. She came back to herself abruptly, slamming back into her own body.

It was like hurtling into a brick wall. She bent over, gasping. The world rushed back in on her—the warm humid air of midday, the heat reflecting off the cars and motorbikes parked along the five-foot way, the stench of the drains.

The man panting at her feet was not the man who'd chased her down in the forest, but a frightened boy, cowering away from her. The skin on the back of her neck throbbed as though it had been scalded, and her hand ached.

She looked down to see blood seeping from the wound in her palm.

Sherng stood outside the entrance to the restaurant.

"What the hell?" he said.

MOLE BOY BROKE loose as Jess stared at Sherng.

"Stop!" she shouted pointlessly.

Sherng stepped neatly out of the way as Mole Boy darted past. The waiter yelped and took cover. Jess lunged after Mole Boy, but it turned out there was someone right behind Sherng—a guy in a green T-shirt, built like a brick wall. He didn't flinch when Mole Boy crashed into him, but caught him and pinned his arms to his sides, as smoothly as though they'd planned the maneuver in advance.

"Boss, how?" said Green T-shirt.

Sherng jerked his head.

"Can you deal with him? People are staring," he said. "Call Pooi Mun to come."

He turned to Jess. "What was that all about?"

"Who is that guy?" said Jess.

Green T-shirt was steering Mole Boy away while talking into his phone. She couldn't see what was in his other hand, but he must have been holding some effective enforcer of good behavior. Mole Boy went quietly, his face blank.

"His name's Razak," said Sherng. "He works for me."

"Works for you? You've got thugs too?"

"Razak's my bodyguard," said Sherng sharply. "You're the one who told me to bring one, remember?"

Jess had forgotten.

"Oh," she said. "I didn't think you'd do it. I mean, what kind of threat do I pose?"

"Given you were waving a knife around when I showed up," said Sherng, "I actually think it was good advice!"

"It's not my knife," said Jess. "I took it off Ah Tat. He's the one who jumped me."

It hadn't been real until she said it out loud. A chill swept over her. She started shaking.

"You knew that guy?" said Sherng, but Jess wasn't listening.

She said, "He would have hurt me, if I hadn't—" The world tilted around her. "If I hadn't—"

The knife clattered on the ground. Jess swayed. Sherng gave her his arm, steadying her. She heard the waiter saying, "Miss, come inside," and felt the blast of air-conditioning as she staggered into the restaurant. Someone pulled out a chair for her and got her a glass of water.

If I hadn't let the god in, she'd been going to say. She had drawn on the same wild power that had come to her when she was struggling against the Monkey God, but this time it had been different. This time she had drawn blood, and she had won, and she would have killed that guy if Sherng hadn't shown up.

Jess looked at the gash in her palm. Her blood. She'd made the sacrifice she had promised, after all—but it hadn't released her from her bond. It had drawn her even closer to the god.

"Are you OK?" said Sherng. Then, his tone changing: "Shit, what happened to your hand?"

Jess yanked her hand away when Sherng reached out.

"I told you, he had a knife," she said. Her voice broke. She looked down at the table, furious.

There was a brief silence while Jess tried to will the water blurring her vision back into her tear ducts. A woman in a black suit came and addressed Sherng in low tones. Probably the manager, telling him to get out or they'd call the police. Jess waited to be thrown out, but the woman went away.

Sherng turned back to her. He said carefully, as though Jess was having a breakdown, "How about we try to stop the bleeding? I'm not going to touch you," he added, when Jess instinctively withdrew. "You can do it yourself—ah, here."

The woman had come back with a roll of paper towels. Sherng tore some sheets off and handed them to Jess.

Jess pressed the sheaf of paper towels against her wound. Her hands were shaking, but the pain helped ground her a little.

She raised her head, blinking. The urge to weep had passed. The restaurant seemed suddenly weirdly busy, full of people standing by tables, talking.

"Who was that?" she said, but the woman was back again, this time with a first aid kit.

"Thanks, Pooi Mun," said Sherng, taking the kit. "How are we doing?"

The woman crouched next to his chair.

"All under control," she said. She spoke good English, with the accent of a primary Chinese speaker. It gave her words a kind of clipped efficiency that matched her appearance. "We managed to catch some of the customers outside. Maybe got some witnesses who got away already, that one no choice lah. But majority we have captured. The captain is very helpful. We talked to the waiters also. I will keep an eye on social media. The one hard to manage is WhatsApp. But at least the names all that, people don't know. Miss is low profile, means easier to handle."

"Do we know if people got any images or video?" said Sherng.

Pooi Mun said, "Two people here took. We made sure they delete already. But maybe miss knows if there's more . . . ?"

"I wasn't really paying attention," said Jess. "Um, sorry, who are you?"

"Oh, my bad," said Sherng. "This is Pooi Mun, she works for my—for us." Jess noted his discomfort over mentioning his dad. She wondered if he suspected Ah Tat of being sent by Ng Chee Hin. "She's helping to manage the situation. I figured you wouldn't want this in the press or on social media or whatever."

"Oh," said Jess. "So you're, like, their fixer?"

"Fixer?" said Pooi Mun.

"Fix—no! She's an executive assistant." Sherng ran his hands through his hair. "'Fixer'! You think this is *The Godfather* or what?"

"I mean, you literally have a team of professionals to help you with cleanup," said Jess. "Normal people don't have that."

"If you don't want me here, you can tell me," said Sherng. "I can go. Do you want me to go?" He sounded more defeated than exasperated.

"No," said Jess, after a moment. She let out a breath. "I'm sorry. I appreciate the help, I just . . . why are you helping me?"

"You're asking me," said Sherng grumpily. "I also don't know."

Jess was getting annoyed again. "It's not that I'm not grateful. But you have to admit it doesn't stack up. You're sweeping in saving the day, when the last time we met—"

I tried to choke you, she was about to say, when Pooi Mun interrupted.

"Mr. Ng," she said, "do you mind if you all go off? That way easier to manage. If you stay here, you'll draw attention only."

Now that Jess looked at the other customers, she could see they were staring at Sherng. She shrank down behind the bright blue and yellow menu propped up at the center of the table.

"Yeah," said Sherng. "We'd better get out of here." He paused, glancing at Jess. "Will you let me take you home? You can take a Grab or something if you prefer. We'll follow."

Let Ng Chee Hin's son find out where she lived? Jess could imagine how Ah Ku would react to that. Or Ah Ma—if she ever heard from Ah Ma again.

"There's no way we could talk at my place," said Jess. "Let's go somewhere else." She looked at Pooi Mun. "Got any ideas?"

POOI MUN'S IDEA was a quiet corner of a Starbucks in a nearby mall. It might have lacked the charm of Tau, but its advantages were evident: huge glass windows looking out on the Saturday afternoon crowds. Great for people watching—and great for being seen.

Jess wasn't sure which of them was supposed to be reassured by the fact they were so visible. Sherng? He didn't seem scared of Jess despite the whole "tried to choke him to death" thing. But then, why would he be? He only had to snap his fingers for a team of staff to rush to his aid.

Of course, he didn't know about the Black Water Sister.

Jess hunched over her panini. *Don't think about her.*

She should know by now that her mind wasn't a locked room. If she wanted to avoid drawing the god's attention, she needed to watch her thoughts.

"Pooi Mun's amazing," she said, to distract herself—and any spirits listening. She glanced down at her hand in its white bandage. Pooi Mun had bound it up, working with practiced ease. "How did you guys find her?"

"I poached her from my friend's skincare company," said Sherng. "He still hasn't forgiven me. She's great, right? The only thing she won't do is call me Sherng." He sighed. "It's always Mr. Ng this, Mr. Ng that."

"Why don't you want her to call you Mr. Ng?"

"It's so formal! It's the same thing she calls my da—" Sherng coughed. "It makes me feel like an old man. I've known her for so long already. She's my friend, not just my coworker."

Jess saw that he really believed what he was saying. Whoever his dad was, whatever his true motivations were, Sherng wanted to be liked. Jess could use that.

"Why did you agree to meet me?" she said. She glanced around. They were way off by themselves and nobody was paying attention to them. Razak was strategically positioned between them and the entrance, not close enough to overhear what they said, but not too far to step in if needed. He was staring down at his phone, apparently engrossed, but Jess had no doubt he'd be at Sherng's side in a second if she so much as looked at Sherng funny.

She lowered her voice. "I tried to *kill* you."

"I wanted to see you because you tried to kill me," said Sherng. "It seemed out of character for you."

"You don't know anything about my character," said Jess. "What makes you think I'm not a murderer?"

"No offense, but I was there and you're not very good at it," said Sherng. "You had all those guys ready to help you and you stopped strangling me halfway to go off and start whacking the altar. You didn't even try to come after me when I escaped. You had to know if you made the attempt, you had to go all the way. If I got home alive, you were screwed."

"Nothing's happened to me so far," said Jess. She corrected herself: "Except for the guy who tried to knife me, and he's not one of yours."

"Yeah, because I don't have that kind of person on my payroll!"

Jess took a bite of panini to stop herself from pointing out that his father definitely did, even if Sherng claimed not to.

"What happened?" said Sherng. "Why did that guy go for you? Do you know him?"

"About as well as you know him," said Jess. "He was at the temple that day. He was one of the guys who caught you when you were running away."

Sherng blinked.

"That's why," he said. "He looked familiar. So what, he was mad at you for not getting rid of me properly? Why not go after me, then?"

"I don't know. It's not like we talked about it." Jess remembered Mole Boy's expression as he'd come toward her. He had looked like someone determined to get an unpleasant job over with.

"But I don't think it was about you," she said. "I think it was about the god."

"The god?"

"The altar I destroyed," said Jess. "It had a god inside it."

"Oh," said Sherng. "Oh *shit*." He paused. "I did some digging. There are some weird stories about that temple. I'm surprised my dad was willing to get involved."

Jess glanced at him. "Is he superstitious?"

"Not really," said Sherng. "It's just messy. He doesn't like messy. But there's a lot of money riding on the Rexmondton Heights development. He's not the kind of guy to let stories put him off a good deal."

The reference to the development reminded Jess that she had been going to ask him what Sejahtera was planning to do about the accident at the site. It felt like it had taken place a long time ago now, even though not quite two weeks had passed.

More to the point, she was beginning to feel it no longer mattered. The main source of the problem, the Black Water Sister, had shifted her attention elsewhere, now that her altar had been destroyed. The construction workers didn't have to worry about her anymore. Jess should know.

Even so, she asked.

"I told him about the accident," said Sherng. "But we didn't have a chance to talk it through. Then that whole thing at the temple happened, where you, um . . ."

"Tried to strangle you," said Jess. "Does your dad know about that?"

Sherng looked away, uncomfortable. "No. No, I didn't tell him about you."

"I owe you one there," said Jess. "I wouldn't be here, talking to you, if your dad knew what I tried to do."

Sherng didn't deny it.

She'd have to get off her ass and send those photos to someone who could make use of them to put pressure on Ng Chee Hin. It didn't look like Sherng was going to be of much use.

"What are the stories you heard about the temple?" said Jess, because she didn't want him asking about the photos.

Sherng shrugged. "Oh, you know. Mediums doing black magic. Beautiful women who appear at night, but they're ghosts who want to kill you. Russell Lee's *True Singapore Ghost Stories* kind of stuff."

Jess's expression must have made it obvious that he'd lost her.

"Sorry," he said. "I forgot you're American."

This made Jess laugh despite herself. "I'm really not."

"You're not Malaysian lah, I mean," said Sherng.

That was also true. She wasn't Malaysian or American. Just as she wasn't straight but she definitely wasn't gay, if anyone was asking. She wasn't her family's Min, but she wasn't the Jess who'd had a life under that name, before her dad had gotten sick. Her beautiful life, with her beautiful girlfriend, her friends, her creative projects, her ambitions.

It all seemed far away now. No wonder Ah Ma had found it easy to get into her head. She was a walking nothing—a hole in the universe, perfect for letting the dead through.

She shivered.

"You're in trouble, right?" said Sherng. "What's going on?"

He looked sorry for her. It made Jess want to punch him, but it also made her want to cry.

She couldn't trust Sherng, but he was the only person she had to trust. He had been there at the temple, had seen what she had done. He'd seen it for what it truly was—something being done *to* her. He wasn't family, wasn't even really a friend. They owed each other nothing. That meant, maybe, she could talk to him.

"You mentioned a woman in your message," said Sherng. "You said 'she' wasn't coming back for a while. What did you mean?"

Jess looked down at the uneaten third of her cooling panini. She hadn't been able to finish it. Her stomach hurt.

She said, "Why didn't you tell your dad about me?"

She meant, *Give me a reason to trust you.*

Sherng was quiet for a moment.

"You know," he said, "I don't believe in ghosts and spirits. I'm almost the only one out of my friends and family who's a skeptic. Malaysians are so superstitious. Everything that happens, it must be because of hantu.

"But what I saw at the temple that night . . ." He shook his head. "I can't explain it. Unless everyone else is right, and I've been wrong all this time."

He looked Jess in the eye. "Who was it who attacked me? It wasn't you, was it?"

Jess hesitated.

But she needed somebody to talk to. Somebody who would believe her, whom she could confide in without worrying about exposing them to danger, or freaking them out. An ally—one she didn't need to protect.

"You know the real reason why I asked you to come to the garden temple?" she said finally. "It was my grandmother's idea. She came with me that day."

Sherng's forehead furrowed. "Then she went off, is it? I didn't see her."

"No. You wouldn't have," said Jess. "She died last year."

EIGHTEEN

Jess only had Ah Ku's home number, because that was the number Ah Ma had known. She rang on Monday, hiding in the bathroom at the office.

Inevitably, a woman's voice answered. Not a young woman, either, which meant it had to belong to her affronted aunt.

"It's Sze Min," said Jess. "Poey Hoon's child. Is that Ah Kim?"

"Yes." The voice sounded distinctly unfriendly.

"Sorry I didn't come in to greet you the other day, Ah Kim," said Jess. "I didn't want to disturb you. Ah Ku needed someone to drive him back, otherwise I wouldn't have come to your house without warning. I'm sure you were busy."

There was a pause. Then:

"Stay in US so long, still clever to speak Hokkien. Not bad ah," said Ah Kim. She sounded gruff, but also genuinely impressed.

Jess enjoyed half a second of relief. Then Ah Kim said:

"What happened to Ah Ku's motorbike? Did he gamble it away or what? When he went out to meet you that time he had a motorbike, when he came back don't have already. Don't say you don't know. You didn't drive him there, so must be you were there when he lost it."

"Uh," said Jess, but she was rescued by Ah Ku himself. She heard him saying:

"I told you already, the motorbike broke down. Ah Hock took it back to his house. No need to interrogate your niece, like police only. You think she stole it or what?"

His voice came down the line. "Eh, Ah Min! Calling for what?"

"I need to talk to you," said Jess. "Can we meet?"

Ah Ku cleared his throat. "Cannot lah, Ah Min. After what happened at the temple that time, I better not go out so much. After that bastard comes after me. Cannot talk over the phone ah?"

Jess glanced at the door. She'd chosen to make her call in the customer bathroom at the back of the showroom. The staff bathroom was right next to Kor Tiao's office, and she'd figured her chances of getting interrupted by customers at nine a.m. on a Monday were pretty slim. She wasn't hearing anything on the other side of the door, but she lowered her voice.

"It's kind of difficult," she said. "I want to talk to you about Ah Tat."

That got his attention. "You know where Ah Tat is? He's supposed to go to the shop today, but they all say he didn't turn up. Not answering his phone also."

"He attacked me on Saturday," said Jess. "Had a knife and everything. I guess he didn't tell you?"

There was a brief silence. The silence of shock, thought Jess—or the silence of someone who had just been found out? After all, Jess had witnessed Ah Ku's participation in an attempted murder. He might want to get rid of her, too, especially if he intended to try again with Sherng.

Ah Ku had said he'd only done it because of Ah Ma. It wasn't clear what reason he'd have to want to off Sherng now, given he seemed resigned about having to move the temple. But what did she actually know about his motives?

"Where do you want to meet?" he said finally.

Jess let him choose. She was half expecting him to invite her to his house, which would have been awkward, but it seemed he didn't want to bring this business home any more than Jess did. He asked her to come to a kopitiam not too far from his place, though it wasn't till the weekend that he'd be able to meet.

They fixed on Saturday, which meant there was a whole working week to get through before Jess would be able to see him. But it was a weirdly peaceful week—the quietest she'd had since she'd arrived in Penang, untroubled by gods or ghosts or portentous dreams. Maybe the blood Jess had spilled while fighting off Ah Tat had propitiated the Black Water Sister for a time.

She avoided looking at the cut on her hand. It tended to send her mind down unfruitful avenues, wondering what the god might want from her next—and when she would come to demand it.

Jess arrived early for her meetup with Ah Ku. The kopitiam was in a corner lot at the end of a row of shophouses, open to the elements on two sides. The tiled walls were covered with posters advertising beer, soy milk, bird's nest and various other delights, as well as the mandatory Chinese painting of a herd of horses. There was a row of hawker stalls selling noodles, rice, kuih and drinks along one side of the restaurant. A TV affixed to the wall was playing some K-drama, subtitled in Malay.

It was busy, occupied by people eating breakfast. Jess went for a table on the five-foot way outside the kopitiam, positioned so nobody in the restaurant was likely to overhear their conversation. The stall nearest the entrance kept up a helpful din, with noodles sizzling in a giant wok, plates clattering and the uncle and auntie chefs addressing customers in a continual hoarse bellow.

She was already sweating by the time she sat down. She wouldn't be getting any relief from the ceiling fans spinning away indoors from here. But the table was visible from the restaurant and the road. Half of Penang would see it if anything . . . happened.

Not that she thought anything would happen. It was Sherng who'd been worried about that. When, sitting in that Starbucks, she'd told him about Ah Ma and the god and everything that was going on, he said:

"You need to talk to your uncle. He's a medium, he's the temple caretaker, he knew your Ah Ma best. If anyone is going to know what can be done about this Black Water Sister, it'll be him."

Jess had hesitated. If she called Ah Ku, she might have to speak to Ah Kim, who was probably still mad at her and her mom. But Sherng misinterpreted the pause.

"I can make sure you guys are watched," he said. "If you're concerned about safety. Razak can be there. He can make sure your uncle doesn't try anything."

Jess gave him a weird look. "I'm not worried. He's my uncle."

Sherng gave her a weird look right back. "He drugged you and tried to implicate you in a murder."

"Yeah, but that's because Ah Ma made him do it."

Sherng frowned. "How old is he, fifty? You can't blame his mom for everything he does."

"You haven't met my grandmother," Jess had said.

She looked around now, checking the faces of the people around her and in the street. She'd told Sherng that she was meeting up with Ah Ku but she didn't need backup; she would let him know how it went. It didn't look like he'd sent Razak to watch her.

Which was a good thing. It would have been creepy if Sherng had ignored her refusal of his offer. She was perfectly safe, Jess told herself.

She tried not to look at the two red tablets affixed to the pillar by the table. There was a small ledge under each tablet, for offerings. The altar at the top was dedicated to Ti Kong, the Jade Emperor; the one at the bottom to Tua Pek Kong, the God of the Earth. The gods followed you everywhere on this island.

Ah Ku was only five minutes late. Jess stood and waved to get his attention.

"You want a drink, Ah Ku?" she said. "I'm going to order another teh peng." She'd drunk most of her iced tea. The glass sat in a little pool of condensation on the table.

"Don't need," said Ah Ku. He sat on the plastic chair Jess had pulled out for him. "What's this about Ah Tat disturbing you?"

Jess told the story, watching him—though she left out the part about having been on her way to see Ng Wei Sherng.

Ah Ku didn't look especially surprised, but he didn't look alarmed, either, as Jess assumed you might if you'd been found out in a plot to murder your niece. He mostly looked disapproving.

"This Ah Tat, he hangs out with these no-good kids," he said. "They all talk big, want to show off. They're always going to this so-called medium. He's just a samseng who likes to act tough. Must be he advised Ah Tat to do. After you spoiled the god's altar, Ah Tat was very scared. I gave him charms to fix his luck, but he was still worried. The medium must have told him he must take revenge on you to make the god happy."

Ah Ku sighed. "Stupid boy! He doesn't know ah, the god doesn't need his help to take revenge? If she wants to punish, she'll punish. He doesn't need to interfere. Don't worry. I'll scold him. He won't disturb you again."

It was like Jess had told him Ah Tat had borrowed her phone and smashed the screen, rather than that he'd come at her with an actual knife. Annoyed, she said, "There's no need to scold Ah Tat. He's not going to try again after what we did to him."

Ah Ku looked amused. "You know how to scare Ah Tat ah? Small girl like you!"

"It wasn't me who scared him. It was the god." Jess said deliberately, "Black Water Sister." The name made her heart thud against her chest, a hollowness opening in her gut.

But its effect on Ah Ku almost made up for that. He stared, horror wiping his face clean of all other expression. "What?"

"She helped me deal with Ah Tat," said Jess. "He's fine, but he'll be avoiding me from now on." In the ensuing silence she flagged a waiter down and ordered a second teh peng. "You sure you don't want anything to drink?"

"What do you mean?" said Ah Ku, waving the waiter away. He lowered his voice. "The god came?"

Jess waited till the waiter had gone back into the restaurant before saying, "Black Water Sister wants me to be her medium. That's why I needed to talk to you. Can you tell me about her?"

Ah Ku twitched at the god's name. "Ah Ma told you what she's called?"

Jess nodded. She'd been wondering about the name. "Why is the god called that? She died where the temple is now, didn't she? In a forest." She thought of the pond in the garden temple, crowded with dozy terrapins. The water had been more of a cloudy brown than black, but maybe at night . . . "Is it because of the turtle pond?"

"Pond? What pond?" said Ah Ku. "The temple is in Air Itam mah. Air hitam is Malay, means—"

"Black water." The prosaic explanation startled a laugh out of Jess. "Right. I should have guessed."

Ah Ku gave her a look of reproof. "You're in this situation and you can still laugh? You don't know only. This is very serious. How do you know the god has chosen you to be her medium? You had a dream or what?"

"Yes," said Jess, after a moment. "I had a dream about her. I went to a temple and they told me it meant she wants me as her medium."

Ah Ku ran his hands through his thinning hair, looking troubled. "Cham, cham, cham. Gone case already. I thought the god wanted to punish you after you spoiled her shrine, but I didn't realize this is how."

"Is it a punishment?" said Jess, genuinely curious. She knew how she felt about the affair, but she'd thought Ah Ku might be more positive. "The temple told me it's a blessing."

"What temple? Who told you?"

"It was Master Yap's temple in Balik Pulau," said Jess. "Master Yap talked to me through a medium."

"Oh, it's the god who said, is it?" said Ah Ku. "This point, you must ask humans, not gods. Any medium can tell you it's not an easy life. Some more, this big sister . . ." He shook his head.

"What?" said Jess. "Is she worse than other gods?"

Her uncle didn't answer. He cast his eyes down, looking troubled.

As they sat in silence, the waiter came back and put Jess's teh peng on the table. Ah Ku started fumbling for his wallet, but Jess had already got some change out in preparation. She paid before Ah Ku could.

She cut off his objections, saying:

"Ah Ku, I need your help. All of this—gods, ghosts, spirits—I don't understand. I'm fighting for my life and I don't *know* anything."

Tears rose unexpectedly to her eyes. Her first instinct was to hide them—but Ah Ku struck her as someone who didn't like seeing girls cry. As embarrassing as it was, she let a tear roll down her cheek before wiping it off on the back of her hand.

"No need to cry lah," said Ah Ku, goaded beyond endurance. "It's not so bad. When I was sixteen I already started dancing Kuan Kong. You look at me. I'm OK what."

"But this god is different," said Jess. "Right?"

As Ah Ku hesitated, she said, "I need to understand her. I need to know how to get away from her."

"If she chose you, there's no such thing as getting away," said Ah Ku.

Master Yap had said the same thing. But Jess felt a kick of disappointment in her chest, as though, unbeknownst to her, it had been harboring a secret hope that Ah Ku would have a solution if she only asked.

After a moment he said, "If it's a big god, it's not so bad. One of the high gods, like Kuan Kong, they're not so violent. Their intention is good. They have more power, spiritual power. So it's simple. If it's a ghost, that's different. In a way, easy also. You go to the temple, ask for a charm, can chase the ghost away already.

"But this big sister, she's not a ghost. She's not a god like the high gods. She's in-between. Being her medium is very difficult. Only someone like Ah Ma can handle."

"Because Ah Ma was tough?" said Jess. What was it Dad had said about Ah Ma? *Things other people don't dare to do, she can do.*

"Because she had no choice," said Ah Ku grimly. "You think if she can choose, she'll pray to such a spirit? Ah Ma was scared of the big sister also. But what to do? No other god can help her."

"She was sick, yeah, I know," said Jess. "But why—"

"Sick what sick!" said Ah Ku. "She was angry. Ah Ma had a hard life. Not like you. Your mother and father take care of you, right or not? Nobody looked after Ah Ma. Because she was poor, she was a woman, people didn't treat her well. She didn't like that. She wanted to give them back."

Jess blinked. "Wait, what? I thought Ah Ma became a medium because the god healed her when she was sick."

"Your mother said, is it? She won't know one lah. Your mother stayed with Ah Chor. Hardly saw Ah Ma back then."

"It wasn't my mom," said Jess. "Ah Ma told me she had snake disease when she was young. She almost died, but the god saved her. She said that's why she had to serve the god."

Ah Ku looked wrong-footed, like he'd been caught doing—or rather, saying—something he shouldn't.

"Ah, correct, correct," he said hastily. "Ah Ma had snake disease. Forgot already. It was before I was born, that's why."

"You didn't forget," said Jess. "Ah Ma lied to me, didn't she?"

Ah Ku wasn't a great actor; his face said everything Jess needed to know. Still he made a valiant attempt. "No, no. Ah Ma is your grandmother. Where got she'll lie to you?"

"Ah Ma would definitely lie to me," said Jess. "She did, if you remember. At the temple? She told me we should get Ng Wei Sherng to pray to the god and then she tried to kill him?"

"That one is because she knew you wouldn't understand."

"Why did Ah Ma become the god's medium?" said Jess. "What did she want that the god could give her?"

But she knew. Even as she spoke, she knew. Ah Ku had already told her the answer.

"She wanted revenge," said Jess. "Against who? Ng Chee Hin?"

Surrendering to the inevitable, Ah Ku said, "If it was that bastard, long time ago he'd be settled already. The god is very effective. That's why Ah Ma served her for so many years. Even after she passed on, she still has to jaga the shrine."

His voice cracked. To Jess's shock, she saw he was crying.

In a panic, she shoved her hand in her back pocket and found a grubby tissue. "Do you want . . . ?"

But Ah Ku declined it, producing his own pack of tissues.

"Even after she died, she has no chance to rest," he said. "She's forced to stay in this world so she can serve the god. It's pitiful, you know or not? Ah Ma has children to pray to her, but because of this, end up she is like a hungry ghost only." He dried his eyes without embarrassment, blowing his nose in the same tissue when he was done.

"Ah Tat is a small boy. He doesn't know anything also," said Ah Ku. "Actually, I'm happy you did the god like that. Nobody else is willing to fight her. Now you destroyed the altar, there's no reason for Ah Ma to stay here anymore. She can move on to her next life. Whatever happens to the temple, the court case all that, she doesn't need to worry. It's not her problem."

"Right," said Jess acidly. "Because it's my problem now."

Ah Ku didn't pretend to fail to understand her dissatisfaction. "If it's not yours, whose problem should it be? You're Ah Ma's granddaughter. Your mother is her eldest child. By rights you should help Ah Ma. You didn't go and see her when she was alive, but at least you can help in this way."

"Oh, you've got to be kidding me," said Jess in English. Switching back to Hokkien, she said, "You want to blame me for not visiting Ah Ma? I was living in a different country!"

"You all came back for holidays what," said Ah Ku. "Got time to go to Cameron Highlands but no time to see your grandmother. If you know how to respect, you will visit. Don't need to give this excuse or that excuse."

Jess was about to point out that she had yet to reach the age of majority the last time she'd visited Malaysia while Ah Ma was alive. But a fleeting expression in Ah Ku's eyes gave her pause. It was a gleam of self-satisfaction.

Jess was being played.

Focus, Teoh, she told herself. What was Ah Ku trying to distract her from?

"You haven't told me who it was Ah Ma wanted revenge against," said Jess. "If it wasn't Ng Chee Hin, who was it?"

While Ah Ku hesitated, she ran through what she knew about Ah Ma's life.

The difficulty was that Ah Ma was the kind of person who accumulated nemeses. In fact, almost the only concrete things Jess did know about her were her enemies. Ng Chee Hin. The scrap-rubber-selling boyfriend who had dumped her after leading her into a life of petty crime. The husband who had beaten her and left her with babies to raise. Ah Ma loathed babies, Jess knew that from the dreams . . .

There was the answer, staring Jess in the face. She might not know much about the facts of Ah Ma's life, what had happened, whose names had belonged to which faces. But she knew about the *inside* of it. She knew what Ah Ma had been willing to show her.

And what Ah Ma had held back.

"It was Ah Kong, wasn't it?" said Jess. "She wanted to get back at him."

Ah Ku looked comically dismayed, like Wile E. Coyote realizing the ground had run out beneath him. "What?"

"Ah Ma was scared of Ah Kong," said Jess. The dreams of Ah Ma's life in those stifling rooms had given her that much insight. Those nights she hadn't dared think of, throughout the interminable days . . . "She would have hated that. She must have hated him for how he treated her. So she asked the god to help. That's the truth, isn't it?"

Ah Ku's expression was all the confirmation she needed.

"What did the god do to Ah Kong?" said Jess.

There was a long moment where she wasn't sure if Ah Ku would answer, or if he would push back his chair and leave.

"You must understand," said Ah Ku finally. "It's not she held a grudge. Because he did her, she must do him back. It's not like that. She was a lone woman. She had to stand up for herself.

"No man will let his wife take his children and go off. Some more Ah Kong, when he's angry, he'll anyhow behave. If Ah Ma tried to leave him, he'll don't know do what. It was, what they call? When the robber comes but you whack him and he dies, you won't go into the lockup. It's OK, because he tried to do you first. They call what?"

"Self-defense," said Jess, in English because she didn't know the term in Hokkien.

Ah Ku nodded.

"'Self-defense,'" he repeated. "That's why she prayed to this god to help her. Because this big sister is not like the other gods. Not nice, the way she died. When a spirit dies like that, because someone killed them, they're very fierce. Very hungry. Some more she has no children, nobody to pray to her."

"Hungry," said Jess. She felt a little dizzy. The noise of the kopitiam was starting to get to her. Her stomach turned at the smells—the savory aroma of food cooking in oil, the rich stink of the drain running along the five-foot way. "For offerings, or . . . ?"

"People," said Ah Ku.

Jess's mouth was dry. She didn't feel up to drinking her tea, but she scooped out the ice and sucked on it, grateful for the chill on her tongue.

"I thought Ah Kong died in an accident," she said.

Before Ah Ku could answer, they were interrupted by a disturbance. The uncle and auntie at the stall near their table had paused their frenetic activity over the wok. Customers craned to see what was going on.

A small group of police officers were mounting the steps to the five-foot way. Ah Ku had barely turned to look when he was surrounded.

One of the police officers said to him, in Malay:

"Mr. Lim, it's been a long time." His voice was courteous, even pleasant. "We'd like you to come to the station with us, please. We want to ask you some questions."

Ah Ku seemed to recognize him too.

"Eh, Sergeant, what is this?" he said, somewhat less pleasantly. "I'm having tea with my niece and you come and disturb me. You cannot simply kacau decent citizens for no reason."

The police officer's expression didn't change. It was attentive, with a slight smile in the eyes—the smile of a man who holds all the cards.

"I'm an inspector now, Mr. Lim," he said. "We have a warrant. You look well. You haven't been taking any substances, have you?"

You couldn't see Ah Ku's bandaged ribs beneath his T-shirt, and Ah Ku was evidently in no mood to share.

"At my age, if I'm not in hospital, considered good enough already," he said. "'Substances' all that, you should know I stay away from that nonsense. You can come to my house and look also. The only substance you'll find is kelulut honey."

"Our investigations show that's not the case," said the inspector. "My colleagues found five hundred grams of cocaine at your residence this morning."

Ah Ku jumped up, bristling with hostility. The police officers shifted on their feet. "What are you saying? I don't have that kind of thing. You're trying to bluff me, is it?"

"We can show you the evidence at the station," said the inspector. He added as an afterthought, "Your wife and child are there also. You can ask them. They were there when our team found the drugs."

Jess had never seen Ah Ku so furious. He had been calmer helping Ah Ma attempt a murder.

"Whatever you found, it's not mine," he said. "I where got time to deal in that kind of business? I hardly left the house for the past few weeks. Went to the temple to pray only. I have an injury, the doctor told me to rest at home. Must be somebody went and put those things there while I'm out . . ."

His voice trailed off as the timing sank in.

Jess knew what was in his mind when he turned to look at her, because the same thought had come to her. If Ah Ku had been set up, it had been by someone who knew he was going to be out of the house just then.

Ah Ku looked incredulous, but not like a man betrayed by someone he had trusted. It was more like he'd stepped on a length of garden hose and found it was a cobra.

Jess said, "Ah Ku, I didn't . . ."

She checked herself. Who even started up with the denials before they were accused, unless they were guilty?

Ah Ku only said, "Ah Yen's supposed to be starting uni in October. She got a scholarship. Your cousin!"

"Mr. Lim," said the inspector, "will you come now? We don't want to bother people here, yes?"

He nodded at the uncle and auntie at the stall next to their table. They had stopped cooking and were watching, their faces stern. They met his eyes but didn't smile back.

"You can pay first," said the police officer. "Or maybe your niece can help settle the bill."

"I didn't do it," said Jess. Her voice sounded small, younger than she was. "I didn't know, Ah Ku."

But her protestations sounded hollow, even to herself. If she was part of a scheme, it wasn't one of her devising—but she knew whose it was.

Ah Ku wasn't listening anyway.

"I'll come," he said to the police officers, and they led him away, a thin man in a faded T-shirt, squinting in the sun. Jess kept her eyes on him as they got in the car and drove away, but he didn't look back.

"HEY," SAID SHERNG, "how did it go?"

"What the *fuck* did you do?" said Jess.

Sherng didn't react to getting sworn at. He only said:

"Where are you?"

This bastard, thought Jess. *This useless fucking bastard* . . .

She hadn't known what to do after the cops took Ah Ku away. There was nowhere at home she could have the kind of conversation she was planning to have with Sherng. It had to be private, but there was going to be shouting.

So she'd walked, passing restaurants and sundry shops and homes where, behind rusting grille doors, old men in white singlets watched Cantonese dramas. She'd ended up on a quiet road of old buildings that hadn't yet been turned into hipster cafés or boutique hotels.

She was sheltering from the sun under the five-foot way, standing between a shuttered shophouse and a joint with saloon doors like a bar in a Western movie, full of men playing mahjong. She wasn't too worried about being overheard by them. They were engrossed in the game and making a lot of noise themselves. It was unlikely their first language was English, anyway, and her American accent would probably make her speech impenetrable to them.

"You said I should talk to him, he leaves his house for the first time in weeks, and suddenly he gets busted for drug possession? You must think I'm an idiot."

"Wait, what happened?"

"The cops came and took my uncle away," said Jess. Humiliatingly, her voice cracked. She pressed the butt of her palms into her eyes until the prickling died down.

"While you were talking?" Sherng said. "That's crazy. Are you OK?"

He wasn't convincing. There was something half-hearted about the performance, as though even Sherng didn't really want her to fall for it.

Jess blew out a breath. "I *am* an idiot for trusting you. Was this the plan all along? To get at my uncle through me? Is that why you started talking to me that day at the temple?"

"No, I—Jess, there was no plan," said Sherng. This time he sounded sincere. Jess could almost believe he meant it. "I didn't even know the medium was your uncle, until . . ."

His voice trailed off.

"Until I tried to kill you," said Jess. "And you decided to use me to resolve your property dispute. Well, you've done it. You fucked my uncle over. There's nobody left to stand up to your dad over the temple. My uncle's family never did anything to you. My cousin might lose her scholarship for something that has nothing to do with her. But I guess you wouldn't worry about that!"

Jess heard Sherng take a deep breath.

"I know you're upset," he said. "And I know he's your uncle. But is it really so implausible that he's a drug dealer? He used drugs on you, remember? It's not like he's squeaky clean. The fellow has a record."

Even amidst her anger, that gave Jess pause. Could Ah Ku have been lying about the drugs? It wasn't like she knew what he got up to, how he made his money, what lines he was willing to cross and why.

But she remembered his face when he'd heard about his family being detained—the rage and fear. It had been the terror of one seeing the foundations of his life threatened.

"No," said Jess with absolute certainty. "He didn't do it. They said they found the drugs at his house. He wouldn't have left that kind of thing there, not with my cousin at home. That's why it was convenient that I got him out of the house, right? So you could arrange for the stuff to be planted while he was out."

"Look, I didn't arrange this, OK?" said Sherng. "Even if I wanted to get your uncle in trouble, it's not like I could simply send out police to take him down. You think I'm the chief of police or what?"

"I didn't think you did it," said Jess. "I think your father arranged it. You told him about me and he saw how he could use me."

Sherng didn't say anything. Jess went on, "But why? It's not like your father even needed me to fuck with my uncle. He could've done that all on his own. You didn't need to go through that whole rigmarole. Pretending you wanted to help, pretending you gave a shit! I even held off on going public with those fucking photos of the accident at the construction site, because I thought you might actually do something about it."

"I am going to do something," said Sherng defensively. "I've just been busy, it's been CNY and—"

An unpleasant thought had struck Jess. "What happened to Ah Tat when your guy took him away? He's not going to be found in a monsoon drain or something, is he?"

"What? No! My staff let him go." Sherng blew out a frustrated breath. "Jess, forget about your shitty relatives. Your grandmother doesn't care about you and your uncle was enabling her. What they made you do . . . if they knew anything about my father, they knew that was putting you in insane danger. You keep calling me his son, but you don't know what that means. I'm his *only* son."

"I don't care what you—"

"You should care," said Sherng. "Listen to me."

Something in his voice made her shut up—an urgency that she hadn't heard in it before.

"I'm my father's only son," Sherng repeated. "Everything he's worked for depends on me. I'm not just his kid. I'm the future of his business. You think he cares about Rexmondton Heights? That's small change in comparison. *I'm* his biggest investment.

"Pa's not what people think. He's willing to forgive a lot. He's not interested in picking fights. But what you tried? That pissed him off. You don't want to know what would have happened if I wasn't standing up for you."

"You're right," said Jess. "I don't want to know what horrible revenge he was planning because you ratted me out."

She'd finally pushed Sherng too far.

"You are being a real bitch right now," he said.

"Oh, I'm a bitch?" said Jess. "You exploited my trust to entrap my uncle, and I'm the bitch? That's fucking rich!"

"Jess—"

"My uncle may be a gangster and my grandmother a nutcase, but you're a grown man who doesn't have the balls to stand up to his dad," said Jess, in a vicious whisper so as not to startle the men playing mahjong. "Enjoy the rest of your life kissing Daddy's ass, Sherng. Don't bother calling me. And if your dad wants to try coming for my family again, I'm going to the tabloids and telling them I aborted your illegitimate child. So he'd better stay the fuck away from me!"

She jabbed at the screen and hung up while Sherng was still protesting.

She stood looking at her phone, breathing heavily. It was tempting to fling it into the drain.

But Jess remembered she had passed a phone shop while looking for somewhere to make the call. She would go get a new SIM card before she cut up her current card.

Adrenaline was pumping through her bloodstream as she walked back to find the phone shop. People passing her looked her in the face, then averted their eyes quickly.

She didn't know what they saw, but it didn't matter. It wasn't like she knew them. It was strange being out by herself, anonymous. Nobody's daughter or granddaughter or niece or cousin.

She had never screamed at anyone like that in her life—never let loose to the extent she had, ripping into Sherng. Sharanya was always hassling her about her reluctance to express her feelings: "What's so wrong about being a normal human being with emotions?"

But Jess didn't want to think about Sharanya just then. She shoved the memory down.

She didn't need anyone to tell her she used humor to mask her emotions and puncture serious conversations. She did that on purpose. She had a lot of good reasons for being repressed.

Being constantly low-level furious was nothing new. But letting herself show how mad she was—lifting her self-control long enough for the fury to escape—that was a novelty.

It felt good.

Of course, now Jess had really screwed herself over. She knew Ng Chee Hin was out to get her and she had lost herself the one ally who might be able to make a difference to that.

Still.

"Fuck that guy," said Jess aloud.

She was a couple of blocks away from where she remembered the phone shop being when a storefront display caught her eye. KEDAI BARANGAN SEMBAHYANG, proclaimed the sign above, followed by a row of Chinese characters and finally, the English version: PRAYER GOODS STORE.

Behind a window huddled some statues of Kuan Yin, their eyes downcast. Each one had a hand upraised, the third finger touching the thumb.

Jess pressed her palm against the glass.

She could imagine her mom praying to Kuan Yin for help getting Jess out of her predicament. The Goddess of Mercy was popular in Penang. She was an easy god to worship—compassionate, unvengeful.

But Jess needed someone with sharper edges than Kuan Yin. A smaller, meaner god.

Staring blindly at the glass, she saw in her mind's eye Ah Ku's back as the cops had led him away, the construction worker Kassim's face when he'd looked at her photos of the collapsed scaffolding. It all led to one place.

The Black Water Sister might be terrifying and murderous, but at this point the main thing she seemed interested in fucking over was Jess's life. Ng Chee Hin's sphere of malign influence was far wider.

And he was human. A rich, powerful, criminal human, but human nonetheless. That meant Jess might have an edge, resources and abilities he wouldn't be expecting—so long as she was willing to do what Ah Ku and Master Yap and Ah Ma had all said she had no choice but to do anyway. To accept her fate.

It would be a sacrifice of her very self. She understood the Black Water Sister well enough now to know that the god would demand nothing less.

But would it even be much of a loss if Jess surrendered herself to the service of the goddess? It wasn't like she had much of a life left to her. She'd probably just been dumped. She hadn't gotten any of the jobs she'd applied for. So long as she was bound to her parents—and it was a lifelong bond—she would never be able to do the things she wanted, pursue her passions, be open about loving women. How much worse of an indenture could the Black Water Sister's service be?

It didn't matter anyway. Jess had a responsibility to fix the mess she'd made. And she knew one person who could help her do it.

She went into the shop.

NINETEEN

Jess went to the office the next day, even though it was a Sunday. She spent a few hours ferreting through the cabinets, but she didn't get anywhere.

On Monday she waited till the office manager had finished her morning gossip with the accounts guy before sidling up to her desk.

"Puan Salmah," said Jess, "do we have any files on the Rexmondton Heights project? You know, the Sejahtera Holdings development in Air Itam."

"Wah, you're very pro talking bahasa now ah!" said the office manager. Kor Tiao's staff treated Jess with tolerant kindness, like she was someone's child who'd been brought in for Take Your Kids to Work Day. Jess guessed she effectively was, though the condescension was a little grating given in her first couple of weeks at work she'd revamped and updated their website, a job the last guy hadn't managed in the three years he'd been with the company. "Rexmondton Heights . . . that's the one you and Mr. Teoh went the other day, right? What files you want?"

"I want to contact the developer," said Jess. "We need to get a release signed by Sejahtera so we can use the photos I took."

"Oh, like that you can call our contact," said Puan Salmah. "Let me find for you the details." She started typing and clicking around on her computer. "When you went to the development that time, you got see anything?"

Jess blinked. "See anything? Like what?"

Puan Salmah lowered her voice. "They all say that place is haunted. Somebody died there, long time ago. People say got a lot of accidents on the site. One of the construction workers almost died."

Jess was fairly sure her face hadn't given anything away. "Jeez. Where did you hear that from?"

"Got a lot of rumors," said Puan Salmah. "You didn't have any experience?"

"Nah," said Jess. It was surprisingly easy to pretend she was amused. It was like playing herself, as she'd been before Ah Ma had started talking to her. "We're lucky we didn't go at night, I guess."

"They should call the bomoh to cleanse the site," said Puan Salmah. "Never mind how nice it is, who wants to live in a haunted condo? Nah, here."

She wrote down a number on a Post-it note and gave it to Jess. "The name is Miss Cheah. Nice girl. You call her."

There were customers in the showroom, so Jess couldn't retreat to the bathroom to make a call as she had done before. She ended up in a corner of the parking lot, huddled under the minimal shade of a starveling tree. At least it was quiet, even if it was blisteringly hot.

She'd played around with the voice-changer app she'd installed on her phone yesterday, so she wouldn't get slowed down by having to figure out how it worked. She dialed the number Puan Salmah had given her and waited, squinting in the sun.

"Wei?"

"Can I speak to Miss Cheah, please?"

"Yes, speaking."

Jess had heard the voice before. It took her a moment before her brain supplied the image—the woman at Tau, quietly cleaning up the mess Jess had made. What had Sherng called her? Pooi Mun.

Sherng had said she was his dad's executive assistant. Jess should have expected this.

She was extra glad she'd paid for the app.

"Miss Cheah, I'm calling from the Moral Uplifting Society about Dato' Ng's donation," she said, in her best attempt at a Malaysian accent.

She didn't want Pooi Mun to link her back to the girl who'd met up with Sherng; it would look too suspicious. She didn't want them tracing her back to Kor Tiao and his company either. Her original plan had been to say she was representing the construction workers on the Rexmondton Heights site, but there was too much of a risk they'd refuse to take her call. A recent press report on Ng Chee Hin's charitable activities had given Jess a better idea.

"My boss asked me to call you. We want to discuss how to allocate the funds," she said. "Is Dato' Ng available for a meeting this week?"

"Your boss is Mr. Tai, is it?"

Had the article mentioned a Mr. Tai? Jess couldn't remember.

"Yes," she said recklessly.

There was a long pause. Unease uncoiled in Jess's stomach. She wiped the sweat off her upper lip with her sleeve.

"Mmm," said Pooi Mun finally. "Must be this week ah?"

No indication so far that she'd recognized Jess's voice. That was promising.

"We're getting requests for the funds already," said Jess. "Mr. Tai wants to settle it quickly. We could do next week if—"

But Pooi Mun was already talking. "For expedited meeting, usually requires purchase of five units, total price is hundred fifty ringgit. But because you're a charity, I can give you discount. For three units, I can book you in to see Dato' Ng on Thursday six thirty p.m., or next Wednesday eleven a.m. Three units is only ninety ringgit."

"I—what?" said Jess. "Units of what?"

"Oh, Mr. Tai didn't tell you?" said Pooi Mun. "It's a chlorophyll drink, one unit is five hundred ml. It's very good, health drink. Mr. Tai said it helped clear his acne."

Jess wondered if she'd somehow hit her head and blacked out during the call. She seemed to be missing some vital context.

"I'm sorry, I'm new, so I don't really know how all of this works. Did you say we have to buy chlorophyll to see Dato' Ng?"

"For expedited meeting," Pooi Mun corrected her. "If you don't mind waiting, that's a different matter. If you don't want to buy the chlorophyll, next slot is . . . end of April, I can see he's quite free."

"End of April? That's two months from now!"

"Dato' Ng is very busy," said Pooi Mun.

"Why does he need to sell chlorophyll for the chance to meet him?" said Jess, baffled. "Isn't he a multimillionaire?"

"You want to see him in April, or this week?" Pooi Mun's tone was frosty. "It's up to you, miss. If you want this week, I take cash or Maybank2u."

Oh. That made more sense. Ng Chee Hin's executive assistant was running a side hustle. Pooi Mun was evidently even smarter than she looked.

"I'll pay," said Jess hastily. "Thursday evening would be great."

"You WhatsApp me the payment confirmation, and then I'll book in with Dato' Ng," said Pooi Mun. She gave Jess the number she was to WhatsApp. "My desk is outside Dato' Ng's office. You can pick up the chlorophyll after your meeting."

The voice-changer app wasn't going to deceive Pooi Mun in real life. If she sat outside Ng Chee Hin's office, it didn't sound like Jess was going to be able to avoid an encounter, but at least she could avoid prolonging it to pick up chlorophyll she didn't even want.

"Uh, I'll have to leave to get to an urgent appointment after the meeting," said Jess. "Could you ship the stuff to me? I'll pay for shipping, obviously."

Pooi Mun was pleased to assist. "Send me your address. I can arrange."

"Cool, thanks," said Jess. "Appreciate it. I've been meaning to eat more healthily. This stuff is good for your skin, you said?"

"Oh, it has a lot of benefits," Pooi Mun assured her. "Detox, help you lose weight, fight cancer. Many clients come back and make repeat order. After you try, if you want more, you Whats-App me. For repeat client, I offer discount."

"Sounds great," said Jess. "I'll be sure to let you know."

THE NEXT STEP was to use the supplies she'd gotten from the prayer goods store.

Jess wasn't sure where to start, so she looked up instructions. The internet proved worse than useless. The first few pages of search results consisted of web pages set up by Western pagans, offering wholly unsuitable template prayers. Addressing her target audience as "Blessed Ancestor" or starting off by giving praise to the Sacred Universe would have been a total failure to read the room.

She waited till it was midnight and everyone was asleep before she set up in the bathroom adjoining her bedroom. She put the joss sticks she'd bought in a glass she had smuggled up from the kitchen, arranged oranges on a plastic IKEA plate and poured Chinese tea from a thermos into a mug. A Chinese teacup would have been better, but she didn't know where Kor Kor kept those.

She felt like the only person awake in the world as she struck a match and lit the joss sticks. She sat back on her heels when she was done, watching the joss sticks send thin scented curls of smoke to the ceiling.

She didn't have a picture of Ah Ma. She'd have to do the best she could with what she had.

Jess crossed her legs, getting comfortable on the bathroom floor. She closed her eyes and brought up an image of Ah Ma. A woman translucent in the sunlight, shifting between ages, the only unchanging features her bone structure and a pissed-off expression.

Jess focused on the image. It was kind of like doing yoga—having to tense muscles she hadn't known she had, trying not to forget to breathe.

Her mind's picture of Ah Ma grew clearer and clearer, until she could see all kinds of small details she hadn't consciously registered. The flaking skin on Ah Ma's thin lips, the fine hairs in her eyebrows, the wiry texture of her hair, the mole on her chin . . .

The Ah Ma in her mind opened her mouth, showing small, yellow teeth. She spat, in a voice trembling with rage:

"You *bad child*!"

Jess opened her eyes and saw her grandmother, the fluorescent light shining through her.

"Ah Ma," said Jess.

THE FIRST THING Ah Ma did was kick over the mug of Chinese tea.

At least, she tried. The mug wobbled. She growled and drew her foot back again. Jess grabbed the mug.

"It's for you, but if you don't want it, that's fine," she said. She paused. "Wait, how come I can see you?"

But Ah Ma was too busy swearing at her in Hokkien to answer.

"You want to give me offering, give XO better!" she snarled.

"We don't have XO," said Jess. "If you want some, I can get it next time—"

"You give XO also I won't drink," snapped Ah Ma. "How can I accept offerings from you? Your own family you're willing to betray. You pray to any god also, they won't want to listen to you!"

"Ah Ma, I need your help," said Jess, but Ah Ma wasn't listening.

"I thought you're a good girl. I thought you made friends with Ng Chee Hin's son is because you want to help your family. How I know actually you wanted to help them? They bully your uncle also you don't care. It's because they gave you money, is it? Or you helped them for free, because you like the boy?"

"I don't like boys," Jess pointed out. "You know that."

"You're not ashamed ah? Your uncle is in the lockup," said Ah Ma. "You know what the police are like or not? Even if he didn't do anything, they will beat him unless he gives them money. Where got your uncle has money to give? He doesn't sell drugs. Long time hasn't done already. He doesn't like that kind of business. Fixing cars, you think can earn a lot ah? Some more he has a daughter going to university. But you don't care about Ah Ku or Ah Yen. You're selfish, like your mother only!"

Jess kept her face fixed in a pleasant expression, though it was starting to ache.

"You've seen Ah Ku?" she said. "How is he?"

"He's in prison. You think very comfortable ah?" Ah Ma tried kicking the plate of fruit Jess had piled up for her, giving it all she had. Two oranges rolled off the plate, catching up behind the toilet.

"Were Ah Kim and Yew Yen there too?" said Jess. "The police said they took them down to the station."

"Went home already," said Ah Ma. "They wanted to stay with Ah Ku, but he told them to go. Even if they sit outside his cell, what can they do? If the police catch you selling drugs, you're dead, you know!"

"I know," said Jess. It was pretty much the only thing she knew about Malaysian criminal law. Every flight she'd been on to Malaysia had taken care to remind passengers that the punishment for drug trafficking was death. "That's why I called you. I want to save Ah Ku."

"Save him?" scoffed Ah Ma. "You're the one who got him in trouble in the first place."

"I know," said Jess again. "I trusted Ng Wei Sherng. That was my mistake," she added, raising her voice; Ah Ma was eager to explain what an idiot Jess had been to do *that*. "This was Ng Chee Hin's plan and his son helped him. I can deal with them and get Ah Ku out of jail, but I need your help."

"Oh, you want to fight Ng Chee Hin now?" sneered Ah Ma. "Last time I asked you to do, you don't want. Now you want to call me to beat that bastard for you?"

"I was going to ask Black Water Sister, actually," said Jess. "But I thought I'd get your advice first. You're the one who knows her best."

The name of the god pricked her tongue on the way out. Jess felt a twinge at the back of her neck, where the god had left her mark on her.

But it was worth the discomfort. She had shocked Ah Ma out of her fury. The ghost stood staring down at her.

"What?" said Ah Ma.

"I'm going to offer her a life," said Jess. She paused, letting surprise and doubt color Ah Ma's expression before she said, "My life. If she helps me in return. That's what you did, isn't it? You promised to serve her, if she helped you handle Ah Kong."

Ah Ma said sharply, "Ah Ku told you that, is it? He shouldn't simply talk about other people's business."

"What did you have to do to get the god to help you?" said Jess. "Did you just ask?"

Ah Ma looked her over, as though Jess had surprised her. Jess half expected her to start laying into her again, or storm off without answering.

Instead Ah Ma said, "You want to kill that useless bastard, is it?"

Jess looked away under her gaze. "I'm not—all I want to do is scare him off. Get him to leave Ah Ku alone."

But the memory came of her standing over Ah Tat with his knife in her hand, dark exhilaration thrilling through her blood. It would have been easy to use the knife.

"What happened with Ah Kong?" said Jess. "What did the god do to him?"

Ah Ma squatted, bringing her face closer to Jess's. The hair tangled over her ears was dark again, but her face was neither young nor old. Her skin was smooth, but her shoulders were rounded, weighed down by care. She could have been twenty-five or forty-five.

"Ah Kong died in an accident," said Ah Ma. "He was riding his motorbike and a car hit him. He died on the road there. No chance to go to hospital also. The driver of the car was OK. Hardly damaged the car."

Her voice was calm, her face expressionless. "Ah Kong, half the time if he's awake, he's drunk. Knowing him, sooner or later this kind of thing will happen. That's what everybody said."

Jess wasn't sure what Ah Ma was trying to tell her. "So the god had nothing to do with it?"

"It was the god who caused the accident," said Ah Ma. "Ah Kong was very lucky. All his life, no matter how useless he was, somehow it turned out OK for him. If not for the god, he would have lived until very old. But this big sister is clever. The way she did it, nobody can know. You believe or not?"

Jess stared. She couldn't read Ah Ma's face, didn't know what to think. If Ah Ma had been praying for her husband's death, it would have been natural for her, an uneducated woman, to take the accident as the fruit of her efforts—the gift of a vindictive god.

Yet the god was real. She could take control of your body, give you the strength to strangle a man, or stab him. Jess had felt that.

But could the god move the hand of fate? Nudge a speeding car so it crossed paths with a man on a motorbike?

What Jess thought of as her own mind—a rational place, under her control—said no.

But there was a deeper part of herself that she didn't control—a roiling sea just beneath the level of consciousness, from which unsuspected creatures emerged sometimes in dreams. And that part said maybe.

It was tempting to suppress that part, pretend it wasn't there or didn't matter, as she had done all her life. But if she was going to fight Ng Chee Hin—and win—it was that part of herself that would do it. The part where the god lived.

"Believe or don't believe, it doesn't matter," said Ah Ma, taking Jess's silence for incredulity. "That's the power of the god."

"Why didn't you ask her to run a truck into Ng Wei Sherng, then? Why use me?"

"Because the god wanted to send a message to that useless bastard," said Ah Ma. "Ah Kong was different. Nobody needs to know. This one, she wanted Ng Chee Hin to understand she is the one who did it. Then only he won't go and disturb her altar.

"But now no altar already." Ah Ma straightened up, cracking her back as if it ached, though it wasn't like she had a real spine.

"Ah Ku was thinking of moving the temple," said Jess. "He said the other gods wouldn't mind."

"Correct. I told Ah Ku also," said Ah Ma. "For the other gods, any place is OK, so long as the feng shui is good. It was only this big sister who needed to stay near the tree there. Now there's no point for the temple to be there. It's bad luck only. Without the altar, what is the god except a hungry ghost?"

She gave Jess a sharp look. "You better watch out. After you spoiled the shrine, you think the god will want to help? You'll be lucky if she doesn't curse you!"

"Oh, she'll help," said Jess.

There was something strange about her voice. It was like the words rode on the breath of another person.

Ah Ma's head whipped around. She looked at Jess as though she had noticed something new about her and was outraged not to have registered it before.

"Your aura is not the same already," she said accusingly. "What happened to you?"

"I went to consult a medium," said Jess. "At Master Yap's temple. Do you know it? It's in Balik Pulau."

Something flickered in Ah Ma's face. It was gone before Jess could pin it down, but if she had to guess, she would have said it was unease.

"Balik Pulau? I don't go there. Too far." Ah Ma was attempting nonchalance, not very successfully.

"I called out to you, you know," said Jess, watching her. "When I was there. You didn't hear me?"

It was interesting having Ah Ma be the one who was trying to catch up for once. Jess was enjoying the novelty.

"Where did you go after I destroyed the shrine?" she asked. "Were you running away from the god?"

Ah Ma bristled. "Why I need to run away for what? I'm not the one who spoiled the shrine. If anybody needs to run away, it should be you! But no point you run also. The god will sure catch you."

The scolding seemed to work off some of Ah Ma's bad temper. She said, less grumpily, "I went to see your cousins. Ah Ku's children, Ah Yen they all."

Jess blinked. "Oh. You found another medium?"

It should have been a relief. Instead it made her feel curiously desolate. She didn't want to be anybody's medium, but it wasn't great feeling replaceable either.

"I tried to talk to them. But they couldn't hear," said Ah Ma. "I even went to KL and talked to Ah Ling, the older girl. Like nothing like that. If I can go to UK, it'll be different. The boy, Ah Ping, out of all the children he's closest to me. He can see spirits also. If I can talk to him, he'll sure hear me. But even going to KL already was not easy. I was so tired. Felt sick, like I had fever like that. I had to go back to the columbarium to rest."

"What columbarium?"

"The place where they put me lah. They burned the body already, but the ashes they put there," said Ah Ma. She paused. "I heard you call Ah Ma, but how can I come? If I come also, I can't help you. You think I can fight Tai Seng Ia? He's one of the biggest gods. If I try to fight him he will straight off wallop me!"

Ah Ma looked *guilty*.

Jess hadn't been prepared for this. Nothing Ah Ma had said or done previously suggested she felt she owed anything to Jess.

"You went to see Tai Seng Ia for what?" said Ah Ma. "I went off already what. You got what problem to ask him about?"

Jess noted Ah Ma's tacit admission that she was a problem worth seeking divine help to resolve.

"There was the god," Jess reminded her. "I was scared of her. I thought Tai Seng Ia could help. But the medium there told me there was nothing to be done. He said the god wants me to be her medium."

Ah Ma nodded, as though Jess was only confirming something she had already guessed. "Makes sense."

"Does it? I wrecked her shrine!"

"When I came back from KL, I was thinking, 'How come I feel so bad?'" said Ah Ma. "I talked to you when you're in US also and I was OK. The big sister sent me to you, but why? You didn't help me protect her temple also.

"Then I realized. Must be she didn't choose you for Ah Ma. She chose you for herself. She wanted me to bring you to her."

Ah Ma paused. She seemed to have more to say, but was having difficulty bringing it out.

"If I knew," she said finally, "I wouldn't have taken you to the temple. But it's too late now."

It was the closest she'd ever come to getting an apology from Ah Ma, Jess realized. An idea struck her.

"What if I leave Penang?" she said. "You said you couldn't go too far from the columbarium. She needs to stay near the tree in the temple, right? So if I went far enough, she wouldn't be able to follow me."

The look Ah Ma gave her was all the more withering for its lack of malice. "If you tried before, maybe can. Now cannot already. Now you yourself let the god in. True or not?"

Mr. Sim's hands around her throat, with all the Monkey God's preternatural strength in them. Ah Tat coming at her with a knife.

I had to, Jess wanted to say. *I had to do it, or they would have killed me.*

But there was no point. It was like a little kid protesting, "It's not fair!" Life wasn't fair. That was how it worked.

"How can you tell?" said Jess. She remembered what Ah Ma had said earlier. "Is it something about my aura?"

"Because you can see Ah Ma," said Ah Ma. "Even though this time I haven't opened your eyes also. The god is inside you already."

Jess lowered her eyes. It wasn't like she would have left Penang to flee the god anyway, she told herself—it was easier to think about that than to linger on what Ah Ma had just said. She needed the god.

"You can ask the big sister for help," said Ah Ma. "But are you sure or not you want what she has to give? She's hungry, you know. Scaring that bastard won't be enough for her."

The look in her eyes was distant. "Ah Ma gave her Ah Kong's soul, but even that wasn't enough. She wanted more. But it's not easy to kill. If you're angry at the man, if you can imagine his face when he dies, then only you can do it. After that time, with Ah Kong, I didn't want already."

A memory floated to the surface of Jess's mind. "What about the scrap rubber guy?"

The effect of this was startling. Ah Ma jumped as though she'd stepped on a live wire. She stood for a moment, her mouth working soundlessly, before she sputtered, "Ah Ku told you what about him? How does he know? Who told him?"

"Ah Ku didn't tell me anything. It was my mom." Jess peered at her. Ah Ma had gone old, white-haired and gaunt, her lips drained of color. "Uh, are you OK?"

"Your mother knows?"

"Knows what?"

"You don't pretend to be stupid," said Ah Ma. Joke was on her; Jess was genuinely being stupid. "She knows about that useless bastard!"

Jess couldn't understand why Ah Ma was so shocked. Ah Ma must have known Ah Chor might tell Mom about her erring mother's liaison. It was clear Mom's grandmother had held Ah Ma up as an example of what not to do.

"Yeah. Why wouldn't my mom remember the 'useless bastard'? She remembers you going off with him," said Jess.

Her brain registered what she was missing before her mouth caught up.

That useless bastard. Jess was talking about the scrap rubber guy, the faithless loan shark boyfriend of Ah Ma's hardscrabble past. But Ah Ma only ever used that term for one person.

Jess's jaw dropped.

"The scrap rubber guy was Ng Chee Hin," she said. "Ng Chee Hin was your *lover*!"

Ah Ma was having a realization of her own. Comprehension, then regret, flashed through her eyes in rapid succession. Her face closed down. "What are you talking about?"

If Ah Ma hadn't powered through life on sheer aggression, maybe she would have learned subtler tactics. As it was, she was better at hectoring than lying.

"Is that what this has all been about?" said Jess. "You've been trying to get back at your ex?"

"You're wrong already. You think I'm so sensitive?" said Ah Ma, abandoning denial. "Man is like that, very fast they lose interest. I knew. When that bastard didn't want me anymore, I didn't make noise. I went off and found my own house. Even after Ah Ku came, I never asked him for money.

"The police came and asked me about that bastard, you know?" added Ah Ma. "Promised me this and that. When promise didn't work, threatened this and that. Even then I didn't open my mouth. He cannot say I simpan dendam.

"But when he tried to take the temple land, when he said the god must go off somewhere else—then I wasn't happy. I followed the god is because of him in the first place. Now that useless bastard wants to get rid of her shrine? Please lah! He didn't want to marry me. Even when he made so much money, one sen also he didn't give me. After all that, I still gave him face. But he's not willing to respect me back. That's why I had to stay, cannot move on to the next life. He must learn."

Jess was only half listening. Something about what Ah Ma had said niggled at her. *Even after Ah Ku came, I never asked him for money.*

Ah Ma had been pregnant with Ah Ku when her husband died. She'd gone to her lover with a big belly. "She didn't even wait to give birth first!" Mom had whispered, scandalized.

No way, thought Jess incredulously. But she didn't doubt the epiphany that had broken upon her. It settled in her mind like a fact, like something she had always known.

It was amazing she hadn't thought of it at the time Mom was telling her about Ah Ma's life—but then, there had been a lot to process in that conversation. What *wasn't* amazing was the fact that Mom hadn't raised the possibility herself. Mom would never breathe the suspicion aloud, if it had even occurred to her. She was curiously blinkered about certain matters. Jess should know.

Jess said aloud, "Does Ah Ku know Ng Chee Hin is his father?"

That was whom Sherng had reminded her of when she met him at his café, the reason why he had felt so familiar. The narrow eyes, the gentle bemused smile. Sherng looked like Ah Ku.

Ah Ma froze.

Jess could tell Ah Ma was considering denying it, but then she looked at her. Jess could practically hear her think, *It's only Ah Min.*

"Nobody knows," said Ah Ma shortly. She didn't bother veiling the menace in her voice when she said, "You want to tell people, is it?"

"Does Ng Chee Hin know?"

Ah Ma raised her chin. Her hair was black again. She looked vulnerable, a defiant young woman, no older than Jess.

"If he doesn't want me, means he doesn't need his son," she said. "If he knows, he'll sure want to keep Ah Ku. But I'm the mother. I'm the one who gave birth to him. That's why. If you do bad things, you'll have bad luck. You make all the money also doesn't mean you'll be happy. You look at that bastard! He's so old but he has one son only, that Indian boy."

Jess saw that this had been Ah Ma's revenge on her ex-lover—a revenge so purely satisfying even murder could hardly compare. She had deprived him of a son. There was probably worse you could do to a man like Ng Chee Hin, but not a lot worse.

Of course, Ah Ma *had* been planning murder as well.

"Is that why you wanted to kill his son—I mean, Ng Wei Sherng?" said Jess. "So Ah Ku could inherit?"

Ah Ma started scoffing, "No lah! Nobody knows he's the son. How can he inherit?"

But her voice trailed off. She looked thoughtful.

"Nowadays they can use DNA test to find out the father, right?" she said.

Jess got to her feet. Her limbs protested at the position she'd forced them into for the past hour. She'd sat for so long in the warm bathroom that her T-shirt was damp with sweat. The place was a mess, and she'd need a minor miracle if she was going to dispose of the joss sticks and ash without anyone noticing.

It had all been worth it. She wasn't sure how she'd use it yet, but Ah Ma had given her a potent weapon.

"I'm going to see Ng Chee Hin on Thursday," she said. "You want to come?"

TWENTY

Jess didn't know what someone who worked at a Moral Uplifting Society would wear. Her experience of Chinese religious institutions suggested a polo shirt would be a safe bet, but given she didn't own any polo shirts, she decided to go formal. She was visiting the fifth richest man in Malaysia, after all.

Most of her wardrobe was in storage, but she had access to a single formal outfit she'd bought for job interviews: a charcoal-gray sheath dress and a black blazer.

When she saw herself all dressed up in the mirror, she looked like a stranger. A serious person, capable of doing a real job. Someone whose life consisted of more than getting jerked around at the whims of gods and spirits.

Even Ah Ma thought she looked good.

"Not bad ah," she said. "But what for you did your hair like that?"

It had caused huge drama when Jess had come home from a clandestine appointment at the hair salon with an undercut and a pompadour bleached platinum blonde.

Mom acted like the world had come to an end. She could hardly have responded worse if Jess had come out as a lesbian.

"How are you going to find job like that?" she'd wailed. "Or get married? The man won't want you, the boss won't want you. You look like—like a *bad girl*!"

Ah Ma was unlike Mom and Kor Kor and the rest of them in that Jess could answer her question with the truth.

"I told you, Ng Chee Hin's PA knows what I look like. I've got to distract her, or she's going to work out something's up."

Jess had done some internet research on the art of disguise. The series of YouTube explainers by a former CIA agent had been particularly helpful.

Pooi Mun had encountered Jess as a teary girl with black hair past her shoulders. She wouldn't be expecting to see Jess in the self-possessed young woman with blond cropped hair Jess now saw in the mirror.

Admittedly the hair didn't really fit her invented backstory, any more than it matched the corporate drag. But it was attention grabbing—and that meant, hopefully, Pooi Mun would have less attention to spare for recognizing Jess.

Ah Ma was skeptical. "You cannot just buy a wig meh?"

"It has to be convincing," said Jess.

Which was true. But the other reason she'd done it was she secretly, unironically loved her new hair. It made her feel brave, edgy. She looked *hot*.

Sharanya's going to freak out when she sees it, said Jess's treacherous brain.

Her mind closed over the thought, burying it. She couldn't afford to dwell on the past. She had to focus on the plan.

She did her face with her mind carefully blank. Pooi Mun had seen her with minimal makeup on, so she went for a heavier look than she'd normally wear for the office. Then she put large plastic-rimmed glasses on her nose.

The finishing touch was the switchblade. She slipped it inside her blazer, just in case.

"Good," said Ah Ma, who'd helped her source the knife.

Sejahtera Holdings was headquartered in a towering office block in glass and steel, more like something you might find in New York or Hong Kong than somewhere in Penang.

Even Ah Ma was impressed. She fell silent as they crossed the pristine floors of the lobby, hung over with the rarefied hush belonging to the holy or the extremely expensive. There was a giant mural on one wall, depicting heritage trades of George Town—rattan weavers, signboard carvers, bookbinders and makers of paper effigies of the gods.

Jess averted her eyes from this last. It was ridiculous to see omens everywhere when she was literally being accompanied by a ghost. The mural must have been Sherng's idea.

"So ugly," said Ah Ma, staring disapprovingly at the mural. "Why didn't they paint it white?"

Jess felt a surge of sincere affection for her. If she had had a material hand, Jess might even have pressed it.

It was six o'clock and a trickle of office workers flowed through the security gates. They had that flattened, preoccupied look people had when they'd already mentally time-traveled to the future where they were chilling out at home in front of the TV. But Jess's hair still got some startled side-eyes as she went up to the reception desk.

"I'm here to see Dato' Ng," she said. She smiled, then regretted it. Was it too American to smile at the receptionist, like asking, "How are you?" without expecting a real answer?

The receptionist gave her a weird look, but her eyes got stuck on the hair—so it was working. The more people stared at Jess's hair, the less they'd be looking at her face.

"You're from what company, Miss . . . ?"

"Miss Khoo," said Jess, picking a surname at random. "I'm from the Moral Uplifting Society. I've got a meeting with Dato' Ng at six thirty."

Her trepidation grew as the receptionist tapped away on her keyboard, frowning a little. Had her phony Malaysian accent given her away? Or did the receptionist somehow know who she was? Maybe Sherng had distributed her photo to everyone in his dad's conglomerate and now the receptionist was notifying security to come throw her out.

If she was lucky. The kind of security detail Ng Chee Hin employed probably didn't stop at kicking people out of places. If Jess's experience was anything to go by, they engaged in a lot of actual kicking.

"Here's your pass," said the receptionist, breaking into Jess's anxiety spiral. "Dato' Ng's office is on the thirty-eighth floor. The elevator is there." She pointed.

When Jess was past the security gates, it became clear why the receptionist had had to point. Only one of the row of elevators went directly to the thirty-eighth floor.

Half of one wall inside the elevator was covered with reflective glass. Only Jess was mirrored in it. Ah Ma, standing next to her, was invisible. They didn't speak.

Beads of sweat formed on Jess's top lip, despite the air-conditioning. In the cold light, her ridiculous hair and giant glasses looked woefully inadequate as a disguise. Her stomach was sour with fright.

To make herself brave, she thought of Ah Ku, the time she'd dropped him off at his house after destroying the god's shrine. The awkward kindness with which he had pressed the money into her hand, the feel of the worn blue-green bills between her fingertips. She had to get him out.

There was another reception desk on the thirty-eighth floor, with shelves on either side, displaying beautiful, expensive-looking things—porcelain vases, wood carvings, ornate silverware.

Behind the desk was a wall of glass. Through it could be seen Penang. Clusters of red and orange roofs were interspersed with greenery, with the occasional high-rise rearing up among the squat white buildings. In the distance could be seen the cloud-wreathed humps of hills and a sparkling gray sea.

The view made something clench in Jess's chest; it felt like sorrow, or love. *If Sharanya could see this*, she thought despite herself. But then Ah Ma said:

"She sit there beside the window all day, must be so hot. Kesian only that girl."

The woman at the desk didn't look uncomfortable. As at both of Jess's previous encounters with her, Pooi Mun came off as someone who had never sweated in her life.

How did the saying go? *Lord, grant me the confidence of a mediocre white man.*

"You said what?" said Ah Ma, the only spiritual authority listening.

Jess was already striding forward, a smile plastered on her face—the smile of someone who was looking forward to her discounted liquid chlorophyll.

"Good evening. I have an appointment with Dato' Ng," she said. "Miss Khoo from the Moral Uplifting Society."

Her palms were sweating as Pooi Mun looked up from her computer. Would she notice that Jess's voice was different from the voice she'd heard on the phone? *It must have been some issue with the line*, Jess imagined herself saying.

But even as Pooi Mun raised her eyes, they veered off to Jess's hair. She blinked rapidly, as though someone had thrown sand in her eyes, before the professional blankness fell over her face again.

"Moral Uplifting Society," she echoed, looking back at her computer. "Yes, six thirty. I thought Mr. Tai was coming?"

"He couldn't make it today, but he asked me to represent him." The YouTube videos had said to distract your interlocutor, engage their attention with something other than you. Jess raked the woman over, hunting for something to remark upon.

But Pooi Mun was totally nondescript. Her suit was so boring Jess's eyes skittered over it. Even her hair was tied back with a plain black band.

"I love your watch," said Jess in desperation.

Pooi Mun looked down at her watch in some surprise. It was an analog watch on a black band, innocent of decoration. "What, this watch?"

"It's so minimalist," said Jess. "Very Muji. Where did you get it from?"

Pooi Mun declined to be distracted.

"I don't remember," she said. "Mr. Tai cannot make it? But you all chose this time. You're the lady who phoned me the other day, right?"

"Yeah," said Jess. She had to hold her nerve. "I'm taking over the medical fund, so I'll be administering Dato' Ng's generous donation . . ."

But Pooi Mun was looking at her now, *really* looking, seeing past the undercut and blond hair and the dignified gray dress and the glasses. Jess met her eyes and knew she was fucked.

"Eh, I saw you the other day," said Pooi Mun, her eyes narrowing. "You're the girl at that restaurant, sell tauhu one. Mr. Ng's friend—"

Jess leaned over the desk and said, in a vicious undertone, "You got your ninety ringgit out of me. Does Dato' Ng know what you're doing? How much have you racked up, selling appointments with him?"

She straightened up. Pooi Mun's eyes were wide, but Jess couldn't afford to leave it there. Pooi Mun had to have nerves of steel or she wouldn't be running this racket. There was no way Jess was even in the top fifty most intimidating people who wanted to see Ng Chee Hin urgently, and presumably Pooi Mun had shaken down all of them.

Ah Ma, Jess thought, *if you try, can you knock something off the shelves?* The object nearest to Pooi Mun was a covered yellow porcelain tub, etched with a profusion of pink and red flowers. *Like that bowl thing?*

"You mean the kamcheng?" said Ah Ma. "That big bowl is called kamcheng. Rich people use at their wedding—"

Yeah, fine, whatever you want to call it, said Jess. *Just do it!*

Ah Ma was already by the shelves. She swiped at the porcelain bowl. It wobbled. Ah Ma swore, reached over and pulled, grunting with effort.

"I'd be careful if I were you," Jess said to Pooi Mun as the kamcheng tipped over.

Only the lid crashed on the floor, but it was enough. Pooi Mun whirled around, real fear flashing across her face.

Jess turned and stalked down the corridor. She could see Ng Chee Hin's office. In fact, she could see Ng Chee Hin himself, because the door to his office was made of glass.

He sat alone behind a large desk, lapped about with space and quiet. He was a relatively handsome variation on the average Chinese uncle, wearing a blue collared shirt. He looked older than in the photos Jess had seen online—but of course, he was only a little younger than Ah Ma. He must have been around Jess's parents' age when Sherng was born.

He was hunched, peering over surprisingly fashion-forward

tortoiseshell glasses at his computer screen. He didn't seem to have heard anything, but he glanced up as Jess approached.

Something must have given away the fact she wasn't just some peon, come to ask him what he wanted on his donor's plaque. He started up, suspicion flooding his face.

Jess thought, *He probably has a gun in that desk.*

But her hand was already pushing the glass door open, determination propelling her onward. Ah Ma followed, a cold draft on the back of her legs.

"Good evening, Mr. Ng," said Jess.

"Who are you?" said Ng Chee Hin. "What do you want?"

Jess looked him in the eye. "My name is Jessamyn Teoh. I'm your son's friend. Sherng said he told you about me."

Ng Chee Hin was already reaching under the desk.

"He's going to shoot you," said Ah Ma.

"I'm here on behalf of my grandmother, Oon Bian Nio," said Jess.

She could hear Pooi Mun's footsteps behind her. She'd probably already called security.

Jess talked faster. "You knew her once. She wants to talk to you."

Ng Chee Hin had put his hands back on the desk. "Oon Bian Nio passed on last year."

"Yes. But she's here," said Jess.

She glanced at Ah Ma and deliberately spoke aloud, switching to Hokkien. "How do you want to prove it?"

Ah Ma was riding high from her success with the kamcheng. She went up to Ng Chee Hin's desk and hurled herself at the cup of Chinese tea on it. It toppled over, drenching his keyboard.

Great. They'd antagonized him already and Jess hadn't even said anything.

"OK, thanks, Ah Ma," she said. "I think that's enough."

"Didn't spill until the computer screen," said Ah Ma regretfully. "Spoiled the keyboard only."

The door swung open behind Jess.

"Dato'," panted Pooi Mun. "Sorry, Dato'! She bluffed me—"

"We just want to talk," said Jess, spreading her hands in the universal gesture indicating weaponlessness. "It's about the accident at the Rexmondton Heights development. And—" She swallowed, but this was her one chance. If it was going to work, she had to play all her cards. "The god called the Black Water Sister."

"The guards are coming now," said Pooi Mun.

"Tell them don't need to come." Ng Chee Hin hadn't taken his eyes off Jess. To her, he said, "You have something to tell me about the problem with the temple there?"

Jess nodded.

"OK. Let's talk," said Ng Chee Hin. "Take a seat, Miss Teoh."

TWENTY-ONE

There was a black leather sofa. Jess perched on it as Pooi Mun left the room. She didn't exactly slam the door as she went, but she closed it with a very pointed click.

"Each of us has the solution to the other person's problem," said Jess. "Your problem is you've got a god screwing with your development. My problem is you put my uncle in jail."

She half expected Ng Chee Hin to deny it. Instead he folded his hands and said:

"Who asked you all to target my son?"

He sounded like a disappointed teacher, except his accent reminded her a little of Jackie Chan. The overall effect was disarming. Jess could feel herself wanting to like him, laugh at his jokes, trust him, even though this was a guy who wouldn't think twice about murdering the crap out of her if she made herself inconvenient enough.

At least she had a ready answer to his question.

"My grandmother did," she said. "She can tell you herself in a second. The god told her to do it. The Black Water Sister, I mean," she added.

"I know," said Ng Chee Hin shortly. She got the impression he didn't like the sound of the name being spoken any more than Ah Ku or Ah Ma did.

He snorted. "You're really like your grandmother, huh? Always talking about ghosts and spirits. I thought Harvard graduate won't believe this kind of thing?"

"I'm surprised you're familiar with my career, Mr. Ng," said Jess.

Ng Chee Hin raised an eyebrow. "My son didn't tell you? I have a very good memory. Especially people who cause trouble for my family, I remember."

His tone was matter-of-fact. Not menacing, because he didn't have to be. Power like his was like a natural law, like the operation of gravity. It didn't need to swagger or threaten. You got out of the way, or you got crushed.

"Oh, I explained that to Sherng," said Jess. A lifetime of deceiving her family in ways big and small had trained her for this. She sounded bright and helpful, not terrified in the least. "He probably hasn't had the chance to tell you, but I saved his life. The god wanted him dead—she possessed me, to try to make me kill him—but I stopped her."

This was a slight massaging of the facts, but she wanted Ng Chee Hin to listen to Ah Ma when her turn came to speak. She had a feeling being told it was Ah Ma who'd personally tried to strangle his son might make him a little less receptive.

Where had Ah Ma gone, anyway? Glancing around, Jess saw she'd drifted to the other side of the room, as if she couldn't stand to be that close to Ng Chee Hin. She was pretending to examine the art pieces on the wall. They were bold blocky paintings of large women in sarongs, vivid-hued and joyful—not really Ng Chee Hin's style. Sherng's hand again.

"If this god wanted to kill my son," said Ng Chee Hin, "why she tried to make you do it? The accident at the site, I hear the worker was possessed. Apparently the spirit made him run under the scaffolding. She is supposed to be a god what. God doesn't need henchman to do things."

"She doesn't," Jess agreed. She found she knew the answer, as sure as if the Black Water Sister had told her. "But if she'd possessed Sherng, he wouldn't have known what was happening. She wanted him to know. She wanted him to be afraid."

Ng Chee Hin's face twitched at that. "What's the god's problem with my son?"

"Why do you want my uncle dead?" said Jess.

"That's why you came to talk to me, is it?" said Ng Chee Hin.

He took off his glasses. She could almost see him deciding to humor her.

Her reason for coming to him was one he could understand and respect, Jess realized. He was taking her more seriously than he would have if she'd simply come to advocate for the construction workers, challenge him on what he was doing to ensure safe working conditions at his development.

Maybe he and Jess weren't so different, after all. She wouldn't have had the courage to confront Ng Chee Hin, knowing what he was under the polish and respectability his wealth lent him, other than for someone bound to her by all the history and debt and mutual betrayals of blood. For her, as much as for Ng Chee Hin, the family bond was incontrovertible.

"I don't have any issue with Barry Lim," he said. "You must understand. I am a businessman. If I decide to do something, it's not because I like the person or I don't like the person. My priority is what is best for the company. I have to think of my business partners and my staff.

"This Barry Lim, if he doesn't bother me, I won't bother him. The problem is he is not reasonable. I am willing to negotiate—even though by law, there's nothing to negotiate also. This land in Air Itam, legally, it belongs to the company. The temple has no right to be there. But we were willing to talk. Your uncle was the stubborn one."

"And because he's being stubborn, you've ruined his life," said Jess.

Ng Chee Hin peered at her, quizzical. "He also tried to attack my son."

"I told you, that was the god's idea. My uncle's a medium. He just does what the spirits tell him to do," said Jess. "Anyway, what about his wife and kids? They didn't do anything."

"If the wife and children suffer, it's because the man is not responsible," said Ng Chee Hin. "Your uncle should have thought of his family. We explained to him also, this is a big development. The government is involved. People will benefit—people need somewhere to live what. If it doesn't go ahead, not only my partners and my company will lose money, we will lose face."

Ah Ma had given up on pretending she wasn't listening and come back over to Jess. She said, "This useless bastard! He can say whatever also. He chose that place is because he purposely wants to insult me. He knew it's my temple back then. You ask him and see!"

Jess didn't really want to ask, but she needed to keep Ah Ma sweet.

"So this was purely business," she said reluctantly. "Nothing to do with the fact that my grandmother was a medium at the temple?"

Ng Chee Hin blinked, nonplussed. "I don't know what your grandmother told you before she passed. But by the time we bought the land, I didn't see your grandmother for a long time already. Penang is an island, there's not much land. The plot is in a good location. Sooner or later it will be developed. If not my company, somebody else will do it."

He added, in a confidential tone, "Actually I held back, to show respect. I let your uncle sue me, didn't rush the process. Until your grandmother passed only, I said, that's enough. But I warned your uncle. He had a chance to clear out and move the temple. He didn't want only. That's why I have to be more drastic. It's not that I want to do. You think I like ah, this kind of thing? If I can avoid, I won't do it."

Jess believed him. Like Sherng, Ng Chee Hin exuded credibility. He gave off an impression of authenticity which, in a man of his age and distinction, came off as something like integrity. She could see how he'd made his way from rubber plantations to highrises, why politicians and civil society leaders might be happy to have their photos taken with him. For a moment she could even understand how someone like Ah Ma, who did not give a shit about anything or anyone, could still be hung up on this guy, lifetimes after they had broken up.

Ah Ma was so angry she had gone all crackly, like the image on a video call when the connection crapped out. She kept going in and out of focus, cycling between the old woman and the young.

"You liar! You want to cheat people only," she told Ng Chee Hin, as though he could hear her. "You call the police to catch my son. You put drugs in his house. You throw him in jail. And now you want to pretend you're so good? Waiting until I die to bully my son, that's called good, is it?"

Ah Ma! thought Jess. *Think of Ah Ku.*

"I am thinking of Ah Ku. I'm scolding this bastard is because of Ah Ku. If it's not for Ah Ku, you think I'll even come into his building?" Ah Ma spat at Ng Chee Hin.

Fortunately for him, ghosts didn't appear to generate actual saliva. He didn't seem to notice.

If you want to help Ah Ku, let me talk to the guy, said Jess.

She said to Ng Chee Hin, "I want to get my uncle out of jail. You want the development to go ahead and make money. It's not going to get completed and it's not going to be successful unless you do something about the god. My uncle's not your problem. She is."

Ng Chee Hin looked at her. "You really believe."

Jess took a deep breath. Whatever she said now, the god would hear.

There was no point in holding back. She was already committed—had been long before she'd even realized it.

"It's hard not to believe," she said, "when the god has made you her medium."

Ng Chee Hin was very still. Jess couldn't read his expression.

"He doesn't know what to think," said Ah Ma.

"How much do you know about the Black Water Sister?" said Jess aloud.

Ng Chee Hin's hand quivered in an abortive movement, as though he had wanted to raise it to silence her. "I know enough."

"Then you should know she's not going to just go away," said Jess. "The workers are unhappy. They've got allies—and they've got evidence. The accident, the safety breaches and the cover-up—it's all going to come out sooner or later. There are already rumors. Even if the authorities decide to stay out of it, even if you're not worried about your reputation, you know what Malaysians are like. You think people are going to want to buy haunted condos? Penang's not *that* short of land."

"You said you have a solution?" said Ng Chee Hin.

"Leave my uncle alone, and I'll get the god to stop making trouble for you. Otherwise . . ." Jess shrugged. "I've heard there's a lot of money riding on the development. You'd better be ready to lose it."

Ng Chee Hin held her gaze for a long moment. Then he looked away, and Jess knew she'd lost him.

"Miss Teoh, I told you, I'm a businessman. I only want to hear about facts. This kind of grandfather stories, I'm not interested. If that's all you have to offer, my answer is no." Ng Chee Hin got to his feet. "Now if you'll excuse me, I have a lot of business to finish today."

"I told you," said Ah Ma. "You think he cares about those Bangladeshis? You should have told him about Ah Ku in the first place."

"Yes, thanks, Ah Ma!"

"I beg your pardon?" said Ng Chee Hin.

"If it's facts you want, there is one more thing you don't know, Dato' Ng," said Jess.

She paused. She'd only have one shot at this.

"I believe what you did to my uncle was nothing personal," she said, picking her words carefully. "I can see you thought it was the right decision. But to make the right decisions, you need the right information. And you're missing a vital fact."

Ng Chee Hin was starting to get impatient. "What are you talking about?"

"When my grandmother came to live with you, after my grandfather died, she was pregnant," said Jess. "Wasn't she?"

It must have sounded like a non sequitur. Ng Chee Hin looked startled. "Even this kind of thing your mother's not ashamed to tell you?"

Jess waited.

"Your grandmother wasn't honest," said Ng Chee Hin. "She wanted to get married, but she didn't even tell me she's pregnant with the other man's son. Later only I found out."

"So you left her," said Jess. "Didn't you think it might be hard for her, having to bring up two kids by herself?"

Ng Chee Hin shrugged. "Your grandmother was a tough lady. I knew she'll be OK one." There was a grudging note of admiration, even fondness, in his voice.

Jess saw that in a way Ah Ma was as real and present to him as Jess was, even if he couldn't see her and didn't believe she was there.

It was a disturbing thought to have about your own grandmother and a man who, in more than one sense, could have been your grandfather—but maybe they really had been the love of each other's life. Maybe that was what true love meant: a bitterness that stayed on the tongue when everything else faded.

Ng Chee Hin's tribute did nothing for Ah Ma but piss her off even more.

"Ah Min, you let me talk to him," she said. "I'll tell him. We'll see whether he believes or not!"

Jess could feel a swelling pressure from the ghost. It filled the room, an oppressive spiritual energy which stole the warmth from the gold lighting and made the shadows fall askew.

It wasn't exactly pleasant, but whatever Ah Ma was doing was nothing compared to having the god around.

Jess said, "Wait."

Ng Chee Hin's eyes were on her, filled with a new wariness. He wasn't afraid yet. That was good. He was a man in whom fear would turn quickly to anger. "Who are you talking to?"

"I already told you," said Jess. But Ah Ma would have her turn. Jess didn't want her on the loose—yet.

She leaned forward.

"If it was me," said Jess, "if it was my girlfriend, I would have wondered. I would have wanted to be really sure about the baby. Whether he actually was another man's son."

It took Ng Chee Hin a moment to get it. When it clicked, his face changed, the eyes turning hard and bright as longan seeds.

Jess had thought she was scared before. Now she realized she had merely been nervous.

Ng Chee Hin laughed, with that blank furious look in his eyes. "Your mother told you this nonsense, is it? You know how many women try to say I'm the father of their children? Women I never met before also."

"But you knew my grandmother," Jess pointed out. "Did you never wonder if the boy was yours?"

"What is there to wonder? She said it's the husband's son," said Ng Chee Hin. "If afterwards she wants to say something else . . ." He shrugged. "I told you, she's not the only one who wants to profit from me."

"Ah Min," said Ah Ma. *"Let me in!"*

"Fine," said Jess aloud. "Your turn."

She closed her eyes and released her grip on herself, letting the boundaries slip between her mind and Ah Ma's.

It was easy to do now that she knew what it felt like to have the god take over. It was almost soothing, giving up responsibility for what would happen next.

When she opened her eyes, it was on a world that bore two faces. To Jess, Ng Chee Hin looked like a stranger—a terrifying old uncle she was forced to sass when all she wanted to do was get out of his office.

But Ah Ma saw in him the ambitious young man she had loved. Till now, Jess would have said neither Sherng nor Ah Ku looked anything like their father. Through Ah Ma's eyes, she saw the resemblance for the first time—the hidden sweetness lurking around the hard line of the lips.

Ah Ma's smoker's voice said from Jess's mouth:

"Where got I profit from you, Ah Hin? If I wanted your money, I won't go and let my granddaughter ask for it. I'll ask you myself when I'm alive, no?"

Jess half expected Ng Chee Hin to react with skepticism—mock Jess, challenge Ah Ma.

Instead he seemed to turn to stone. Only his eyes were alive in that statuelike face, alive with horror.

Jess had forgotten he belonged to a different generation. In many respects, he lived in a different world, one where it would be as foolish to be skeptical about the supernatural as to doubt the existence of cancer. And unlike Jess, he had known Ah Ma when she was living. He recognized her voice.

"Bian Nio?" His voice was gravelly with dread.

"Look so surprised for what?" said Ah Ma. "My granddaughter told you I'm here. You didn't believe? You should know if you do me wrong, you won't get rid of me easily."

"Where got I do you wrong?" Ng Chee Hin jerked to his feet. He was speaking Hokkien now. It was like Jess wasn't even in the room. "I let you stay in my house until you found your own place. You think how many men will do what I did? You have no reason to be angry at me."

"You bully my son, you think I won't be angry?" said Ah Ma. "Your own child also you can catch and put in jail. What kind of man has the heart to do that?"

"He's not my son," snarled Ng Chee Hin.

"You don't believe? You go do DNA test and see!"

"You were pregnant already by the time you came to my

house," said Ng Chee Hin. "How do you know your husband is not the father?"

"I know," said Ah Ma. "I gave birth to the boy myself. I will know one."

"You told your son I'm the father?"

Ah Ma sniffed. "You think I'm so proud ah, want to tell people my son's father is a samseng?"

"You told your granddaughter."

"That one she guessed herself," said Ah Ma. "I never told anybody."

There was no relenting in Ng Chee Hin's face. Jess waited for Ah Ma to speak up, argue, persuade him of the truth, but moments passed in silence.

It became apparent that Ah Ma wasn't going to say anything else. She was stewing over the fact that Ng Chee Hin hadn't given in already. No wonder they hadn't lasted as a couple.

Jess was still present enough in her own body that it wasn't hard to speak.

"Just look at him," she said in English. "Look at him properly. He looks like Sherng. It's obvious once you know."

Ng Chee Hin flinched at the sound of Sherng's name.

"Don't talk about my son." Fury contorted his face. "Get out. You've said enough already. I don't want to hear anymore. You go now and don't come and disturb me or my son again.

"For your grandmother's sake, I'll give you face. You stay away, you don't bother me, and I won't bother you. You want to disturb me some more, you'll regret it. I've been patient, but this is too much already."

If it had been up to Jess alone, she would have turned and run. But Ah Ma kept her in place. Ah Ma was dead; she had nothing to lose.

"You think it's so easy to chase me away, Ah Hin?" said Ah Ma. "You ask my granddaughter. She prayed to so many gods to get rid of me also, it didn't work. Why we came is to help Ah Soon. So long as he's suffering, I won't go. I'll sit here and bring your office bad luck. If you treat our son like that, what else can I do? I am the mother."

Ng Chee Hin was breathing heavily, his face brick red. He looked like he might punch her, or blow her head off, if he did have a gun within reach. It was Ah Ma who kept Jess's neck straight, her eyes fixed on his.

"If he's really my son," he said, "why you never told me until now?" His voice sounded like he'd been swallowing broken glass.

Ah Ma put her hands on the desk, which would not have been Jess's choice. She would have preferred to avoid any sudden moves.

But Ah Ma was pleased, Jess realized. In fact, "pleased" was understating it. In a way, this was what she had been waiting for her entire life.

"I didn't tell you," said Ah Ma, with vicious satisfaction, "because I *hate you*."

There was a suspended moment when Jess really, genuinely thought she was going to die. Then:

"I see," said Ng Chee Hin.

The words were like the pricking of a blister. The tension oozed out of the room.

Jess felt her body relax. Ah Ma had been worried too.

"Then there's nothing to fight about anymore," said Ng Chee Hin. "I do you, you do me back. I don't owe you anything already."

"What about my son?" said Ah Ma, but Ng Chee Hin said:

"I'll settle Barry Lim. By tomorrow he'll be back home. All charges dropped. Enough or not?"

"I got ask you for money meh, even when he's small?" said Ah Ma. "I never asked you for anything. I never said anything against you. I left you alone. All I'm asking is you leave our son alone also."

Ng Chee Hin moved in a way that suggested he was about to hold the door open for Jess. She was loath to jump in given how badly it had gone last time, but . . .

"How do we know we can trust you to do it?" said Jess.

Ng Chee Hin reached under his desk without answering. Jess shrank back, but he only took out a phone. He squinted at it, holding it away from his face the way old people did, and dialed a number.

The call was in Cantonese, which Ah Ma didn't understand any better than Jess. She could only distinguish Ah Ku's name. The person on the other end of the line started arguing, but Ng Chee Hin cut them off, speaking brusquely, and hung up.

"Tonight itself they'll let him out," he said in English. "Tell his wife to go to the police station to pick him up."

He pulled open the door with an air of finality.

Jess wondered if Ah Ma was going to say anything to him— fling out some defiant last word—but she was quiet as Jess passed through the door. It was only once they were down the corridor that Ah Ma said, *Bastard*. She sounded almost wistful.

BY THE TIME they stepped out of the elevator into the lobby, it was past eight, according to the clock hanging over the reception desk. The desk itself was empty, the receptionists gone.

Jess was at the security gates, waving her pass ineffectually over the sensor, when a voice said behind her, "You're having problem, ma'am?"

Jess started, stifling a yelp. The man who'd addressed her was thin and dark-skinned. He held a mop in one hand, but in the other he was already raising his pass. The security gate beeped, swinging open.

"Thanks," said Jess, feeling stupid. She stepped through.

"Working late, is it?" said the cleaner affably.

"Uh, yeah," said Jess.

She glanced at her phone. No panicky messages from Mom asking where she was. That was good. Jess had told her parents she was going for a job interview. She'd have to tell them it had been promising, they'd kept her for an hour and a half, but in the end they had decided to go for someone with more experience. That sounded legit, if depressing.

The cleaner was leaning on his mop, in a mood to chat. "You must be tired, hah?"

"Yeah," said Jess, inching away. "You're going to be here late? Have a good night."

The cleaner nodded. "My shift is until two a.m. I'll go back and sleep, then wake up eight o'clock to talk to my children before they go to school."

It probably only took around five minutes for Jess to extricate herself, but it felt longer. When she was finally out of the building, she rolled her shoulders, the tension inside her chest easing. The relief was so intense it felt like joy.

It had been light out when she'd gone in, but dark had fallen while she was talking to Ng Chee Hin. It was warm but not hot, a light breeze ruffling her hair. A thick underwater smell, half seaweed, half sewer, wafted from the sea. Gurney Drive was busy, the road almost as bright as day under the street lamps, cars zooming past. But there were no other people around.

"Ng Chee Hin wasn't that bad," she said, like a kid insisting they hadn't screamed after a roller coaster ride.

"Call Ah Ku," said Ah Ma. She didn't seem to share Jess's exhilaration. "Check if the police let him go or not. I don't trust that bastard."

"Ah Ku might not have his phone on him," said Jess.

But she did need to call Ah Kim so she'd know to pick up Ah Ku from the station. Jess had been planning to order a Grab home, but she didn't like the idea of being overheard by the driver. She'd call now.

Through the glass door she could see the cleaner in the lobby, mopping the shining expanse of cream tiling. She stepped aside so he wouldn't see her if he looked up and called the number for Ah Ku's house.

"Wei?"

Jess had braced herself to speak to Ah Kim, but the voice on the line was younger, a girl's voice. Jess said, "Yew Yen?"

"Who's this?" said the voice in Mandarin, cautious.

"It's Jessamyn," said Jess in Hokkien. What would Yew Yen call Mom? Mom was her father's sister. Kor Kor was Dad's sister, so . . . "Kor Kor's daughter."

"I know," said Yew Yen, switching to Hokkien. Jess remembered that not only were they Facebook friends, she was the cause of Ah Ku being busted by the cops and thrown in jail. If Yew Yen might not have immediately recollected who she was a couple of weeks ago, she definitely knew now. "You're calling for what?" Her tone wasn't friendly.

"They're letting your dad out of jail," said Jess. "Can your mom pick him up from the police station?"

"What?"

"Let me talk to Ah Yen," said Ah Ma. She hadn't disentangled herself from Jess yet, so she didn't have to wait for her to agree. Jess found herself saying in Ah Ma's voice:

"Don't need to ask so many questions. Faster call your mother to go get your father. You think the lockup is so comfortable ah, like hotel like that?"

There was a brief shocked silence. Yew Yen said, "Ah Ma?"

Jess covered the phone with her hand. "Warn me before you do that!" she whispered.

Ah Ma was unrepentant. "If I didn't do, she'll hang up on you. At least now she's listening."

Jess rolled her eyes and said into the phone, "Can you ask your mom to WhatsApp me when she's picked him up?"

"That was Ah Ma's voice," said Yew Yen. "Is she there?"

"I can explain later," said Jess. "But I need to get home—"

"Can you ask Ah Ma," said Yew Yen urgently, "what should we do with the idol?"

"What? What idol?"

"The idol of the god." Yew Yen lowered her voice. "Black Water Sister's idol. Ah Tat went back to the temple and found it. He used superglue to fix. He managed to find all the pieces, so it's OK, just cracked only. What should we do with it?"

Jess looked at Ah Ma.

Ah Ma shrugged, feigning indifference. "How am I supposed to know? You're the medium. You ask the god lah."

Jess waited. If she knew anything about Ah Ma, it was that she wasn't good at keeping her opinions to herself.

Sure enough, Ah Ma couldn't resist the temptation to advise. After a moment she said, "Most likely the god will want you to rebuild her shrine near the tree there. If you fix the altar, you'll need an idol."

The memory of the bodhi tree at the garden temple flashed through Jess, the rich smell of earth and leaf fall rising in her nostrils. That smell, the shape of the tree's spreading branches against the sky, the vines rustling in the breeze—they were all mixed up with death, the Black Water Sister's ignoble death as she bled out into the dirt.

Jess wanted to tell Yew Yen to throw the idol away, or bury it. But the god still had her in her grasp. Now, with Ah Ma's prosaic ghost by her side, she felt as safe as she ever would. But tomorrow morning she might wake to find the god standing at the foot of her bed. She'd always be lurking at the edge of Jess's vision, if Jess didn't do something about her.

"Ah Ma says hold on to it for now," she said. "I'll come by tomorrow to check in on your dad and pick up the idol."

"How come the police are letting him go?" said Yew Yen.

Jess hesitated. How much did Yew Yen know about everything? She couldn't see Ah Ku disclosing much more to his kids than Mom had to her. But maybe Yew Yen had picked things up, growing up here, that Jess had had to have explained to her.

"I talked to Ng Chee Hin," she said.

An intake of breath. "And he just let Pa go like that?"

"Well," said Jess. "Ah Ma helped."

Yew Yen was silent.

"Thanks, Ah Min Chee," she said finally.

It felt weird to be called "elder sister," a sign of respect Jess didn't deserve.

"Don't thank me yet," she said. "Get your mom to pick him up first. Don't forget to let me know, OK?"

She hung up and opened the Grab app.

"What are you doing?" said Ah Ma.

"Ordering a taxi."

"Nowadays everything is through the phone," said Ah Ma. "If you don't have the phone, I think you cannot do anything."

Jess made an affirmative noise. Grab was applying surge pricing, but she requested a cab anyway.

She was starting to come down from the adrenaline high of her encounter with Ng Chee Hin. Her feet hurt in the cheap black heels she'd gotten from Bata as part of her corporate drag, and she could no longer see the cleaner in the lobby.

For some reason his disappearance spooked her. It was like she'd dreamed him up.

She thought of home and bed with intense longing as Ah Ma grumbled about young people and technology, sounding for once like a normal grandmother. First a shower, then Jess would slip into soft, faded old shorts and a T-shirt. Maybe she'd watch some Netflix in bed before going to sleep. She could almost feel the texture of the blanket against her bare legs.

The shrill cheep of her phone startled her out of her reverie.

"Who is it?" said Ah Ma, watching her expression.

"Pooi Mun," she said. "Ng Chee Hin's assistant."

"Don't pick up," said Ah Ma instantly. She paused. "Why she call for what? Better pick up."

Jess had gone through the same internal back-and-forth. The phone hadn't stopped ringing. She accepted the call, raising the phone to her ear with a sick rush of anxiety. "Hello?"

"Where are you?" said Pooi Mun. "Are you in a public place?"

"I—what?"

"You must go to the place with a lot of people one," said Pooi Mun. She sounded breathless, like she'd been running—or like she was scared. "Go to Gurney Plaza. You know Gurney Plaza? It's the shopping mall. Turn left and walk. Don't go into any car. Don't talk to anybody."

"What's she saying?" said Ah Ma.

"I don't understand," said Jess. "What are you—"

"You shouldn't have come here," said Pooi Mun. "You don't know ah, who is Dato' Ng? If you told me, I would have warned you. You're a young girl only. You better go now! Go!"

The line cut out. She'd hung up.

A car was pulling up to the sidewalk where Jess stood. The light from the entrance of the building shone on its windows. The car was full of people. Men.

The certainty of having made a hideous mistake settled at the pit of Jess's stomach. She turned to run, to find a well-lit place where she'd be among people, anonymous and safe—but it was too late. The cleaner had come up behind her.

TWENTY-TWO

The cleaner shoved Jess into the car before getting in himself. She fought, screaming her throat raw, even though she knew there was nobody around to hear.

She only shut up when someone hit her—a casual open-handed smack, like she was a naughty child. She sat gasping, her head ringing.

She was hemmed in, with the cleaner on her right and another man on her left. There were two other men in the front. The car smelled of cigarette smoke and sweat.

It was dark enough that it was hard to distinguish the men's features. But then the car passed a street lamp. Orange light washed in, illuminating the driver's face in the rearview mirror. It was Chief Thug, the man who'd beaten up Ah Ku at the garden temple.

They moved out of the street lamp's glow and the night blanketed them again.

Jess was going to die.

She dug her fingernails into the flesh of her thighs, trying to think over the incessant siren wail of her terror.

The self-recrimination was almost as loud. How could she have been so fucking stupid? Did she really think she could beard Ng Chee Hin in his den and walk out unscathed? The plucky girl detective, trumping the gangster with a damning clue.

What an idiot. She was never going to get away with it. She knew too much and she was totally defenseless.

She looked under lowered lids around the car. She didn't see any knives or guns, but that wasn't to say the men didn't have weapons, hidden on them or stashed away.

Nobody said a word. It was like she wasn't even there.

Well, they had her and they were going to do whatever they intended to do. What did they need to talk to her about it for? It wasn't like her opinion mattered. Unless she made it matter.

She cleared her throat. "Where are you taking me?"

She said it in English, sounding as American as she could. Her accent, her tone, said, "I'm the most important person here. I'm not just from a first-world country. I'm from the *biggest* fucking country, the best in the world, and you'd better respect me or we'll bomb the shit out of you, because that's what people like us do to people like you."

The men ignored her. Jess's body stiffened, the muscles going rigid, anger drowning out fear.

She'd dealt with these losers before. There had been more men in the garden temple that first night, the night she'd met Ah Ku and chased off the men who hurt him. She could handle these assholes. She had the forces of the underworld on her side.

Ah Ma! She kept her mouth shut, but the call went out from every part of her, body, mind and soul. She was almost surprised the men didn't hear it. *AH MA! Help me!*

It was like dropping a stone in a well and waiting to hear the *plop*. Waiting while long moments passed, until the truth couldn't be avoided any longer.

Ah Ma wasn't there. Jess was alone.

"I said, where the hell are you taking me?" said Jess, raising her voice.

She sounded more hysterical than authoritative. The guy on her left seemed amused.

"Is OK, is OK," he said soothingly, in Chinese-accented English. He put his hand on her knee. In the dim light she could make out a smile on his face.

Jess looked at her knee with his hand on it as though if she tried hard enough she could detach it from the rest of her body with the power of her mind.

She'd been trying not to think about what they might do to her before they killed her. Her stomach bucked and heaved. Maybe she could puke in their faces. That might put them off.

Without looking up from the road, Chief Thug said crisply, "Jangan bising. Don't make noise."

He didn't need to say "or else." Jess had no leverage here.

The creep shut up, but he kept squeezing Jess's knee. His fingers were knobbly and cold from the AC. So she wouldn't keep staring at them and wishing she was dead, she turned her eyes to the cleaner.

He was looking out of the window. If anyone had asked, she would have said he was the one she wanted to stab the most. Even more than Chief Thug, because he'd smiled at her and made small talk, all the while intending to help murder her. But there was something in his face that she hadn't expected.

He was the weak link, Jess realized. She'd asked about his kids. Were they in elementary school?

"In primary school, yes," he'd said. "They're in Bangladesh."

"You must really miss them," she'd said. It had sounded dumb, inadequate, but she hadn't known what else to say.

To the other men, Jess was nothing more than a warm body to

fuck and dispose of. To the extent that she was a person, she was someone who'd pissed them off, humiliated them when they were doing their job. But she'd talked to this one guy about his life. She'd met his eyes. To him, she hoped, she was a human being.

They drove on in silence. Jess's disorientation subsided a little, though fear was an insistent pulse beneath her thoughts. She hadn't driven around Penang enough to know the streets well, and they looked different at night, but she thought they were going toward George Town.

That was good. There would be people there, witnesses who would make it harder for the men to hurt her. She'd have to be ready to act.

She had her plan clear in her mind by the time they were approaching George Town. As she'd expected, the narrow roads were still busy at this hour, lined with mamak stalls and backpacker bars thronging with people. Pedestrians crossed the road with minimal acknowledgment of the traffic. The car slowed down.

Jess couldn't pause to think or she would get scared. She shifted in her seat to shake the creep's hand off her knee, moving her arm across her front as though to protect herself. Her hand slipped under her blazer.

The creep gripped her knee harder, smiling meanly. That made it extra satisfying when she drove her elbow into his side, grinding the bone into his flesh to make sure he felt it. She lunged for the door, throwing herself over the cleaner and fumbling for the lock.

Shouts broke out around her. Where was the fucking lock? She felt hands swarming up her body and kicked back, her heel smashing into flesh. She hoped it was the creep's face.

She felt the lock under her fingers, flicked it open and grabbed the door handle. She'd managed to get her legs under herself, losing a shoe in the process. Her knees were on the cleaner's bony lap. He seized her around the middle. A small part of Jess's mind noted that he was avoiding touching her chest.

She had the switchblade she'd hidden in her blazer open now. It was no time for regret. She slashed the blade across the cleaner's arm. He yelled, letting her go.

The door swung open, thank *fuck*. Some asshole was holding on to her ankle, but she stabbed at his hand, heard him scream, pushed herself off the cleaner and hurled herself out of the car.

The road slammed into her. She tumbled like a kicked stone. The glow of headlights passed over her, vehicles screeching as they came to an abrupt stop. A chorus of indignant honks rose into the air.

She found herself on her back, looking up into Ah Ma's face.

"You're lying there for what? Run!" said Ah Ma.

Jess didn't have the breath to answer out loud, but luckily she didn't need breath to yell at Ah Ma. *Where the HELL have you been?*

"There was something inside the car there, blocking me," said Ah Ma. "Couldn't go inside. Must be those bastards went and asked a bomoh for help. These foreigners, their magic is tajam— very sharp. Shouldn't get involved with them."

Well, it's too late now, isn't it? Jess pushed herself up, but this proved to be a bad idea. Putting weight on her wrists sent red agony pulsing through her. She stifled a scream.

"Faster run," said Ah Ma. "They're coming!"

Jess looked back, though the movement made her head spin. The car had pulled over. Chief Thug and his men were getting out.

She was on the edge of the road, near the drain. A motorbike passed so close the exhaust gusted over her face, a warm stinking wind drowning out the stench of sewage for a moment. She didn't know where her knife had gone.

"I can't move." Her voice came out in a rough-edged whisper, scraping her throat. "It hurts. Can you help me?"

Jess felt a delicate almost-sensation, like the wind ruffling her hair.

Ah Ma said, frustrated, "Cannot. That thing is still blocking. If I'm a god, it's different. But I'm just a human. How can I fight these foreign spirits? You have to move yourself. If they catch you, you'll hurt even more, you know!"

Jess started crawling, her body screaming in protest.

The shophouses immediately nearby were closed, their shuttered facades like a row of tombstones. But light radiated from the edge of the next block. Some kind of restaurant, not busy, but open. All she had to do was make it there.

It felt like a million miles away, like she was traversing the Sahara, though only a few storefronts lay between her and the restaurant.

When I get to the five-foot way, I'll stand up, she told herself.

She got to a pillar and leaned on it while pulling herself to her feet. But when she tried to take a step, her ankle gave way. Something was wrong with it.

She fell against the pillar, her shoulder catching against the Ti Kong altar and knocking a glass bowl off the ledge. She heard it smash on the ground.

Just what she needed. Another damn god pissed off at her.

As she got up again, something came down on her back, flattening her out. Her face crashed on the tiles. Hands grabbed her, dragging her off the five-foot way.

She traveled bumpily over unforgiving ground. Chief Thug must be holding her, because she couldn't see him—only the other men, following. Their faces showed nothing, neither malice nor anticipation nor dread.

They were taking her to the narrow, ill-lit back passage between the rows of shophouses, where they were less likely to be disturbed at their work. The air coming out of the passage was redolent of garbage, even more than the main road. It smelled like a place where things and people came to die.

There was someone standing at the entrance to the alley. A woman. Jess opened her mouth to scream, beg for help, but then she recognized her. It was the Black Water Sister.

The god met her eyes. Her face was a question—or rather, a statement.

It said, *You can submit yourself to me, or you can meet an ugly death at the hands of these men.*

You can kill, or you can die.

Jess was being borne past the god, a twig on the swift current of a stream. She had a moment to decide.

She'd told Ah Ma she was going to offer the god her service. She'd claimed the role of the Black Water Sister's medium when speaking to Ng Chee Hin. Jess had drawn on the god's powers, tasted her suffering, died her death. Arguably it was a done deal.

But until this moment, she hadn't consciously surrendered. When the god had helped her before, Jess had been in control—or at least, it had felt like it.

This time, she couldn't deceive herself. This would be going to the god, clear-eyed, and saying, *Do what you will with me, and these men.*

Either way—whether she offered herself up to the god in exchange for salvation, or whether she let the men take her, alone, into the darkness of the alley—she was going toward a death. Jess didn't know how much of herself would survive the process, what of her would come out the other side.

But you had to die before you could be reborn.

Jess put out her hand. She was too far from the god to reach her. But she felt the god's answering touch—a cool hand laid on the back of her neck, five fingertips resting lightly on her skin.

Jess's head fell forward.

"Sister," she whispered.

THE MEN TOOK Jess down the alley. The noise from the main road was muffled here. There was nobody around except Jess and the men who were going to kill her.

The god had touched her. Hadn't she? The terrible shining certainty began to recede from Jess.

She'd got it all wrong. The Black Water Sister didn't want her as her medium. The god had been waiting for this all along. This was Jess's punishment for destroying her shrine.

Chief Thug threw her on the ground. Jess rolled instinctively, curling up like a touched millipede, so when he kicked her it caught her in the back and not the stomach.

It still hurt. Jess drew her knees up in the fetal position, whimpering. Blows landed on her upper back, her neck, her shoulder, her ear. The god wasn't going to help her. Nobody was coming. She cut her lip on her teeth and felt her mouth filling with blood. She was going to die.

There were raised voices above her. The men were shouting, quarreling among themselves. She couldn't make out what they were saying. She should crawl away while they were distracted, but she had scarcely formulated the thought when she was hauled roughly to her feet.

Someone shoved her in the back. She staggered over tarmac onto the cracked concrete slabs that covered the shallow drain running along the back of the shophouses. The rich stink of the drain rose in her nostrils.

A man pushed her against the wall. The exposed brick scraped her cheek. He fumbled at the hem of her dress, pulling it up.

"No," said Jess, "*fuck you*." She struggled, trying to pull her dress back down, trying to break free, but she wasn't strong enough.

She heard herself babbling, praying, "Sister! *Sister!* Kill them! Fucking kill them all! Kill me. Let me die. Please, oh God, oh God."

She felt air on the back of her thighs. Her underwear was exposed. The man kicked her legs apart. Jess had never been touched except in love or lust, never fucked anyone she didn't want to. All her life she had been treated as something precious, someone who mattered. Maybe that was why the Black Water Sister was angry at her.

"I'll give you whatever you want," said Jess. She wasn't sure if she was talking out loud or inside her head, but it didn't matter. "Anything. All the blood you want. All the lives. You can fucking bleed these assholes dry. Sister, please!"

A heavy hand held her down. She could hear the man fumbling with his pants, the zipper coming down.

There was no answer to her pleas, from the god or the men. But suddenly a great calm descended on Jess, flattening her fear and anger until it was as if they had never been.

She didn't need to make a big deal of this. It had happened before. Men were like that. They couldn't control themselves. It would be over fast. It wouldn't hurt much, so long as she relaxed. Afterwards, when he had calmed down, things would be better. He would do something nice for her to show he was sorry, like tapau her favorite charsiu for dinner. All she needed to do was empty herself of terror and anger and the will to resist, become a still vessel for his rage. He was doing this because he loved her.

But he doesn't love me, thought Jess suddenly. *He's not—why would he love me?*

He was her husband, came the answering thought. Of course he loved her. That was why she had married him. It hadn't been for money, he never had money even now. She was the one who worked. It was her wages that would pay for the charsiu.

It was like the drive in the dark car, a street lamp flashing past once in a while, illuminating the interior and revealing the passengers' faces to one another. Occasionally there was a burst of lucidity, light washing through Jess's mind and laying its contents bare.

She wasn't alone in her head, Jess realized. There had been no need to call out to the Black Water Sister. The god was here with her, inside her.

With the realization came a sense of her life and the Black Water Sister's, parallel streams running alongside each other until they joined together. For a suspended moment the two of them stood outside time, in the space between the god's past and Jess's future.

Here, they—she—could see everything clearly. The outcome of her past had not been inevitable, just as what was happening to her now could be avoided, quite easily. Before, she had died alone, but now there were two of them, welded into one—dead and alive, flesh and spirit, past and future.

And she didn't have to put up with what was being done to her. *You didn't have to put up with any of it*, thought Jess.

She wasn't frightened anymore. She reached back for the man's hand.

But of course she'd had to put up with it, argued the voice in her head—the god's voice, though it felt like Jess's own. What else could she have done? Left her husband and gone back to her family? Her family would have told her that a woman's place was with her husband. They would have scolded her for making a fuss about a few small quarrels . . .

But now they were dead. And she was still here.

She pried the man's fingers from her neck. He was protesting, but the protests trailed off when she crushed his hand in hers. The bones ground together with a satisfying crunch. The man screamed.

She turned, jerking him forward, pulling him off-balance. He lurched into her. She put her mouth on his jaw as though she was kissing him and bit down until her teeth met bone.

The coppery taste of blood bloomed in her mouth. She spat and pushed the man away, kicking him between the legs so he doubled over.

After you are dead, the boundaries between you and other souls grow thin. She could feel the man's agony. It was divinely irritating, a sensation like picking at a scab.

Without difficulty she took a knife off another man who was coming toward her. She stabbed him in the gut, but something stopped her from making sure of the death. She pushed him gently to the ground and stepped over him to get to the next man, the blood singing in her veins.

She had never felt like this before, in life or in death. No one else had ever offered her such a wondrous sacrifice—these men's bodies for her to break and bloody and use, as hers had once been used; their suffering a banquet for her to pick over at her leisure, their pain a salve for her own unceasing torment.

A great tenderness welled up inside her for Jessamyn, a profound love for this strong young body that would let her do all she wanted. She would do the girl justice. She was going to enjoy the night.

TWENTY-THREE

Jess came to herself slowly.

She was lying in a bed. The air on her face smelled unfamiliar, but it was cool and dry enough that she had to be indoors. She opened her eyes and looked up at a nondescript beige ceiling.

She was in a hospital ward. She turned her head and saw Ah Ma.

"Ah Min?"

For once Ah Ma's image held steady. Her hair was gray and brittle. She was in those pajamas old Chinese ladies always wore, and her face was concerned. It made her look like the kind of grandmother who cooked you nice food and nagged you about your weight and stayed in her grave once she was dead.

"Ah Ma," Jess meant to say, but her voice fluttered away from her. She felt terrible. What had they been doing with her body?

She remembered the god's pale face in the darkness, the promise in it—and the threat. What had *she* been doing with Jess's body?

"Ah Ma," Jess tried again. This time the words came, scraping her throat on their way out.

For the first time ever, Ah Ma looked glad to hear her voice.

Relief crossed her face. She said gruffly, "Now only you come! You know or not how many times I called you?"

"What time is it?" said Jess. Her voice sounded thin and creaky, the voice of someone who had barely survived a grave calamity. "How did I get here?"

"Ambulance lah then. You think what, the god flew you here?" said Ah Ma. "She doesn't give chance to her mediums. If it's down to her, you'll still be lying there in the morning. Lucky thing there was no block anymore. Must be the god chased away the foreign spirits when she entered you. After she went off, I went inside you and took you out to the main road so people can find you. You were bleeding, you know! The doctor had to staple you up, like exam paper like that."

Jess's head hurt. Memories of the night came back to her in bits and pieces, like a bad dream. Chief Thug's face right up against hers, so close she could see every bead of sweat, his blood warm on her hands. The guy who'd pretended to be a cleaner, sobbing like a child.

"Where is she?" she said.

She didn't need to specify whom she was talking about. Ah Ma knew.

"How I know? I'm not the medium anymore. She ran off back there in the alley, after she finished playing with those men." Ah Ma shook her head. "You were covered in so much blood, the doctor thought you must be dying. Didn't realize it was other people's blood. Your mother almost fainted when she saw you."

"What?" Jess sat up, but she regretted it immediately. The movement sparked off a series of explosions, pain lighting up all along her body. She looked down and saw a cast on her right forearm, covering her wrist and ending before her fingers. There was another cast on her left ankle, the one that had betrayed her when she was running away.

But she was in clean clothes—her own faded T-shirt and shorts, imbued with the familiar scent of the detergent Kor Kor used.

"My mom came?" Jess touched the soft weave of her shorts with her good hand.

"The hospital called your parents. Your mother brought you new baju to wear. Your old one, the dress, she threw away because of the blood. Didn't even want to clean it." Ah Ma sniffed at this wastefulness. "She cried the whole time she was washing you. She and your father stayed here for a few hours, then they went back to rest. They didn't sleep last night. Worried because you didn't go home. Your mother is like that, the mind is not strong."

"She is strong," said Jess. "She was. She's had a tough few years, that's all." The thought of her parents looking after her made her feel like a kid again, treasured and safe. She wished they were still there. "Why didn't they wait for me to wake up?"

"They did," said Ah Ma. "Only after they talked to you, your parents went back."

"I woke up before?" Jess had no recollection of this. Maybe it was the head injury. "I don't remember talking to them."

"It wasn't you who talked to them," said Ah Ma. "It was the god."

"What do you mean?" said Jess, but her body already knew the answer. She felt cold, nausea rising in her throat.

"I called you again and again, but your spirit don't know went where already," said Ah Ma. "When you opened your eyes, it was the god who was there. She didn't say much. She was quite confused, or tired, maybe."

The god had sat in Jess's body, talking to her parents while she wasn't there. The idea chilled her to the bone. The god belonged to dark alleys, violent men, nighttime and desperation. She wasn't supposed to seep into the daytime. She wasn't supposed to take over any more of Jess's life.

"You said she went away after she—" Jess swallowed. "After she dealt with the guys who kidnapped me." She didn't want to think about the men—what they'd tried to do to her, or what the god might have done to them. "Did you summon her back?"

"Why I want to call her for what? I said already, I was trying to call your spirit to come back to your body. Instead she came," said Ah Ma. "This is happening is because you didn't follow protocol. When you invoke the gods, you must do it properly. Carry out the rituals. Then when you don't want the god anymore, ask them to go back. But you simply do only. Whenever you felt like it, you called her. The god is not like a contractor, you call when you need them to fix the toilet or what."

Jess seized onto irritation with relief, grateful for any distraction from her mounting dread.

"I wasn't the one who invited her in in the first place," she said. "That was you, if you've forgotten! I only called on her when I got attacked."

"I also suffered. You think I didn't suffer?" said Ah Ma, never one to shy away from a fight, even when her opponent had multiple broken bones. "Ah Kong, after he drank he went crazy. Anything also he wasn't scared to do. One time he picked up the iron when it was hot and threw it at my head! So many times he almost killed me.

"But I tahan. I didn't call the god just because I'm scared. These spirits, when you ask them to come, it's like inviting your friend to stay at your house. You invite too often, they'll start to think they can come whenever they want. You let this big sister enter you so many times, she thinks your body is hers already. Your body also cannot tell what's the difference between your soul and her soul."

The joy of battle drained out of Ah Ma.

"You watch out," she said heavily. "Next time she goes inside you, could be your spirit cannot get back in. Sometimes it's like that."

Jess stared, petrified.

She knew Ah Ma was right, better than Ah Ma knew it herself. After all, it was Jess who had crossed the boundary between herself and the god, letting it be crushed under the need of the moment.

The Black Water Sister had been in her head, but it hadn't stopped there. For a time they had been the same person. Jess had felt the god's hurt that was her rage that was her hunger. A soul who died the way she had could never be at rest.

Now that she had Jess as a channel for that hunger, she would never let her go. That dark fury would consume Jess until she burned down to nothing. Her body might live on, but she would end up as insubstantial as the dead herself—a hungry ghost, exiled from her own life.

"Ah Ma," she said, "you have to help me."

"You think I won't help if I can?" said Ah Ma tetchily. "Even if you're a gay, don't listen, scold your grandmother, you're still my granddaughter. And you taught Ng Chee Hin a lesson. After what happened to his men, hah! He won't dare to say grandfather story this or grandfather story that. He'll know how to respect!

"But I can't do anything. Who am I to fight the god? That useless bastard." Her tone made it clear she was talking about Ng Chee Hin again. "In the end you beat him, made him lose face. But because of him, you've ended up losing even more. He won't even know how much you suffer. Same as Ah Ma, last time."

She meant herself as a penniless young woman, not much older than Jess, but already widowed by her own volition, abandoned by her lover and charged with the care of two children.

Jess was in a pretty bad state, but she couldn't imagine dealing with a situation like that. She felt a sudden rush of fondness for Ah Ma—this ornery, redoubtable survivor who'd never stopped being mad about the bad hand life had dealt her.

"I'm not asking you to fight the god," said Jess. "I need you to get me out of this hospital, that's all." She looked at the cast on her leg. The idea of getting out of bed was daunting. "I'm not sure I can walk with this thing. But you could help me."

"You want me to go inside you and help you walk?"

"You did it when you got me out of that alley, right? Even if it hurt, you wouldn't feel it."

"That's different. That one no choice," said Ah Ma. "Now you're safe in the hospital, the doctor is looking after you, you should rest. If you move here move there you'll hurt yourself only."

"So I should lie here and let her take over?" said Jess. "If it's a choice between hurting my leg and losing my soul, I'm going to take my chances with the leg."

"You want to fight the big sister?" said Ah Ma. "After you gave her those men's blood, she is very strong now. Even the big god will find it hard to beat her. You ask Tai Seng Ia to chase her away now, maybe he can't do it also. You think you can?"

Jess shivered, even though the AC wasn't that strong and she was already sticky with sweat under her clean clothes. She'd mostly been managing not to think about the men, but she couldn't avoid the question any longer.

"What happened to those guys?" Jess took a deep shaky breath. "Did I kill them?"

"You think I went to check if they're alive or not? I ran off as fast as I could."

"Ah Ma."

"I don't know," said Ah Ma. "The god was rough. She made sure those bastards bled. But she didn't get to play with them for long. Your body couldn't tahan. Anyway, if they die, they die. Why do you care so much? It's the god who did it what."

Jess wasn't convinced. In her patchy memories of last night's violence, it was another force that had fought those men, that had struck and hurt and stabbed with a strength she didn't possess. But the fierce triumph that had coursed through her veins, the vindictive satisfaction—that had been her own, as much as the god's.

She looked at her bruised hands. They had been cleaned. She could imagine Mom patiently wiping them, giving loving attention to every crease, careful of every inch of skin. But the nails were still encrusted with dried blood.

"I can't live like this," whispered Jess. She cleared her throat. "I have to do something."

"But you want to go where?" said Ah Ma, her voice rising. Someone who didn't know her would have thought she was working herself up into a fury. Jess thought, *She's softening.* "I told you already, even if you leave Penang, you cannot run away from the god."

"I'm not planning to run away," said Jess. "I want to go to the temple."

"And do what? You destroyed her altar already. What more is there to do? You want to cut down the tree? Offend some more gods?"

"I want to talk to her, that's all. Are you going to help me or not? Don't forget, I got you in front of Ng Chee Hin," Jess added. "So you could tell him what you thought of him."

An involuntary smile spread across Ah Ma's face at the recollection. She tried to hide it, turning down the corners of her lips, but her face had already betrayed her and they both knew it.

She raised her hands. "Fine. If you want to go and break your legs, who am I to stop you? But if end up you get cursed because you don't want to listen to Ah Ma, you don't blame me!"

"I won't," said Jess. If her plan didn't work, soon there wouldn't be much of her left to blame anyone. But she didn't say this. "Thanks, Ah Ma. Let me call Ah Yen. Where's my phone?"

Ah Ma pointed at a small table at the bottom of the bed, where

Jess's phone lay, along with a couple of containers of food and a note in Mom's handwriting. Jess scooted down the bed awkwardly and picked up her phone.

She avoided looking at the note. She couldn't afford to lose focus right now.

"You want to call Ah Yen for what?" said Ah Ma.

Jess was busy searching for the contact in her phone. Ah Ma had to repeat herself before she answered.

"To check she's at home," said Jess. "We've got to go to Ah Ku's house first. I'm going to need the idol."

TWENTY-FOUR

Yew Yen was the only one there to greet Jess when she arrived at Ah Ku's house.

"Ma and Pa are napping," she said.

It was the first time they were meeting in real life, not counting any encounters they might have had when Ah Yen hadn't been able to hold up her head yet. But she was familiar. Less from Facebook, more from an indefinable family resemblance—a something in the shape of her face and her mannerisms that made Jess feel like she had known her for much longer.

It wasn't clear if Ah Yen was having the same experience of recognizing Jess as family. The two casts and the crutch Jess had appropriated from the hospital proved too much of a distraction. It took a while to get her to stop exclaiming about Jess's injuries and back onto the topic of how Ah Ku was doing.

He was fine, said Ah Yen. The police hadn't hurt him. He was tired, but glad to be home.

"Good," said Jess.

Ah Yen looked worried. "You're going to do what with the idol?"

Jess had tucked the statuette unceremoniously under one arm—
it was the only way she could hold it and her crutch at the same
time. Her cousin was starting to look a little dubious about the wisdom of handing it over to her.

"I'm going to bring it back to its proper place," said Jess.

She didn't actually know what she was going to do. But she had
given the Black Water Sister her sacrifice and more. Not only the
blood of the men who had attacked her in the night, but her in-
nocence, her clean hands. Before all of this, she had been a normal
person, someone who had never been violent, who hadn't known
what it felt like to wipe another's blood off her own face.

She was owed something for that loss. She meant to demand it
from the god. And if she was going to find the god anywhere, it
would be at the garden temple.

Her Grab car was waiting, so she declined Ah Yen's polite suggestion that she come in and have a drink. But Ah Yen stopped
her when she turned to go.

"Nah. Take with you." Ah Yen held out a yellow cloth with
Chinese characters on it, printed in red.

"What is it?"

"It's a charm," said Ah Yen. "Put in your pocket, or your bra
also can. Important thing is to keep it close. It'll protect you, if
there's a fight or what. It was blessed by Kuan Kong. Pa gave us
all one."

She told a story about a time Ah Ku had almost been in an accident. "He was waiting by the roadside and suddenly a car
swerved and came onto the pavement where he was standing.
Lucky thing it missed him! Pa had the charm in his pocket. When
he looked at it afterwards, it was torn in half."

Jess was a little amused, but mostly touched. "Thanks."

She fingered the charm in her pocket as the car drew up by the
hawker center outside the garden temple. The dinner rush hadn't

started yet, so the place was quiet, foreign workers snoozing with their heads down on the tables.

The intolerable heat of late afternoon had subsided, the sun low in the sky. The air was soft, though not yet cool. This was the time when people started getting off work and went to the park or the beach.

The Grab driver opened the door for her and helped with the crutch, but Jess noticed he avoided touching the idol. He looked Malay. But she had learned by now that in this part of the world, being the follower of any given religion didn't exclude a healthy respect for other gods.

She made sure to tip him in the app before moving on. Best to settle her worldly business now, while she was in control.

Mostly in control. Ah Ma was driving her body, forcing the unwilling muscles to work, the heavy feet to move despite themselves. Jess's body twanged as she hobbled up the steps to the temple, but the pain was muffled, like the noise of a quarrel drifting over from a neighbor's house—easy to ignore.

Getting to the top of the steps, emerging into that green space dominated by the bodhi tree, was like entering a dream. Towering over the little shrines, the tree looked monstrous and unlikely, an alien growth from another planet. The vines looked as though they might seize on you if you went among them, coiling and strangling.

Since the boundaries had softened between her and the god, Jess's vision had sharpened for the things other people couldn't see. There had been no need for Ah Ma to open her eyes this time. She saw the temple's habitual occupants with a clarity that was a little unnerving as the sky turned blue with twilight. The spirits drifted around the garden, loitered on the paths, hovered over the plants—but not the bodhi tree. They left that alone.

As before, they paid Jess and Ah Ma little attention, for which

Jess was grateful. She only had it in her to deal with one god that day.

"So how?" said Ah Ma. She had been subdued since they left Ah Ku's house, speaking only in a mutter, as though she was afraid of being overheard by the idol.

"Do you remember where her altar was?" said Jess.

She couldn't see any trace of the destroyed shrine, but Ah Ma led her without hesitation to the precise crevice among the roots. The vines fell back in place behind them, screening them off from the garden and its gods and spirits.

Ah Ku must have arranged for the tiled base of the altar to be removed. The only sign that it had ever been there was the rectangle of earth it had stood on, bare of the tangled grass and weeds that covered the ground everywhere else.

Wobbling on her good leg, Jess bent and placed the cracked idol on the ground between the roots. It looked small and weirdly vulnerable without the shelter of its shrine.

"Now what?" said Ah Ma. "You want to pray, is it? Like that should have gone to buy joss sticks, fruit all that. You think the god will listen if you don't give an offering? Gods are like humans. Nothing is for free."

"She'll listen," said Jess.

But as she put her hands together to pray, doubt rippled through her. What was she going to say to the Black Water Sister, if the god even condescended to appear? *I gave you what you wanted. You owe me.* It sounded less convincing in her head now, with the god's tree looming over her, than it had in the hospital.

She closed her eyes, trying to put fear away. A deep breath.

"You have to make yourself empty," said Ah Ma. "So the god can come."

Jess said, without opening her eyes, "OK."

Another breath. The sound of air rushing through her nostrils filled her ears, drowning out the murmuring voices of the spirits, the screech of the cicadas and the occasional bird's cry.

"Must try not to think about anything," said Ah Ma. "Clear your mind. If you worry about this and that, you won't be able to focus."

"Yes, OK, thanks, Ah Ma!"

It took her a little while to rediscover the quiet inside her. She called up the image of the Black Water Sister in her mind—the broad, ordinary face, with its narrow eyes and cautious lack of expression.

Jess hadn't realized before that the blankness of the god's face wasn't a divine characteristic. It was a defense mechanism. In life the god had never been able to afford to be natural, to allow her emotions free rein. She hadn't lost the habit of guarding herself in death. She was . . .

Like me, thought Jess, surprised. She trembled on the brink of an epiphany, a revelation that might change everything. Power welled up inside her, like a golden bubble, expanding.

Come to me, she thought, her entire being engaged in the summons. *Come now . . .*

"Eh, you came back?" said a male voice in Malay.

The cresting wave collapsed on itself, the power dissipating. Jess's eyes flew open.

She was prepared to curse out the speaker—man, god or ghost as he might be—but when she saw his face, the "fuck off" evaporated off the tip of her tongue. It was the Datuk Kong, the one they'd met at the construction site, who had saved the migrant worker Rijaul.

Concern clouded his face. "Why you came here? You know or not, *she* is around?" He paused, his eyes narrowing. "Eh, you're not the same already. What happened to you?"

"So sibuk for what?" snapped Ah Ma. "It's none of your business. Why don't you go back to your altar instead of disturbing people? You don't need to jaga those workers meh?"

"The hantu didn't bother them since you all came that time," said the Datuk. "Somebody came and destroyed her altar. Since then she's been going here and there, looking for the fellow."

"But she's here now?" said Jess.

"Don't talk to him!" said Ah Ma in Hokkien. She lowered her voice. "You didn't see ah, got all those spirits over there? After they hear you, then how? If they realize what you're doing, you think you'll be able to come back to your body? People will sure come and take it!"

"What are you talking about?" Jess started saying, when Ah Ma took her arm.

It wasn't like the previous times Ah Ma had touched her, or tried. This time she felt *real*. Her palm was cool and dry against Jess's flesh.

Looking at Ah Ma's hand on her arm, Jess saw that the cast on her right hand had vanished. So had the cast on her foot. The ambient background pain that had dogged her since she woke up in the hospital was gone, miraculously sloughed off.

Ah Ma put her hand on Jess's shoulder, turning her so she could see her own body, crumpled over her crutch. Its face was pale and bruised, its eyes shut in prayer.

"Holy shit!" gasped Jess. Her body stayed still; the lips didn't move. She glanced at Ah Ma and the Datuk, panicked. "How do I get back in? I—what is that?"

Wisps of dark mist rose from the idol of the Black Water Sister, nestled in the crook of the roots. As Jess watched, the wisps came faster and thicker, till the statuette was shrouded in billowing smoke. The smoke solidified, coalescing into the form of a woman.

The Black Water Sister stood by her statue, looking down at

Jess's praying body. The five marks of the god's fingerprints could be seen on the pale nape of Jess's neck, red and inflamed.

It was weird. Even though Jess was in spirit form, her terror felt as physical as ever, an acid roiling in her stomach.

But she couldn't run now. This was what she had come for.

"Sister," she said shakily.

The Black Water Sister turned.

"I gave you your sacrifice," said Jess. "Will you listen to me now?"

The god held Jess's eyes for a long moment. She smiled, deliberately.

Then she turned and ran.

"Shit!" Jess started off after the god. But there was her body, kneeling undefended among all these spirits . . .

She paused. "Could somebody really steal my body?" she said to Ah Ma.

"You go," said Ah Ma. "I'll stay here and jaga."

"No, you go with the girl," said the Datuk Kong. "I will watch her body, make sure nobody enters."

They stared at him. The Datuk Kong said, "I live in Penang so long, you think I cannot understand Hokkien? That time I was fighting this hantu, protecting my devotees, you tried to help.

"You were useless," he added. "But Datuk can see your intentions are pure. Don't worry about your body. I won't let anybody kacau. Afterwards, if you are free, maybe you can make some offering to me."

"What offering you want?" said Ah Ma.

"Nasi dalca with mutton kurma and kerabu kacang botol," said the Datuk Kong promptly. "Can find at Pak Din's stall at Jalan Jelutong. Just put in Waze. And one air bandung." A look of yearning crossed his face. "Long time since I've had air bandung!"

Ah Ma frowned. "Mutton also want? You think this girl has a lot of money ah? Nasi should be enough already—"

"It's a deal," said Jess. "Come *on*, Ah Ma."

They saw the god as they crossed the bridge over the terrapin pool, the muddy water reflecting the darkening sky overhead. The god stood under the zinc roofing where Ah Ku had regaled Jess with chrysanthemum tea the first time she'd come to the temple. She had her back to them, but as Jess approached, she turned and opened her arms.

She was smiling, still. It was the first real expression Jess had ever seen on that face, and it was mean as hell. Did Jess want to challenge her? the smile said. Then she was going to get what was coming to her.

Jess pulled back, trying to slow her pace. But the god drew her like an iron filing to a magnet. An irresistible momentum bore her on, while behind her Ah Ma shouted fruitlessly, "Stop, stop!" She rushed into the Black Water Sister's arms and darkness overtook her.

MOM AND DAD were sitting together in Kor Kor's living room, hunched over a phone.

"What's up? You guys broke Facebook again?" said Jess. She found it amazing how bad her parents were at phones, given they weren't *that* old.

But when they turned and she saw their faces, she knew something terrible had happened. Her heart went cold inside her.

"What's wrong?" she said. "What did the doctor say?" The cancer had come back, she knew it. She'd known they weren't really safe.

But that couldn't be it, because the cancer had never gone away. For a moment she'd thought Dad was in remission. Where had that idea come from?

Her head felt weirdly foggy, her thoughts confused. The back of her neck twinged. She reached back to touch it, but her fingers flinched away. The skin there felt raw and tender.

Dad was sick, she told herself. How could she have forgotten?

That was why he looked so shitty, wearing the hat he'd worn all the time when he was going through chemo because he was self-conscious about his hair loss despite his dad jokes about looking like the Rock. It was too hot in Malaysia for that hat. She should get him a cap or something. Why hadn't she thought of it before?

Then she saw what her parents were looking at and forgot all about hats.

It was a photo of her, one she'd never seen before. She was with Sharanya, and it was unmistakable what they were doing.

Shame crashed over her like a wave, stealing her breath. For a moment she couldn't speak, but she had to, she had to take that look off their faces—

"It's not—" *Me*, she wanted to say, but it would have sounded ridiculous, because it was so obviously her. "Where did you get that from?"

Mom got up. There were tears in her eyes, and her nose was already red. She came toward Jess, looking soft and sad.

When Mom looked like this, she hugged Jess and sobbed on her shoulder. It had happened plenty of times since Dad lost his job and got sick. Jess braced herself for it, but she needed to have braced herself a lot more, because what happened was Mom hauled off and slapped her.

Jess put a hand to her stinging cheek, shocked.

"How can you do this kind of thing when Dad is so sick?" said Mom.

"I'm not," Jess protested. That was true, she thought, or at least kind of true—close enough to the truth to count. She hadn't seen Sharanya in months, and they'd barely even sexted in all that time. It turned out having a sick father and going through a familial financial crisis was a major libido killer, who knew?

Sharanya had dumped her now anyway. That memory was another nasty shock, like having freezing water dumped over her.

"We're not even together anymore," said Jess. "Mom—Mom, listen to me!"

Mom had turned away, gone back to Dad's side and burst into tears.

"Enough, enough already," said Dad, but it wasn't clear which of them he meant.

Mom kept talking, an unstoppable stream of words coursing from her. "So lose face! You all young people think of yourself only. Even if you have no shame, you don't know how to think of your mother and father ah?"

"But nobody knows," said Jess, by which she meant *nobody important*. She'd been careful to keep the relationship a secret from anybody who might have passed messages back to her parents' circles. Not even all her friends knew.

"Kor Kor sent us the photo," said Mom. "Now she wants us to move out. Said she doesn't want her family to be exposed to this kind of lifestyle. Cannot blame her also."

Jess felt like she was going crazy. Nothing anyone was saying made sense. "My lifestyle? You mean being an unemployed shut-in with no friends?"

The levity was to distract her from the wound of Kor Kor's rejection. She'd never asked herself what Kor Kor would think of her being gay. All of that lay in an unknown country, beyond anywhere she had ever planned to travel.

"Look, that's all over now," said Jess. "I'm done with that part of my life. I'm looking after you guys now. That's why I came back to Malaysia with you."

"Better if you didn't come back. Better if you stayed in US," said Mom. "Must be I did something bad in my past life. I didn't bring you up properly. It's my fault."

"No lah," said Dad wearily.

"It's our fault," Mom insisted. "See lah! Go to US some more!

Min was exposed to Western lifestyle too young. If we stayed in Malaysia, let her grow up here, this won't happen."

Dad said, "We went to try to improve Min's life. Give her a better future. Who knew it'll turn out like that?"

"Dad," said Jess painfully. "I'm sorry. But you guys don't understand. Sharanya doesn't even—"

Want to be with me anymore, she was going to say, but Dad cut her off.

"Don't need to say so much," he said. "I don't want to hear." He put his head in his hands. Mom touched his shoulder.

"Painful, is it?" she said softly. "You want a drink? I made herbal tea, I'll bring for you. You drink, then lie down and rest."

"Don't need," muttered Dad. "I'll just go to sleep."

Jess went to help him up, but he withdrew his hand from her, quite gently. He turned to Mom, who took his arm. They walked slowly to the stairs while Jess stood, stupid and empty, feeling like she'd been beaten clean like a carpet. The shame was crushing, unbearable.

At first she didn't hear the voice. But it spoke again:

Use the charm.

It was Ah Ma's voice in her head.

What? thought Jess. She stared at Dad's bowed shoulders, Mom's hand on his arm.

The charm Ah Yen gave you, said Ah Ma. *Use it! Look in your pocket!*

Jess remembered touching the yellow cloth, moved by this small show of support from a relative she'd never met before. The charm, of course . . . she reached into her pocket.

But the charm would be back with her body where she'd left it, praying at the temple. She didn't remember getting home from the temple. What had happened? Had she found the god?

She looked up and saw the Black Water Sister watching her

through the glass of the sliding doors. The back of Jess's neck started to throb.

Her surprise was muted. The Black Water Sister's presence seemed inevitable at this moment where her life was going awry. The god stood where she had appeared before, when Kor Kor had tried to cast her out. Jess had promised her a sacrifice then.

Well, the god had had her sacrifice. What was she doing here now?

"Better if I died in US," Dad said to Mom, his voice soft but horribly distinct.

"No, no," said Mom.

Jess froze, humiliating hot tears rising in her eyes. But her hand was already in her pocket. Her fingers brushed the charm.

The dream split open. Memory rushed back.

Dad *was* in remission. Nobody had ever taken nude pics of her and Sharanya, and even if they had, it was incredibly unlikely Kor Kor would have got ahold of them.

The Black Water Sister was *fucking with her*.

Jess's hand squeezed into a fist around the charm.

She spun around, heading for the god where she stood behind the glass.

Suddenly Ah Ma was next to her, panting, "I shout shout shout so many times, you never answer. The god blocked your ears, is it?"

"I didn't hear you," said Jess grimly. "That *bitch*!"

The living room seemed suddenly vast, but Jess crossed it. The glass of the sliding door and the metal grille and the wall around it melted away as she hurtled toward the god. She threw herself on the Black Water Sister, slamming bodily into her. They crashed into the ground together.

The god was small and fine-boned—she'd grown up eating rice and not much else. Physically she was no match for Jess, with her sturdy body nourished on American milk and Chinese meals lovingly cooked by her mom, her body that had never had to go hungry.

Of course, neither of them was embodied, but for the moment the god had forgotten that. Terror flashed across that impervious face. She flinched away from Jess, raising scrawny arms to shield herself.

Jess had been furious enough to do something terrible, the kind of thing that would be unthinkable in her normal waking life but seemed plausible, even necessary, here. Like strangle a woman who was already dead.

But the movement of those thin arms gave her pause. It reminded Jess how the Black Water Sister had died, what she had endured. Men like Master Yap became divine after living revered lives, dying serene deaths and getting promoted by the Jade Emperor. Women like the Black Water Sister became gods because their lives were so shitty, their deaths so hideous, that people prayed to them to avert their vengeance. Because they had died with all that fury left to spend.

The moment of unbidden sympathy gave the god time to remember she wasn't actually weaker than Jess. She shoved Jess off her. Jess landed on her side, jarring her shoulder, but: *I'm not in my body right now*, she thought, and the pain evaporated.

She rolled onto her feet. The god was already scuttling away.

At first Jess was chasing the god, but suddenly they were running side by side, outdoors. Trees lurched out of the darkness. The ground was covered with slippery leaf fall, wet from rain. Roots emerged abruptly from the ground, slowing their progress. Stray twigs snapped and rolled under the soles of their feet.

Then there was only one of her and she was running alone in the forest, her heartbeat loud in her ears. Behind her a man was shouting, swearing at her.

"Useless. Bitch. Whore. I hate you. I'll kill you."

The words had been flung at her so many times that they had lost their sting. She was sobbing as she ran not because of them, but because she knew what was coming.

She couldn't keep up her pace. She was going to fall. He was going to catch her. And then . . .

But she'd been here before. She had died this death many times. Death meant being crystallized in horror, unable to break free, except when she could find a living soul to give her respite. When she was in another's head, occupying their warm living body, her terrible death gave her power—a power that came from the fear and belief of the living.

She liked it when they asked her to do things—poison healthy minds, blight lives, cause accidents. Best of all was when there was blood, blood that she drew, in exchange for her own spilled blood that had never been paid for.

She tripped over the root of a tree, as she had known she would. Anger clawed at her throat, all the more terrible for being ineffective. She fell, bashing her cheek against the tree trunk, rough bark scraping her skin.

This was how it would always go. This was why she could never move on, never forgive, never rest. Her death was a debt owed by all the world. She would make every living soul pay penance for it if she could.

"You have to help her settle it. No choice."

The voice was new. The girl looked around, confused.

It was an old woman who had spoken. She was wiry, hardy-looking, her thin face stern under cropped gray hair. She had never been there at the girl's death before, yet there was something familiar about her.

She pointed. "Look."

She was gesturing at the girl's hand. The girl found it was curled into a fist, so tight her fingers were cramping. She opened her hand and saw a piece of yellow cloth lying on her palm, with red writing on it. A charm.

"Make him pay," said Ah Ma. "The big sister helped you when those men came after you. Now you help her."

"I don't have a weapon," said Jess, or the Black Water Sister. She wasn't sure, at that moment, which of them she was.

Ah Ma glanced back. "He's got one what."

The Black Water Sister's lover came through the trees, moving fast despite the uneven ground. It was so dark he was mostly sound—twigs crunching, heavy breathing. He'd stopped yelling. As he approached, a stray beam of moonlight caught his face.

He was skinny and ordinary-looking. Jess wouldn't have taken a second look at him if she'd passed him in the street. He didn't look crazed, or even especially angry. His face was tense and absorbed.

He grabbed her roughly and slapped her once, twice. Her head rocked on her neck from the force of the blows. Pain resonated through her body, but it was distant, not her own. She was looking out for the knife.

He pushed her against the tree that had felled her. The trunk was knobbly against her back. *It's the same tree*, she thought. *The bodhi tree. It didn't grow from her blood. It was here all along.*

What a thing a bad death was. It made a mythology that caught up in its wake old trees and young women alike, the violence of it reverberating through the years.

At least this time, the death wouldn't be hers.

The moonlight gleamed off her husband's knife as he took it out. She reached out and seized the knife with the hand holding the charm, wrapping the cloth around the blade.

The knife slipped out of her husband's hand easily. With a strength she could never have had before she died, she brought her knee up into his stomach. She heard him gasp.

As he faltered, she pushed him off her, shoving him to the ground, and Ah Ma held him down.

Now. Now! she thought. Exhilaration bore her up. She felt like she could fly. *I want to do it!*

Hunger roared inside her, bottomless and fierce. She would make this slow. She would relish every moment. Only his anguish, long drawn out, could soothe hers.

Jess watched the Black Water Sister fall to her knees, crouching over the man who had killed her, crooning in delight.

"Help me, sister," said the god.

Jess gave her the knife. Ah Yen's charm fell away, fluttering to the ground. She focused on it, letting it take up her field of vision, staring so hard that the Chinese characters started to blur.

Jess felt the Black Water Sister's movements in her own body. The muscles in her arm tensed as the god raised the knife over her murderer. She tasted the god's hunger on her own tongue. When the knife fell, when the man's blood soaked into the earth, finally she would be at peace.

That was what the god thought. But as Jess stared at her charm, the fug in her mind seemed to clear. It became easier to decouple herself from the god.

This is pointless, she thought.

The Black Water Sister was dead and so was her murderer. There was nothing to be done about that any longer. It was too late.

So what? Jess didn't have to intervene. She could let this happen. He wouldn't be the first person whose murder she had enabled, probably, and he was already dead. Maybe his blood would sate the god, even if none of this was real.

Jess wanted to stand by. She wanted to be done with all of this. And a small part of her wanted to see the man die, slowly and in pain. It would be some return for all that had been done to her and the god and Ah Ma and Mom and Dad and those men under the hot sun at the construction site . . .

It was like she kept dropping off into a poisonous daze, her mind blurred by the Black Water Sister's ancient rage. She bent so she could touch the charm, feel the fabric under the pads of her fingers. Clarity returned.

The Black Water Sister's murderer had nothing to do with all that suffering—in one sense. In another, he and what he represented had everything to do with it. But if Jess knew anything, it was that his tools—the knife, darkness, secrecy, violence—were useless to end that suffering. That was why the Black Water Sister was still bound to the horrible moment of her death, unable to escape the soil that had drunk up her blood. It was like she was under an evil spell, but it was a prison of her own making.

Who had said that? It didn't matter. They were right. Jess had to find another way out.

The Black Water Sister might be a god now, but before her appalling death, she had only been a girl. Jess had felt from the inside her powerlessness and her fury, her endless grief. If she didn't do something now, the girl the Black Water Sister had once been would be trapped here forever, striking at shadows in her own mind.

"Sister," said Jess. "Sister!" She seized the god's hand holding the knife, pulling it back. "Stop!"

"What are you doing?" said Ah Ma. She kept the man pinned with ease, but that was no surprise. Ah Ma was a ghost, but the man was even less than that—the impression of a person in a dead girl's heart. "Don't interrupt!"

The Black Water Sister turned to look at Jess. Her face was the impassive god's face again, the face that had watched Jess the first time she'd walked into her temple, that had peered into Kor Kor's house, that had terrorized Jess's dreams. And she was angry.

Fear stopped Jess's voice. But—

What's the worst she could do to me? she thought.

She remembered Dad's curved back, his low voice saying, "Better if I died." The Black Water Sister had already done her worst and it was Jess who had given her the ammunition. That horrible fantasy belonged to Jess.

It was hers, and that meant Jess could survive it. That was true for the god as well.

"Sister, he's dead," said Jess. Her voice came out small and wavering, a mere thread of sound. She cleared her throat and tried again. "He's already dead. Listen to me!"

"What are you talking about?" said the Black Water Sister. She tried to tear her hand away. But Jess held firm, even though the back of her neck was aching again, the god's marks on her burning.

"He can't hurt you anymore," said Jess. "And you can't hurt him. He's gone."

The Black Water Sister shook her head. "You're lying! When did he die? You tell me that!"

"He died a long time ago," said Jess. "It's been more than a hundred years. Sister, it's time to put it down. There's nothing you can do about it anymore. I'm sorry."

"I don't believe you," said the Black Water Sister. "You're lying."

But she did believe Jess; she couldn't not. Their souls had cleaved together so that for a short time they had been the same person and their minds had been one. The god could feel the truth of what Jess said.

The man lying on the ground disappeared. Ah Ma blinked, disconcerted at being deprived of her captive.

"He's dead?" said the Black Water Sister. "Really?"

"Yes," said Jess. "He's never coming back. You're safe."

The Black Water Sister stared at Jess.

"He's gone," said the girl, and it was no longer a question. Her face crumpled.

"But I loved him," she said. "I loved him."

Her voice came out in a wail. She brought her hands up to her face and slapped herself, the noise startling in the dark forest.

Jess took the girl's hands in her own so she couldn't hurt herself again.

The girl was sobbing so violently she was shaking. Jess put her arm around her shoulders, pulling her close. A sweaty human smell came from her hair—her hair, which was wet, because Jess was crying too.

"It's OK. It's over now," said Jess, again and again. "You're going to be just fine."

TWENTY-FIVE

When Jess visited the garden temple for the last time, she went with offerings. She had learned that much by then.

They drove round to the sales office first, where the Datuk Kong's altar was. Jess had taken care to come on a Sunday, so the office itself was closed. The joss sticks had burned down to stubs in the incense urn in front of the little statue, but the spirit wasn't totally forgotten. A packet of cigarettes had been left there for him.

Jess unknotted a blue plastic bag, releasing a warm delicious scent onto the air. She'd eaten before she had come, but the smell almost made her wish she was hungry. Pak Din's nasi dalca lived up to the hype. It made sense that even a spirit might crave it.

She set the food out before the statue, carefully balancing a plastic bag of neon-pink air bandung next to the rice. She lit the joss sticks she'd brought and closed her eyes, recalling the Datuk's image—the kindly, wrinkled face above the crisp white baju.

Enjoy, she thought. The prayer was in English. She'd lost her Malay in the weeks since she'd last been here. Her improved facility in Hokkien, weirdly, had stuck with her.

Maybe it wasn't that weird. Her family and their friends spoke Hokkien around her all the time. She probably would have gotten better even without Ah Ma.

The garden temple itself was quiet, bathed in sunshine. It was just after lunchtime and the heat of the sun was almost tangible.

Jess couldn't help feeling a twitch of apprehension as she walked between the shrines, but nothing happened. She no longer saw spirits. No statues sprang to life. No gods or ghosts started whispering in her ear.

She lit the rest of her joss sticks for Kuan Kong, waving them in the air before planting them in the incense urn before his altar. She paid her respects to Kuan Kong whenever she saw him now—quick prayers when she saw his idol at the back of a restaurant or overseeing a checkout counter. But until now she hadn't had the chance to light incense for him, in thanks for the charm.

There was one last god to visit.

Her steps slowed as she approached the bodhi tree, but all she felt when she stepped into its dappled shade was the relief of being out of the glare of the sun. Leaves cast flickering shadows on the grass. A breeze lifted the vines before letting them drop again.

She picked her way among the roots, circling the tree. And there she was, propped up on the ground between roots like miniature petrified rivers—the Black Water Sister. Cracked and worn, but still there.

The idol was nothing more than a statue now—an empty house. Someone had left an offering in front of it, a small pile of oranges. They should have saved the fruit for one of the other deities in this crowded garden. The god wasn't coming back.

Jess didn't pray or burn incense. She'd given the Black Water Sister all she had to give her, and the god had taken from her all she would take. She stood looking at the idol, remembering.

It had been dark by the time she'd woken up in the garden temple, her crutch on the ground next to her, the day she had escaped from the hospital. Ah Ku had been bending over her, shining a flashlight in her eyes and yelling, "Ah Min ah! Wake up!" about an inch from her face. Blinking, she'd seen her parents behind him.

He'd brought the whole gang—Mom and Dad, but also Kor Kor, Kor Tiao, Ah Kim and a shamefaced Yew Yen. Ah Ku had reamed Ah Yen out when he woke from his nap and heard that Jess had taken the god's idol off to the temple by herself. He'd called Mom up on the phone and they'd all come out to find her en masse.

That was a few weeks ago. Since then it had been hard to get any time alone. Jess had had little excursions out of the house with the family—trips to the cinema, kopitiam breakfasts, picnics at the beach. She was aware of a conspiracy to keep her entertained, as though she was a small child.

She'd gone along with it, even enjoyed the sensation of being lovingly smothered. She knew she was being treated gently. Kor Kor had suggested having her exorcized by her pastor, but the subject was dropped without Jess even having to say anything. She suspected her dad had intervened, but she hadn't troubled herself to find out. She'd felt like she was recovering from more than physical injuries.

Her unpaid employment by Kor Tiao had ended by mutual agreement. She hadn't exactly been hustling since then. She'd figured applying for jobs and doing something about the photographs of Penang she'd accumulated could wait for when she was feeling less like warmed-over crap.

But maybe some benign deity had finally taken pity on her. As she was idly scrolling through her emails one day, she saw that the job at Sharanya's university had come up again.

It had felt like a sign. She hadn't heard from Sharanya since they'd fought. But Jess had sent in an application, feeling like she was putting a question to the universe.

They'd invited her to interview. She'd done it over video call, the camera carefully angled so the interviewers couldn't see either of her casts. And they'd offered her the job.

She'd hesitated when she first got the call. Her fantasies about bumping into Sharanya on campus and getting back together with her shriveled up in the light of reality. Would Sharanya think she was stalking her? Was Sharanya even still moving to Singapore? Probably she was. Arrogant to think she would've changed her plans just because of what had happened between them.

Jess had wrestled with herself for half a day before sitting down and sending off an e-mail accepting the job. Teaching Singaporean freshmen wasn't what she'd dreamed of doing, and Singapore wasn't where she'd dreamed of living, Sharanya aside. It was going to be incredibly awkward when, inevitably, she encountered Sharanya there.

But it was the only offer she'd gotten. And it was time to move on, do something new. Rediscover who she was when she wasn't ensconced in the mildly stifling embrace of her family.

That e-mail had been the end of her dormancy. After that she'd messaged the construction worker, Kassim. It turned out the NGO he'd been working with had done a social media campaign about the accident at the site, featuring Jess's photos of the collapsed scaffolding and an interview with Rijaul.

The Facebook post had tens of thousands of shares. The NGO had called out the mainstream media for their silence on the incident, but that had since changed. Jess scrolled through links to multiple newspaper articles about the scandal on the NGO's Facebook page. It had drawn media attention in Bangladesh as well. Kassim and Rijaul had even gone on TV a couple of times.

The developer had given a press conference in response, with Ng Chee Hin himself speaking on behalf of the company. Jess flinched away from the sight of him.

The construction workers were considering legal action. There was a fundraiser. Jess donated a princely sum on the strength of the salary she would soon be earning.

A few days later, she announced she was going out.

The boot was off Jess's foot and she was feeling remarkably like herself. Even the marks the god had left on the back of her neck had faded to pale ovals, hardly to be made out. In time she thought they would disappear.

"Where you want to go?" said Mom. "Dad got some errands to run, but afterwards he can take you."

"I'm craving nasi dalca," said Jess. "Yew Yen knows a place. She's picking me up, so Dad won't need to drive me." Jess was definitively banned from using Grab or any other taxi service. If she wasn't being driven by a trusted relative or family friend, she wasn't going anywhere.

So far the trusted relative category hadn't included Ah Ku and his family. Jess hadn't seen much of them since Ah Ku had found her in the garden temple. But Mom couldn't really prohibit Jess from seeing her cousin. Ah Yen was OK—young, blameless, on her way to college.

Mom said, discontented, "When you got eat nasi dalca before?"

"Never," said Jess. "That's why I want to try it. I'm not going to be in Penang for much longer."

Her parents took some convincing, but eventually they agreed she could go. Jess only had to show them exactly where Pak Din's stall was on Google Maps and promise she wouldn't be out for more than a couple of hours.

It was fine. It wouldn't be like this forever. It was only because they were worried about what Ng Chee Hin might do.

Jess wasn't. Ng Chee Hin wasn't going to do anything to her. There had been no retaliation so far for what she'd done to his men, and Jess had a feeling there wouldn't be. Ah Ma wouldn't have left unless she was sure he was no longer a threat.

Jess hadn't heard from Ah Ma since that last encounter with the Black Water Sister. She'd been waiting for her—expecting to hear that raspy voice in the quiet moments before she fell asleep, or while she brushed her teeth, watching herself in the mirror.

But the voice hadn't come, even when Jess brought a bottle of cognac to the columbarium where Ah Ma's remains were. For the first time since she'd arrived in Malaysia, Jess was alone in her head.

It wasn't like she wanted Ah Ma in her head. But it would have been nice to have closure. A debrief. Maybe even some praise for how she'd dealt with the Black Water Sister, oblique and grudging, the way Ah Ma said anything nice.

But there was nothing. After all, what did Ah Ma have to stick around for any longer? The god's shrine was gone. The god herself had been laid to rest. There were no debts left to pay off, no scores to settle. Jess was going to be fine.

With Ah Ma falling silent, it was like Jess had stepped out of her domain—crowded with gods and ghosts, spirits and secrets—back into the ordinary sunlit realm where the worst thing she was likely to take away from the temple was mosquito bites.

She preferred this world, overall.

Navigating the steps was the worst part. Jess took them slowly, favoring her good leg. This required so much attention that it was only once she'd reached the first landing that she looked up and saw Sherng, standing at the bottom. She froze.

Sherng had already seen her. His expression was so comically dismayed it almost made Jess laugh.

After a moment the expression passed. Sherng reorganized his face into a look of impersonal friendliness, like he'd spotted an old classmate whose name he didn't remember.

"I almost didn't recognize you with that hair," he began. Then: "What are you doing?"

Jess peered at him over the top of her phone. "Recording. What's it look like?"

He wasn't coming any closer. That was good.

"Why are you—" But Sherng wasn't a complete idiot. He flushed as understanding dawned. "There's no need to record me. I'm not going to attack you!"

"Good to hear." Jess didn't put down her phone.

Sherng cleared his throat. "Listen, I heard about what happened. With the—when you visited my dad's office. I'm sorry."

He was trying to meet her eyes, but Jess didn't look away from the phone screen. It stripped the moment of detail. You couldn't really make out Sherng's expression.

"Are you going to—" Sherng paused. "You're not going to try to hurt me, right?"

Jess had been determined to keep her cool, not let fear or anger make her mouth off. That resolution went right out of her head.

"Am *I* going to hurt *you*?" she said. "How many staples do you have in your head? I had seven!"

"The other guys don't look great either."

Jess narrowed her eyes. "Am I supposed to feel bad about that?"

"No, I was just—" Sherng raised his hands, in frustration or apology. The phone screen stole that nuance as well. "Sorry. Forget I said that."

Jess let a beat pass, then another. Sherng didn't look like he was going anywhere.

"So your dad's men are still alive?" said Jess.

Sherng blinked. "You didn't know?"

"How was I supposed to know? I was busy nursing a head injury."

"I don't know what you know, Jess," said Sherng. "I don't know what you're capable of. What you did to those guys . . . you scared the shit out of my dad."

Jess felt something inside her unclench. Turned out she had been worried after all. "Really?"

"Trust me, you don't have anything to fear from him," said Sherng. "We had a big fight about the whole thing. He made me promise to stay away from you. He'd be freaking out if he knew I'd run into you here."

"You going to tell him?"

"No, Jess," said Sherng. "I've already fucked up enough for a lifetime."

Jess let her silence stand as agreement. At least Sherng didn't seem to be expecting forgiveness.

"I can tell you why he sent those guys after you," he said. "Do you want to know?"

"I thought it was obvious. I pissed him off."

"It wasn't that," said Sherng. "He wouldn't—not just because you annoyed him. I know you have no reason to believe me, but he doesn't do stuff like this. But you had him spooked. He didn't want you going off telling everybody about, you know, your uncle. He wants me to inherit the business. He's got it all planned out."

It took Jess a moment to get it. "He thought my uncle was going to, what? Fight you for the inheritance?"

"Don't get me wrong. I don't have a problem with it," said Sherng. "If it's your uncle's right, that's fine. I said that to my dad. But he didn't agree. This is a big deal for him. I told you, I'm his biggest investment."

Jess lowered her phone.

"How do you feel about that?" she said.

Now that she was looking at him directly, she could see the resignation in his face.

"He's my dad," said Sherng. "What can I do?" He sighed. "Look, can we go somewhere to talk? It's damn hot here."

"No, Sherng," said Jess, not unkindly. "I'm not going anywhere with you."

She started hobbling down the stairs again. He came up the steps, saying, "Eh, let me . . ."

"No," said Jess.

Sherng stopped. He looked forlorn, but also a little annoyed that she wasn't letting him restore his self-image as a good person.

It gave Jess a petty pleasure, but it was also a reminder that she needed not to push it. Sherng feeling he owed her something was good, but it could morph all too easily into him resenting her for not forgiving the debt.

As she passed him, Sherng said quietly, "My dad gave in, by the way. I'm getting the temple."

Jess paused. She should go, but she was curious. "Aren't you still waiting for the judgment?"

"The temple committee isn't going to win," said Sherng. "My dad's getting out of the development anyway. He's decided it's too risky. But he's promised to carve out the temple plot so I can have it. He wasn't so willing at first, but there haven't been any incidents recently. With the, you know, the god." He hesitated. "Did you have anything to do with that?"

Jess considered her answer.

"Everything," she said.

Sherng nodded, letting out a long exhale.

"I've told my dad I'm going to get priests involved, do all the rituals, get approval from the gods," he said. "We'll make any donations that are needed. We're going to consult on layout, make sure the altars are preserved. We want to do it properly." He looked at her sidelong. "What do you think?"

"I'm not in that business anymore," said Jess. "You'll have to talk to my uncle. You two probably have a lot to talk about."

Sherng looked rueful. "I thought you might say that."

Jess was about to move on when he said, "I know you didn't like my idea about turning this place into a café. But keep an open mind, yeah? Come and see the place when it's done. You might be surprised."

"I'm leaving Penang, actually," said Jess.

"Oh," said Sherng. "Where are you going? Back to the US?"

Jess shrugged. It wasn't like she didn't think he could find her if he looked, but she didn't need to offer up the information. Singapore wasn't that far away.

Just far enough for a new start.

"Is it because—are you leaving because of my dad?"

"I'm moving for a job," said Jess.

"Oh, great. That's great," said Sherng. "But I want you to know you can come back. You don't have to worry about, you know." He gestured at her, a vague, comprehensive wave intended to capture her various injuries—broken ankle, fractured wrist, incipient PTSD and all. "I mean it. I'm really sorry about what happened. It's not going to happen again. I'll make sure of it."

"OK." Jess could tell he wanted more, but she couldn't bring herself to thank him, even if that would have been politic.

"I would have WhatsApped you before to tell you," said Sherng. "But I wasn't sure you wanted to hear from me."

There was no point telling him she'd changed her number. He'd find out if he tried using it, and it wasn't like she was going to have a Penang number for much longer anyway.

"I've got to go," said Jess.

"OK. OK," said Sherng.

She was at the bottom of the steps when he blurted, "I wish we could have been friends."

Jess looked back up at him.

"Me too," she said. She realized she meant it.

Yew Yen was waiting in the car park, humming along to K-pop and editing selfies. She showed one to Jess as she got in the car.

"Nice," said Jess. "I like the cat ears."

Ah Yen started up the car.

"Some guy came, looked like Malay like that. Did you see him?" she said. She pointed at a silver BMW, parked in a shady corner of the lot. "Looked like he was going to the temple. Father must be rich, man. See his car!"

Jess looked.

"No," she said. "I didn't see him."

JESS GOT HOME well within her allotted two hours. Ah Yen stayed for a drink and a snack, chatting affably with the uncles and aunties.

Jess knew she should smile along, do her bit, but she was too keyed up to make small talk. She had one item of business left for the day—one final thing she'd committed to doing. It was putting her on edge, even though it didn't really matter if she didn't get to it today. It had been overdue for years.

Nevertheless, having worked herself up to it, she wanted to get it over with. She gave up on socializing and excused herself, sneaking up to her bedroom. She checked her phone for the first time in a couple of hours and saw Sharanya had messaged.

It would have been one in the morning where Sharanya was. They were the kind of messages you only sent at one a.m.

Hey. I'm sorry I didn't reply to your messages. I needed some time.

I've been thinking a lot about us. I realized I was holding on to a lot of resentment I didn't tell you about, because of everything you had going on. I wanted to hold a space for that, for you. But I needed to make space for myself too. And for you to hold that for me.

I don't really know where I'm going with this. You're probably mad at me for going AWOL for so long. I just wanted to let you know I've been thinking about you. And I miss you.

Jess's knees gave out. She sat down on her bed and reread the messages until the words began to run into one another.

I miss you too, typed Jess.

Her fingers hovered over the screen.

I've had time to think, too, she wanted to say. *I'm moving to Singapore and I came out to my parents. Can we talk?*

But that wasn't all true yet. And she was giving up lying from now on. That was the whole point.

She put the phone down and went back downstairs to play host.

When she came back to her room later, she saw her phone sitting on the bedside table. She knew there wouldn't have been any further messages from Sharanya—she was probably asleep now— but she couldn't resist checking, just in case.

Nothing new. Jess was busy staring at her phone, estimating the earliest time by which Sharanya was likely to wake up and check her phone, when Mom came in after a cursory knock.

"Min, for dinner ah—eh, what's that?"

"What's what?" Jess followed Mom's line of sight. There was a big brown moth on the wall, next to the window. "Oh."

Mom hated creepy-crawlies of all kinds, which was weird given she was the one who'd grown up in this bug-ridden climate.

Jess got up. "I'll get rid of it."

"No, don't need to do," said Mom. "Leave it alone."

"It's fine, Mom." Jess riffled through the desk, looking for a sheet of paper to scoop up the moth with. "I won't kill it. I'll let it out of the window."

"No need. Better don't touch," Mom was saying when Dad poked his head around the door.

"What's the matter? Why are you all quarreling?"

"Not quarreling lah," said Mom.

"I'm going to get rid of this moth, but Mom wants to keep it as a mascot," said Jess.

Mom rose to the bait, predictably. "What mascot? I'm just saying, this kind of thing, don't need to do one."

"Moth? What moth? That moth?" said Dad, though it wasn't like there was more than one to choose from. "Mom is right. Better don't kacau. Don't need to test."

"Test what?" Jess started to say, when it clicked. "Wait. Is this a superstition?"

As far as Jess could tell, all Chinese superstitions were about either money or death, and the ones about death were nearly impossible to learn about because talking about death was taboo. Her parents were cagey enough that this had to be a death one.

"People say if the moth fly into your house, cannot chase or kill them," Mom said finally. "They're the spirit that passed on, the spirit of your ancestor."

"Ah," said Jess.

She looked at the moth. Maybe this was Ah Ma's idea of closure. If so, it sucked. There didn't seem to be anything special about the moth. It was just an insect. Its wings were vibrating slightly, as though it was thinking about taking off.

"What if you off the light?" Mom suggested. "Then the moth will see the light in the road and want to fly out. Moths like light."

So Jess turned off the AC and the lamp and opened the window, and they sat waiting in the blue half-light of evening, watching the gentle shiver of the moth's wings. They didn't talk, at Mom's command ("if the moth knows we're here, he'll think we're going to turn the light back on").

It was peaceful, if a little boring. Jess was half expecting Dad to go off to watch TV or something, but he stayed where he was, his hands on his knees. His silhouette in the darkening room had the solidity of a boulder covered in moss—something that had always been there and would be there for many more years.

Jess put her head on Mom's shoulder, breathing in the clean scent of shampoo and lavender talcum powder. She wished she could bottle the moment.

She remembered the nightmare the Black Water Sister had tried to frighten her with—her parents with their backs to her, hurt written all over them.

Maybe it would be like that. Even if it wasn't, even if it went better than Jess could let herself hope for, everything would be different after tonight. Nothing would ever be the same again.

But she knew she'd survive it. That was one gift the Black Water Sister had given her.

Dad's breathing had changed, becoming stertorous. Jess was about to prod him to see if he'd fallen asleep when Mom whispered, "There!"

The moth was flapping its wings. As they watched, it flew to the edge of the window, paused, then fluttered out into the night.

Mom laughed, delighted as a child. "Nah, see! It worked!"

Dad started, snorting. "Hmm? What?"

"The moth is gone." Jess went to look out of the window. There were insects buzzing around the streetlight, but they were too small for any of them to be the moth. It had as good as vanished. "Who do you think it was?"

"Aiyah, this is just superstition lah," said Dad. "People say only. Doesn't mean it's true."

"You want to eat what for dinner, Min?" said Mom. "Dad can tapau for us, or we can go out and eat. You want to stay at home, or you want to go out?"

Jess reached through the grille to pull the window shut. She could see herself in the glass. She looked nervous, but she was braver than she looked, braver than she'd known she was before she had first heard Ah Ma's voice.

You had to die first before you could be reborn.

"Mom, Dad," she said. "I've got something to tell you."

ACKNOWLEDGMENTS

In the process of conceiving and writing this book, I consulted a number of sources on Chinese popular religion and spirit mediumship, including Cheu Hock Tong's *The Nine Emperor Gods* and his work on Datuk Kong, Vincent Liow Ken Hua's *Confessions of an Ex-Taoist Medium: The Truth Revealed* and 界线 (*Between Two Worlds*), directed by Ashley Thio. But this book owes its greatest debt to Jean DeBernardi's work in this area, particularly her book *The Way That Lives in the Heart: Chinese Popular Religion and Spirit Mediums in Penang, Malaysia*, which, among other riches, gave me the garden temple and the Black Water Sister her name.

I am grateful to my agent Caitlin Blasdell; my editors Anne Sowards and Bella Pagan, as well as Rebecca Brewer, Miranda Hill, Georgia Summers and the wider publishing teams at Ace and Pan Macmillan; the Idlers by Bamboo for brainstorming sessions and high-quality chat; Seet Yan, Alina Choong and Maxine Lim for Rexmondton Heights, the lowdown on Penang housing stock and other lore; Kate Elliott for an Ameripicking beta; Charis Loke for a Penangite review; Mom and Dad for the scrap rubber guy and information on construction sites; Helen Smith for the Chan family tree and details of snake disease; and Bernadette and Martin Auger for looking after the baby so I could write.

Thank you, finally, to my family and Peter, for everything you give me every day. I love you.